Praise for Andi

'A mistressclass in combining humour and lovely
characters, all wrapped up with a cracking story'
Jo Brand

'Witty, joyful and a truly uplifting celebration of friendship'
Beth O'Leary, bestselling author of *The Flat*

'As soon as I start
humour and atten
both realistic and

'A massively entertaining tale of wingwomen recharging
each other's love lives. Funny, spiky and fab!'
Beth Morrey, bestselling author of *Saving Missy*

'A debut novel that I'll return to again and again.
An absolute triumph and I loved every word'
Susan Calman

'This brilliant warm book had me laughing from the
first page and I couldn't put *Asking For a Friend* down'
Lucy Vine, bestselling author of *Hot Mess*

'An ultimately feel-good story about female friendships
full of heart and humour. So relatable, I loved it!'
Angela Griffin

'I LOVED it. Funny, sparky and written with so much heart'
Daisy Buchanan, author of *Insatiable*

'A loving tribute to female friendship bursting
with funny lines and loveable characters'
Lucy Porter

'A fresh, funny, relatable page-turner from the ever brilliant Andi Osho – for anyone who's ever navigated the dating world and needed the sisterhood'
Deborah Frances White, *The Guilty Feminist*

'A delightful read, a beautiful paean to female friendship – genuinely funny and full of heart'
Roisin Conaty

'As hilarious as Andi's stand-up while feeling like a lively night out with brilliant friends'
Sara Pascoe

'From the first page, you can guarantee laughter. This book is hilarious, warm and an absolute page-turner. I loved it!'
Angie Le Mar

'A hilarious, laugh-a-minute, laugh-out-loud, relentless romp through dating, women and friendship. Brilliantly vivid and relatable characters. Brilliantly written, fun and joyous!'
Shazia Mirza

'Wise, witty and warm. Everything Andi Osho touches turns to gold'
Richard Osman, bestselling author of *The Thursday Murder Club*

Andi Osho is an award-winning stand-up comedian, actor, writer, filmmaker and lover of shoes. Her acting credits include *Shazam!*, *Lights Out*, *Curfew*, *Death in Paradise*, *Eastenders*, *Holby* and *Kiri*. As a stand-up, Andi wrote, performed and toured two sell-out Edinburgh shows, played at the O2 in London and has appeared on *The Late, Late Show*, *Mock The Week*, *Never mind the Buzzcocks*, BBC1's *Live at the Apollo* and more. Basically, she's done a bunch of stuff. *Asking For a Friend* is her debut novel.

Stay in touch with Andi on Twitter @andiosho and on Instagram and Facebook @theandioshow

Asking
for a
Friend

ANDI OSHO

ONE PLACE. MANY STORIES

HQ
An imprint of HarperCollins*Publishers* Ltd
1 London Bridge Street
London SE1 9GF

www.harpercollins.co.uk

HarperCollins*Publishers*
1st Floor, Watermarque Building,
Ringsend Road, Dublin 4, Ireland

This edition 2022

1

First published in Great Britain by
HQ, an imprint of HarperCollins*Publishers* Ltd 2021

Copyright © Andi Osho 2021

Andi Osho asserts the moral right to be
identified as the author of this work.
A catalogue record for this book is
available from the British Library.

ISBN: 978-0-00-847895-7

MIX
Paper from
responsible sources
FSC
www.fsc.org
FSC™ C007454

This book is produced from independently certified FSC™ paper
to ensure responsible forest management.

For more information visit: www.harpercollins.co.uk/green

This book is set in 11.2/15.5 pt. Bembo

Printed and Bound in the UK using 100% Renewable Electricity at
CPI Group (UK) Ltd, Croydon, CR0 4YY

To my fabulous female friends.

CHAPTER 1

Jemima

Jemima had been staring at the same text for a good five minutes. 'It's me', it read. Two innocent words that made her palms sweat like a politician turning in their expenses. Though her phone said the texter was UNKNOWN, they weren't. That number had been seared into her memory from all the other 'It's me's that had pinged, uninvited, into her inbox over the last two years. Just then, the three dots of doom began their 'incoming text' cancan.

Guess what?

Urgh. Jemima hated guessing because she hated surprises. Even fortune cookies gave her palpitations. Furthermore, this wasn't any old 'guess what?' from any old number. This SMS projectile was from Miles, the ex that wouldn't go away. Double *urgh*.

He was constantly showing up on her phone, even if it was just random 'LOL's on her Facebook posts. She'd deleted his name from her phone contacts ages ago. Perhaps it was time he got the chop on social media too, Jemima grizzled as she watched a stewardess move through the cabin serving pre-flight drinks.

'Prosecco?' said the stewardess, proffering her tray with a playful wink.

'Cheers,' Jemima said as she took a glass.

However, staring at Miles's text, she could have done with the whole bottle. Jemima necked her drink in one. Its cheap plonk bubbles immediately effervesced in her throat, threatening to shoot out of a nostril. She spluttered, glancing around the half-full airplane cabin as she tried to choke to death discreetly. Though her dad was American, she was as British as binge drinking and sarcasm so drawing attention to herself, even when dying, felt inappropriate. Finally, satisfied she'd been largely ignored by the boarding passengers, she slumped back in her premium economy seat, fingers tight around her phone. Why did Miles always do this? They'd broken up two years ago! She'd bought a new boiler, started dyeing her hair Deep Mahogany to hide her roots and had had twenty-six periods since then. Yet every time it felt like she was getting her life back on track, up he'd pop like a bad game of Ex-boyfriend Whack-a-Mole. She deleted the text. *Whack.*

Things were good, Jemima reassured herself, despite this pebble in her shoe. Finally, at the age of 42, life felt like it had some order again. Work was on track – sort of. She was doing okay financially… well, kind of. For a clean sweep, all she had to do was muster the courage to bat her niggly ex away once and for all and she'd be good. As she thought, half-heartedly, about how she might do that, another message from Miles whooshed into her inbox, this time with an accompanying photo. 'Great. Now with added attachments,' she groaned.

Number 62 is finally off the market!

Jemima bristled as she peered at the picture of the 'fixer-upper' property at the end of her street. With its overgrown front garden, faded green door and grubby windows it looked more like a crime scene than a potential investment. But what really bothered Jemima about this photo was, it was another reminder how close Miles *still* lived to her. When they'd been together, living on adjacent streets had been cute. Friends were always telling her how they had 'the best of both worlds'. But when their relationship had imploded, 'the best of both worlds' became hell on earth. A wave of anger rippled through her. She'd really loved him. More than anything she was angry at herself for letting him in, for forgiving the missed birthdays, broken promises and tired old let-downs. She'd excused his self-centeredness as ambition and his narcissism as self-care throughout their three-and-a-half-year relationship. His weekly threading appointment alone should have rung alarm bells. The day after, his eyebrows were so impeccable, he looked like a cruise ship magician. Jemima wished she'd listened to her girlfriends, Simi and Meagan, but she'd been in love. She couldn't hear them, that is until who Miles was became a noise she could no longer ignore. And so they'd broken up, a street apart. At the time, Jemima had desperately wanted to move apartments but just couldn't afford to, so instead had concocted strategies to avoid bumping into him – including an extra half-mile walk to a different tube station. Jemima shuddered at the chronically recent memory of diving into Number 62's overgrown shrubbery when she'd seen Miles approaching from the other end of the street. She was pulling privet twigs from her hair all the way to the tube and even now, wasn't entirely sure it *was* Miles. That was nearly seven weeks ago and was, for Jemima, the last straw… well, twig. She needed to get away. For years, Rebecca, an old work colleague, had been inviting Jemima to visit her in Los Angeles. That afternoon, privet leaves still entangled in her neat bob, Jemima had finally accepted the invitation. Within a week, she had booked her flight, packed a bag and was gone – one of the few benefits of being a self-employed writer. If she needed to, she could escape at a moment's notice.

'So, business or pleasure?'

Jemima looked up to see the prosecco stewardess casually leaning on the seat in front.

'Err… bit of both. Did a bit of work, a lot of drinking mimosas. I didn't expect to like LA so much and now I keep thinking about… ' Jemima trailed off.

'Hun, I get it,' said the stewardess as she cooed a friendly welcome to a train of passengers shuffling down the aisle, 'Seen that face a million times. Looking for a fresh start?'

Jemima shrugged. It was a thought that surfaced whenever things got tough. Extracting herself from troublesome situations had become her go-to solution and something of a speciality. Dad dies suddenly? Run away to university. Fall out with your boss? Become a struggling writer. Even in Brownies, the ceaseless pressure to acquire a sleeve full of badges had led her to quit and join the Sea Cadets. Of course all this only ever gave her temporary respite, like the moment between jumping out of a frying pan and into the bowels of a raging volcano. The reality was, university had been a nightmare, she'd almost lost her flat trying to make it as a writer and the Sea Cadets had only taught her one thing: she was a first class landlubber. But having relied on her vanishing skills for much of her forty-two years, Jemima didn't know any other way even if she did leave

4

other people's misery in her wake. She ran her fingers through her hair, holding it in a tight bun as she overheated.

'Fresh starts are good but… all that glitters is not gold. My cousin Bradley moved to Culver City and ended up joining the Latter Day Saints. Now he's a missionary in Vanuatu. He's had malaria four times,' said the prosecco stewardess, taking a wistful sip from one of the glasses on her tray, 'Anyhoo, I'm Susan. Yell if you need anything!'

Jemima watched Susan head to the galley kitchen, bemused.

She thought she'd got lucky finding a cheap flight home at late notice but she was beginning to see the cost – tangy prosecco and slightly bonkers cabin crew predisposed to over-sharing. In need of a distraction, she closed her eyes, transporting herself back to the sea views from Rebecca's Santa Monica apartment. Just picturing those vast beaches made her feel better. From the moment she'd stumbled out of LAX airport into that LA sunshine, she'd felt a calm descend. Her father, a Philadelphia man, had always held a deep mistrust of Los Angelenos, in part, on account of 'their teeth being too white'.

When Jemima had first arrived, she'd wondered if, aside from her ebony skin and long legs, she'd also inherited her dad's mistrust. But though there were some dazzling dental displays and a few too many fairy lights everywhere for her liking, she'd felt an unmistakable sense of belonging. When she introduced herself as an author, even if the person hadn't heard of her literary debut, *Beverly Blake Investigates*, they were so thrilled she was living her dream that she began to wonder why she wasn't that enthused on her own behalf. And after a week in LA, her shoulders dropped and tension ebbed away. Far from being the devil's playground for people with brilliant-white teeth, LA was a chilled-out city filled with artists and possibility. *She loved it.* And of course there was no Miles which made even an average city great. By that criterion even Milton Keynes was superb.

By the end of her second week, Jemima had forgotten about crouching in pissy hedges and was instead noticing things like house prices and parking, details holidaymakers pay little mind to but people considering relocating did. She'd gasped at the thought. Could LA be more than just a getaway retreat? Her friend Rebecca was certainly surviving, in fact she was thriving. And Jemima wouldn't have to wait for a job offer as Rebecca had. Because of her dual citizenship, she could move whenever she wanted, it was just a case of… what? *Nothing.* It was clear Miles wasn't going anywhere but maybe she could. If she organised a short-term let of her place, she could be settled in LA by spring.

Of course, while her besties Meagan and Simi were on board with an *LA vacay*, getting them behind her emigrating would take a lot more convincing. They wouldn't let her go without a fight and why would they? They'd been best friends for over a decade and were so entangled in each other's worlds, it was hard to know where one began and the other ended. Jemima smiled to herself as she remembered the first time they met, a stand-up comedy course she had signed up for to help her writing. Quickly she learned stand-up was not her bag and the best thing hadn't been learning The Rule of Three but finding, in Meagan and Simi, two great mates. At the time, Jemima remembered thinking, it shouldn't have worked. There was her, a social hermit, aspiring actress Simi and 19-year-old gum-popping go-getter Meagan – an unlikely combination. But as they wrote Puns and Pull Back and Reveals, it became apparent they were laughing at each other's material a lot more than anyone else – like, a *lot* more. Jemima chuckled as she recalled the first cracks appearing in Meagan's steely exterior. She was a tough cookie who turned out to also be a funny and fiercely loyal firebrand. Then there was Simi who had a heart of gold that saw the best in everyone. Jemima couldn't resist. On day one, the girls had shared a secret wink noticing almost everyone else on their course was a twenty-something lad in skinny jeans with an arsenal of jokes about their own penis. In those three months, Jemima learned thirty-eight euphemisms for masturbation but while new synonyms were handy, by far, her biggest take away had been her bond with Simi and Meagan in whom she found her left and her right arm. It was the girls who would piece her back together again after she and Miles broke up. Jemima who'd loan Simi thousands to support her acting, almost financially crippling herself. Simi and Jemima who'd comfort Meagan after her parents' divorce. The girls with whom Jemima would celebrate her first book deal, and she and Meagan who'd listen to Simi analyse her procession of boyfriends who all went from being *maybe* The One, to *definitely* The One, to *why wasn't he* The One? Poor Simi, Jemima sighed. She so wanted to be in love but every attempt ended in utter heartbreak and this weekend, it had happened again. To say Simi rushed into relationships was an understatement. Just days after getting together with city-working, cycling fanatic Oscar, Jemima had caught Simi practising her married name signature. A fortnight after, she and Meagan moved Simi into his Chiswick flat and now, just twelve months on, it was over. Jemima scrolled through her texts to Meagan's last message:

They've split up. Get home now.

And with just six words Jemima had cut short her LA trip and was heading back to London to be with her broken-hearted friend. Consoling Simi was a two-woman job and Jemima needed to get to her before Meagan started suggesting things like *getting under someone to get over Oscar.* Right now, Simi would barely be capable of getting out of bed, let alone into someone else's. Jemima sat back and exhaled, noticing how shallow her breathing had become. She hated seeing her friend in pain and would cross a hundred time zones to take it away but Simi's break-ups – and there had been many – always brought back everything she had gone through with Miles. The girls sometimes teased her about her compartmentalised life. From her chronically tidy flat to the meticulously organised apps on her phone, Jemima had everything in its place. Even her love life had its own special spot, a forgotten, dusty corner at the back of her mind. But it was what she needed for a peaceful life. Not letting anyone in again was not weakness; it was Jemima's defence against suffering as Simi was now or how she had with Miles. Jemima suddenly flashed back to hiding from Miles in that stinky privet hedge and her breathing shortened again. All at once, life didn't feel compartmentalised but like a maze and she was a lab rat scurrying back and forth trying to escape. Jemima clamped hold of her arm rests, searching the cabin for the exits, only calming once she'd spotted the glowing green sign behind her. The grip of panic, as always, had been swift. The impulse to bolt painfully familiar, her one and only answer – always.

'Postscript,' said Susan, appearing behind her. 'If you do decide to relocate and you want something fun to do, Bradley said the Latter Days are always looking for more members. The LA chapter is super small, like, tiny.'

Susan moved off again, closing overhead bins as she went. The thing was, Jemima mused as she buckled her seatbelt, if she joined she too might get shipped out as a missionary to Vanuatu where there absolutely, definitely was no Miles. Exposure to four strains of malaria was a small price to pay for that.

CHAPTER 2

Meagan

Meagan snatched up the book of wallpaper samples, barely taking in one design before snapping to the next. Too flowery, too many patterns, too Liberal Democrats! She flung the swatches across the bed and flicked though the carpet samples instead. They were even worse.

'Too pub-carpet, too corporate, too refurbished-council-building. No, no, NO.'

'Trouble in paradise,' Todd murmured into his pillow.

'Sleep,' said Meagan, brushing her hand over his face.

'Yes, ma'am,' said Todd as he snuggled closer.

Meagan rolled her eyes.

'*60 Minute Makeover* has a lot to answer for,' she scowled. 'They make it look like a refurb can be knocked out in an afternoon.'

'Maybe I can—' Todd began.

'I don't need help, cheers,' she said, wedging a pillow barrier between them.

How many times did Meagan have to tell him, she didn't need assistance and certainly not from her 'friend with benefits'.

As with everything else, she would figure it out – somehow. She sighed wearily, as she leafed through a ceiling tile brochure. Three months back and Meagan had been delighted to sign the lease for her new West End office. After seven years of running her comedy talent agency from rented desks and her mum's garage, it finally had a place to call home. In truth, she knew an agent didn't *need* Soho premises. Nowadays, getting bookings for her comedians was all done via email. If she'd been willing to look outside of Central London, she could have acquired an office twice the size at half the price but what was exclusive and swish about that? Meagan was all about the look, and what a fabulous look a W1 postcode was. After months of searching she'd found the killer spot, sixty square metres of unloved office space at the back of a Soho Square building.

Now all Meagan had to do was refurb it to her exacting standards. And there was no way she would hand that task over to anyone else no matter how many times Jemima bleated '*hire a project manager*'. Meagan could handle this on her own. That's what she did – handle things. And anyway, this job was just cosmetic. She was basically giving her office a boob job.

'Shall I get the papers?' Todd said propping himself up.

'You want me to change your litter tray?' said Meagan.

'Only if you need me to top up your saucer of milk.' Todd grinned, his hand snaking towards her under the duvet.

'Top bants, Toddy, but I have to get this right. It has to say Meagan Leslie. Big, ballsy, brassy. Like, go big or go home,' she said, dumping his hand back on his side of the bed.

The truth was, Meagan would have liked nothing more than to ride him like a ten-speed racer but she had to concentrate. Three months on and her refurb was not going to plan. She'd spent hours chasing suppliers and battling contractors, all while working off a desk made out of lever arch files. But she had to be strong. If she panicked as mere mortals would, she'd end up drafting in a stranger who would inflict all kinds of hotel-lobby awfulness on her and that would not do. When an act walked through her door, she wanted them practically licking her Louboutins desperate for her to represent them. She wanted them to believe only she could win them that career-defining, star-making TV panel show slot. She wanted them to leave her office convinced that Meagan Leslie and Partners was a top-flight agency and not the one-woman band it actually was. Of course, there were no partners. She didn't need randoms screwing things up. Meagan had learned the hard way that the net result of letting people in was Bruce-Willis-in-Space levels of disaster. It left you exposed and, after Parker, Meagan was never going to let herself feel like that again.

Dating a comedian, it transpired, wasn't as funny as she thought it would be, especially one who turned out to be married. It was a tough lesson but at least one good thing had come from it: Meagan's meticulously thought-out life plan. While other women stumbled into domestic captivity, knee-deep in carrot and leek baby mush, yoking themselves to someone they barely knew, Meagan was patiently moving through her five-phase plan. The first phase, which she'd inventively titled Phase Fun was about exactly that. Parties, parties and more parties. But it had ended the minute she turned 20 and phase two had kicked in. The aim was simple: crush it at work. And the best – indeed only – true measure of her success was when all twenty-four of her clients were employed. Currently there was only one outstanding: Simi. Meagan smiled at the thought of her mate earnestly throwing everything into becoming an actor. If only she'd give stand-up a try. If she got good, Simi would fly off the shelves. Meagan just knew it, but that wasn't what she wanted. Simi wanted pathos and dramatic pauses, mystery and suspense. However, with no agent, she was a million miles away from her dreams. Meagan often wondered if she'd done the right thing, taking Simi on as a client. Comedy was her wheelhouse, not acting. She preferred its immediacy and, frankly, straightforwardness. But if she hadn't signed Simi, how else was she going to progress? All Meagan needed to do was find one great role for Simi and she'd be flying high just like her comedians. How hard could getting acting work be? Occasionally casting directors would enquire about her acts. One even auditioned to be the next Doctor Who. As long as Simi did everything Meagan told her to, her career would transform in no time, which meant Meagan could move on to phase three of her plan: a relationship. Everyone had her pegged as anti-love but she wasn't. She was simply *pro-chronology*. And though she was deeply ensconced in phase two of her plan – getting it on at work – it didn't mean she couldn't get it on with Todd every now and then.

She peeked over her pillow barrier. He was dozing, mouth open. She smiled despite herself then picked up the carpet swatches and started from the beginning. As wintery afternoon rays spilled in through the half-open curtains Todd draped his hairy arm across her waist and let out a contented sigh. Meagan looked down at him. Of late, he'd got a lot more… snuggly, which was absolutely not part of their deal. In fact, in the beginning, he'd been more vocal about the no-strings thing than she had.

Just then, Meagan's phone rang. Her long chestnut weave

tumbled over her shoulder as she grabbed for her phone. Todd reached over and began massaging her neck.

'I'm on the phone, knobhead,' she said, batting his hand away.

'I should report you,' he said as he lay back down.

Meagan kissed her teeth, the long, rasping sound letting Todd know to zip it.

'Simi?' she said, sitting up, phone to her ear.

To the uninitiated, Simi's breathless sobs were unintelligible but, like the parent able to decipher their toddler's every gurgle, Meagan was well versed in decoding Simi's talk-crying.

'Okay, so last night your tarot lady said Oscar doesn't want kids… then this morning you had *The Talk* and now it's over and – alright, darling. Okay, okay. Don't worry, I'll be there in an hour,' Meagan said before hanging up.

Meagan knew the Simi-break-up drill well, and what emergency supplies were required – red wine, pizza and lots of tissues. Meagan pushed Todd's hand off her curvy, mocha hips ignoring his tuts. Even when there wasn't a crisis of the heart to deal with, she never hung around for more than an hour and he knew that.

'What's happened, Simi locked herself in her vestibule again?' Todd quipped.

'That could happen to anyone!' Meagan said, her eyes narrowing.

No one mocked her friends. That was her job.

'I thought we could have brunch or something,' said Todd as he watched Meagan dress.

'*Brunch?* This isn't *The Real Housewives*, babes. Besides if we have brunch, next it's dinner then I'm staying the night. Nah fam, this way we get the best of each other. I never have to watch you shave and you don't have to see me take a shit.'

'Lovely,' Todd laughed as he tucked his hands under his head.

Meagan slipped on her skirt and silk blouse, her mind already on Operation: Love Fool. When Simi's relationships ended she was by her side quicker than a first responder, but seeing Simi repeat the same pattern over and over again was becoming more frustrating for Meagan. She whipped open the curtains to let in some light.

'Meagan!' said Todd as he yanked the duvet over his naked body.

'It's the middle of the afternoon and I need to do my face,' she said touching up her already flawless make-up.

Todd collapsed in on himself like a badly folded napkin, 'You'd miss me if I wasn't here.'

'And where would you go?' Meagan laughed leaning in to kiss him.

'I might find myself a new friend, one who wants these benefits.' He smiled, cupping his manhood in his hands.

Meagan stared down at him. Now he wasn't excited, it looked like a clenched fist. Of course it wasn't about size or aesthetics. She and Todd were a good fit and she wasn't about to surrender access anytime soon.

Meagan patted his crotch and winked, 'Just don't let him get into any fights.'

'He does not look like a clenched bloody fist! Stop saying that!' Todd wailed after Meagan but she was gone.

Out in the corridor she let his door click closed behind her as she slipped on her coat and then, pulling out her phone, pinged a six-word text to Jemima.

They've split up. Get home now.

CHAPTER 3

Simi

'But *whhhhyyyyyyyyy?*' wailed Simi as snot trickled onto Meagan's designer mini-skirt.

She had been sobbing into Meagan's lap since she'd arrived a few hours earlier and the tears showed no sign of abating. Occasionally she'd resurface like a blue whale rising to clear its blow hole. Then she'd emit another pitiful '*whhhhhhyyyyyy?*' only to drop back down into the murky depths of her despair.

Two weeks into the new year and Simi was already experiencing her *worst* break-up *ever*. This was stare-at-his-Facebook-profile bad. This was Toni Braxton-on-repeat rotten. This was Jack-and-Rose-at-the-end-of-*Titanic* terrible. Except Simi wasn't Rose shedding a single tear for the love she'd lost, no, Simi was the actual ship, a colossus sinking under the weight of all the tragedy. Another wave of grief hit her. *Jack could totally have fit on that board!* she whimpered as she imagined fighting tooth and nail to drag Oscar onto that much-discussed driftwood. Or perhaps Oscar was the iceberg, their paths destined to collide. She was always being told she was too dramatic. Her black friends said it was a black thing. Her actor friends said it was an actor thing and her mum said it was a black actor thing, but this situation was *titanic*. Her response was completely proportionate! Simi sniffled as she wrapped her arms around Meagan's waist and quietly began warbling, 'My Heart Will Go On'.

'Simi… *Simi*?'

Simi blinked her eyes open just as she was about to launch into the big middle eight.

'Why don't you have a shower, babes? You'll feel better,' Meagan offered.

'I don't want to take my pyjamas off. He bought me them for Christ*maaaaas*,' Simi grizzled.

Suddenly she understood why Jackie Kennedy had kept on her infamous pink Chanel suit that fateful day. She decided, however, to keep the macabre revelation to herself. If people thought she was dramatic before, then comparing her break-up to a presidential assassination might tip the scales against her.

Simi whimpered as she looked down at her Cat in the Hat pyjamas wishing she hadn't been wearing them that morning when she and Oscar had had *The Talk*.

With her revolving-door romantic life, she'd grown wearily accustomed to that conversation.

Granted, *The Talk* wasn't always a bad thing. Simi smiled wistfully as she remembered *The Talk* she'd had with Jason. They'd gone from dating to boyfriend and girlfriend over pizza and beers while watching *Rent!* in his dad's basement. Next came Ade, who she'd ended up living with after an argument about filling the dishwasher turned into *The Talk*. However, overwhelmingly, *The Talks* consisted of a lot more 'it's not you's than 'I do's.

Since turning 30, five short years ago, Simi totted up that

she'd fallen stomach-churningly head-over-heels in love four times! She'd thought *he's the one* four times and every relationship had gone soul-crushingly wrong.

'I tell you what, Meagan,' she sniffled, 'Gabrielle got it wrong in that flipping song of hers. Dreams *don't* come true. Where's my happy ever after? The BAFTA, the husband, the kids, the overweight chocolate Labradors?'

'You want fat dogs?' Meagan asked looking down at her.

'My tarot lady was riiiiiight. Oscar *never* wanted children. She saw it all,' sobbed Simi.

'You can't let some Sideshow Sally tell you what's what in your life,' said Meagan.

'But she was right! She's always right,' said Simi before slumping back into Meagan's lap.

This was pointless. Her need for spiritual guidance was one thing neither Meagan nor Jemima understood. They'd stopped coming to Simi's tarot nights years ago probably because they already had everything figured out. Jemima was a successful author and Meagan had her ten thousand phase plan but Simi still felt lost. Her acting career was so tenuous it required inverted commas and though she had adored Oscar, something had been off. Even she couldn't ignore the way he stalled or changed the subject whenever their future came up in conversation. So she'd decided to get answers from the only thing she trusted, a spread of randomly selected occult cards. When would they marry and how many children would they have? She hoped for three but would settle for twins and those chocolate Labs. The only thing Simi wanted as much was a BAFTA… and to be met at the airport by a driver with a nameboard.

The night of the reading Oscar had politely made his excuses, leaving Simi and her actor chums to eat a little, drink some more and have their fortunes read by Rosalie. But when Rosalie had laid out Simi's cards, there'd been no sign of children with Oscar – at all. Simi had laughed, mainly out of shock. Next door, she could hear the others giggling and chatting whilst, here in the back bedroom, her life was imploding.

'So he only wants *one* child?' Simi had asked as she stared at a card showing a crumbling tower.

Rosalie had smiled sadly. 'Let's see what the next card says.'

She turned it over revealing a skeleton on a black horse… holding a scythe.

'Oh,' she'd said.

Afterwards, numb from the reading, Simi had returned to the living room and chatted with her friends as though none of this had happened. She oohed and aahed as one shared Rosalie's prediction of a forthcoming work opportunity involving buffalo. She clapped excitedly for her acting chum Alice who had received a message from the other side saying not to worry about her teeth. Who knew the spirit realm could be so specific? And when they'd all asked about her reading, Simi had slapped on a grin, said it was all about change then changed the subject.

The following morning in bed Simi had turned to Oscar. She'd mustered all the courage she could to ask the one person who actually had the answers she sought.

'Do you want children… with me?'

The plainness of his 'no' had shocked her.

And so there and then, in bed, just that morning, wearing Dr Seuss jammies, Simi and Oscar had broken up. Oscar had gone to his friend's place to give Simi room to pack and Simi had wallowed in misery until Meagan had run to her rescue as she always did. Simi stared at the pile of collapsed cardboard boxes propped up against the living-room door that Meagan had arrived with. That's how together she was. She had turned up with boxes. Even Amazon couldn't have got them to her quicker. But how was Simi supposed to pack when her entire world had fallen apart? How could she start folding T-shirts when her life was in tatters? She closed her eyes and clung even tighter to Meagan who'd been stroking her hair while checking emails on her phone. Simi took a breath and launched into the middle eight of 'My Heart Will Go On'. It was time.

As she was about to hit a high note, another email alert beeped on Meagan's phone above Simi's head, 'Interesting… ' murmured Meagan.

Simi stopped and looked up.

'No, babes, it's not Oscar but if you have a shower I will tell you what it is,' said Meagan.

Simi slumped back down.

'Come, Simi. You don't want Jem seeing you like this.'

'Jemima's in LA,' Simi exhaled.

'No, babes. I texted her when I left Todd's earlier. She'll be home tomorrow,' Meagan said, cupping Simi's face in her hands.

'For me?'

'Who else would she cut short her escape-break for?'

'You?'

'Apart from me,' Meagan laughed.

'Can I have a shower in my pyjamas?'

Meagan tutted then pulled Simi close.

'Fine. Keep them on – for now. I'm gonna make up the spare bed.'

'You're staying?' said Simi blinking away her tears.

'It's a big day tomorrow. We're gonna wash that man out of your hair… literally. Then we'll pack you up and get you out of here. I know it hurts now but this is gonna be good for you.' Meagan smiled.

Simi hugged Meagan as tears fell but they were grateful tears. Meagan was here and soon Jemima would be too. Natural order would be restored and they'd once again be a three.

CHAPTER 4

Jemima

Jemima glanced along her empty row and grinned. Takeoff was in less than twenty minutes and the two seats beside her were still empty. It wasn't that she didn't like people, well it was a bit but really she just *loved* space. She felt pangs of jealousy for Robinson Crusoe. Imagine, a whole island to yourself.

As she contemplated that solitary existence, the plane's PA system crackled to life. 'Good evening, ladies and gentlemen, I'm Captain Ted Striker!' the announcement began, followed by a warm chuckle. 'A little cockpit humour there. No, I'm Captain Brett Lambert and on behalf of my crew, thank you for choosing Wow-Oui Air... not many people do. Anyway, I'm delighted to welcome you aboard this 19.20 flight from Los Angeles to Brussels.'

A panicked murmur spread throughout the cabin.

'Only joking. We are, of course, heading to London... *Ontario*. Kidding. London, England.'

Good God, thought Jemima, now wishing she *had* paid the extortionate last-minute premium to fly with a normal airline.

'We're just awaiting one last connecting passenger and we'll be on our way. Until then, I'll leave you in the capable hands of our cabin crew led today by Ms Susan Burke. If you ask nicely, she'll give you a massage. Joking. But I can guarantee a happy ending when we land in London at approximately one p.m. *GMT*. Ice and a slice in mine.'

Jemima grimaced and began arranging her blankets and pillows on the vacant seats beside her. She barely noticed the last straggler making his way down the opposite aisle apologising as he bashed people with his hefty rucksack. Finally, she looked over. What was it with some people and time management? she tutted. And that bag was definitely over the size allowance. '*Selfish*,' she murmured as the straggler began checking row numbers. Keep moving, keep moving, she silently chanted, as she watched him search for space in the overhead bins, stopping briefly to wipe his curly brown hair out of his eyes.

'Please, no,' Jemima muttered to the gods of seat allocation as he started rearranging bags in the bin above *her* row.

As he reached up his T-shirt lifted revealing a taut, sun-kissed tummy. Vain, Jemima thought, as she observed him charmingly involve other passengers in the bag reshuffle. Vain and *late* she decreed noticing his muscular arms. Just then the straggler caught Jemima's eye. She snatched up a tattered duty-free magazine and leafed through it. A blur of spy equipment and pink lipsticks flashed before her. She wished that just once, duty-free would stock cosmetics vaguely suited to her ebony skin tones. That, however, was a battle for another day. Right now, her sights were on The Straggler – the worst of all Batman's nemeses.

His annoyingly jovial bag palaver finally over, he took his seat – on Jemima's row!

Noooooooooooooo, she wailed inside as she watched him get

comfortable in what had been occupied territory. Well, he'd better not talk to me, she ruled.

'Hey. Chance,' he said, reaching across the two empty seats to shake hands.

'Chance?' said Jemima with zero warmth.

'Yeah, you know like the Abba song. Take A—'

'Yeah, yeah. I've heard the word "chance" before,' said Jemima, observing his Australian accent, with unnecessary disdain.

'You reading that upside down on my account?' he quipped. Jemima looked down and realised she was indeed holding the magazine the wrong way up.

She snapped it shut, flustered.

'Is this your stuff?' Chance said pointing at Jemima's detritus.

'Sorry,' she said, indignantly. 'I thought the row was empty.'

She collected up her things and stuffed them under the seat in front.

'My bad. Bloke on my last flight had a heart attack and I had to do CPR. Cracked his rib but at least he's alive, eh?'

'Lucky you were there,' Jemima replied. *Show off!*

'Cabin crew, arm doors and cross-check and if you left the iron on, I hope your house doesn't burn down. Joshing! I hope it's razed to the ground and you get a mighty insurance payout. Right, here we go!' the captain hooted.

Chance leaned across the seats, 'This guy's a laugh.'

His sarcastic aside at least, was one thing Jemima could agree on. She nodded ungenerously then clamped her headphones on and scrolled through the music selection. She needed calm, soothing tones to help her drift away from row twenty-eight, from this chatterbox and from their 'comical' captain. Finally she found what she was looking for, Bach's Cello Suites. At school, she'd made a few half-baked attempts to learn this and in adulthood it was her go-to when she needed tranquillity. As they taxied for takeoff, Jemima caught one last inappropriate cockpit broadcast about using breast milk in the tea, before the cellos whisked her away.

Halfway through Suite No. 5 Jemima felt a tug on her headphone cord and turned to see Chance waving at her. With a quiet sigh, she lifted one ear pad.

'Wanna chat?' said Chance.

'No,' said Jemima in an alternative reality where she freely spoke her mind.

However, in this reality where she was steeped in British awkwardness, she slipped her headphones off and with a pinched smile said, 'Sure.'

Instinctively, she scoped the cabin again for exits. Even at 36,000 feet Jemima was always looking for a way out.

'So you a big fan of old Johann Sebastian?' Chance asked, 'I could hear it through your headphones, the music from that bank commercial, right?'

'Sorry. I can turn it down if it's too loud. It's my favourite piece of music. Helps me to… block out the drone of the plane,' she said.

'Oh, if that's what you need I've got something much better,' Chance said as he surreptitiously looked around the cabin before handing Jemima a slender hip flask, '100mls of liquid gold.'

'Oh, no, thank you,' said Jemima raising a hand.

Chance thrust the flask into it.

'Come on. It's a long flight,' he nudged.

'I know,' Jemima replied looking down at the thin flask.

Cautiously, she put it to her lips as though it were a vial of anthrax. The syrupy alcohol slipped down her throat. She had to concede, it was good.

'Tequila.' Chance grinned. 'Picked up some good shit in Mexico.'

Jemima took another micro-swig. The airline pillows were too small to put over Chance's face so mild inebriation might be the only antidote to ten hours next to him.

'So, what takes you to London?' Chance asked scooching over one seat.

Jemima withered. Was this a chat or a talk show interview?

'It's home,' she said.

But the words caught as they came out. Yes, she loved her little flat and was looking forward to its familiar solitude but thoughts of LA just weren't going away. Beaches, beautiful skies and a clean slate awaited. Her mother would have no objections. Jemima relocating would give her another part of the world to visit. It was Simi and Meagan who would need convincing. But as Jemima considered the reality of putting such a distance between her and her two best friends, it made her heart ache.

'What about you?' she said redirecting the conversation. 'What takes you to LA? Surfing?'

Chance laughed looking down at his scruffy T-shirt and jeans.

'Right. You are looking at Australia's best, worst surfer. Honestly, I suck at it. In your face, stereotypes,' he said winking at Jemima.

'Sorry,' she said, quickly.

As a black woman, she knew how grating even positive prejudices were, yet here she was laying one on this guy with a trowel.

'So, what do you do?' she asked turning back to Chance who, if he were offended by her presumptions, was being kind enough not to show it.

'Occupational therapist. I help people recover from injuries and stuff. Got a little practice in Stokey,' he said, taking another sip of tequila.

Jemima froze.

'Stokey?' she quizzed, her voice ascending half an octave.

Stokey was what the locals called Stoke Newington and was where she lived!

'Yeah, above the coffee shop on Apone Parade.'

'Azi and Rania's place... Nostromo... ?' Jemima spluttered.

'That's the one! You know it?'

'Not really,' Jemima lied.

Know it? Not only was it minutes from her flat but she'd written two and a half of her three books there. Why had she never spotted him?

'Err how did you get into occupational therapy?' she quizzed.

As she once again shepherded the conversation, Jemima noticed his warm smile wane and in its place something deeper appear – was it pain, regret? She couldn't tell but clearly, this wasn't just a job to him. Chance picked at his flask, for a moment taken by his thoughts.

'My brother lost his leg in Afghanistan. I felt helpless, like I wanted to do something but I didn't know what so I trained as an OT. And I wanted to support people in the same boat as Pete so I started my charity, Man Up. We give OT to wounded vets. See,' Chance pulled his faded T-shirt tight showing her the Man Up logo.

Jemima nodded earnestly but inside she was squirming. She'd been so mean when his only crime was to sit next to a snide, seat-hogging misery-guts. She took a hit of tequila and handed the flask back, 'So what took you to Mexico apart from the search for really good tequila?'

Chance laughed, his infectious smile, returned. 'Only the best wedding *ever.*'

Jemima listened as Chance described Pete's journey to recovery, how it had begun in their parent's home in Adelaide and continued with a trip to Los Cabos where he'd fallen in love. Chance explained how at first he'd been worried when his brother had left but the minute he'd seen Pete and Lula together, he'd known they were destined for each other. Jemima smiled though something was bothering her. Yes, it was a gorgeous story but it was also oddly familiar.

'Sometimes you can just feel it, when two people fit. Don't you think?' said Chance, handing the flask over.

As their fingers brushed against each other Jemima felt her breath falter. She looked up at Chance, noticing for the first time that his eyes were different colours, one green and the other hazel or was it brown… ?

'I do,' she said.

'Huh?' said Chance.

'What?'

'You said, you do.'

'Do I? I mean, did I?' said Jemima, ruffled.

Her eyes darted around the cabin, 'Did they turn the air conditioning off? It feels like the air is… can you feel that?'

'Feel what... ?' asked Chance.

'Like, hot. Feels like a heat. A hot heat,' Jemima gabbled, looking behind her to see if the bathroom was empty.

You're not going anywhere, the red occupied light glowered back.

'So you were saying, Peter got married?' she stuttered trying to look at him without looking at his eyes which were... hypnotic – purely in a freak-of-nature kind of way.

He did. 'I love a good wedding, but this one... Blubbed like a little girl,' said Chance.

'Or boy,' Jemima said.

She groaned at herself. Halfway through a story about Chance's disabled brother's life-affirming wedding was probably not the time to thrust her equality politics on him.

'Eh?' said Chance.

'Nothing.'

'I could barely get through my speech,' he continued, smiling at the memory. 'Pete was determined to walk down the aisle despite everyone telling him he wasn't ready. Even I had my doubts. The whole chapel held their breath as he got out of his wheelchair and onto his crutches. But with each step, the applause and cheers got louder and louder. I swear people in the street must have thought we were watching the footie.'

Chance paused, as though struck by an idea. He reached into his carry-on bag, pulled out a hardback book and passed it to Jemima. *Pete Dasos: A Walk on The Mild Side*, the cover read. Jemima turned it over in her hands. She had seen it before. She flipped the book over to see who the publisher was. *Shit.* Hudson Hicks Books – the same publisher as her! She hurriedly handed it back.

'No, no. Have it,' he said pushing the book towards her. 'He decided to write his life story and what do you know, he got published. Look inside.'

Jemima opened the well-thumbed book and Chance leaned across, leafing through to the foreword.

'He wrote me a frigging dedication. I mean, in my top ten best things ever it's like number five, four, three, two and one. When I saw it, I cried like a… like a little boy,' said Chance winking.

But despite his delight, Jemima could see he was welling up. She went back to the book to give him some space. As her hand glided over its glossy sleeve she couldn't help feel a twinge of jealousy. Hudson Hicks Books often sent her new releases. Jemima always loved a freebie, however, she didn't appreciate how often Eve Lim, her passively pushy editor would enclose notes pointedly detailing how well each book was doing and how much romance said books contained. It irritated Jemima specifically because romantic storylines had been the source of an ongoing battle between her and Eve since Jemima's second book a year ago.

And that's where she recognised Pete's story and his book from. Eve had sent his autobiography with a note declaring it a veritable love fest which only the stone-hearted would be able to resist. The book had sat unread somewhere in Jemima's flat since she'd received it. She pushed Chance's copy into her bag.

'Honestly, you read that and I promise, you will fall in love.' said Chance.

Jemima looked up at him, her cheeks suddenly burning.

'With Pete and Lula… ' said Chance. 'Anyway, enough about all that. What do you do to keep the wolf from the door?'

Oh brilliant, thought Jemima, her least favourite question.

Writer was one of those professions, like actor, where if people hadn't heard of you they'd silently categorise you a pointless failure and a glassy-eyed indifference would descend. Jemima had even tried lying but that hadn't worked out.

'A goat herder? Wow and what do you produce?'

'Yoghurt and... cheese. Yoghurt cheese.'

'Would I have heard of your brand?'

'No.'

Glassy-eyed indifference.

And now there was the added complication of Jemima sharing the same publisher as Chance's brother. This plane was too small to contain his potential excitement if that information grenade was tossed in.

'I write novels about a woman who investigates insurance fraud. I used to be a junior investigator. Anyway, you've probably never heard of them unless you buy your books from charity shops but I was number nineteen in *What Insurance?* magazine's top twenty insurance-based novels, so...'

Confession over, Jemima braced herself for the judgemental axe of Chance's glassy-eyed indifference.

'Wait, you wrote those *Beverly Blake* books?' he said clicking his fingers to spur his memory. 'You're Jemima Abeson? I frigging *love* them! What do you mean "charity shops"? Your first book was on *The Times* bestseller list. Tell me there's gonna be a third one. The way *Mysteries* ended I was like, come *on*!'

Jemima tentatively dipped her toe in the pool of adoration. The water was warm. It was a rare treat to meet a fan who was a real-world normal person and not an insurance investigator eager to correct her factual inaccuracies. *It's a made-up story*, she always wanted to bellow at them.

'I'm close to finishing the third one.' She smiled.

'Mate, that's awesome!' said Chance. 'And will Beverly find out what's in lock-up 639? Actually, I don't want to know. Man, this is intense!'

Wow, he really did know the books, thought Jemima.

'I won't spoil it but let's just say, it picks up with her heading to Swindon,' she teased.

'God, I've got so many questions!'

And he really did. Through the drinks service and evening meal, Chance interrogated Jemima on every detail of her novels. And as the cabin lights dimmed, Jemima realised his voice, rather than grating, was actually pretty sexy – from an objective point of view, she clarified to herself for no reason. And his eyes, the hazel, green and brown seemed to almost glimmer in the subdued light. But it wasn't so much his eyes, more the way he looked at her. And she'd clearly had more drinks than she'd thought because she was starting to feel flirty. That hadn't happened for a very, very long time. Jemima breathed Chance in. He smelled like… running. Not in a bad way. It was the aroma of hard work and life and skin. He smelt like earth, like a forest. Jemima bit her lip. Given they were random strangers, would a mini-flirt be such a dreadful thing? She ran her fingers through her bob, twirling a finger around a stray strand.

'Look, I've gotta ask,' Chance said leaning in, 'why doesn't Beverly have a special someone?'

Jemima's smile flickered and Chance immediately back-pedalled, 'I'm being nosy. You've got to keep some stuff under wraps. I get it.'

Jemima turned to him tugging her finger from a tangled knot of hair.

'It's my publisher,' she sighed, 'they're not happy with Beverly's love life which is obviously ridiculous. Eve, my editor, loved the will-they-won't-they between Beverly and her boss in the first book and she wanted me to take it further in the second book, *Mysteries*.'

'But you killed him,' said Chance.

Yeah, alright, Mr Super Fan, thought Jemima. What he didn't know was that when she'd sat down to write her second book it was just weeks after breaking up with Miles. There was no way Jemima could write about romance when hers had come crashing down around her, and so she'd turned Beverly's complex and rich world into a strict procedural. Jemima focused all Beverly's dogged determination on tirelessly unearthing insurance fraud and busting open criminal underworlds. Romance was a distraction. And though Eve did everything she could to steer Jemima back towards the passion and intimacy of book one, Jemima was adamant. Besides, who could argue with the five star reviews for her debut and broadsheet write-ups that noted the 'Nordic sparsity of Abeson's storytelling' and 'the stripped back single-mindedness of the lead character'?

'They were practically telling me to remove the romance,' Jemima argued, 'but then *Mysteries* came out and those same critics said my "sophomoric offering was a let-down". "*Dry*" was the word that hurt the most.'

Jemima looked away from Chance, remembering how crestfallen she'd been after her agent, Shaheena had forwarded the reviews. Mediocre write-ups were almost worse than getting panned. Having your book described by a *Guardian* critic as, 'the worst use of paper since their nephew tried to print out the Internet', at least made for entertaining dinner party conversation. 'Dry' was just awkward.

And so, after Jemima had killed off Beverly's boss in *Mysteries*, Eve had ramped up her campaign to resuscitate Beverly's love life to save the latest instalment, *Beverly Blake Discoveries*.

Prior to her LA trip Jemima had delivered a draft to Eve hoping the minuscule crumbs of amour she'd sprinkled on the story would be enough to satiate her. They weren't, and Jemima bristled all over again just remembering Eve's feedback.

'Jeeeeeehm. It's *Eeeeeve*.' Eve had said as she'd inhaled on that bloody e-cigarette, 'Darling, this latest draft is veh, *veh* good.'

Eve was so posh it was her assistant's job to pronounce the 'r' in very.

'Ummm… Latest?' Jemima had asked. 'It's the *final* draft.'

'*Riiiiiight*. Of course. Just got a couple of *suggesteroos* for a more *final,* final draft.'

Suggesteroos, Jemima snorted. They were demands masquerading as suggestions about as convincingly as a wolf in a sheepskin jacket.

'Thing is, Boo, we love how you've upped the stakes. Powerful stuff. And her getting a cat, *veh* moving but, when I said Beverly needs more emotional intimacy, I meant, you know, man intimacy not cat intimacy. Without the boss, Beverly's world feels small. All she does is work and you know, all work and no *plaaaaaay…* '

Every word Eve uttered had made Jemima's blood boil.

'We just want people to like *haaah* again,' Eve had offered.

'So, being brilliant isn't *likeable*?' Jemima had snapped.

Surely Eve wasn't suggesting readers can only like Beverly if she's fawning over some bloke? She's Beverly Blake not Bridget-bloody-Jones! Jemima made a mental note to slip that in at the earliest opportunity. Witty ripostes usually took her a day to formulate so it was great to have one in the back pocket.

'She's become brittle, Jem and… highly strung,' said Eve.

'So a good seeing-to'll sort her out, is that it?'

'Plus,' Eve had pressed on, ignoring Jemima, 'this'll mean there's been two books with not a snog or a fumble between them! It's becoming… *repetitaaaave*.'

And there you had it. What had remained unsaid had finally been uttered, leaving Jemima in stunned silence. She knew she was no Xandria Bishop, the hot new author and recent winner of the Booker Prize. Her debut novel, *The Cave*, which was set entirely in a vagina had sent shockwaves through the publishing world. But despite none of Jemima's books being set in anyone's reproductive organs she trusted her creative instincts. Beverly did NOT need a man.

'MAYBE I SHOULD SET THE WHOLE THING IN MY VAGINA?!!' she'd barked at Eve.

In hindsight, Jemima wished she hadn't been sitting in the window of Nostromo when she'd yelled that down the phone. The sensation of her voice bouncing off the glass and echoing around the quiet café still felt very recent.

'Look, Jemima, all we want is a good shafting.'

'I'll think about it.'

'That's all I ask. We love you Jem-J and would hate to lose *yoooooou*.'

And with that, Eve had taken a sharp inhale on her e-cigarette and hung up, 'Laters!'

The casual 'Laters!' had left Jemima so fuming she hadn't picked up on Eve's parting, 'hate to lose you'.

'That sucks,' said Chance.

'My editor just won't let it go. She's desperate for Beverly to fall in love but it's crazy, isn't it?' Jemima said, knowing that as a connoisseur of the books, Chance would understand.

But instead of empathetic nods he was smiling.

'I really liked her boss, Kane. Beverly was good with him. And just when things were gonna get hot and heavy, boom, he died. Don't get me wrong, great twist that he was behind the Swindon fraud and I love that you focus on how brilliant and driven she is but wouldn't it be great if she had, I don't know, *some* kind of encounter? Nothing serious but, you know.'

Jemima's face turned to thunder. 'Want Beverly to shag some random, eh? Maybe a guy she meets in a bar or on a plane—'

Chance looked at Jemima confused, 'That's not what I meant. It's just, apart from her cat, now she's got no one—'

'Mr Tinkles is not no one! And anyway, the book is about her work not her bedroom.'

Chance put his hand on Jemima's wrist. 'What I meant was, it was great to see another side to her. The fans miss that.'

Jemima turned squarely to him, '*Real* fans love her for who she is not who she's with.'

Nice. She'd remember that one too. She whipped her hand from under his, unclipping her seatbelt, 'and IT'S BEVERLY JONES *NOT* BRIDGET BLAKE! I mean Blake. It's Beverly Blake. Oh whatever!'

Bollocks, she exhaled as she flounced off to stew beside the exit.

CHAPTER 5

Simi

'*Jeeeeeem*, you came back – for me,' whimpered Simi.

Jemima was one of the only things, aside from Meagan, keeping her afloat and now all three of them were back together, everything was as it should be – apart from her heart which Oscar had exploded into a million pieces.

'Of course I came back, angel,' Jemima said as she held Simi.

And just as Simi's tears were about to subside, she saw Jemima's suitcase nestled in the corner of the room and started crying all over again. 'You came all this way – with a suitcase!'

Jemima kissed Simi's forehead and wiped away her tears. 'I did. Now, look, Meagan said Oscar will be back soon. Shall we finish packing?'

'You mean start,' murmured Meagan looking back at her stack of collapsed boxes.

'I *caaaan't*,' Simi keened as she let herself slip out of Jemima's grip and onto the floor.

Jemima scrambled to keep hold of her as Meagan buried her head in her hands. 'Babe, we've got to—'

'I really, *really* thought he was the one, guys. He was kind, faithful and clever. Well he wore glasses… ' said Simi from her puddle of despair as she remembered their initial spark.

His dreamy cappuccino complexion – which Meagan unkindly referred to as decaf – his precious overbite and lean body, had all made her swoon. The girls always badgered her about sleeping with guys too soon but when Oscar, this black, bespectacled dreamboat, had invited her back to his place, who was she to say no? Simi loved how in sync they'd been… at first. When she was down after an audition, he'd miraculously appear with a red velvet cupcake – her favourite. When they were picking a TV show to binge-watch, they'd always choose the same one. With Oscar, it felt different, like they were going somewhere. So why had everything fallen apart?

'What have I done to deserve this? I'm kind to animals and I buy a poppy every year!' Simi sobbed.

'Darling, you're a dime and the minute you're packed and out of his place, you'll realise that,' said Meagan thrusting a thumb in the direction of the door. 'So shall we?'

'She's right,' said Jemima trying to scoop Simi up from Oscar's hardwood floor. 'We should probably head down to the basement and—'

'Pack? Ha!' said Simi letting her head loll back until it came to a rest on Jemima's shoulder.

'Oh no you don't,' said Meagan as Simi's entire body collapsed into their grasp.

'Just leave me be, girls. I've had a good life,' Simi said looking back at the sofa like a dying dog searching for a quiet place to howl its last goodbye.

'Jemima,' she said earnestly holding Jemima's face, 'to you I leave my collection of self-help books. Read them, especially

The Girl Who Tried to Outrun her Shadow. It's a novel but you know how sometimes they can be metaphors… '

'Simi,' barked Meagan. 'Allow it, man! You have to pack or do you want Oscar to see you looking like this and smelling like French onion soup?!'

'No… but… ' said Simi.

'You said he's coming back at seven, right?' Meagan said tapping her watch.

'Yeah?'

'Well, it's already gone six!'

Simi's eyes turned to saucers. 'What?! Frig!' she bawled, barging past Meagan and practically traversing the stairs on the balls of her feet. 'What are you waiting for? We have to pack!'

CHAPTER 6

Meagan

Moments later Meagan's slingbacks were clacking down Oscar's wooden basement steps. At just over five foot one, flats were out of the question no matter the task at hand. Even when she broke her foot skiing, her compromise had been cork wedges. To Meagan, flat shoes were a *reverse* heel and looked brain-numbingly uncomfortable. She glanced over at Jemima's Converse pumps. Of course *she* wore flats. Her primary concern was always a fast getaway.

All three of them looked around Oscar's dark basement at the neatly piled boxes, old bike parts, unloved forgotten furniture and other crap people keep in the hope of one day needing again. Meagan folded up her sleeves and began lugging boxes upstairs. This was the third time they'd moved Simi out of a boyfriend's flat and whilst she was well versed at handling the practicalities of Simi's crises, inside she was beginning to fume. Why did women put themselves in this situation, moving into a guy's place only to render themselves homeless when, inevitably, the shit hit the fan? It wasn't that she was opposed to cohabiting – after all that was phase four of her life plan. It was the power imbalance that infuriated her. Even when Parker had teased a shared future, on this point Meagan had been clear – no one was moving in with anyone else. They would buy a new place *together*. In the end it had turned out to be academic. But at least she'd given it some thought. She was certain most of Simi's issues lay in the fact that she didn't have even a hint of a game plan. She was always either getting into something or coming out of it and in between, kissing an awful lot of frogs. Meagan glanced at the pathetic silhouette of her bereft friend, her chunky afro still sculpted into the shape of Meagan's lap from the day before. She tensed. This was what her mother had been like when she'd separated from her dad. Meagan was determined, she would never let anyone have that kind of power over her.

'Guys, come on,' said Jemima clapping her hands. 'We haven't got long.'

She was right. They had to crack on. Meagan hoisted up another box of books. The quicker they sorted this the sooner everything could get back to normal. She wanted Jemima to get back to complaining about the injustices of the world, Todd to stop ruining good sex with his yammering and cuddles, and Simi to go back to being her normal, scatty, law-of-attraction loving self. She wanted her to be able to say Oscar's name without hyperventilating but most importantly, she wanted her to go back to work – and soon – because the *interesting* thing that had popped up on Meagan's phone yesterday very much involved Simi. Call it luck or fate but somehow Meagan had secured Simi an audition for IPC, a company who made some of the biggest shows on television. And if it weren't for this bloody break-up, Meagan would be discussing that with Simi rather than heaving boxes of Deepak Chopra books up Oscar's rickety basement stairs.

'Nice of him to box everything up for you, I s'pose,' Jemima said as she gathered an armful of yoga mats and headed up.

'Yeah,' Simi said, 'except… he never made room for me – in the flat.'

Meagan looked at all Simi's neatly packed belongings.

'Unbelievable,' she sneered and just as she was about to launch into a colourfully worded rant, Jemima came thundering down the stairs.

'He's back!'

Simi sniffed her armpits and ran a panicked hand over her pyramid of uncombed afro hair.

'He's early, isn't he?' she hissed, darting around the room like a trapped ant.

'It's gone eight. He's not early. We're late!' said Jemima, hovering halfway down the stairs.

'Hide me!' cried Simi, turfing Oscar's camping gear out of a trunk.

She pulled a dusty groundsheet over her head and collapsed into a ball.

'Simi?' Oscar called from upstairs.

Jemima and Meagan stared at the pathetic, quivering plastic sheet.

'Tell him I'm not here!' Simi hissed.

'You're not,' Meagan murmured as she clacked up to the ground floor.

'Hey, Oscar!' trilled Jemima trotting behind Meagan, straining to sound casual.

In the hallway, Oscar propped up his bike. He unclipped his helmet and wiped his face, still glistening with sweat. Meagan arched an eyebrow at his skin-tight, bright red and yellow cycling outfit. Dork, she sneered to herself. *Stringy, decaf dork.*

'Where's Simi?' Oscar asked peering down the basement steps as Meagan blocked his path.

'Not here, babes. Prepping… for a role… new IPC show with Bradley Tyson and Cameron Christiansen,' she said nonchalantly, ignoring Jemima's glare.

So it was a big, fat fib. So Simi hadn't even auditioned for, let alone got the job. There was no harm in making Oscar jealous in the meantime.

'Cameron Christiansen? Is she the actress from that mermaids and zombies thing?' Oscar asked.

Meagan crossed her ankles to stop herself kicking him. For his taste in film alone, Simi should have canned this guy ages ago.

'No,' Meagan said through gritted teeth, 'she's the actress from that winning-an-Emmy-last-year thing.'

Meagan felt a sharp jab in her back and conceded she may have lost track of her objective.

'Anyway, we just came to get Simi's things,' said Jemima stepping in.

'Fair enough.' Oscar nodded, moving towards the basement.

'We're good,' said Meagan, casually resting her hand on the doorframe in front of him.

Oscar's eyes narrowed, 'Not that I don't trust you. I just want to make sure our things aren't mixed up.'

'But it's so dark down there. Don't you get umm… scared?' said Jemima.

Meagan glowered at her as Oscar moved past them.

'Pathetic!' she scowled, clipping Jemima around the back of the head, fluffing her bob.

Stick to correcting people's grammar, she wheezed as she flapped down the stairs after him. In the basement, Oscar took a deep breath. After a quick scan of the room he started handing bags and boxes to Meagan and Jemima who were battling hard to keep their cool as they ferried everything up to the landing. Oscar smiled sadly at the space where some of Simi's belongings had been before noticing his unpacked outdoor gear.

'You know that's *my* camping kit?' he said, pointing.

'As if. Black people and the outdoors,' Jemima smirked, play-punching Oscar.

He stared back at her rubbing his arm, '*I'm* black.'

'I mean, of course. Jokes.' Jemima nodded vigorously as she and Meagan watched Oscar collect up what Simi had strewn everywhere in her desperate bid to hide, their alarm rising.

He placed everything in the trunk then reached for the ground sheet. Without thinking, Meagan leapt forward, wrapping her arms around him. She buried her head in his chest, her face contorted with sadness, 'I'm going to miss you!' she wailed.

Oscar froze looking down at Meagan before nervously patting her head.

'Don't touch the weave,' Meagan corrected before returning to her wailing.

Oscar tried to wriggle free but like a Chinese finger puzzle, the more he did, the tighter Meagan's grip became. Just as he got an arm free, Jemima clamped herself to him from behind.

'I'll miss you too!'

'I... ' began Oscar, confused, 'I didn't think you liked me.'

'We don't like you, Oscar. We *love* you,' Meagan said looking up at him adoringly, 'and it would really help if we could have a moment alone – for closure.'

'With her things… in the basement?' he asked.

'Yes,' Meagan suggested as she led Oscar to the stairs, Jemima still clamped to his back.

'Okay. I'll… I'll be in the flat,' he said, climbing the steps.

Meagan watched Oscar's feet disappear and once he was out of sight, she whipped the groundsheet away where Simi cowered, brow crinkled and eyes damp.

Meagan raised a silencing finger, 'No, babes. No time!'

Simi's tears promptly retreated as Meagan, with Navy SEAL efficiency, including her own tactical hand gestures, hustled them and Simi's remaining possessions up the stairs and out.

'Go, go, go!' she barked as they bustled Simi into the back of her Mercedes like a diplomat in hostile territory.

And once Jemima had made sure everyone had their seatbelts on, Meagan floored the accelerator, 'Where to, Simster?'

Simi stared blankly back at Meagan. Typical, she seethed. No plan.

CHAPTER 7

Jemima

Meagan sped through a set of changing traffic lights, giving the finger to a motorist who'd dared to use the road at the same time as her. She rounded a corner crushing Jemima against the passenger door.

'Are you *sure* you don't want me to drive?' Jemima whimpered.

Meagan grabbed her water bottle. 'You drive like a blind cabbie in a funeral procession.'

Jemima inhaled in shock. 'I am an *excellent* driver!'

'Please. You get overtaken by rollerbladers,' Meagan said swigging from the bottle.

'At this rate, we'll end up in our own funeral procession,' Jemima grumbled as her boring life flashed before her.

Simi, who had been sat on the back seat in a deathly silence, finally spoke. 'He knew I was there. He could feel me.'

'He could probably smell you,' mumbled Meagan.

Jemima threw a stern look across the car at Meagan as she violently swerved around a cyclist.

'He did. He knew I was there,' Simi said again.

Jemima checked her pockets for tissues in anticipation of the sorrow that threatened.

'We had a connection,' said Simi as a tear tumbled down her face.

'Right, that's it!' Meagan said, skidding into a taxi rank and stopping inches from an idling cab.

Jemima and Simi lurched forward like crash test dummies as Meagan thumped the brake button and turned sharply to Simi. 'Babe, you might have had a connection but it's time to hang up.'

Jemima braced herself hoping that, for once, Meagan's tough love might be administered kindly.

'Wake up to yourself!' Meagan barked in Simi's face, flicking her forehead with a *thock*.

Nope, it was going to be angry drill sergeant all the way, sighed Jemima.

'You weren't living together. You were his lodger. Your stuff wasn't even in the flat. It was in the boxes we dropped you off with A YEAR AGO!'

'But—' Simi started; however Meagan was on a roll.

'No, Sim. If you've got this amazing connection and he knew you were there, why didn't he fight for you? He was practically helping us pack. SCREW. THAT. GUY,' she said punctuating each word with a handclap.

Behind them a black cab pulled into the rank, tooting at them. Meagan gave him a dismissive wave then turned back to Simi who sat in stupefied silence. Jemima looked at her and her heart lurched.

'I'm sorry, darling. Meagan's right. Screw him,' she said.

'Damn straight!' Meagan boomed. 'You HAVE TO TAKE CONTROL! You let every boyfriend set the pace of the relationship then you just dance to the beat of his drum! They decide when you get to see each other, when your first time is, when they meet *your* friends and family. It's mental. Every guy you have EVER dated has made you into what they want and then they chuck you out when *you* ask for something. And it starts All. Over. Again.'

'But I left him… ' Simi began.

'Constructive dismissal, babes,' Meagan snapped. 'He creates the conditions to make it untenable but you have to do the deed. Full Metal Coward. Do you need Jemima to write it down in black and white so you can see how your history repeats again and again?! Change the backstory, Sim! Do a U-turn. Switch it up. Something. Please!'

Jemima watched Simi take it all in, her face unreadable. They'd both tried to say this to her for years but the message had never got through. Instead, they'd just taken their place on the sidelines ready to rush in the minute their player was down. But this time was different. The intent behind Meagan's words shocked even Jemima. She held her breath watching Simi who was no longer crying. In fact, her face was… clear.

'I am a disaster area,' she whispered, as though seeing the whole picture for the first time.

'You are not a disaster area. You just need to… love you,' Jemima cooed trying to smooth over the crude, broad strokes of Meagan's vitriol.

'No, Jem, I am. I'm Fukushima, the Bermuda Triangle and a Primark sale all rolled into one. I keep picking guys who won't let me set my boundaries,' Simi panicked.

Meagan clutched her temples. Jemima had seen this before. It was like Simi had heard you but not heard you at the same time. Meagan often lamented that discussing relationships with Simi was like having a political discourse with a vacuum cleaner. A lot was going in but it was mainly rubbish.

'It's not about a guy *letting* you set your boundaries. You set your boundaries and if he doesn't like it he can Foxtrot Oscar,' explained Meagan.

Just then the cabbie in front pulled out of the rank sending the drivers behind into an indignant, honking frenzy. Meagan blew them an inflammatory kiss which caused Jemima to scrunch down in her seat, mortified.

'Set boundaries? Just like that? What if he doesn't like those boundaries? What if he wants to change them? What if he likes me more with different boundaries?' Simi asked oblivious to the drama unfolding around them.

'No, Simi. I mean it. No,' Meagan repeated with the futile strictness of someone talking to a baffled puppy.

Meagan suddenly stopped. She reached across and thocked Simi on the forehead again.

'Awwwww!' Simi wailed.

'Meagan!' said Jemima.

'She wants to go back to Oscar and try *setting boundaries*. I can tell. She thinks if she says she doesn't want kids and marriage and a house in the country, he'll get back with her and then eventually they'll have kids, a marriage and a house in the country,' said Meagan.

Jemima looked back at Simi who was doing her best innocent face but looked more like a toddler caught with their hand in the biscuit tin. How was Meagan able to spot a seemingly insignificant detail and turn it into a three-act narrative?

Simi began welling up again. Jemima reached between the

seats putting a reassuring hand on her knee. It broke Jemima's heart to see Simi try so hard only for the happy-ever-after she longed for to elude her every time. However, perhaps there was a positive to come from this. Maybe it was a chance to take time away from men. It would be tough for Simi who would probably need some sort of relationship methadone – like Kettle Chips or *Orange is the New Black*, but if Beverly Blake could survive without a man, surely Simi could too.

Jemima went to speak just as a queuing taxi tooted at them long and loud.

'Alright, alright,' said Meagan.

Behind them, the cab drivers looked like they were about to combust. Jemima turned to Simi who was still staring at the floor. Seeing her crammed in the back seat with her scrunched up afro, Cat in the Hat pyjamas and knees practically around her ears, surrounded by her belongings, would have been comical had it not been so tragic.

'Okay, Sim,' said Meagan her tone finally softening. 'Where are we going?'

'Oh… ' said Simi.

Jemima knew exactly what that meant. Simi didn't have anywhere to go so she would be coming to stay with her. Her heart sank. Of course she wanted to help her friend, it was just that after fourteen hours of planes, trains and automobiles, she just wanted to get home and close her door on the madness of the world. She was so delirious with jet lag, she could barely remember the alphabet. Jemima peered across at Meagan, who probably already had an airtight excuse teed up as to why Simi couldn't stay with her.

'It's okay, Jem. There's a MegaMotel ten minutes away. Just drop me there,' said Simi off Jemima's silence.

Jemima sank back in her seat. There was no way she could let Simi stay in a hotel more famous for Legionnaires disease than a good night's sleep.

'It's fine, you guys. I actually like MegaMotels,' mumbled Simi.

Jemima sighed and her face broke into a kind smile. 'Don't be silly. You're staying with me,' she said.

'Great, sorted,' said Meagan. 'You know I would have let you stay at mine but I don't want to jeopardise our client/agent relationship.'

Jemima peered past Simi out of the back window where the cabbies were now shoving a community police officer in their direction.

'I think we should get out of here,' she said.

'On it,' replied Meagan as she swerved out of the taxi rank, beeping indignantly at a bollard.

Jemima squeezed Simi's hand, embarrassed she'd even considered abandoning her in her hour of need. Everything would be okay in the end, she reassured herself. As Meagan whipped through a red light, Jemima just hoped that end didn't happen in the next thirty-five seconds.

CHAPTER 8

Meagan

Meagan looked around Jemima's compact flat. The way everything matched was unnerving. Is that what happened once you passed 40, your entire life became more and more coordinated until you and your soft furnishing were indistinguishable, Meagan wondered as she deposited the last boxes in Jemima's living room. Behind her Simi slowly shuffled in, her whiff preceding her.

'Right, lady. Shower,' said Meagan.

Enough was enough.

'I don't think I can, Meag,' whimpered Simi.

'It wasn't a question, mate,' said Meagan. 'You've already lost a boyfriend. You don't want to lose me and Jem too.'

'Meag?' blubbed Simi.

'It was a joke,' she replied steering Simi towards the bathroom.

One day, Meagan groused, the world would get her sense of humour and life would become infinitely easier for everyone. She closed the bathroom door behind Simi and listened. There it was: the sound of running water – followed not long after by a pitiful rendition of Toni Braxton's 'Un-Break My Heart'.

'You got her to take a shower?' said Jemima as Meagan walked back into the living room.

'She smelt like a steak bake, babes.'

'Well, now she needs something to eat,' Jemima murmured like a soap opera surgeon proposing a life-threatening procedure. She pulled a twenty pound note from her purse, 'Let's get some food and cook her something.'

Meagan stared at the money then back at Jemima.

'Cash, *cooking*? This ain't the Seventies. If you tweet a pizza emoji to Domingo's they'll be round in twenty minutes with a nice hot meat feast,' she said pulling out her phone.

'Fine,' Jemima moaned. 'She needs something. All I've got in that fridge is a block of parmesan and some vaginal probiotics.'

'You don't want her thinking about her vagina. That'll just remind her of Oscar,' said Meagan.

'Everything reminds her of Oscar.'

'Maybe because he *is* a vagina,' said Meagan coldly.

Jemima snorted as she went back to tidying Simi's belongings. Meagan watched, bemused. Even though these weren't her things, Jemima was still determined to find a place for everything because – everything had its place. It wasn't personal. It was just Jem. Luckily for Meagan, Jemima's love of her personal space would play nicely into her scheme to get Simi back to work and, specifically, auditioning for the IPC role she'd been waiting to discuss. She just had to play it very, *very* delicately. Meagan nudged Simi's box of bongo drums with her foot.

'Be fun having Simi's drumming circle around,' said Meagan as she leafed through an old copy of *The Stage*.

The record scratch in Jemima's brain was almost audible.

'Eh?' said Jemima.

Meagan tapped out a paradiddle on one of the bongos and grinned at Jemima.

'Tell you what would get her back on her feet and moving on – a date. The best way to get over a bloke is to get under another one, right,' she said.

'Then that's sex. That's not even a date!' Jemima interrupted as she popped up from behind a pile of Simi's things.

'S'right. Cut to the chase.' Meagan beamed.

She knew this was a bad idea. Suggesting it was merely a stepping stone en route to her long con. If she'd been alone she'd have let out a cartoon evil laugh.

'I mean, I want Simi to find her own place eventually but that is a terrible suggestion,' said Jemima.

'What's a terrible suggestion?' said Simi now trussed up in towels.

'Nothing,' said Jemima, darting a stony glare at Meagan.

'Tell me,' said Simi, hope flickering in her eyes.

Jemima disappeared behind the boxes.

'Well,' began Meagan, metaphorically cricking her fingers, 'you know what they say is the best way to get over someone?'

'Therapy?' suggested Simi earnestly.

'No, dummy. Getting under someone,' said Meagan with a wink.

'Terrible suggestion, terrible suggestion!' Jemima moaned from her box fortress.

Simi looked at Meagan confused as though her brain were literally buffering.

'But… I just… '

'You need to get back on your feet and a date would be a great way to do it,' said Meagan.

'That's an awful idea,' said Simi.

'Told you,' came a muffled rebuff from behind the boxes.

'I couldn't ask someone out. What would I say? "Hi, I'm damaged goods. Want to spend an evening speculating on why my ex didn't want children?"' said Simi slumping into Jemima's sofa.

'Good point,' said Meagan as she pretended to think though alternative solutions. 'What if we ask guys out for you?'

Jemima poked up from behind the boxes, looking horrified, 'Nice. Nightmare upgrade.'

Meagan stifled a smirk.

'You're right. My bad. I'm just trying to help,' she said putting an arm around Simi's shoulder, 'Wait, here's a thought – why don't you try getting stuck into work?'

'My reception job?' Simi asked, puzzled.

'No, not your survival job. Your real job. Acting,' said Meagan.

Simi's face crinkled. 'I don't think I can… '

'Sweetheart, I don't think you *can't*. What is it you actors say? *Let Doctor Theatre work his magic*. What better tonic is there than the smell of a crowd, the roar of the grease paint. Jemima was just saying that work might take your mind off things… '

'I… I… did I?' stammered Jemima.

'Well, you said that dating was a bad idea,' Meagan corrected.

'But that doesn't mean… '

'Do you think it would work, Jem?' asked Simi.

Meagan sat back and let the rest of the conversation take its course. This was an inelegant hustle but it had worked. Jemima was always a soft touch for Simi's doe eyes. She wouldn't tell her no.

Jemima pulled open a box of books. 'Do you want me to alphabetise these?'

'It's just there was an interesting development... ' Meagan said, drawing Simi back in to soft-sell her the idea of going to this audition.

For the most part, Meagan was enjoying this relatively new challenge of being Simi's agent. Because they were friends there was a shorthand that made things easier. Sometimes, however, like today, where the lines were blurred, it made things take ten times as long. Given Simi's current state, Meagan had to keep it light but that was going to be tough given that the casting director who had offered Simi the audition was none other than the esteemed Antonia De Silva. Even Meagan knew what a big deal she was. It was the first audition to come from her office and not a contact to be squandered. And if Simi made a good impression, it could mean big things for Meagan's comedian clients who had thespian ambitions too. However, if Simi no-showed, who knew when or even *if* Antonia would offer any of Meagan's clients an audition again. The most frustrating thing was, Simi was perfect for the role and this IPC show had BAFTAs written all over it. Meagan just wished opportunity had knocked when Simi was not a walking power ballad. She took a breath.

'So, it's called *Clash of the Crown*. It shoots in Ireland and it's a new fantasy period drama.'

'Yeah. I heard you fibbing to Oscar about it but it's too soon,' said Simi, towelling her hair.

'It's a really great role,' Meagan said with a clenched jaw, 'and they've already confirmed it's going to series.'

'Can I see them next month?'

'Next *month*?' Meagan growled about as breezily as a force nine gale. 'Darling, they're shooting in five weeks. You'd be playing Bradley Tyson's lover and you'd have at least one scene with Cameron Christiansen.'

Meagan looked at Simi, fuming. Most actors would bite her arm off at the elbow for this.

'I can't, Meagan. I'm sorry. What if I have to do a scene about a break-up? Or a scene with a character called Oscar? Or worse, play a character who's *won* an Oscar? Who'd pick up the pieces of me then?'

Meagan listened to Simi's bizarre logic and gradually softened. Dealing with hardened comedians all day, she had forgotten that actors were a different breed – their vulnerability, much closer to the surface.

'You're right, Sim. I'm sorry.'

'Thanks, Meag. I really appreciate it,' said Simi, dropping her wet towel onto the sofa.

At the sight of this, Jemima let out an unintentional squeak, her eyes locked on the soggy towel. 'Maybe you should… consider it.'

Meagan looked over at Jemima, then back to Simi and the towel slowly depositing a damp stain on the sofa.

'I mean it's not every day you audition for BAFTA-winning producers,' Jemima added.

Meagan smiled innocently. 'I'll ping you the details and you can decide in the morning.'

CHAPTER 9

Jemima

Jemima sat up in bed sipping her coffee while Simi sang to herself in the living room. Last night after Meagan had shared details of Simi's big audition and, as always, ladled on her unsolicited acting advice, Simi had definitely brightened. She'd dispensed with the power ballads and this morning had graduated to revenge songs.

As Jemima pondered a leisurely stroll to Nostromo to shake off the jet lag, her phone *grrrr grrrred* insistently, jolting her from her ruminations. *Shit.* It was Eve. She'd been expecting her call but not for at least a fortnight. Just before leaving LA, Jemima had sent Eve an inflammatory new draft she'd been working on throughout her trip. If all went to plan, it would end the 'romance' conversation once and for all. Instead of resisting Eve's 'suggesteroos' as she had done for so long, Jemima's new tactic had been to lean into them – hard, giving Eve *everything* she wanted. In fact, she had given Eve so much of it, Jemima hoped she would decide she didn't want it after all. But how had she read it so quickly? Jemima had only sent it ten days ago. Perhaps, she speculated, Eve had got just a few pages in before realising the error of her ways. She could be calling to apologise for ever mooting concerns about the amorous content of Jemima's books.

'Soooooo sorry, *Jeeeeeeeehm!*' she'd probably mewl with her elongated, downward inflection that sounded like she was offering condolences. Jemima grinned, took a deep breath and answered the phone.

'Jemima. It's Eve.'

Jemima sat up, Eve's clipped tone surprising her.

'Are you alright?' she asked.

'I just finished the draft you wrote in LA. Is *that* what you were doing with your time?' Eve said spitting out the words like an unexpected pubic hair from a night she'd rather forget.

'Look, I know you're cross… ' Jemima began.

'Cross? *Cross*?' Eve spluttered, 'The draft you sent before was bad enough, like a nun's bloody diary, but this one – it's basically *Debbie Does Dallas* the novel!'

'I just took your notes and ran with it,' Jemima said as she heard Eve angrily leaf through the manuscript.

'"Beverly pulled Nigel close, growling, 'I want a damn good shafting!' He rodded her with his big, fat rod,"' Eve read before pausing.

Clearly she was waiting for some form of explanation or worse, apology but Jemima held her ground. Eve pressed on, picking out excerpt after excerpt which Jemima imagined were circled in red ink that pressed four pages deep.

'"Beverly bounced on his towering inferno screaming, 'You're on fire!"' hissed Eve. 'And what the bloody hell is "doming"?'

'I thought this was what you wanted?' Jemima said with faux indignation, battling the giggles.

'Jemima, this is *obscene!*'

And just as she thought it couldn't get any better, Jemima heard the unmistakable *click, click* of a lighter. Eve was smoking – a real cigarette!

'What's more, I have to say… in places, it's just spiteful,' Eve said, wounded.

Jemima's smile flickered. Hurting Eve had not been her intention.

'"Shag me likeable"?' quoted Eve, 'I'm trying to help you, Jemima but this is… It's like a literary "up yours".'

Jemima sat forward, in a panic. She'd been shot in the foot but only just noticed she was holding the gun.

'It was silly of me, Eve. I'm sorry,' Jemima back-pedalled feeling like an utter imbecile.

She'd spent over a month producing something completely worthless and for what – to make a point?

After a long, long pause Eve huffed, '*Okaaaaaay.*'

Jemima exhaled at the return of those unmistakable, elongated vowels but the relief was slight. She still owed Eve one completed manuscript that would most certainly be her last with Hudson Hicks if she didn't come up with something fast. She'd squandered so much time creating this filth fest that to get a new draft to Eve, Jemima only had – she silently gasped – a month.

'Don't worry, Eve. Bad joke. I've been working on the real draft for weeks. In fact, I think I've fixed the problem,' she lied.

'How?'

Jemima began overheating as she scrabbled around in her brain for a response. She wasn't a romance novelist. She was a hard-nosed-insurance-investigator novelist. Nothing more, nothing less. She hadn't the first clue how to write flings and flirtations. What she had included in that first novel had been inspired by her relationship with Miles but the thought of drawing from that well, made her shudder. And even if she did go there, it would completely change Beverly's characterisation. She was a lone wolf not a love bird.

'Jemima?' said Eve into the long silence of Jemima's mind whirring into hyper-speed panic.

'History!' Jemima blurted, her thoughts literally forming microseconds before they tumbled from her mouth.

Hadn't Meagan said something to Simi about changing the backstory, rewriting history? Could that work for Beverly? Jemima frantically speculated.

'History… is a backstory… it repeats,' she dry-gulped.

'*What?*' said Eve.

'Sorry. Dodgy connection… with my brain. Haha. No. What if… I mean, that is to say, what I've been doing is… ' she stammered, 'I'm weaving Beverly's love life in as… backstory.'

'Go *oooon*,' said Eve with the suspicion of a child who'd asked for candy but been given kale.

'That way we both get what we want. Yes! We both get what we want. I'll make her past as romantic as you like while I get to keep the Beverly I love in the present… I'll use it to… explain why she is the way she is!'

'No sleaze,' Eve said sharply.

'Definitely. No mentholing, no tea-bagging and absolutely no doming,' promised Jemima.

Eve went quiet as Jemima waited, praying she'd go with it.

'*Aaaaaalright*,' said Eve.

Jemima silently punched the air. 'And as this was just, you know, a bad joke, we probably don't need to tell Shaheena about it… '

As a habit Jemima didn't like to keep things from her woe-fully indiscreet agent but she knew, if Shaheena got wind of this particular draft, news of it would spread across the industry like gonorrhoea around an assisted-living complex. It was never intentional but in literary London's rumour mill, Shaheena was the miller, her apron dusty with its tittle-tattle — even if it was about her own clients.

'Fine but I want that draft, Jem-J. I want that draft,' said Eve hanging up.

Jemima listened to the sound of her pulse pounding in her ears. That was close. However, now she'd got herself a reprieve, how was she, a relationship cripple, going to fix this full-fat fail and create a believable, romantic backstory for her beloved Beverly? This could turn out to be the most high-stakes shag in the history of literature.

Eve's default advice was always to use one's own experiences but, having spent the past two years trying to obliterate her relationship with Miles from her memory the last thing she wanted was to commit it to print *forever*. And anyway, Miles and the random few that preceded him were hardly befitting of Jemima's beloved heroine. Furthermore, how could she forget, Miles also worked in the industry and was very, *very* well connected. It would be painfully easy for him to acquire a copy of the manuscript. If he recognised himself he could halt publication all together. Jemima grizzled. She loved being a writer. She wasn't bothered about awards or recognition. All she wanted was to be on a beach and see someone engrossed in *Beverly Blake Investigates* or perhaps catch the eye of a busi-ness woman on her morning commute blasting through the 254 pages of *Beverly Blake Mysteries*. Even when she'd seen her first book in a bargain bin at the airport, she'd wanted to tell anyone who would listen, *I wrote that! Those half-price words are mine!* And now it was all slipping away. This career-defining, make-or-break nightmare was exhausting. She flopped back into her plump pillows and reached for her cold coffee. She had a month to deliver this book or that would be it for her and Hudson Hicks. She knew it. She opened up the browser on her laptop and did what any writer under pressure would do – started planning an escape route. Without thinking, soon Jemima was googling 'LA apartments'. Her time at Rebecca's place really had planted a seed within her and it was starting to germinate. Perhaps Santa Monica was the ideal escape not just from Miles but also Eve and her looming deadline.

'Jem!' Simi called from the living room. 'Where's your printer paper?'

'In the cupboard by the TV,' replied Jemima, one hand poised to close her laptop.

She listened to Simi clutter around before cautiously returning to her search for a new life.

'And where's your printer?' called Simi.

Jemima sighed. She shut her laptop and headed next door. Perhaps helping Simi prepare for her audition was the distraction they both needed. Given that the casting was in the morning and Simi was only now printing the script, this was probably an all-hands-on-deck situation.

CHAPTER 10

Simi

Simi sat in the narrow, white corridor outside the audition room. As she muttered through her lines a bead of sweat trickled down her back. Even though Jemima had rehearsed with her for hours, she was still terrified. Simi loved acting but hated every aspect of auditioning. The pressure, the camera that silently judged you and the oh so 'casual' chat at the beginning. Every actor knew it wasn't a real conversation. It was the casting director's way of finding out if you were a handsy weirdo who might grope their principal cast. Were it any other audition, Simi would have passed but once the possibility of working with BAFTA-winning producers was dangled, she had been helpless to resist – heartbroken or not. So, here she was, waiting to perform four pages of dialogue as a 'kind doxy' in the hallowed offices of Antonia De Silva. Simi didn't even know what a doxy was. In her last-minute haste she hadn't bothered to check. All she knew was the show was medieval, involved unicorns and was called something like *Crashing Clowns* – which didn't sound very BAFTA-winning to her.

Just then, the main door swung open and Sandra Scott strode

in, her luscious, black locks bouncing around her shoulders. Everyone knew Sandra Scott. She was that one actor who instantly sucked hope out of the room because she was that actor who *always* got the job. Simi had even seen some girls leave audition waiting rooms the moment she walked in.

Sandra commandeered a group of seats and dabbed powder on her perfectly made-up face before throwing a warm, toothy smile Simi's way. Up yours, you perfect goddess, Simi bristled before reaching into her bag for her love-emitting rose quartz crystal. Meagan and Jemima always dismissed her new-age trappings but for Simi they were as vital as water. She carried her rose quartz everywhere, running her fingers over its smooth surface anytime she wanted to drive out negative thought and usher in something more... kind. She smiled back at Sandra sweetly.

As Simi's loving zen returned, the audition-room door sprung open and the previous girl was shown out by Gabe, Antonia's wiry assistant. He glanced up and down the row of waiting actresses, his thin face revealing nothing until his gaze reached the last seat.

'Sandy, come through!' He beamed before hugging Sandra and gesturing for her to go right on in and follow her dreams.

Sandra feigned surprise at her egregious queue jump. She then pulled a box of Krispy Kreme donuts from her bag and presented them to Gabe as she glided into the room. *A bribe???* fumed Simi as two actresses upped and left. Surely Antonia wouldn't fall for such a shallow ruse?

'Krispy Kremes? Love that!' gushed Antonia as the door slammed shut.

An hour later, after Simi had listened to the murmured voices of Sandra and Antonia chatting about everything from climate change to the latest series of *Doctor Who*, the door opened and Sandra breezed out. She blew Antonia a kiss then gave Simi a supportive thumbs-up and left. Simi threw a thumbs-up back. *Biiiiiiiiiiiiiiiiiiiieeeeetch*, she seethed as the door bumped closed behind her. She quickly rubbed her crystal.

How was she going to follow that? She didn't have any sugary treats with which to bribe Antonia. Maybe she could go with the classic Sandy opener – a hug. *Disarm with charm.* Gabe beckoned Simi in and she launched herself at Antonia who was holding a piece of donut in each hand. Simi quickly adjusted, grabbing Antonia's shoulders.

'So great to meet you!' Simi squealed. 'Strong arms!'

Antonia looked at Simi who was practically nose to nose with her.

'Pop yourself in front of the camera, dear,' she said working herself free and neatening her salt-and-pepper up-do which Simi had shaken loose.

'Gabe will read with you,' said Antonia as Gabe positioned himself between Antonia and Simi like a human shield.

Simi sat down, her back now damp with sweat.

'Off you go,' said Antonia.

Wait, no banter? Simi panicked. She didn't expect the Graham Norton-style interview Sandra had been privy to but didn't Antonia want her thoughts on climate change? How would she know Simi wasn't a grabby weirdo without 'The Chat'?

Simi leaned in. 'By the way, new Doctor Who – best choice. A guy at my agency got seen but he couldn't do a Welsh accent.'

Antonia stared back at her. 'When you're ready, dear.'

Simi glanced at Gabe who looked ready to march her out in

a headlock if Antonia said the word. She gulped as she reordered her script pages.

'Ready when you are!'

Simi paced down the street in a vain attempt to shake the embarrassing funk the audition had put her in. She had intended to simply go as far as the nearest burger bar but somehow her feet had carried her out of Soho, through Holborn and towards The City. Another shame shudder rippled through her as she replayed her absurd *Doctor Who* banter and even stranger response when Antonia had asked if she was, 'comfortable with scenes of a sexual nature...'

'The more sexual the better!' Simi had flailed.

Why hadn't she read the character description? If she had, she'd have known about the scenes of a sexual nature and that a doxy was a prostitute! As Simi read and reread the Google definition on her phone, the blood drained from her cheeks. She had based her entire audition on the idea that a doxy was some kind of medieval clown. No wonder Antonia had looked at her like she was crazy when she started juggling mid-scene. Simi stopped and look around her. Across the street was a building she knew only too well. Oscar's office. This is where her feet had carried her. As workers scurried in and out, making their lunchtime dash, she knew she shouldn't be here. She knew it but she also knew that one brief glance of him, even if it was from a distance, would make her feel better. That's what they did. She'd feel crummy after an audition and he'd say something sweet to take the crumminess away. Tears brimmed as she realised that was gone forever. Just as Simi felt the first sob about to rock her, a flash of yellow and red across the street caught her eye. She scuttled out of view, peering from behind a wall. It was Oscar. Nausea bubbled in her stomach. Instinctively she raised a hand to wave but then stopped. It had only been three days since she'd seem him but he looked... different. She watched him chain up his bike as another cyclist pulled up beside him, lassoing their ride to the same rail. Simi knew Oscar liked a lunchtime ride but he'd never mentioned a riding buddy. The other cyclist was even skinnier than Oscar and as he whipped off his helmet, auburn hair cascaded down his back and Simi realised he was a she. Simi raised her hand again. But as she did, Oscar put his arm around his companion's waist. Simi's mind raced and just as she had convinced herself they were simply overly tactile colleagues, they leaned in and kissed. Simi stumbled back as, across the street, Oscar pulled a paper bag from his pannier and he and his... lover shared a red velvet cupcake.

Simi sagged against the wall, its cool, hard surface barely keeping her upright. There was nothing to gain from looking again but she just had to. She turned back but they were gone. She scoured the street left and right. Immediately, her mind tried to explain it all away. With so much passing traffic could she be sure it was Oscar? Plus she was exhausted and was due an eye test. But she knew what she had seen. First she was numb then embarrassed. This had been happening right under her nose but she had so wanted her relationship to be something it wasn't, she hadn't seen what it was. Simi became aware of the stickiness of tears on her cheeks. How many more times was she going to feel this way? Heartbroken over *him*. Not Oscar but all the hims. The Jasons, The Ades and the Azads. All of them had led her to the same place – tear-stained and devastated. This needed to change; she needed to do *something* and whatever that was, it would start today. She had major league man problems and she needed to bring in the big guns. She pounded out a WhatsApp message to Meagan and Jemima.

We need to meet up. 2NITE!

CHAPTER 11

Jemima

Since sending Simi off for her audition that morning with a good luck hug and pack of tissues, Jemima had been trapped in a Facebook/Twitter/Instagram loop. All the while, behind her open browser pages lurked the unchanged Beverly Blake filth fest draft. As she liked her fifteenth kitten photo the klaxon ringtone she reserved for her agent sounded and she groaned.

'Hi Shaheena.'

'So,' Shaheena said with gleeful reproach, 'something you want to tell me?'

'Nope. Just plugging away at the script,' Jemima said, tensing.

'A script in which you've made Beverly a *scatologist*?' Shaheena said in a scandalised whisper.

Jemima face-palmed at her naivety. Of course Shaheena had found out about her misstep with Eve. She had an information network that could rival MI5's.

'We have a problem, Jemmy. I heard through the vine of the grape that Hudson Hicks are thinking of giving you the old Spanish archer, you know, *El Bow*,' said Shaheena.

'I know,' said Jemima weakly.

'So, what are you doing about it?' Shaheena yelped.

Like Meagan, Shaheena was an agent who had little time for the hand-wringing of creatives. She was about solutions. If Hudson Hicks wanted romance, Jemima needed to serve it up with a side order of *lurve*. Even Jemima's dilemma over how to source material was simple to Shaheena.

'Nick it!' came her tinny bark down the phone.

According to Shaheena, bookshelves were brimming with authors who'd ransacked other works for inspiration. Even the much-lauded *The Cave* was just *Star Wars* meets *Pride and Prejudice* set in a cervix, or so Shaheena claimed.

'Look, Jemmy, whatever Hudson Hicks wants, Hudson Hicks gets because as far as other publishers go, it is slim pickings out there so crack on!' she said signing off.

Jemima wilted back onto her bed. 'Balls.'

She opened her laptop again hoping for an insight, a spark, anything. Options that were a definite no-no included stealing from other authors, returning her advance – the last of which she'd spent on her LA trip – and volunteering for the one-way manned mission to Mars. If she'd had more time, perhaps she could take a specialised writing workshop, read some sample texts, start from scratch but she had less than a month. She needed a rock solid solution – fast. She'd already established that her love life was too pitiful to be a legitimate source. Eve would be more appalled by a draft concocted from that than the filth fest. But if she couldn't use her own experiences, was there somewhere else she could turn? She needed detail and emotional authenticity or it just would not work. She sighed heavily. The only love lives she knew as encyclopedically as her own were Meagan and Simi's.

For a moment, she let her mind wander, imagining what Beverly would be like if she'd had their chequered relationship history – the heartbreak, the mishaps, the highs and lows. Between the two of them, that would certainly give Beverly a past colourful enough to satiate Eve's desire for romantic tension. But would Simi and Meagan even let her use their stories? Perhaps if the details were far enough removed from the truth, they wouldn't even need to know… But then Jemima remembered Troy. She'd been on the same comedy course where the girls had first met. Their bourgeoning friendship with her had faltered, however, once they discovered she was spinning their private conversations into comedy gold. Not only that but she was performing her newly nicked material on the open mic circuit – for the public! She hadn't even had the decency to change their names. Meagan had been so livid she'd wanted to eject Troy from the group quicker than a protester at a parliamentary committee meeting. Yes, they were all mining their lives for material but they were using their own stories and *only* sharing them in the safety of the course room not to a braying audience. After that, Troy remained, at best, a satellite friend but they never discussed anything classified in front of her ever again. Jemima speculated on what was worse, being ostracised by Meagan and Simi or demoted to *acquaintance*?

Her fingers froze over her keyboard as a text alert chimed.

She glanced at the screen. Miles. Again.

I miss you. Are you in London? Mx

God, he was like ants. She wished there was a powder she could put down to permanently get rid of *him*. She didn't hate him.

She didn't even dislike him. It was just that every text took her back there, to the pain, the hurt. She snapped her laptop closed and grabbed her coat. She needed a break and knew exactly where to go – Nostromo. Jemima loved its shabby chic decor. She loved the old, mismatched wooden tables and cosy chairs. She especially loved the recovered airplane seats that had been transformed into a comfy two-seater sofa, quickly becoming the must-have spot. Even the light that flooded through its huge windows was cleansing and restorative. But what Jemima adored the most were the owners, Azi and Rania, a young Egyptian couple, who'd made it their mission to create a sanctuary for artists in need of inspiration. They treated every customer like a friend they were yet to make, another reason Jemima loved them and their shop. She had spent so many hours there, poring over her novels, that it had become her second home.

'You're back!' Azi and Rania said as Jemima walked through the door.

Jemima smiled. This was the one silver lining to her writing predicament – having a place like this to figure things out. She took her latte and planted herself in her usual window seat, basking in Nostromo's roughly-put-together charm and the quiet murmur of its customers. Opening up her notebook she once again pondered her dilemma. Staring back at her was one word: Miles. She scored it out with a thick, black marker and thought back to her other possibility. The girls. Perhaps they would agree if they were unrecognisable. That had been Troy's mistake. If Jemima wrote some sample passages for them, it might help. Then again, if Simi and Meagan saw a sample and vetoed the whole thing, she would be screwed. No, if she did this and it was a big *if,* she had to present them with the finished article so they knew exactly what they were dealing with. Jemima began mulling over stories from the girls' current situations. Immediately, Meagan's 'arrangement' with Todd came to mind. She wondered if Beverly might have had something similar in her past. If she did, unlike Meagan, she would at least know his last name. Or maybe, like Meagan, Beverly had once loved a married man. At the time Meagan had brushed it off as a fling but when it had ended Jemima knew her feelings went much deeper than that. Parker. Jemima wasn't sure if that was his first or last name. She only met him once. What she did know was that Meagan had loved him and since then, any man who got entangled with her was always kept at arm's length. There was always a reason, the most hardy being Meagan's 'plan'. Though she daren't say it, Jemima wondered if it wasn't a plan at all but some kind of defence. Against what, she wasn't sure, but there were definitely morsels she could plant in Beverly's past. Jemima then thought about Simi and seeing her things neatly piled up in Oscar's basement. Beverly would never have allowed that to happen… *unless*, thought Jemima, it was the catalyst that turned her into the solitary, work obsessive she'd become… A quiet excitement brewed as ideas coalesced. Perhaps Beverly had lived with a man once but he had never shown her the respect she deserved. Maybe the experience had hardened her. That was justification for her transformation into the single-minded insurance sleuth she now was. Jemima had to admit, that was a pretty solid backstory. As she began scribbling down more ideas her attention was taken by a medic in blue scrubs outside helping a tall, athletic-looking man on crutches into a cab. Something about the doctor captivated her. She watched how, with absolute patience and good humour, he guided the man into the car. The taxi pulled away and her heart lightened at the display of generosity. But as she enjoyed the goodwill afterglow, she saw the doctor step back into a pile of poo so big it looked like a baby rhino had deposited it.

'Oh dear,' Jemima chuckled guiltily.

Literally, sod's law. The doctor turned to scrape his clog on the pavement edge and Jemima gasped, recognising him straight away. It was Chatterbox Chance from the plane. It all came racing back. His practice was upstairs! She siphoned her drink into her to-go cup and shrank down in her chair. Outside, Chance was attempting to clean his shoe by dragging it along the ground in a second-rate moonwalk. Finally conceding defeat, he tried to lob his clog into a rubbish bin with his foot. It looped up in the air and circled back, missing him by inches. If this had been a stranger, Jemima would still be whooping with laughter but it was Chance and frankly she was still embarrassed about their testy exchange on the flight home. Under the feeble guise of packing away her things, she ducked down, awaiting an opportune moment to make a speedy exit. Five Mississippis later, she peeked over the table top. With no Chance in sight, she bolted for the door, her bag thwacking several customers as she fled. And just as she was within grabbing distance of the door, she ran directly into… Chance. Milky coffee splattered over her top and his scrubs.

'Oh my god! I'm so sorry!' he said scrabbling for napkins.

'It's fine!' Jemima said trying to flick the excess liquid from her shirt.

'Please. Let me buy you another?' he said, mortified.

Jemima looked at him. Despite being keen on escaping she was a little irked he didn't recognise her. Then again it was probably for the best or next, she'd be stuck talking to him and they'd end up married… *What?* Where did that come from?

'Holy shit!' Chance exclaimed. 'Jemima. It's me – Chance – from the plane!'

'The plane... ' she said pretending to search for the recollection.

'Remember, I work upstairs,' he said. 'You live nearby?'

'I'm just passing through,' she lied.

'Well then I *definitely* have to buy you a coffee if I might not see you again. This is our reunion!' Chance beamed. 'Hey, Azi, two coffees, hon.'

'Great,' Jemima said with the warmth of a coroner and suddenly feeling possessive of Azi and Rania.

They were *her* friendly neighbourhood purveyors of fine coffee. She won them fair and square in her quasi-divorce from Miles. She stewed as Chance headed for the coveted airplane seats.

'Just like old times.' He winked.

Jemima had forgotten how annoyingly happy he was. He'd be great for Simi, she surmised as Azi followed behind with their drinks.

'Aaaaah. Couples are always drawn to the love seats,' Azi sighed as she set down their coffees.

'We're not—' Jemima interjected.

'I know.' Azi smiled. 'Anyway, I'll leave you to it.'

There was nothing to leave them to, Jemima wanted to insist but Azi was already gone. They were just two strangers, joined by a common coffee stain. Jemima turned back to Chance – unsure what to say. 'So you work. . .'

'Upstairs. Only been there a few months... but I have seen you around,' Chance said, sipping his coffee.

Jemima paused. 'Really?'

'Yeah, well…' said Chance, a little flustered, 'I always notice interesting-looking people – not in a creepy way.'

He laughed, his cheeks flushing red.

'Well, it's not like I *never* come here,' Jemima said. 'I write here… from time to time.'

She cringed, hoping that somehow this might course-correct her earlier fib.

'And instead of writing you got dowsed in coffee. God, I'm so embarrassed,' Chance winced.

'It's okay,' said Jemima placing a hand on his.

He looked up and she quickly moved it away.

'I'm just getting some ideas together,' she said holding up her notebook.

Chance looked at it as though it were a lost passage from the Bible. It intrigued Jemima how people deified the writing process when ninety-five per cent of what she produced was unusable garbage.

'Can I read some?' Chance asked.

Can you read stories I've borrowed from my friends before I've even asked them? Jemima thought. *Errr. No.*

'I'm in the middle of a rewrite,' she said closing her notebook. 'I'm giving Beverly a backstory.'

Not that she owed him an explanation. Frankly, she owed him an apology. When he'd made suggestions about her book on the flight she had bitten his head off.

'A backstory is great and do you think this backstory will include… a guy? Just asking,' Chance said, his hands shooting up in defence.

Jemima smiled. She often forgot that fans loved Beverly as much as she did and wanted the best for her too.

Chance set his coffee cup back on its saucer. 'In the second book she was pretty down on love but I reckon there's more to it. My brother, Pete, says, "Cynics are closet romantics who've had their hearts broken".'

The thought lingered like the scent of dying flowers as Jemima and Chance locked eyes.

'Great, well... ' said Jemima standing, 'thanks for the coffee but I've got to get back to it.'

'Totally. Listen, sorry again. Can I make it up to you?' Chance asked, standing too.

'You already did,' she replied pointing at their empty cups.

'I can do better than that. How about dinner?' he pitched.

Jemima looked into those warm eyes as his face broke into a sun-kissed smile.

'I need to crack on with this draft,' she said looking away.

'No worries.'

Jemima said her hasty goodbyes to Azi and Rania, feeling Chance's gaze on her. She scurried out of the door, not looking back.

CHAPTER 12

Meagan

Meagan was feeling pretty pleased with herself. Not only had Simi managed to drag herself to the audition that morning but now she even wanted to meet for a drink. Normally Simi went into a deep post-break-up hibernation so this was proof; Meagan had been right – as always. The audition was just what Simi needed. Meagan's vibrating phone shook her from her self-congratulations. She stared at the screen, perplexed. It was Todd. They never spoke on the phone.

'What's wrong?'

'Just calling to say, "hey",' he replied.

Meagan kissed her teeth, making a mental note never to take a call from him again. What happened to just texting a time and place to meet? Brevity was a turn-on. Phone calls were not.

'Todd, babes, I saw you this morning.'

'Which was lovely. I just wanted to see how your day went?' said Todd.

Meagan stared at her phone. Was this some kind of prank?

'Has something happened?' she asked.

'No… ' said Todd.

'So you're just calling to, what, talk to me?'

'Yeah.'

'About what?'

'Not about anything. Just to chat. All the kids are doing it. I really think it's gonna catch on.'

Meagan frowned. Yes, she was aware *some* people liked chatting on the phone but Todd had failed to read the memo that stated she was not one of them. Meagan slowed as she arrived at Ripley's. She looked through the bar's large windows eyeing the fancy vintage decor. Jemima and Simi had nabbed a table and were studying the wine list. She stiffened. The wine at Ripley's was supposed to be excellent. She had to end this bizarreness with Todd and get inside before the girls ordered something awful.

'Sorry, Todd. Gotta go,' Meagan said squinting through the glass. 'I think Jemima's about to order some Napa Valley swill and I'm not here for that. Bye. Text me. Bye!'

What was with him? she griped as she yanked the bar door open and strode over to the girls' table. First snuggling and now phone calls? He'd obviously forgotten how good their deal was. No last names or sweet nothings. Just good sex and plenty of orgasms.

'What's up, bitches?' She grinned, snatching the wine list from Jemima and turning to their waiter. 'If she's ordered Californian wine, scratch it.'

The waiter looked down at his pad and crossed out the order.

'Hey!' Jemima bleated. 'That Chardonnay is delicious.'

'It's oaky muck,' said Meagan as she scanned the wine list. 'Okay let's have the 2010 Sangiovese.'

Meagan snapped the weighty wine list closed and handed it back to the waiter who disappeared to fetch their order.

'That's really expensive,' said Simi.

'It's on me.'

'Oh well in that case, Chardonnay is disgusting!' Jemima grinned.

'It's to celebrate your triumphant audition. Soooo, how was it?' Meagan asked.

'A nightmare. I'm never auditioning again,' said Simi.

Meagan nodded with feigned empathy. Simi said this after every audition.

'There's something else,' Simi said. 'We're doing your dating challenge thing – tonight.'

'Wait. Back up a minute. What challenge?' said Meagan.

'The one where you find me a date. You're right. I'm a disaster. I have no idea what's best for me when it comes to men. But you do. You both do,' said Simi.

Meagan turned to Jemima for an explanation.

'She saw Oscar… with someone,' said Jemima mouthing it like she was naming a venereal disease, 'but let's not be too hasty, Sim. I mean you don't want to revenge date.'

'It's not revenge. It's reinvention!' Simi said flailing her arms.

Just then the waiter arrived, deftly dodging Simi's flying hand. He set down their bottle of wine and three glasses, and popped the cork. With ceremonious flair, he presented the bottle to Meagan.

'Just pour it, babes. Shit's going down here,' she instructed. 'Simi. What happened?'

Simi bowed her head, embarrassed, as she recounted her sighting of Oscar, his auburn-haired companion and that incriminating red velvet cupcake.

'Oh, Sim. That sucks,' said Jemima leaning in to hug her.

'No, Jem,' said Simi pushing her back, 'I've been so blinkered, I didn't see this at all!'

'Let's go round his gaff. Find out who this scrub is. Get medieval on her arse,' said Meagan, crushing her coaster.

Meagan had been waiting for an excuse to dismantle Oscar and cheating on Simi was an even better reason than his grotesque cycling gear.

'Hang on. How do we know it's not just a friend?' said Jemima putting a calming hand on Meagan.

'A friend that he goes on bike rides with… and snogs in the street… ?' said Simi.

'Oh,' Jemima replied.

'So who is she?' Meagan asked.

Simi pursed her lips. 'I think her name's Sophie. He introduced us once when I met him for lunch. He said she was his team leader. I checked her out on Insta. She has three thousand followers. How is that possible? She works in a bank.'

'It's the hair, babes. Gingers stick together. It's like a cult. So, what do you want us to do?' asked Meagan, hoping Simi would suggest ordering five hundred pizzas to her office.

'I don't want you to do anything. Oscar's the poop. I can't do anything about him so it's time to make a change in me – today,' Simi said gathering herself.

Meagan looked at Simi properly for the first time that evening. The rawness of the break-up was evident but there was also a steeliness. No matter what life threw at Simi, she always fought her way back.

'I think there's something in your idea about you asking guys out for me. I could learn so much just by dating someone I would never normally consider,' Simi implored.

Jemima shook her head. 'Darling, think this through. You've *just* got out of a relationship. The body is still warm. Why would you want to get into something now?' she said trying to wedge herself between Meagan and Simi.

'This isn't about finding a boyfriend. It's about retraining my brain to not keep making the same mistakes. If I ask the guys out, I'll just go for another version of Oscar or Jason or Ade and the same thing will happen over and over again until I'm Zsa Zsa Gabor, dead and divorced a billion times,' said Simi.

Meagan sat back sipping her wine as Jemima continued her futile attempts to derail Simi's plans. Just because Jemima was terrified of men it didn't mean Simi had to be. Meagan admired Simi's desire to recalibrate and if she could help her move on from Oscar, she would. She'd only concocted this idea as a way of getting Simi to go to her audition but actually, it might do her some good. They had sat by the sidelines for long enough. It was time to get on the court and give Simi some much-needed coaching.

'Jem, don't you want to help me?' Simi said, taking Jemima's hand.

'Of course I do. I just think there's better fixes than pestering random men.'

'Such as?' Simi asked.

'Well, I'm not the expert,' Jemima floundered.

'Exactly. In fact, you could do with a little help yourself,' said Meagan as she gave their waiter the nod to fetch another bottle.

This was no longer just a regular night out and for that, they needed more wine.

'I'm fine as I am, thank you,' said Jemima crossing her arms.

'Shit. There's Miles!' hissed Meagan, pointing to the other side of the bar.

'What, where?!' said Jemima, eyes wide as she dived under their table, 'Did he see me? Is he looking?'

'Meagan. That was mean,' said Simi. 'He's not here, Jem.'

Jemima slowly emerged, straightening her sweater and glaring at Meagan. 'Not funny.'

'I wasn't trying to be funny. I was proving a point. You *both* need to change it up,' she said taking a triumphant gulp of wine.

Jemima made one more nervous sweep of the bar before sitting back down and taking a large mouthful of wine too.

'She's right, Jem,' ventured Simi. 'It's been two years and you haven't had a single date.'

'I've been busy,' said Jemima.

'Ptttthh,' Meagan said rolling her eyes.

'Let's be honest. We could all learn something from this,' said Simi looking at Meagan.

Meagan looked around the bar ignoring Simi's gaze. The game or challenge or whatever, was about fixing Simi's love life not hers. Everything in Meagan's world was just as she wanted it.

'Simi's right, Meag. Meagan?' Jemima said firmly.

'You've been seeing Todd for four years but you're not even boyfriend and girlfriend,' added Simi.

'For the gazillionth time, I'm not *seeing* Todd. We have sex. Regularly. That's it.'

The waiter discreetly switched out their wine bottles, showing no signs of acknowledging the conversation. Jemima gave him a polite smile.

'You've been exclusive for a whole year,' Jemima argued.

'*I've* been busy!' Meagan deflected.

'Ptttthh,' said Jemima sitting back with a self-satisfied smirk. 'Whatever.'

Okay, so she *hadn't* slept with anyone other than Todd in the last twelve months. She'd been too busy to find a replacement. And anyway, why would she? Who eats burgers when they've got the keys to a steak house? But that wasn't 'seeing each other', that was screwing. Maybe Todd was getting a bit hazy on that detail. Was that why he'd been more clingy of late? He thinks they are a thing? If so, Meagan needed to shut that down, and dating other guys was a sure-fire way to do it.

'Okay, I'm in,' Meagan said, slapping the table. 'How's it going to work?'

'Wait, what?' blurted Jemima.

Meagan shrugged as Simi rummaged in her bag for her crumpled-up audition script. On it were a scrawled network of notes.

'What?' Simi said, looking up at Meagan and Jemima's confused expressions. 'I made some notes while I was waiting for you.'

Meagan wrapped her hand around her drink and sat back. What kind of sweet hell was this?

'So first, I thought we could make a list of your guy friends and—' began Simi, pen poised.

Meagan sat bolt upright. 'HARD no, Simi. For real. Forget it. My friends aren't just friends, they're work associates and I don't wanna mess with that by tangling them up with you two. No shade,' she added off of Jemima's offended scowl.

'That's not fair. You met Todd through Jemima,' Simi wailed.

'Errr, slow your roll. Yes, he works at Hudson Hicks but I caught that fish all by myself,' Meagan said folding her arms.

Simi looked to Jemima for help.

'It's true,' said Jemima, 'Meag hooked up with him after that

85

first Hudson Hicks party we went to and the rest, as they say, is her story… '

Simi sagged, resting her head on her hand, 'Well, if friends are out, how are we going to find dates for each other and break each other out of our patterns?' Simi pleaded.

'What if we set up online dating accounts for each other?' said Jemima.

Meagan leaned back in her chair, looking around the bar, which for a weeknight was buzzing.

'We need to think of this as an experiment, and for that we need fresh samples but you two are overthinking it,' she said. 'Internet dating is a long ting. Messaging back and forth til you get ghosted. Who's got time for that? Let's just bowl up to someone. *Yes or no, mate? Yes? Cool. No? Your loss.* IRL. Face-time. Old school stylee!'

'Yes!' said Simi. 'Let's get out there and face-time! For each other! And change our shit!'

'Yes, Sim! And there's no time like the present,' said Meagan, clapping her hands and whistling for their waiter, 'Three sambucas, my good man!'

'Oh my god, what are we *doing*?' said Jemima.

'This is great. I love it!' squawked Simi. 'What's IRL??'

CHAPTER 13

Jemima

'So we're literally going to walk up to a bloke and go, "Excuse me, my friend fancies you"?' Jemima said, sniffing her sambuca with suspicion.

It reeked of liquorice and bad choices.

'Yeah,' said Meagan gulping her shot.

'I'm so excited!' squeaked Simi, 'Let's come up with some rules of engagement.'

'Because this will be a battle,' Jemima murmured, feeling like that cowardly soldier who knows there's no escape other than going over the top.

This wasn't what she should be doing with her Wednesday nights. She should be planning loft conversions and going on wine-tasting holidays not embarking on a game of My Friend Fancies You. This was going to be horrific for her. Men would love having a 29-year-old like Meagan bouncing towards them but being ambushed by a 42-year-old recluse was a different story. Jemima groaned as Simi excitedly smoothed out her overturned script pages, to take notes. Meagan tapped the table for quiet.

'Okay, rule one, we always ask guys out for each other, never for ourselves. So for example, I'll ask someone out for you,' said Meagan pointing at Jemima, 'you ask someone out for Simi and she'll ask someone out for me. Round Robin.'

'Perfect,' said Simi scribbling on her crumpled papers, 'and it's important the guys know who we truly are so, rule number two, no fibbing or exaggerating. No telling them I have a fake leg or that I'm an Olympian,' said Simi glaring at Meagan.

'Fine. I've got a rule for you, no falling in love,' Meagan said staring right back at Simi.

Simi broke Meagan's gaze and diligently noted that down, 'Three. No… falling… in… love.'

Jemima rolled her eyes. If any of them were likely to do that, it wasn't her.

'Question,' she interjected raising a hand. 'If we don't like the guy, we can veto, right?'

Simi considered this. 'That sounds fair… '

'Of course you can't!' barked Meagan. 'The whole point is to get you two out of your comfort zones and meeting different guys or in your case, Jem – a guy.'

'Rule number four?' asked Simi revelling in her role as secretary.

'You betcha, Simster,' said Meagan.

Jemima necked her shot and thumped her head on the table. Why couldn't Simi go to therapy like a normal person? 'How long do we have to do this for?' she grumbled.

'Well, in *Change Your Life, Become a Wife*, it says—' began Simi.

'There is NOT a book called *Change Your Life, Become a Wife*?' Meagan said, eyes wide.

'Just listen. It says that changing a habit takes twenty-one days but changing your life takes ninety,' Simi said enthusiastically.

Jemima's heart began to race. This was the worst idea since that 3D *Jaws* sequel. She wouldn't be able to take three days of this let alone three months. She panicked, looking around for an escape route. Meagan gave her a comforting pat on the knee, though to Jemima it felt more like the reassurance you give a lame racehorse who knows its fate.

'Relax, Jem. Let's do a month,' said Meagan. 'That's plenty of time to change our habits.'

How was it that a few days ago Jemima had everything locked down but now worms were spewing from the proverbial can all over the place. Through not just gritted teeth but a gritted body, Jemima clinked glasses with Simi and Meagan, agreeing to at least give it a try.

'Jem, it's just a date. You never have to see them again if you don't want to,' Meagan said, nudging her.

Jemima sighed, her tension eventually subsiding. Maybe she could bear a few platonic evenings out?

'Fine. Let's give it a go,' she conceded.

'Perfect! I'll start,' Simi said scraping back her chair.

'Wait, now?' bleated Jemima but Simi was already standing.

'I saw a guy earlier who would be perfect for you,' said Simi before disappearing into the throng.

Jemima watched Simi head off trying to look sassy and confident and not heartbroken and betrayed. The head held high was good but the swinging shoulders was more Eighties-soap-star than she probably intended. Nineteen seconds later Simi returned in defeat.

'I— I don't know what I did wrong,' she said looking back at the two guys she'd literally left scratching their heads.

Meagan indicated to the waiter to bring three more shots as Jemima quietly hoped Simi's swift defeat would show her the madness in this. Maybe now she might consider therapy or at least unfollowing Oscar on Instagram. How many cycling photos can one person truly like? She rested her hand on Simi's arm and was just about to administer some gentle but firm love when Meagan piped up.

'Tell you where you went wrong. You've got to look like you don't give a shit,' she said. 'Like Jemima. See?'

'That's just my face!' Jemima said.

It wasn't that she didn't give a shit, she just wasn't convinced what Simi needed after the end of a relationship was even more rejection, even if it was on someone else's behalf!

'Come on, Jem. You have a go. Watch this, Simi. You'll see what I mean,' said Meagan.

Jemima gawped at her with the expression of a death row convict who'd just heard the executioner's keys. *Fine.* Two wipeouts were bound to end this insanity. Jemima wobbled to her feet. Steeped in sambuca, she unsteadily scanned the bar. Way over on the other side, she spotted her mark. He looked like a nice enough guy and that would do. Jemima made her way over. She'd had enough drinks to give her false courage but not so much that a nightclub sounded like a good idea. As she approached with a full bladder and empty mind, she decided to opt for her father's usual opening gambit of tapping someone on the shoulder and saying, 'Excuse me, young man!'

As she prodded the tall stranger in the back, his whole table, work colleagues she presumed, turned to look at her. *Shit*, gulped Jemima. Now she was up close, her mark looked exactly like Oscar! He had the same cappuccino skin and was thin, tall and athletic just like Simi's ex. She definitely had to fail. If she brought this guy over, Simi would either fall madly in love or think Jemima was some perverse psychopath intent on compounding her misery. She looked back at Meagan who was waving at her to get on with it. Jemima caught her balance and yanked Oscar 2.0 aside.

'This is going to sound weird but I'm going to ask you out for my friend and you have to pretend you're not interested,' she hissed at him.

'I'm not interested. I'm married,' said 2.0 holding up his wedding ring finger and turning away.

Jemima grabbed his hand and tried to shove it in his pocket, 'No one can see that!'

'But I want them to. That's why I wear it – so strangers like you know I'm married,' said 2.0 as he looked back to his friends for help.

'Don't worry about them,' said Jemima turning 2.0's face back to hers. 'Shhhhhhh. Listen, listen, you just need to let this play out and I'll go away.'

'You promise?' said 2.0 as one of his colleagues appeared by his side.

'You alright, Deon?'

'I honestly don't know,' he said.

His colleague gave him the internationally recognised look for give-me-the-signal-and-I-will-rugby-tackle-this-lunatic-for-you then returned to their table where everyone pretended to talk while eavesdropping. Jemima pressed on.

'You ready?' she said rubbing her hands.

'And you promise you'll go away?'

'Exactly!' She beamed. 'Okay, so Dane—'

'Deon...'

'Exactly, would you like a date with my friend?' boomed Jemima before whispering behind her hand, 'then you look at her and shake your head so they can see.'

Deon looked over at Simi who was straining to see him through the crowd.

'No thank you,' he said shaking his head.

'Do it more,' Jemima said, 'and then wave your hands like, *no*. This is acting 101, Dave. It's got to read across the whole space.'

Jemima remembered Simi saying something along those lines when describing theatre acting.

'I'm not interested,' bellowed Deon waving his hands.

'Bravo,' said Jemima in a whisper that could have been heard in a helicopter.

She patted him on the back, shoved him towards his friends and left. Behind her, Jemima heard the sound of crashing glass and knew she'd shoved him too hard. Cringing, she decided to just... keep... on... walking.

'What happened?' Meagan asked Jemima as Deon beckoned over a waiter and pointed in their direction.

Jemima watched as the waiter approached and braced herself, ready to defuse the situation. This place was in her top three best haunts. She couldn't get barred for harassing men!

'Sorry, Sorry,' she said placing a hushing finger on her lips as only noisy, drunk people do.

The waiter smiled patiently. 'No worries. Just, please, don't bother people,' he said clearing the assortment of glasses from their table.

Jemima mimed hushing everyone as he left.

'Right, well we tried but you heard the man. We're bothering people,' she said, sitting back down.

'But what happened over there?' Simi asked, ignoring her.

Jemima crossed her fingers under the table. 'He said he thought it was, and I quote, *weird and not what he expected from three adult women persons* then he made me promise to go away.'

Meagan stared at Jemima. 'He said that?'

Jemima gave an overzealous nod before turning to Simi. 'But he did say you were incredibly beautiful and if he saw you on a dating website, he'd be more than interested.'

Simi clutched her chest. 'Aaah, so sweet!'

See, there *were* times when lying was okay, Jemima reassured herself.

'We gave it a shot but probably best we quit while we're behind,' she said, sweeping up her drink.

Without a word, Meagan vanished into the crowd. *Damn*, thought Jemima. If anyone was going to succeed at this, it was her. Five minutes later Meagan returned with Gil, an uncomfortable hybrid of hipster chic and millennial awkwardness.

'Jemima, meet Gil. Gil, this is Jemima. Like I say, she told me – she fancies you,' said Meagan before dusting her hands of the two of them and dragging Simi off to another table.

Jemima looked from Meagan to Gil and back again in horror. What had just happened? A moment ago she was on the way to burying this idiotic game and now she was on a date! She eyed up Gil, clocking his tattoo sleeve, hipster beard and lumberjack shirt.

'Watcha,' he said sitting. 'Your home girl said you're a writer. I write content for an Internet start-up so, you know. Great minds.'

He clicked his fingers back and forth, indicating the simpatico. Jemima looked over at Meagan with a glare that said both, *help* and *you bloody cow!* Meagan turned away with a broad smirk.

At Jemima's table, Gil was filling the conversational void by talking about his top five breakfast foods and passion for the new cereal restaurant which had opened near his Shoreditch office.

'Cheerios, Weetabix, Cornflakes, Rice Krispies, porridge, obvs. Pop Tarts, actually that's six,' he yakked.

Jemima had been planning on having a coffee to sober up but listening to Gil's waffle was doing a much better job. As Gil rambled on, she spotted Simi get up from her table with that same intent she'd had earlier. Jemima had to stop her. They'd already been warned to stop bothering people. *If* they were going to play this game at all, it had to be in a place they had never been or never would again. That was non-negotiable.

'Okay, Gil, lovely to meet you. We must have cereal sometime,' Jemima blurted before staggering over to the girls' table and stopping Simi in her tracks.

'Thank God that date's over,' Jemima said pulling Simi back into her chair. 'Probs best we knock it on the head for tonight though.'

Simi glared at Jemima.

'That was the introduction,' she scolded. 'You can't have the date the night you meet.'

'What?' exclaimed Jemima looking back at Gil as he raised his mason jar of pale ale at her.

'You mean I have to spend a whole *other* evening… with him? *Why?*' wailed Jemima.

'Rule number five. Girl Code. No woman left behind. If two of us get dates and have them that night, the last one would be left on her own and we can't do that.'

Jemima's head thumped onto the table again.

'Then we need better dates. You matched me with a lumbersexual manboy,' she moaned.

'At least I got you someone,' said Meagan.

Simi raised her hands to quell the bickering.

'Okay, Jem. We'll chalk this one up as a test. You don't have to see Gil again but we need to figure out how this thing is going to work. Meag, come over to Jem's tomorrow. We can create a playbook and you can give us some tips.'

'You lot might be beyond help,' said Meagan.

Feeling Simi's doe eyes burning into her, Jemima nodded glumly no longer possessing the energy nor the sobriety to fight this.

Meagan waved her credit card at the waiter and once the bill was paid they slipped on their coats and headed into the icy January night. Jemima sucked in the cold air as though it were the common sense she'd left at the door earlier that evening.

'Relax, you wally. They're just men,' Meagan said prodding her. 'Besides, all this dating drama will be good for your book.'

Jemima smiled noncommittally as they hugged their goodbyes and Meagan went off to dome, teabag and spider with Todd or whatever they did that left her waddling the next day.

Moments later, an Uber arrived and Jemima and Simi clambered in.

On the way home, as Simi snored in the crook of her arm, Jemima mulled over Meagan's parting words. *This dating drama will be good for your book…* It hadn't occurred to Jemima that *this* experience might actually be of use. Though Beverly would never play a game like this, by Jemima playing it with the girls, it did give her a window into their love lives and their attitude towards relationships. Coupling these insights with their stories might give her the material she needed to finish her book. But how should she broach this without getting consigned to the naughty step with Troy – forever. She wound down her window to let the breeze sober her up. Simi stirred, repositioning herself onto her lap as Jemima stroked her hair.

'Thanks for tonight, Jem. I already feel better,' said Simi and she nodded off again as their 4.9-rated driver whisked them home.

CHAPTER 14

Simi

Simi gawped at Meagan from across the kitchen. Tonight was supposed to be about dropping dating knowledge not major league bombshells.

'But if Bradley Tyson has been fired from *Clash of the Crown*, who's going to replace him?' Simi asked, her mind somersaulting at the possibilities.

Perhaps the producers had realised they need someone with more cachet, perhaps even, BAFTA-winning cachet. Simi grinned as she speculated over potential replacements. Would they go for Darius Wallington, an African American acting titan? They'd be lucky to get him though. He hadn't done television in years. Maybe they'd entice Rhys Goswell who'd just won a Golden Globe for playing a neuro-diverse superhero. Or perhaps they'd go the other way, plucking some unknown from obscurity, giving them the break they'd long dreamed of.

'Don't worry, babes. The replacement is even better than Bradley. Now, let's talk about the game,' said Meagan waving a tub of ice cream at Simi. 'I brought your favourite.'

Simi's eyes widened, 'Wait, you know who it is? Spill!'

Meagan set down the tub and took a breath, looking back and forth between Simi and Jemima.

'So… they're rewriting Cameron Christiansen's part. She's replacing Bradley – which is great.'

Simi blinked at Meagan as her brain tried to process this new information. 'But… so… there'll be scenes of a sexual nature… as a prostitute… with a lady… woman?'

'On some level, yes, exactly but apart from that, everything's the same,' Meagan said popping the lid on the ice cream. 'This is that fancy stuff you have to leave out for—'

'The SAME?!' screeched Simi.

'Can you pass me the mixed herbs?' Jemima asked.

Momentarily distracted, Simi rooted in the cupboard. She handed a jar to Jemima who stirred her Bolognese sauce, clearly electing to sit this conversation out.

'Honestly, Sim. It's not a big deal,' said Meagan, hands on hips.

'Then why didn't you tell me?!'

'Because I knew you'd freak out,' Meagan carped.

'I'm not freaking out, it's just, I haven't even done… stuff with a girl *in real life* let alone on set, in front of a crew!'

'Well maybe you should get some practice, in case you get the job!' Meagan winked.

'Meag!' Simi wailed.

Of course this was no big deal to someone as uninhibited as Meagan but for Simi it was. She wasn't sure she was ready for *scenes of sexual nature* – with anyone.

'Honestly, I don't know what all the fuss is about. May I remind you, kissing a girl feels just like kissing a boy – just less scratchy. I went lez for my first six months of tech college,' declared Meagan.

'It's not about that—' Simi protested.

'And secondly,' Meagan continued, with a silencing finger, 'there's nothing wrong with being a prostitute.'

'Please don't tell us that's what you did with the last six months of college,' said Jemima.

'Alright, keep cooking, *Ainsley*,' said Meagan. 'Look, Sim, you're overthinking it. Once you're skin-to-skin, it's like belly buttons. Everyone's just an innie or an outie. Plus, don't forget, Jodie Foster played a prostitute and she got an Oscar nom. Big picture, babes. And now you're back in the saddle, you can audition again. Speaking of which, I've snagged you a humdinger of a casting this Friday.'

'The saddle? My foot's barely in the stirrup! May I remind *you*, I am a cuckquean,' Simi said.

'See,' said Meagan, 'you already sound medieval.'

Simi grimaced. This was typical Meagan, just barrelling ahead. Simi wanted to believe Meagan knew best but she was growing tired of it.

'Shouldn't you… check with me first? It feels like stuff just happens without me knowing,' said Simi.

'Like when?' Meagan asked folding her arms.

'Like when you changed my casting age to 17 and I got called in to play a sixth former. I was 30!'

Jemima stifled a giggle as Simi recalled her abject humiliation.

'What can I say, black don't crack!' said Meagan as though playing the statement to a crowd bigger than just Jemima and Simi.

'All I'm saying is, shouldn't this be more of a democracy than… a… a dictatorship?'

Meagan's mood shifted and right away, Simi wanted to backtrack.

'I mean, you're not Pol Pot, It's just… ' she said, her toes curling up inside her trainers.

'Paul who? The guy who won *Britain's Got Talent*?' said Meagan. 'Listen, Sim, I'm grafting my arse off here. The acting game, it's not like comedy. Everything takes ages so sometimes I cut a couple of corners. That's how I get the job done but I'm trying my best coz you're my girl,' Meagan said pulling Simi in for a bear hug.

Simi's cheeks warmed and she was instantly disarmed. *My girl*. Those words meant a lot.

In the marathon to make it to the top, Simi was leagues behind Meagan's other clients. In fact, she was lucky to still be on her books. The least she could do was stop griping and turn up to a few auditions.

'Sorry, Meag. You're right. It's fine.'

'Sweet, now can we discuss this dating mad ting or what?' Meagan laughed.

'Double yes!' Simi said, clapping as Jemima carried on stirring her sauce.

CHAPTER 15

Meagan

'I just don't think the best place to play this game is a gelateria,' said Jemima folding her arms.

'Just say ice cream shop and stop being such a ponce,' Meagan tutted.

It didn't matter where they were, they just needed to get going, she huffed. Once they had, Simi could start to forget about Oscar and Meagan could start drip-feeding news of her dating escapades to Todd so that he would calm the hell down with his unrequited love-in.

'What's wrong with this place, Jem?' Simi asked, jabbing a spoon into her cookie dough gelato.

'There're children here!' Jemima blurted, gesturing around her.

'So? We're not about to hump a bloke on the counter!' Meagan gassed. 'This isn't about finding someone to go IKEA shopping with! This is just practice.'

'Well, either we'll get dates or get arrested for cradle snatching. Actually, rule number six. No breaking the law,' Jemima declared.

'I'm gonna break something in a minute,' said Meagan slapping her hand. 'Enough with the moaning, Jem. For real. If you're gonna do this, you can't be moaning the whole time. You're giving me tinnitus.'

Meagan looked around the West End shop and its bustling Saturday afternoon crowd. This place was fine. No one knew them, it was busy and there were plenty of men. Granted a lot of them looked like they were on a gap year but what did that matter. After the woeful display at Ripley's this was exactly what they needed – a safe place for a trial run.

Jemima sighed. 'Believe it or not, I'm fine about the game, I just hoped we'd be approaching people who were of voting age and how come this place is so busy? It's freezing outside.'

'You know what it's like, teenagers and northerners never feel the cold,' said Meagan.

She clapped her hands together. It was time to put into practice what they'd come up with at Jemima's a few nights earlier over wine and a pretty decent spag bol.

'Okay, Simi, you go first. You're going to find someone for Jemima. Think about who she is and what she needs. Not what she wants,' Meagan cautioned, 'what she *needs*.'

Simi thought for a second. 'Well, for a start he's got to be anally retentive about recycling and correcting the grammar on takeaway menus.'

'I did that once!' Jemima said raising her hands in defence.

Meagan laughed, scanning the room. She spotted a young guy in thick, dark-framed glasses having an animated discussion with his friends and gave Simi the nod.

'Him,' she said cocking her head his way.

'He looks about 12 years old!' said Jemima.

'I'd say early twenties,' Simi said, squinting.

'He's got a skateboard,' Jemima hissed.

Meagan craned to look. 'Environmentally friendly transportation. Right up your street!'

'I mean, I know this is a trial run but I could actually see you together,' said Simi.

'Simi!' said Jemima.

'I know, I know. Okay, here I go.'

Simi pushed her chair back, sights locked on the target.

'And remember, Sim, it's all about psychology with men,' said Meagan. 'They're a wolf pack.'

'But at Jem's you said they were monkeys,' Simi replied, her nose wrinkled in confusion.

'Both,' Meagan confirmed. 'You train them like a monkey and they hunt like a wolf.'

'And they have good memories, like elephants?' Simi said helpfully.

Meagan rolled her eyes. This was like an arse kicking contest between two one-legged idiots.

'Just go,' she said shoving Simi towards the bespectacled skateboarder.

Meagan watched her leave before turning back to Jemima. 'So, spill the tea. What's new?'

'Oh, you know, writing and more writing,' Jemima said stirring the dregs of her melting gelato.

'I dunno how you do it,' said Meagan. 'Days, weeks and months on the same project. I'd go mad. Comedy's quick. In and out. Done.'

'Well, generally speaking, I love it. It's just, at the moment I've hit a bit of a brick wall.'

'Writer's block or something?' asked Meagan.

Jemima took a spoonful of her melting ice cream. 'It's this whole romance thing my editor was going on about.'

'Oh yeah. You want me to do something about her?' said Meagan who was still waiting for the nod from Simi to take care of Oscar's red-haired harlot.

She'd even brought her Super Soaker to work just in case.

'No, Meagan. Jeez, you're like a bloody mob boss. She just wants more romance in the book and I'm finding it hard to write, that's all,' said Jemima.

Meagan looked at her friend, the demands of her job clearly weighing on her.

'You know why you're finding it hard, babes? Coz *you* haven't had any romance since Rapa Nui,' Meagan said, her attention caught by Simi who was in a lively exchange about skateboards with Jemima's potential date.

'Don't call him that,' said Jemima.

'I'm sorry but Miles is the spit of those Easter Island statues. His head is *massive*. Completely disproportionate to his body,' said Meagan.

'It's not just about Miles,' Jemima snapped.

Meagan stopped. 'Well what is it?' she said side-stepping Jemima's irritation.

'Sorry,' Jemima said, shifting in her seat. 'It's just, I've got less than a month to finish this book and… I've been searching for a solution. The thing is, I… I was wondering how you would feel about me using—'

Just then a loud crash reverberated around the gelateria. Meagan and Jemima turned to see Simi face down in the lap of a middle-aged couple as a skateboard trundled to a halt by the shop entrance. Simi tried to detangle herself, only to get more wrapped up in the folds of the woman's dress. After finally working herself free, she picked up the skateboard and wordlessly returned it to its owner before dashing back to Meagan and Jemima. The sound of teenage laughter echoed around them.

'We have to leave!' Simi said, barely containing her abject embarrassment.

Jemima and Meagan needed no further instructions. They gathered up their things and scurried from the scene of the crime only slowing once they'd reached the tube station.

'You were literally face down in that woman's lap!' Meagan shrieked, hardly able to breathe she was laughing so much.

Jemima collapsed in peals of laughter at the image.

'I mean I thought you might crash and burn, but not like that!' Meagan wheezed.

'What were you thinking, darling? Skateboarding indoors – on tiles?' Jemima said, battling to stem her laughter.

'He said it had slow wheels!' said Simi as the girls dashed into Leicester Square tube station, zigzagging around the weekend tourists congregating in the ticket hall.

Jemima pulled out a handful of tissues and dutifully cleaned the creamy gloop from Simi's neck.

'Well, that was a disaster,' said Simi as she checked behind her ears for any last remaining gelato.

'And you know why, right?' said Meagan.

'Please, don't mention the skateboarding again!'

'Because you were pretending to be like him. You're 35. You don't skateboard. Don't pretend you do,' said Meagan.

'Then what should I have done?'

Meagan sighed. There was more to this dating game than

she'd imagined but she'd never had to deconstruct her technique before. She wasn't even sure what she did that worked or what the girls did that didn't. So far they'd had three wipe outs. She'd had the only score – with Gil. Meagan thought back to when she'd approached him. The first thing she recalled was smiling. As a sufferer of resting bitch face, that was compulsory so as not to terrify strangers. She'd been confident but polite, after all she was interrupting his night. He could equally have just won the lottery or lost his job. She remembered touching his arm to get his attention. They always seemed to like that. Their conversation had been brief – an introduction, a compliment and then she'd gone straight to discussing Jemima. She'd spoken about her as though she were highly prized, an exclusive opportunity he'd be a fool to pass up. And most importantly, Meagan had been willing to walk away.

She turned to the others who were staring at her, awaiting the guru's wisdom.

'You're not gonna like it,' she said.

'We don't stand a chance, do we?' said Simi.

'Here's the thing,' Meagan said. 'What I did, a hair flick here, a compliment there, it worked because it's me.'

Simi slumped. 'So we have to be you to do this?'

'No. You have to be *you*,' Meagan said.

'Noooooooooooo!' wailed Simi. 'That's what got me into this mess in the first place!'

Jemima gave Simi a consoling pat.

It was tough but that was the truth of it. Meagan shrugged. If Simi played the game using her usual tactics – mutating herself into what she thought they wanted, it would be an even bigger shit-show than earlier. They had to be authentic *and* transparent, get themselves out of the way so the guy could see through them to who they were being hooked up with.

'If you're a miserable cow, then they'll think that's what's in store for them when they meet us,' Meagan said nodding Jemima's way.

'And if you're desperate, guess what?' she said, giving Simi a kind smile.

Simi nodded, mulling over Meagan's words. Even Jemima appeared to be taking it all in rather than coming up with some snarky comment.

'Right then,' Jemima puffed, 'we need more coaching. And if we're really doing this, we have to talk about the type of guy we'd like to meet – or not meet.'

Jemima was clearly still smarting from her brief encounter with the copywriting lumberjack, Gil, thought Meagan. It was fair enough. She'd spent the best part of a week batting away his request for a *proper* date. As commuters swirled around them, Meagan linked arms with Simi and Jemima.

'Okay, but let's get out of here,' she said and they headed towards the escalators.

'You start, Meag. What do you want?' Simi asked as they descended to the platforms.

Without thinking, Meagan replied, 'He's gotta be fit, live north of the river and own a decent car.'

If she was going to spend two, possibly three hours in someone's company, plush leather interiors were non-negotiable. Jemima and Simi followed her in silence as they moved through the crowd to some empty seats. They obviously hadn't considered this at all.

'Come on, Simster, what are you looking for?'

Simi thought for a second then rummaged in her bag to retrieve a thick, blue notebook stuffed with magazine cuttings and Post-it Notes. Meagan stared down at it. She was wrong. Simi had given this way too much thought.

'What. Is. That?' said Jemima planting herself on the other side of Simi to get a better look at the Keanu Reeves collage on the front cover.

'My cosmic ordering book,' said Simi as though it were obvious. 'I've had it for years. It's like the Argos catalogue but it comes from the Universe instead of the stock room at the back.'

She leafed through the pages until she reached the section on partners which was three times denser than the others and brimming with photos.

'You want the Universe to deliver you Keanu Reeves?' Jemima asked.

'What if you're out when he arrives?' said Meagan.

'I guess they'll leave a card,' said Jemima, '"Sorry, we tried to deliver The One but you were out. We left him with a neighbour."'

Simi snapped her book shut.

'You asked us a question but my answer's not that simple.'

'Sorry, Sim. Go on,' Meagan said as though coaxing a hissy cat from under a sofa.

Simi cautiously reopened her book on the relationship section. The pages were thick with notes, lists and collages. It looked more like Simi was on the cusp of discovering time travel than dreaming up her best life.

'First and foremost,' Simi began, spreading the pages open, 'he needs to appreciate the arts, you know, visit galleries, go to the theatre – but not musicals. I'm done with that. It's a red flag. Oh and he has to love music but his music collection can't have more than five *Best of* albums. Maybe he could even be in a band. It'd be great if he worked in the entertainment industry too and was successful, you know, broken the US market – and was famous… '

Meagan went to speak.

'Oh and I'd like him to have *really* good hair and he *has* to be spiritual but not a hippy,' Simi continued.

After thirty minutes of Simi detailing her perfect man, Meagan had lost the will to live and Jemima didn't look far off. Fourteen tubes had screeched in and out of the station and the platform guard was starting to eye them suspiciously. Meagan didn't want to rain on Simi's parade but this wasn't cosmic ordering, it was wishful thinking and a far cry from Meagan's meticulously scheduled plan. Hers was grounded in logic not the position of the planets. She'd be married by her mid-thirties, have all her kids by 40 who'd be in uni by her mid-fifties and then she'd be free. She'd travel more, work less and continue to slay in every way possible. Simi should take a leaf out of her book and put *that* in her bizarre catalogue, thought Meagan.

'Simi, you're basically describing Keanu Reeves,' Jemima said. 'Maybe just choose a couple of things to get us started.'

Simi scanned her reams of notes. 'Spiritual – and the *Best of* album thing.'

'Got it,' said Jemima tapping her temple.

'What about you, Jem?' Simi asked.

'No weirdos,' Jemima said straight away.

They all nodded. That, they could agree on.

'Oh, frig! I'm late for my monologue class,' said Simi looking over at the platform clock.

She snapped her book shut and gave the girls a goodbye cuddle.

'Tell them there was a late-running skateboard.' Meagan grinned.

'Funny. So, what are you two going to do with the rest of your day?' Simi asked.

'You mean who!' Meagan winked.

Simi pulled out of their hug.

'Sorry, Meag, but no side pieces. That's got to be rule number seven. You need to get rid of Todd,' Simi reprimanded.

'What? *Why?*' Meagan spluttered over the roar of another incoming tube.

Giving up sex so she could date was like giving up chocolate to eat more fruit. It was ridiculous.

'Because if you've got a backup, you're not invested,' Simi explained crossing her arms.

Jemima rubbed Meagan's arm. 'I'm sure you can survive one month without Todd the Rod.'

'How am I supposed to make him jeal— I mean, how will Todd know to back off if he doesn't know I'm seeing other people?' Meagan said.

'I think, if you stop seeing him, he'll get the message you're not seeing him,' said Jemima.

Meagan scowled.

'I'm not *seeing* him and if my vajayjay heals up because of this, there will be consequences. Thanks for ruining my afternoon, Simi,' Meagan griped.

'It'll be good for you!' said Simi before blowing them a kiss and heading off to her class.

Meagan slumped against the tiled wall, glowering at weekend shoppers and tourists bustling around her.

'Fancy a drink at mine?' said Jemima.

'Well, seeing as I'm not going to be getting any, might as well,' Meagan moaned.

Jemima laughed and linked arms with Meagan as they hopped onto the next train. But Meagan was not laughing. No sex with Todd... for a whole month. She made a mental note to buy a large pack of batteries on the way home.

'So, did you know about Simi's... book?' Jemima said over the beep of the closing doors.

'I did,' said Meagan, slowly pulling herself from her funk. 'Did you see the *Terry* pages?'

'Yeah, what was that about? There were more pictures of him than Keanu.'

'Did I ever tell you about the time Simi stalked a guy at college... ?' Meagan said.

CHAPTER 16

Jemima

It was an hour since Meagan had left but Jemima was still sitting by her open window waiting for her bedroom to stop spinning. Whilst Meagan's hollow legs enabled her to drink like a rugby player, Jemima had reached her upper limit way sooner. As she forced down one more gulp of water before bed, her mind was working overtime. All day she'd been deliberating over her book but Meagan's recollection of Simi's college obsession had unwittingly thrown Jemima a lifeline. She was intrigued by what Beverly might be like if she had the same compulsive past. Jemima closed her window and pulled out her notebook, scribbling down what she could remember. She winced at the thought of Terry sitting Simi down, asking her to leave him alone. That must have been mortifying but the fact that he'd brought along a witness... *Ouch*. Ideas cascaded as Jemima then imagined a young, innocent Beverly back in college, deeply in love with a boy who would never reciprocate. She envisioned the secret love letters Beverly would write but never send, her desires, her vulnerability. How, Jemima wondered, had Meagan got Simi to confess such personal information? This had never once come up in the ten years she'd known Simi. Jemima knew how. Meagan had an unnerving ability to extract information – from anyone. Jemima paused. That trait was ideal for her increasingly complex heroine. Also, what if, just like Meagan with Parker, Beverly had loved once but never again, now burying her vulnerability under a tough veneer? The tipping point for Meagan had been when Parker had decided to stay with his wife. She'd been utterly crushed and, when she recovered, a new Meagan had risen up from the ashes – a Meagan with a plan, a Meagan who relied on no one, a Meagan who was brittle…

'Oh my god,' Jemima whispered.

Hadn't that been the exact word Eve had used to describe what Beverly had become? Jemima was onto something. More info on Parker would help galvanise this, setting up how her leading lady had become the woman she is today. But, thought Jemima, that intensity would now have to be offset with humour. She grinned as she recalled the many quips and stories Meagan had shared over the years. A particular favourite that had left Jemima and Simi howling was how Meagan often described Todd's manhood as *a clenched fist*. She'd said going down on him was like 'being in the ring with Anthony Joshua', and how after three minutes she'd half-expected to hear a bell. Previously, Beverly had been painfully serious but with this humour she would now be able to laugh at herself in a way Jemima had never allowed her to. A smile spread across her face. Regardless of how unsuccessful they'd been at getting dates, the game itself was proving to be a great vehicle for getting the girls to open up. It was giving Jemima the material she so desperately needed. If they continued, she might even have a chance of finishing her book within the deadline. Excitement bubbled at the thought of crossing that elusive finish line and handing in a final draft. As inspiration coursed through her, she opened her laptop and began to type.

Paragraph upon Meagan-and-Parker-inspired paragraph flowed onto the page. Still on a roll, she then switched and began detailing Beverly's college obsession. This was great material. As she wrote, an image of a young, insecure and deeply in love Simi jostled its way into her mind and her face fell. If Simi read this, she might feel humiliated all over again. Jemima hit delete. That story would never go in the book and if she used other stories, it had to be with the girl's go-ahead. Her attempt to broach the subject at the gelateria had been seriously hampered by Simi faceplanting into that woman's lap. Nonetheless, Jemima had to ask and soon. The girls loved her and wouldn't want her book to fail. She might have to do some convincing but she would get them onside in the end.

As she put away her laptop, her phone pinged. It was one in the morning. Either it was Meagan sending some wildly explicit GIF or… she peered at her phone and her smile waned. It was Miles.

You back?? Would love to buy u lunch Mx

Jemima tapped out a reply.

In LA. Sorry!

She flung her phone back onto the night stand, wishing she was in LA. The idea of an ocean separating her and Miles was a dream. As she wriggled under her duvet, she wondered, had she *always* opted for flight whenever her back was against the wall? Staring up at her ceiling, Jemima thought of all the ways her mother constantly tried to protect her from extremes of emotions. Her earliest memory was when she was just 5 years old. They were visiting her grandmother's house and they passed a police cordon. A man had fallen from a fire escape. His body lay in the street covered by a grubby blanket as police took statements and onlookers gathered. A curious little girl with no knowledge of life and death, Jemima had wanted to look. However, the moment her mother had seen the flashing red and blue lights she'd covered Jemima's eyes and led her on an extra twenty-minute walk around the block to reach their destination. Even when they were out of view of the fallen man, her mother had kept Jemima's eyes closed, her feet barely touching the ground until they reached her grandmother's doorstep. Jemima had always seen her flight instincts as moving towards something, not running away but now she wondered, were her LA fantasies really about a fresh start or was she just looking for the long way around – again?

Jemima pulled her mac collar up around her ears as she paced down the street. The sunshine was intrusively joyful for a head still woozy from a night of wine and gossip with Meagan. Her sole mission that morning: a decent coffee. She hadn't been into Nostromo since her dousing from Chance and she was now literally craving an Azi latte. Half-awake and unshowered, she had decided to make her stealthy reconnaissance while it was still early and, hopefully, quiet.

'Hey, Az. My usual – to go. Cheers,' said Jemima, darting a furtive glance around the shop.

'Wow! You look like poop!' laughed Azi, as she glugged milk into her steamer jug.

'Thank you!' said Jemima, pulling her coat even more snugly around her.

If Azi thought she looked crappy now, imagine if she discovered she still had a pyjama top on.

'Forgive my wife,' Rania said with a roll of her eyes, topping up the pastries.

'She knows what I mean. She's so bloody gorgeous normally, with that beautiful skin. And she never ages. What are you? Seventy, seventy-five, eighty?' Azi asked.

'Alright, more coffee, less back-handed compliments,' laughed Jemima.

Behind her the *pshhhp* of the door made her turn automatically. Her jaw clenched. It was Chance. Azi plonked Jemima's to-go cup in front of her and Jemima snapped it up, her grin fixed in place. Of all the people to run into looking like this, her head pounding like there was a dress rehearsal of *Stomp!* going on in there, it had to be him.

'Hey,' he said with a broad smile, 'I saw you walk in from my window and I… did you get my message?'

'Message?' asked Jemima.

'Well, if you came in as often as you used to… ' scolded Azi.

'I've been working,' gabbled Jemima.

'This is where you work!' said Azi, flailing her hands at Jemima's window seat.

Jemima felt her pulse increase. She hadn't visualised a specific worst case scenario when she'd set out this morning, but this was a good place holder.

'Azi,' said Rania with her usual, calming tone.

Azi puffed out her cheeks. 'Fine. I have a message. Chance is looking for you.'

She winked coyly which Jemima made a concerted effort to ignore. This was awkward enough without Azi playing some kind of percolated matchmaker. And why was he leaving messages for her anyway? She hoped it wasn't to chat about Pete's book. That was still in her hand luggage – unread.

'What's up? Jemima asked, hiding her concern.

'I was thinking about your romantic predicament – with your book.' Chance paused, clearing his throat. Jemima rearranged her coat as her discomfort increased.

'Umm… Pete's publisher invited him to a big book reading this Thursday but he's delayed his trip to London so he asked if I wanted to go and then I thought, maybe you'd like to come?'

And just when Jemima thought things had reached peak-awkwardness.

She knew exactly whose book was being read because she had the same publisher as Pete and had been invited to the same thing, *Descend into The Cave: A happening with Xandria Bishop.* The pompous event name alone had made her bristle when she'd received the invite from Eve.

'It's a bit of a weird book. Kind of a romance hybrid thing but I thought it could give you some inspiration?' said Chance.

Jemima tried to unscrunch her face. It was sweet of him but this was going to be a hard pass for a kabillion reasons.

'That's very kind of you but—' began Jemima.

'She'd love to go.' Azi beamed at the two of them.

Jemima stared back at her. What the actual *hell?*

'Jem, I haven't seen you writing for days. This will be good for you,' said Azi glaring at Jemima, whose toes were curling into a foot fist.

'Okay. Great,' she mumbled at last.

'Good!' said Azi, slapping the counter and disappearing into the backroom.

Chance turned to Jemima, laughing. 'So, meet you there at seven?'

'Yes! Seven's great!' hollered Azi before Jemima could reconsider, renege or runaway.

'Great,' said Chance.

Jemima nodded, tight lipped. 'Yup. Great!'

'You're welcome, guys! You're so very welcome,' said Azi.

CHAPTER 17

Simi

Simi took in her surroundings, bewildered yet intrigued. Instead of Jemima's swanky pick, Ripley's, where they'd made their first attempt at the game the week before, tonight they were in Bar Dodgem – chosen by Meagan. Simi looked around the rough-and-ready Shoreditch basement bar, still trying to make sense of its strange, fairground vibe. Unlike Ripley's, there were no waiters in pointless half-aprons, no fancy wine lists or flickering tealights. The venue was awash with a murky, pink glow and the staff were so hipstery, the whole place smelt of beard oil. But the weirdest thing was the seating: painted rocking horses. Simi looked over at Jemima who was still trying to calibrate the canter of her bright green steed. At least she was finally on a horse. Initially she'd refused, instead leaning against it like an angry jockey. Meanwhile, beside them, Meagan was at full gallop having a heated call with one of her contractors. Simi's impatience grew. This was their first *proper* attempt at the game since her skateboarding calamity. Instead of watching Meagan verbally dismantle her builder, she wanted to get started. She needed to purge memories of Oscar and his deception and feel love, real love because life without it felt – horrible. Just then she noticed Jemima lean over to hand her a tissue. She was crying again, and she'd thought she was doing so well.

'Thanks, Jem,' she said choking down the sadness.

'Don't be hard on yourself. It hasn't even been a fortnight.'

Simi gripped her hand, its warmth filling her up from her hand to her heart. She looked over at Meagan who had missed her mini-meltdown.

'Glenn, if you don't finish the partitioning *this week* I'm gonna chew your balls like I'm on a *I'm a Celeb* bushtucker trial!' Meagan blared, forcefully rocking her horse back and forth.

Simi took a sip of her cocktail pretending not to listen. Poor Glenn. He was finding out the hard way, you don't let Meagan down. She held everyone to such high standards but often you only found out you had fallen short when you got the tongue lashing of your life. And though Meagan seemed oblivious, Simi knew, like the plan, it had all started with Parker. Meagan was so young when she met him, just 18. The whole thing had been so messy that when Parker told Meagan he was leaving his wife, Simi had actually been relieved. At least he was making a decision. But what was supposed to happen after a month, turned into six then a year until Meagan accepted it was never going to happen and ended it. Simi and Jemima had put their loving arms around her until the pain, at long last, released her. After though, Meagan was never the same. She never mentioned him. It was as though she'd airlifted him from her memories. The effect of him, however, lingered. Whenever there was even an inkling of being let down, this beast arose from within ready to tear off someone's head – or more often, their balls. There was always a Glenn, some poor sap who had failed and found themselves torched by the flames of Meagan's rage.

'Got it? Good!' said Meagan hanging up before he could respond.

The inferno abated, she breezily sipped her cocktail, 'So, what do you think of this place?'

Simi gave Jemima a bewildered look. Just like that, Meagan's fury had calmed to warm embers.

'Love it, really great. Wicked!' she and Jemima chimed.

'And you know what else is wicked?' Meagan said. 'You got availability-checked by Antonia De Silva today.'

Simi stopped rocking her horse. An availability-check was by no means an offer, merely an enquiry but it meant Antonia was still interested in her for the role of Dorothea. Since her fateful audition Simi had done some well-overdue research and discovered that the books *Clash of the Crown* had been adapted from had a huge following. The cast that had been announced so far were amazing and the blogosphere was already abuzz with show gossip. But as quickly as Simi's excitement rose, it plummeted.

'What about these scenes of a sexual nature?' Simi mouthed.

'Oh don't be starting on this lesbian thing again,' Meagan interrupted. 'So you have to get your kit off. It's awks but you could end up in three episodes!'

Meagan crossly pulled her horse back and began rocking so hard it looked as though she might flip over the front of it. Simi withered as she watched Meagan rock back and forth like a demented cowgirl.

'You don't have to go down on Cameron. It's pretend. You know, acting,' sulked Meagan.

Simi slid off her horse and slowed Meagan's to a gentle canter.

'I am grateful, Meag, you know I am.'

Simi sometimes wondered, of the two of them, who found it hardest to balance their friendship/work relationship. If this was any of her other clients, Meagan would have verbally pummelled them into submission. It was probably taking all Meagan's will to keep that rage inside.

'I'm just trying to give you what you want,' said Meagan glaring down at Simi from her horse.

Jemima dismounted her steed too. 'You've done your bit. The rest is up to Simi now, isn't it?'

Meagan shifted her glare to Jemima.

'It's just, you're so capable. Not everyone's like you. You expect a lot,' Jemima ventured.

Simi looked at her. Jemima was on rocky terrain. No one schooled Meagan.

'Perhaps you need to be like an insurance company. You know, have some accident forgiveness. People make mistakes… In some ways, I wonder if your high standards played a part in what happened with Parker?' Jemima said, her face tilted with innocent curiosity.

Simi whipped round to face her. What on EARTH was she doing and why was she bringing up Parker? It was like she'd seen a *Don't Poke the Bear* sign and then shoved a broom into the cage. What did he have to do with anything? Simi watched as Meagan's top lip curled. Jemima deserved whatever inferno was heading her way.

'Loo,' Simi said making a dash for it.

'Oh no you don't,' said Meagan yanking her back.

Meagan rocked her horse, the reins resting in her hand as she glowered at Simi.

'Do you want me to stop putting you up for auditions?'

'I just… ' blurted Simi.

'Yes or no?'

'No.'

'Right then.'

Meagan turned to Jemima. 'You're right. I do expect a lot and if people let me down, they'll hear about it. My life is excellent *because* I have high standards. Take it as a compliment I choose you as my friend. And FYI, what happened with… what happened with him, affected my life for a nanosecond. I'm over it. End. Of. Convo.'

Jemima nodded, looking flushed with embarrassment.

'Now, shall we get on with this game or what?' Meagan said dismounting her horse.

'Yeah, sure, of course,' Simi flustered as Jemima nodded vigorously.

Meagan surveyed the room, eyeing a mark as Simi gawped on in awe. Having spotted her target, Meagan plumped her hair, straightened her top and glided over to him. Once out of earshot Simi exhaled. When Meagan's wrath was singeing someone else's eyebrows it was enthralling. However, when the flames burned closer to home, it was no fun at all.

'You got off lightly. Be careful, Jem. Don't do a Troy,' said Simi pulling her gaze away from Meagan.

Jemima's face froze.

'Remember how she was always asking about Parker,' said Simi.

Jemima exhaled. 'Right, sure, of course. I thought you were talking about the other thing.'

'No, I meant, you know, poking around. I know Troy regrets it… and the thing with the jokes. She just lost her way,' Simi said.

'You still talk to her?' said Jemima, sipping her cocktail.

Simi drained the last splashes of her drink. 'She was always nice to me. I couldn't cut her off like Meag did. And anyway, what Troy did was crappy but not a hanging offence.'

Jemima nodded. 'I agree and you know, that does make me think… '

Simi began rocking her horse again. Jemima obviously regretted casting Troy aside.

'You know, Jem, it's never too late to make amends,' she said with a reassuring smile.

As they rocked their horses, a piercing whistle cut through the bar. They both looked across to see Meagan, standing with a nervous-looking guy, beckoning Simi over.

'I'm in!' Simi beamed as she slid off her horse.

She dashed over to Meagan, remembering, halfway, to act casual.

Five minutes later and Simi was back, brimming with excitement. She high-fived Meagan who had teed up the introduction brilliantly without a single mention of fake legs or Olympic medals. Simi had been charming and not intense at all. She'd let him take her number rather than asking for his, because you know, it was his loss if he didn't call. And even when she'd blurted out a cheesy, '*See you later, alligator!*' he'd just playfully replied, '*In a while, crocodile.*'

It was a slam dunk.

'So what's he like?' asked Jemima.

'His name's Steve. He's agnostic, has three *Best of* albums and works in transport.'

'He's a bus driver, Sim. Don't gas it,' said Meagan.

'For now, but who knows where that could lead.'

'Bethnal Green Bus Garage by the sounds of it,' quipped Meagan. 'But you know what, he's a nice, solid guy and a great way to kick off your new boundary-based love life.'

Simi liked the sound of that. She wasn't concerned with his career aspirations. She just wanted different so she could finally learn, grow and change!

'Right then, Simi,' said Meagan mounting her trusty steed, 'Your turn. Go and nab someone for Mrs Frigidaire.'

Jemima's smile flickered at the dig.

'What should I look for?' asked Simi.

Meagan stroked her chin. 'Well someone a little bit uptight,' she said winking at Jemima.

'Ha, ha,' Jemima said. 'Just get someone like me. Someone I'll get on with.'

'Oh, no, you don't get to choose personality,' Meagan said.

'Fine. Then get me a George Clooney lookalike.'

'*E.R.* George Clooney or *Ocean's Eleven*?' enquired Simi.

'Just get on with it,' Meagan squawked, shooing her away.

Simi looked out into the throng of drinkers. She could do this. She would find an uptight George Clooney circa *Ocean's Eleven*. She moved off with the determination of The Predator looking for a new skull to claim.

The moment Simi saw him, she knew he was the one. His greying Brylcreemed quiff was just visible above the tops of people's heads. He was a good ten years older than everyone else. Instead of the usual Shoreditch uniform of a moth-bitten T-shirt and skinny jeans, he wore a fitted shirt and suit trousers. A city boy in search of a trendy drinking dungeon, Simi decided. She breezed past him for a quick reconnaissance. Initial impressions were good. He was alone, hopefully waiting for a friend not a date. No wedding ring, nice shoes, attractive and he looked like he could read the hell out of a book. Jemima would love this guy.

'Hello,' Simi said casually leaning on the rocking horse next to him. The horse lurched under her weight and she stumbled forward.

'Hello.' He smiled. 'Ride here often?'

'What… Oh,' she laughed, thrusting her hand at him. 'Simisola. It means *rest in wealth*.'

'Beautiful name. I'm Lance. Means *lover of Arsenal*.'

Simi laughed again looking into his sultry brown eyes. I should keep this one for myself, she conspired before remembering the rules and rubbing her crystal.

'Look, I'll cut to the chase. My friend fancies you,' she said.

'It's like I'm 15 again. Tell her to meet me after double French,' he chuckled.

A broad grin spread across Simi's face and she decided to go for broke. She told Lance all about her fantastic but almost unattainable author friend, surprising herself with how easily the patter flowed.

'Plus, she has excellent general knowledge, like Trivial Pursuit good and she volunteers at Christmas. Well she did once and that's once more than me,' Simi said.

'She sounds too good to be true. Where is this dream woman?' Lance smiled.

'Wait there!' said Simi almost in shock as she scurried back to the girls, eyes wide with delight.

'I've got one!' She beamed. 'His name's Lance. He loves books and he keeps making jokes. He's *exactly* like you!'

Practically wrestling Jemima off her horse, Simi shoved her

towards Lance, thrilled at her achievement. It had worked. She'd got herself out of the way and it had bloody worked.

'Well done,' said Meagan with an enigmatic smile.

'Thanks!' said Simi as she scanned the room, calculating how to modify her approach for the different types of men.

Maybe the suit having an animated debate would need his ego massaged. She'd descend upon those students like the party girl from heaven and as for that trio of hipsters, perhaps she'd parachute in with a strident opinion about fine art. *I mean, what is art, really?*

'Listen, I've been thinking,' Meagan said, rocking gently, 'If you really want me to, I'll tell Antonia's office you're not available. Simi?'

Simi watched Jemima and Lance chatting on the other side of the bar. Looking out at Shoreditch's melting pot of punters, she realised that this was what being single but *not* heartbroken felt like. And even if it was fleeting and the sorrow returned, this felt good. She could always come back to this place, this feeling. Yes, the thought of Oscar could still bring her to her knees but those moments would get further and further apart the more she let life in.

'It's cool,' said Simi, 'and thank you.'

'Right, I should hear back from her in a couple of days,' said Meagan, raising a glass.

As Simi leaned in and clinked her drink against Meagan's, Jemima returned, puffing out her cheeks.

'Bloody hell. He can talk the hind legs off a rocking horse,' she laughed, throwing him another wave.

Simi smiled again. What a win. She'd actually got Jemima to enjoy talking to a guy. That hadn't happened for years. As

127

Simi felt the quiet relief of a slowly healing heart she wondered if Jemima might begin to let go of her fears and allow someone in too. Maybe even Meagan could learn to trust again. She wouldn't say it to the girls but she had a good feeling about how this was all going to turn out.

'Happy days,' cheered Meagan. 'Right, Simster, get the drinks in. Jemima, don't get too cosy. You're up.'

CHAPTER 18

Jemima

There was no way she was getting off the hook and Jemima knew it. She had to find Meagan a date. The good thing was, at least their earlier schism had passed. Jemima scolded herself for those clumsy queries about Parker. In her eagerness to engineer the conversation she'd forgotten how sensitive a subject he was. Simi was right, she *had* got off lightly. And her heart had nearly stopped when Simi had mentioned Troy. She thought she'd been rumbled about the borrowed stories before she'd had a chance to confess.

'Be nice,' said Meagan shaking Jemima from her thoughts. 'Play with your hair or something.'

'Right,' said Jemima, her face frozen in an unnecessarily grave expression.

Now wasn't the time to think of Troy. It was time to get Meagan a date. But before she could even get to that, she had to somehow strike up a conversation with a guy in the first place. Even in platonic encounters, she hardened. Look how she'd treated poor Chance. A small smile broke at the thought of him and though she could only just admit it, she was looking forward to seeing him at the reading. Jemima wondered what the girls would make of that. Obviously it wasn't a date and therefore she wasn't breaking their rules. However, if they knew about him, they were bound to get overexcited and turn it into something it wasn't. For simplicity's sake, she would keep it to herself – even though it really *wasn't* a date.

She pushed thoughts of Chance aside, bringing her attention back to the matter at hand. For this game to work and keep the girls sharing stories, she had to be nice to these guys. No more moodiness, snarky comments or treating them with a disdain usually reserved for the brassy cacophony of a Mariachi band serenading you in the street.

'And make sure he's over five foot ten,' Meagan bellowed, as Jemima walked away. 'I'm like Thorpe Park. I've got height restrictions!'

'What happened to no picking for yourself?' said Jemima with a stern look.

Meagan poked her tongue out by way of a reply.

A casually dressed guy precariously carrying four pints crossed in front of Jemima. Meagan shook her head and Jemima continued to scan the bar. What Meagan needed was someone dependable. She needed to learn that not all guys were a let-down. As Jemima hovered by a birthday party doing shots, she caught a flash of broad shoulders and shock of neatly cropped blond hair, and knew this was the guy. Here was someone Meagan could lean on. In fact this guy looked as solid as masonry. Jemima sidled over, her warmest grin firmly in place.

'Helloooo,' she said giving him the ten-thousand-watt smile of a market researcher.

He looked down at her suspiciously. His broad six-foot three frame blocking out the light like an eclipse. His sharp haircut, fitted shirt covering pecs that looked like pillows and his tailored suit would definitely get the thumbs-up from Meagan.

'You must need the fire brigade to cut you out of that shirt,' Jemima chuckled.

'Hmmf,' he sniffed before turning back to his friend.

Bugger. Be nice, be vulnerable, Jemima chanted to herself. She prodded him on the shoulder.

'It's just, you're so toned. Are you a personal trainer?' she asked sincerely.

'Financial Analyst,' he said, his German accent light but unmistakable.

Jemima panicked, wondering where 'German' sat on Meagan's extensive list of deal breakers. Yes, she needed someone to lean on but the Berlin Wall wasn't what Jemima had in mind. Well, it was too late now she resolved, twirling a strand of hair around her finger.

I'm Jemima,' she continued and after an infinitely uncomfortable moment, she prompted, 'And you are?'

'Bruno.'

'Bruno! Bruno the banker. So, what do you do at the bank, Banker Bruno?' she asked, contorting at the sound of her voice.

Bruno huffed.

'Operational Recovery Supervision,' he said, clearly expecting his answer to bewilder her.

'So, you reorganise companies to help them pay back loans to your bank!' Jemima whooped.

Those hours watching Bloomberg TV instead of writing had *finally* paid off.

'Wow, no one ever knows this,' Bruno said, almost cracking a smile. Almost.

'Triv queen,' Jemima beamed, pointing at herself, 'Anyway, listen, Bruno. Here's the thing. I've got this friend. She's pretty hot property but she really fancies you.'

She slowly reeled out the carrot and waited for Bruno to reach for a bite.

'Hmmf,' he sniffed.

'No really, she thinks you're incredibly, you know… '

'No. I do not.'

She was losing him. *Abort! Abort!* her brain yelped and if she was doing this for herself, which would never happen, she would have – ages ago. But now, it wasn't just about her. She was doing this for the girls, *all* her girls, Meagan, Simi and *Beverly*. She couldn't just walk away. Jemima leaned in further. 'Over there. Gorgeous hair, black girl, navy top, just getting on the orange rocking horse.'

That was a phrase she never thought she'd hear herself say. Jemima watched Bruno as his expression transformed from indifference to that of a starving man who'd only just realised he was hungry. She placed a reassuring hand on his shoulder.

'It's strange. She has these ridiculously high standards but for some reason… ' Jemima shrugged, now toying with him.

'What's her name?' he drooled.

Incredible, thought Jemima. Meagan had predicted this. Even a hint of something being unobtainable suddenly made it irresistible.

'Do you want me to bring her over?' Jemima said.

Bruno shook his head and instead downed the dregs of his drink and made his way to Meagan so quickly Jemima could barely keep up. Once there, Jemima stood aside as Meagan and Bruno swapped numbers with the cool efficiency of good-looking, busy professionals. Sure, there was an attraction but they were both masters of the game and neither were giving anything away. Once Bruno had disappeared the girls huddled to debrief.

'German?!' shrieked Meagan.

'You like him, I can tell,' retorted Jemima.

'Even I could see that!' added Simi.

'But German. It's a bit beach-towels-at-dawn,' Meagan said.

The girls laughed and as they dissected the evening, Jemima confessed to herself, she'd had fun. Her book was still her primary motivation but if this helped Simi and Meagan with their love lives too, surely it would all be worth it in the end?

And later, after Jemima and Simi had said their goodbyes to Meagan and were strolling arm-in-arm to the tube, Jemima wondered if dating, just literally, going out for dinner or to the cinema was something she could do. Maybe spending an evening with someone like Lance might be more than just useful but actually enjoyable. As a light drizzle fell, Jemima thought about Beverly. What, from tonight, would be useful for the reimagined version of her leading lady? She went back to the conversation about Meagan's standards. Whilst the pushback had burned, Jemima was in awe of Meagan's unashamed ownership of her ideals. What an amazing trait for Beverly to have – unachievably high standards, not just in terms of a partner but of herself and, indeed, her whole life. Imagine how uptight that would make you, how hard relationships would become, how angry you'd feel when people failed you... Jemima pulled Simi close as a shiver shot down her spine. She was scared *and* exhilarated by the character she was creating. But now, not only was Beverly's history and awesomeness becoming intimidating, so too was the prospect of speaking to Simi and Meagan about using their stories. Her attempt to bring up the book this evening had been just as epic a fail as before. Was she *that* scared? Meagan had not minced her words regarding Troy. To her, she was *persona non grata*. Simi was slightly more sympathetic but even if she said yes, Meagan could still torpedo the whole thing. Jemima exhaled.

'Everything alright, hun?' Simi asked as they entered Old Street tube station.

'Yeah,' replied Jemima forcing a smile. 'I was just thinking about my date – and my book.'

'Ah, don't you worry. Everything's going to be brilliant,' said Simi tapping her Oyster card on the reader.

'Yeah,' replied Jemima hoping she was right.

Jemima paced the Kings Place lobby, unable to shake the ambivalence clouding her. Yes, she had been looking forward to this evening but she couldn't ignore her anxiety – like she was losing control. She decided to focus her mind on Xandria Bishop and the reading of her award-gobbling hit novel. Just as she was relaxing into that thought, she spotted Chance making his way through the crowd. As his eyes searched the room, she automatically smiled. Just like on the plane, he had an ease around people making them instantly warm to him.

Finally he spotted Jemima and made his way over, his smile brightening at the sight of her.

Jemima's cheeks practically burst into flames with pleasure and awkwardness in equal measure.

'Hello, you,' he said hovering for a moment.

If he was contemplating a kiss, that was a no-no. Why? Because this was not a date, Jemima told herself. Tomorrow night with Lance – that was a date. Tonight, Simi and Steve, Meagan and Bruno, those were both dates but this, here with Chance, was not. And if she didn't let him know that from the off, one minute you're air-kissing in a Kings Place lobby and the next, you're living together – *what*? Why did her brain keep making these insane leaps?

'Hello, *you!*' She smiled, thrusting out her hand.

Chance stopped, looked down at it and without missing a beat, took Jemima's hand in his.

Her breath shortened as she became aware of his soft skin, his palms big and spongy.

What was he doing and why was she rooted to the spot looking into his eyes?

'I'm looking forward to this. I think it's gonna be pretty special,' he said.

Jemima pulled her hand out of his clasp.

'Me too. Drink?' she babbled, searching for the bar or an exit, whichever was nearest.

Chance smiled. 'Sure.'

Jemima watched as a barefooted Xandria very deliberately closed her book, made prayer hands and bowed to the assembled audience. The applause was immediate and rapturous.

Jemima looked around her. Had they all been listening to the same reading? Not one review mentioned that *The Cave* was a hodgepodge of incoherent ramblings, puffed-up prose and wildly implausible dialogue. Jemima flinched as the woman beside her leapt to her feet, wiping tears from her eyes, her standing ovation threatening to infect the entire room. Jemima wanted to cry too but her tears were in mourning for the four hours of her life she'd just lost. She gawped as, one by one, people around her began standing until she could no longer see the stage. Jemima looked at Chance for assurance but he too was standing, clapping along with everyone else! She *knew* this had been a bad idea. Granted he was easy on the eye, but even the cult leader Charles Manson was a looker in his youth. And fine, he was pleasant to chat with but they were clearly on different pages if he enjoyed what they'd just been subjected to. She snuck another look at him. Yep, he was still flapping his hands together like an aqua park sea lion. But worse, Jemima had a growing awareness that her being seated was becoming conspicuous. With nowhere to hide, she forced herself out of her seat and begrudgingly applauded. Her petty act of rebellion was to do it so lazily it was essentially a slow hand clap. After what felt like an age, the applause subsided and the assembled audience made their way out of the auditorium. Still in a daze, Jemima followed Chance out of Kings Place. As they emerged onto the street, Jemima stole yet another look at him. After his response to *The Cave*, his love of Beverly Blake's escapades didn't feel quite so flattering.

'Well,' said Jemima, 'That was…'

'Shit,' said Chance checking to see he was out of earshot of other attendees.

'Oh, thank God!' Jemima laughed, clutching her chest in relief.

'Yeah, it was awful,' said Chance. 'Never heard anything like it.'

'But you were clapping?' Jemima wailed.

'Coz I thought *you* loved it. I heard you crying.'

'That was the woman beside me!'

Laughter rippled through them as they realised they'd hated the reading as much as each other.

'God, what was that line she kept using?' Chance giggled, clicking his fingers.

'*And so it begins,*' Jemima droned, mimicking Xandria's monotone voice, her impersonation sending them into more peals of laughter.

As they recounted their favourite pompous passages, Jemima wiped tears from her eyes. Clearly their highbrow captivity had made them hysterical, she thought, as she rested a hand on his shoulder. It felt good – solid. Was this allowed on a non-date night she wondered before pulling her hand away.

'Man, I am *soooo* sorry. I thought that was going to be helpful but I've probably set your writing back a month!' Chance shuddered.

'Don't be silly. I'm glad I came. I've been putting off reading *The Cave*, building it up as this insanely brilliant masterpiece so it's good to see Xandria is a mere mortal too.'

'She seems demonic, putting us through that,' said Chance puffing his cheeks.

Their giggles slowly ebbed away and they continued their stroll through St Pancras Square, Jemima keeping a platonic distance apart. This was nice. Just strolling. Admittedly, it always felt nice, just being with Chance. Jemima felt very… present, by his side.

'Is that a swing?' he said pointing across the square to a giant birdcage installation.

Before Jemima could reply, Chance had already run over. He pulled back the swing seat and beckoned her to follow.

'I'm good,' she called.

'Come on,' encouraged Chance, 'it'll be fun.'

'I'm fine,' said Jemima.

Chance let go of the swing and walked back to her.

It's not that she had a problem with swings. They seemed to give kids hours of pendulous fun. But if there was something that would make tonight feel like a date, surely Chance pushing her on a swing in the middle of Kings Cross on a wintery evening, was it – it had Richard Curtis rom-com written all over it and that wouldn't do – because this was not a date. This was two friends, discussing a novel set in the depths of a reproductive system. Nothing more, nothing less. Chance pushed his hands into his pockets and tilted his head holding her in his gaze. Jemima looked down at her watch, drawing a slow breath. 'I'm going to head off.'

'No worries. I'll walk you to the tube,' said Chance.

'I'm fine,' said Jemima. 'Thanks for tonight. It was very… informative.'

She turned and headed towards the station feeling his eyes on her. She quickened her pace.

CHAPTER 19

Simi

Simi stared at the breadsticks in the middle of the table cursing herself for choosing today to start her low-carb diet. She glanced at her watch. Steve was twenty-four minutes late and with each passing moment, her discomfort grew. The thought of being stood up for dinner was horrific but even sitting alone in a restaurant was excruciating. Flying solo might be fine for Jemima but Simi hated it. Even tonight, Jemima was off on her own, to some book reading. For Simi, however, the idea of doing that made her shudder. She was grateful for mobile phones. At least then she didn't have to sit here looking like a complete Charlie Chumless, she thought, as she fired off a third text update to Meagan who was also on her date.

Wow! She smiled. Just two days, nineteen hours and forty-seven minutes ago, they were scoping out guys in Bar Dodgem and now here she was, on her date – almost. Meagan was out with her German hottie and tomorrow night even Jemima would dip her toe in the dating pool. It was too perfect, well it would be, the moment Steve showed up. Just as the wait was becoming unbearable and Simi was considering having a fake phone conversation, Steve arrived. Simi watched the maître d' lead him over. Should she kiss him and if so, would he be a one or two kiss type of guy? Perhaps he was a no-kiss-at-all man. Perhaps, a hug was more appropriate, she panicked as he approached. But a hug or worse, a handshake like they were meeting to discuss a business loan wasn't what Simi wanted. She wanted *lurve*.

'Hello! *Apols* for being late!' said Steve giving Simi a gentle hug and a kiss on the cheek.

Apols, Simi recited in her head, immediately warming to him.

'No worries. You're a bus driver. I'd expect you to be a bit late – then three of you to turn up at once.'

'Why's that?' Steve asked tucking in his chair.

'Well because… ' A long way away an imaginary klaxon droned. 'Never mind.'

Simi ignored the warning sounds and quickly picked up her menu.

As she browsed the list of dishes her eyes lit up. She loved Fez. The romantic snugs, the ornate North African design, the to-die-for food and friendly staff made it a great first-date destination.

'So,' said Steve.

'So,' said Simi trying to contain her nervous excitement.

She looked at him dreamily. They were on a real world, this-is-not-a-drill date. Meanwhile, across the table, Steve's head was buried in his menu. Occasionally he'd emit a deep *hmmmm*.

''Scuse me, what's "*Meeeeez*"?' he asked a passing waitress.

She looked at him confused, leaning over his menu.

'Oh, *meze*. Small dishes to share.' She smiled before moving off.

Simi bit her lip then pretended to peruse the mezes... even though she knew them by heart. After a while, she peeked over the top of her faux-leather menu to steal a glance at Steve. He was handsome, his face generous and uncomplicated. Simi noted the tight curls of his deep brown hair which had a little too much product on it, his clean-shaven face and mismatched shirt and tie. He'd obviously made the time to go home and change before meeting her and she appreciated it.

'So, what made you want to become a bus driver?' Simi asked breaking the silence.

Steve considered the question.

'I dunno really.' He smiled before returning to his menu. 'Right, think I know what I want.'

He waved over their waiter.

'I will have,' he began, while taking a final look through the entire menu for the tenth time, 'omelette and chips, thank you.'

Simi blinked, her mouth opening and closing as the waiter wrote down Steve's order.

'And for the lady?'

'Ummm.'

Her eyes darted around the menu. Who orders an omelette at a Moroccan grill other than... a vegetarian! Simi gasped. If that was the case, the last thing he'd want is to watch her gnaw through skewered carcass.

'I'll have – the same, thank you. No chips!'

The waiter collected up their menus and disappeared.

'Can't be doing with all that spice,' Steve said once the waiter was out of earshot, 'They didn't have steak, so I thought, omelette's a safe bet.'

So, he wasn't a vegetarian, just a man with the palate of a 3-year-old. Simi tried to push down her disappointment and instead, reminded herself that tonight was about being with someone she wouldn't normally choose, an opportunity to get to know somebody different. It was also a chance to experiment with those boundaries Jemima and Meagan kept going on about, which, if she were honest, she still didn't completely understand.

'Of course, I didn't always want to be a bus driver,' Steve said wistfully into the conversation vacuum.

Ah ha. Earlier he'd probably felt cautious about sharing his innermost feelings but now he was finally opening up, Simi concluded. She rested her elbow on the table and perched her chin on her hand. It already felt more romantic.

'When I was a kid, I wanted to be an astronaut,' he said proudly.

Simi's smile congealed. She herself had lofty career aspirations and whilst she didn't want to dampen anyone else's dreams, *astronaut* was surely an ambition from a galaxy far, far away.

'Not like a normal astronaut. Imagine a fleet of space shuttles that go back and forth to the moon. I'd want to drive one of them shuttles.' He nodded snapping a breadstick in three and putting it in his mouth sideways.

So, a space bus driver, Simi groaned inwardly as she watched him chipmunk through his breadsticks.

After a quiet eternity, other than the sound of Steve munching, their food came. Simi gave the waiter an apologetic smile and picked up her cutlery with a sad whimper. World food was her passion. She cooked and consumed everything from Japanese to Jamaican, African to Asian. Coming to a four-stars-in-*Time-Out* restaurant to eat egg and chips kind of broke her heart. And she couldn't even have the bloody chips! She watched her date plough through his meal like a mastiff excavating a bowl of Pedigree Chum.

'What do you think of the omelette?' Simi said, attempting to interrupt him.

Then again, why ruin a perfectly good meal with conversation, Simi mused as she stared at the top of his head, his plate already half empty. Simi had an uncle who refused to converse over dinner claiming it gave him wind. She wondered if that was the problem as Steve cupped his hand to his mouth in a feeble attempt to conceal a burp. Nope, Simi huffed.

It was time for a radical change in policy. She wasn't going to let Steve vacuuming up his food ruin the evening. It wasn't that he wasn't listening, he just wasn't talking and that was something she could work with. And so, for the rest of the meal she regaled him with her life story. She spoke, uninterrupted, about how she'd become an actor. About her first job, an horrific show called *C-Section! The Musical*. She even told him about her fateful audition with Antonia De Silva. And, credit where it was due, though he wasn't a great talker, largely due to his mouth never being empty, he was a good listener. He nodded and laughed, with a full mouth, in all the right places, seeming genuinely interested. Not as interested as he was in his plate of food but Simi was no longer expecting miracles. Maybe this night wasn't a write-off after all. What was the point of having two chatterboxes in a relationship? She needed to stop looking for perfection and start living in the moment, just being with what was right in front of her. Sure, he was no Keanu Reeves but all you needed was a spark to start a fire. She tilted her head and smiled. He smiled back, burped into his cupped hand and licked his knife.

'Finished.' He grinned.

CHAPTER 20

Meagan

> Good luck with Bruno. Eeeek! Steve's not here. Panic stallions! Sim xox

Meagan stared at Simi's text. What the hell were panic stallions?

> Bloody autocorrect! *stations!

> Oh, he's here!!!! Wooooo! Sim xox

''Scuse me,' said the barman holding the card reader out for Meagan.

'Right, sorry,' she said tapping her card.

She grabbed her cocktails then sashayed through the hotel lobby to re-join Bruno. Hotels were a real turn-on for Meagan so in choosing this as their meeting place, Bruno had made an excellent start. Hotel sex was one of Meagan's favourite things. In fact, she would suggest it to Todd next time they sexted. But then she groaned, remembered Simi's stupid rule. *No Todd allowed*. Oh, how things had changed. It wasn't easy to find a lover that fitted like he did, a lock and key. Her only hope was that her absence would calm his affections sufficiently that, once this game was over, they could get back to what they did best, straight-up shagging. In the meantime, Bruno was easy on the eye even if he was a little grating on the ear.

'Nice hotel. You stay here often?' Meagan asked as she set down their drinks.

'Hmmf,' sniffed Bruno leaning back in his leather single seater. 'No, it's just near my gym.'

They were only two rounds into the date and as delectable as Bruno was, Meagan's patience with that grunt of his was thinning. Since they'd arrived, she'd given a good account of herself. She'd been witty, intelligent and looked *incredible*, opting, tonight, for a low-cut top, tailored slacks and of course, a fabulous, black heel. Her look said, I'm a professional woman who happens to have a great rack. And on arrival his opening play had been strong, just the right dose of chivalry and compliments but what Meagan couldn't stand was how he punctuated almost every sentence with a sniff. How had Jemima not spotted this?

Meagan noticed the dull glow of her phone from inside her handbag. Without a break in conversation she reached in and tilted the screen towards her. It was Todd. Oh for the simplicity of a quick fumble with him right now. If she'd seen him tonight, she'd already be back home in her slanket watching *Scandal* reruns. Meagan smiled tightly at Bruno, trying to focus on the positives. He was tall which, to Meagan, was the hottest thing in the world. She'd once dated a guy who she towered over when in her heels. She felt like Godzilla looking down on the tiny people of New York City. Never again. When Meagan and Bruno had air-kissed upon first meeting, she'd also noticed his deliciously expensive cologne. This was another deal-breaker. A long, *long* time ago, Meagan had dated a man whose aftershave smelt like fly spray. At the end of dinner, she'd half-expected to see dead bluebottles at their feet. Bruno, however, smelt good, looked good, had good hair, good shoes and she could tell, under that fitted shirt, had a *great* body. However, the one thing that was not good at all was his *nasal fluid management*.

'So tell me more about your work,' he said.

She looked into his eyes. That piercing crystal blue was insanely sensual. Should she give him another chance? she thought, as he rubbed his arm gently against hers. There was no denying, he had *game* which he probably needed to counteract the…

'*Hmmf.*'

Okay, I'm done, concluded Meagan, sliding out of her seat.

'Oh no,' she said barely committing to a convincing performance, 'I've just remembered.'

She shrugged on her coat as Bruno stood.

'What is it?' he said. 'Are you okay?'

'Yeah, well, no. Jemima. The woman who introduced us.'

Out of the corner of her eye Meagan could see Bruno's face etched with worry. She groaned inside. Humans made everything take so much longer.

'She's on dialysis and I need to change her thing.'

'Goodness,' Bruno said putting his hand on her shoulder. 'I thought you were going to say, you'd arranged to meet her.'

That would have been a less harrowing excuse, thought Meagan.

'Is there anything I can do? *Hmmf.*'

The guilt instantly evaporated. She tied the belt around her thick coat, texting as she headed for the door.

'No, babe. It's all good!'

CHAPTER 21

Jemima

Jemima walked to the middle of Liverpool Street station's busy concourse, her stress levels peaking. This, she realised, was a far cry from the day before on her absolutely-not-a-date-but-keep-it-secret-from-the-girls-anyway evening with Chance. Yes, she'd been anxious but she'd also felt, was it, butterflies? She looked up at the information board. It was a few minutes after seven. She was almost half an hour early but she wasn't being keen, just cautious. She wanted to see him approaching before he saw her. Liverpool Street had a myriad of exits and Jemima was prepared to use any one of them if she needed to. Just then she felt a tap on her right shoulder. She turned but over her left came a quiet, 'Great minds and all that.'

Jemima *hated* the tap-the-wrong-shoulder gag. 'Good one,' she said with a pinched smile.

'Get here early just in case!' Lance laughed, rubbing his hands together with a loud clap.

Jemima exhaled a nicer smile onto her face. 'So, where to?' she asked.

'My van's outside. Just jump in the back and roll yourself up in the rug,' said Lance.

Jemima looked at him. A murder joke two minutes after meeting? What due diligence had Simi actually done on this individual?

'Only joking. You're too gorgeous to murder,' he said beckoning her to follow.

Jemima went to move but her feet were nailed to the spot. Though Lance was as threatening as a crane fly in a bath tub he just didn't get it. Women had to think about personal safety all the time – especially on dates. All guys had to worry about was if their wallet condom had expired. Murder jokes – not cool. Ahead of her Lance stopped, turning back concerned.

'Are you okay?' he asked.

Jemima hesitated and his face fell.

'I've done it again. So sorry. I've been told countless times to rein in the gags. I overcompensate and start gabbling,' he said walking back towards her.

Jemima looked up at him. His contrition, real and heartfelt, took her by surprise. In her mental Rolodex she slipped his index card out of the total wanker section.

'I just replayed the van thing back in my head. It sounded awful,' he said slapping his forehead. 'I heard something similar at a comedy night and, well… think I'll stick to the day job.'

'It's fine. Let's start over. I'm alright,' Jemima said giving him a friendly jab.

'Or are you *all left*? Sorry. I'm out of control.'

Jemima facepalmed, as they exited the station, a little snort of laughter escaping before she could stop herself.

'Here we are. Thought it might be fun to try something a bit quirky,' Lance said.

Jemima looked up at the restaurant sign.

'Cereal Offenders. Great name, isn't it?' said Lance.

Jemima laughed to herself. This was the restaurant Gil, her lumbersexual date from the week before, had been yakking on about. Clearly, the Universe really wanted Jemima to have breakfast for dinner this month.

'Hey Fast Breakers, welcome to Cereal Offenders, the crunchiest corner of Shoreditch,' said their chirpy waitress.

Jemima looked around at the vast display of cereal boxes on the walls. There was even an entire section devoted to Rice Krispies. There were vintage boxes, novelty boxes, *Star Wars* boxes. A veritable treasure trove of cereal memorabilia. The restaurant itself was filled with rows of tables like a Victorian orphanage. All of them were packed with parties, works dos and rowdy groups of friends with not a single couple in the entire place.

'Came here last week for a mate's birthday. It was brilliant!' said Lance over the din of spoons clunking against bowls.

Jemima looked at him. For some reason, Simi had thought *he* was the perfect match for *her*?

'Okay, Fast Breakers, we've got a table for you. Right this way,' chirruped their waitress.

'After you,' said Lance gesturing for Jemima to go ahead.

She wasn't as keen on chivalry as Meagan and Simi. However, given that fifteen minutes earlier Lance had sounded like a tone-deaf nitwit, the gesture was welcome. Jemima followed the waitress to their table.

'So, tell me about yourself,' Jemima asked as they squeezed onto their bench.

'You mean apart from my razor-sharp wit?'

'Now that was actually funny,' said Jemima as she settled into the evening.

Over their bowls of sugary, multi-coloured hoops, their conversation took the standard first date twists and turns. There were the usual questions about siblings, a momentary detour into school days and a toe dipped into the political hotspots of the day. It was all pretty bearable, Jemima mused, as she grabbed a paper straw from the holder in the centre of their table and slurped up the milk at the bottom of her bowl. She'd forgotten just how good cereal milk tasted.

'Thumbs up?' Lance asked pushing away his bowl.

'I've been pleasantly surprised.'

'I saw your face when we first arrived,' said Lance.

Jemima chuckled. 'Yeah, it just reminded me of someone—'

'Another date?'

'Yes, I'm a *cereal* dater.'

Lance blanched at the pun then went in for a high-five. Jemima duly obliged, taking a small bow.

'This is a really nice turn of events,' said Lance, smiling at Jemima.

'How so?'

'Well, I would never have asked you out. I mean, don't get me wrong, you're lovely but if your mate hadn't come up to me, this would not have happened. I haven't dated for years,' Lance said almost grimacing.

Jemima paused. Though she was ready to call it a night, her intrigue was now piqued. She knew *her* reasons for not wanting to date but what was his excuse? In the interests of her book, she would probe a little further. When she'd had enough she'd simply glare at the door in the way her mother did when she'd had enough of guests.

'So, if dating's not your thing, why did you say yes?' she asked.

Lance grinned. 'It was an experiment. Plus, your friend said you fancied me.'

'An experiment? What type of experiment?'

'I wanted to see if dating was as ghastly as I remembered then I saw you and thought… ' said Lance with a why-not shrug.

'Riiiiiight,' said Jemima, mirroring his shrug.

'Being with someone means giving up too much. I've been married three times. I'm not making that mistake again,' he said.

Jemima blinked at him. Married… *three* times? She couldn't *wait* to hear what Simi thought they had in common.

'Romance is just a temporary hormonal imbalance. You know what a brain scan of someone in love is identical to?' Lance said.

Jemima shook her head not sure she wanted to know.

'An addict,' said Lance sitting back with a worldly-wise nod. 'It's all just chemicals. So now, the minute I get a whiff of it, I'm out of there. Not worth it.'

Jemima was baffled. In her gut, what he was saying felt wrong. There had to be more to it than that, otherwise why was adding romance to Beverly's story such a big deal? And if being in love was just some chemical interchange between two skin suits, what was the point of anything?

'That's so cynical. It's about connection. It's not *all* hormones,' said Jemima.

'You obviously haven't been in love for a while but I bet you know someone who has. Don't they do anything to be with their beau, think about them, talk about them, want them all the time – like an addict?'

Instantly, Simi popped into Jemima's head like a jack-in-the-box. Lance couldn't have described her more accurately if he'd tried. Could he be right? Though Jemima didn't want it for herself, surely the world would be a much drearier place if being in love was simply biological impulses. She shifted in her seat, glaring at the door. Lance had short-circuited her brain. Jemima beckoned the waitress who scuttled over with their bill.

'Hope you snap, crackle and pop back soon!' She beamed as Lance tapped his credit card on her reader.

'Well, thanks for breaking your, you know, rule, to come out tonight,' Jemima said as they made their way to the exit.

'It was lovely,' said Lance, taking Jemima's hand and kissing it. 'And if I'm ever after a fourth ex-wife, I'll look you up!'

'Great... *Cheerios!*' said Jemima striding off down the street in the opposite direction.

In her Uber on the way home, Jemima huffed. What a bizarre evening. At times, she'd found Lance vaguely attractive but the next moment she'd wanted to waterboard him in a vat of semi-skimmed milk. Her car breezed down Upper Street and Jemima noticed all the couples doing normal coupley things or, according to Lance, satisfying their rampant addictions. His comments had really got under her skin. At the next turning the car cruised past Nostromo. On impulse, Jemima looked up at Chance's window and smiled. The lights were off. She wondered where he might be and who he was dousing in coffee tonight.

Not long after, Jemima was relieved to be back home, padding around in her pyjamas. Simi was at a stage combat class and the place was silent. She went through to her living room, staring at a book she'd put off reading for a very long time. She peeled it from the shelf, her fingers tracing the gold letters of its glossy cover.

'*A Walk on the Mild Side* by Pete Dasos,' she read.

It was very kind of Chance to give her his copy of the book and she was glad he had. Perhaps, within its pages, she would find an antidote to Lance's depressing cynicism or maybe just an escape. She headed back to her bedroom, snuggled under her duvet and prised open the book.

Jemima's eyes snapped open. Her bedside lamp was still on, her hand clasped around Pete's book. She'd only meant to read a few chapters but had ended up reading it cover to cover! She looked down. In her other hand was a ball of tissues. She opened the hardback, peering at its smooth, white pages and all at once, she wanted to see Chance. She wanted to talk about Pete and Lula's journey. She wanted to talk about *that wedding*. Quickly, she dressed and headed out.

'Hello?' came the voice, tinny and distant through the intercom.

Jemima hovered, her breath a rising pillar in the chilly morning air. Now, standing outside Chance's practice, this felt like a bad idea made by her sleep-deprived brain. She had a tonne of work to do plus she was meeting Simi and Meagan tonight. She didn't have time for an impromptu book club. She turned to leave.

'Can I help you?' came the voice, it's Australian twang unmistakable.

Jemima stopped, leaning in to speak.

She stared at the intercom. She would return Chance's book another time, she decided as she headed back the way she came.

He was probably busy fixing twisted ankles and untennis-ing people's elbows.

'Jemima!' Chance called from behind her.

Her knees locked, rooting her to the spot.

'Shit,' she murmured before turning around.

'Hey,' said Chance trotting over. 'What a brilliant surprise. You okay?'

Jemima instantly held up Pete's autobiography, a defensive barrier between them.

'I just came to return your book,' she blurted.

'Ah, thanks but you didn't have to. It's lovely to see you though.' Chance smiled.

Bad idea, Jemima, bad idea, she intoned, vowing never to follow her instincts again. Stupid sleep-deprived brain. Stupid instincts. Stupid chemicals.

Chance shivered. 'I've got a break between patients. Fancy a walk?'

'Mmmm,' said Jemima, as though her head was being nodded for her.

Damn those instincts!

'Great! Let me grab my jacket,' he said as he dashed back inside.

Before Jemima could change her mind, Chance had remerged, wrapped in a thick, navy parka and scarf.

'Looks cosy,' said Jemima.

Chance grinned, opening up one side of his coat to let her snuggle inside. She froze.

'I'm kidding,' he laughed, digging his hands deep in his pockets. 'Wow, you guys sure know how to do a cold snap. How's about a couple of laps around the park, get the blood going?'

Jemima relaxed and, once again her invisible puppeteer nodded her head and they walked off down the street.

'So, what did you think of Pete's book?' Chance asked as they rounded the corner to the park. 'I know it's a bit rough in places.'

'It was lovely,' said Jemima. 'You get a few mentions.'

These were both understatements. The book had been enchanting from beginning to end and Jemima had been moved by how much Chance featured. The love between him and Pete was evident. Furthermore, the love between Pete and Lula and the way it inspired him to work to regain his mobility had been... profound. That was the word Jemima had whispered to herself in the middle of the night as she read. This wasn't a book about learning to walk or war wounds and injuries. This was a meditation on love and Jemima had found it unputdownable. Screw Lance and his brain scans. Love was real.

'I do get the odd mention, don't I?' Chance smiled sheepishly.

They walked on for a while, bound by the quiet. This felt so different from yesterday with Lance. There was a lightness whenever she was around Chance, just walking.

'It said in the book you gave up medical school to help Pete,' Jemima said.

Chance's smile flickered almost imperceptibly but Jemima saw it. In her brief glances, she wanted to study him, understand him, know him a little better.

'There was a complication with one of his surgeries. Lula had to work full time and there was no one to look after him during the day so I took six months out, flew to Mexico and... well, you know how life is... A year later, after I came home, I decided to just keep going with my OT practice and set up the charity instead.'

'Wow,' said Jemima as they completed their lap of the park, returning to where they'd begun.

'The way I see it,' said Chance holding onto the railings and watching an old couple throwing breadcrumbs for some ducks, 'it doesn't matter how you give back just as long as you do.'

Once again Jemima's puppeteer took over her body and before she knew it she was putting a comforting hand on Chance. He looked back at her. She could tell, though he would never blame Pete, the missed opportunity weighed on him still.

They both turned back to watch the old couple scatter food for the hungry ducks who waddled and pecked their way through the scraps.

'Don't you hope you can be like them one day... ' said Chance, almost to himself.

'The ducks?' said Jemima.

Chance smiled before looking back at the couple.

'So, dare I ask how the writing's going?'

'It's definitely going,' Jemima replied as her gaze followed the old couple stroll, arm in arm, to a nearby bench.

'Well if you ever need a sounding board, I'm always here.'

'Thank you,' Jemima said appreciating the offer.

'So, is it going so well you'd be free for dinner? I found this amazing Mexican joint. If you liked the tequila I had on the plane, you will love this place. It's got fifty-seven varieties. It's like the Heinz of tequila,' said Chance.

'I... I'm not... ' she stammered.

'Doesn't have to be dinner. Could be lunch? Breakfast – a coffee? A piece of cake? Another walk?' said Chance.

Jemima's stomach tangled up. She could say yes, she thought, as she looked into Chance's gentle eyes. And one day maybe she would but that day wasn't today.

'The thing is… me and my girlfriends are playing this dating game. It's really to help Simi, my friend, change her habits. Point is, we've got these rules. No outside dating.' She shrugged apologetically.

Was it still an excuse if it was true?

Chance stared at her blankly. 'I didn't say… I mean, it's just dinner.'

Jemima's mouth gaped as she frantically replayed the conversation. 'Well you said… '

'I had a nice time at the reading. I just thought we could do something again but no sweat… ' he said glancing at his watch, 'I've got an eleven thirty appointment. You coming?'

He turned to leave and after a moment, a confused Jemima followed him.

After some awkward small talk, they reached his practice.

'Well, see you around,' he said before disappearing inside.

Jemima stared at his closed door. Eventually, she turned and stomped back to her flat, her mind whirring with irritation. Not that she was interested, she stewed, but why *didn't* he want a date?

CHAPTER 22

Meagan

Meagan pulled a pristine album cover from her collection. She blew an invisible speck of dust off the heavy black disc and placed it on the turntable.

'What is Jem up to again?' Meagan asked as she moved the needle across and Stevie Wonder's 'Songs in the Key of Life' spilled from her strategically positioned speakers.

'She stayed up reading yesterday so she's getting an early night,' Simi said picking at the foil of the champagne bottle on Meagan's coffee table.

'No, Sim. We're not drinking that,' said Meagan.

'Well, Todd didn't send it to be an ornament?'

'If we drink it, he'll think I want him to keep sending me stuff. Last week it was flowers, the week before, chocolates. My life's turning into a Nineties R&B video. And anyway, I've got something much better,' she said, pulling a bottle of whisky from the top of her book-free bookcase.

'No way. The last time I had whisky was that New Year's Eve party.' Simi shuddered.

'Oh, yeah. We played drunk lady KerPlunk on you.'

'And I woke up covered in crap!' moaned Simi.

'Okay, you win,' Meagan puffed pushing the whisky bottle back onto the shelf.

She planted herself back on the sofa and popped the champagne cork, pouring two glasses.

'What is it?' she said, feeling Simi's gaze on her.

'Nothing…' Simi began, 'it's just, Todd's being so sweet and you're already, you know, doing it. Why *aren't* you two together?'

'Because I've got my plan! Nothing's gonna get in the way of that,' Meagan said sitting up. 'I'm gonna be 30 soon—'

Simi went to speak.

'And, no,' Meagan said cutting her off, 'I don't want a party this year either.'

'But it's your thirtieth!' Simi pleaded.

'I mean it. Low key to the point of no-existence is how it's always been. Deal?' said Meagan.

'Deal,' grizzled Simi.

'So, that gives me three years to meet someone. I'll have my first kid by 34 and last by 40. Then I'll get married and by my early fifties they'll all be old enough to be left alone without burning my house down. At that point me and Mr Meagan will travel the world, popping back for the odd graduation or wedding. Good, eh?' said Meagan, pleased.

'Yeah…' said Simi.

Meagan knew what was wrong. According to her plan, at 35, Simi was already behind schedule.

'Stop worrying, Simster. Look at Jem. She's not worrying about all that.'

'I'm not sure she even wants to meet a guy let alone have kids,' said Simi glumly.

'Of course she wants to meet a guy. Why else would she put herself through this game?'

'Maybe,' said Simi.

'And I reckon talking about our demons is helping her come to terms with hers so she can meet someone decent.'

'Hmmm, she is asking us a lot of questions about our love lives,' said Simi sinking back.

'Exactly.'

It was the only sane explanation for Jemima's behaviour of late, Meagan deduced. She was wrestling with all kinds of demons including the belief that being part of a couple weakens her. That was what being with Miles had done and was one of the many reasons Meagan wanted to punch him in the throat.

'You know what, Sim, we need to up our game,' Meagan said setting her glass down. 'Jem needs us to find her someone who'll show her two is more than one, not less.'

'Ooooh I like it. Poetic. But two *is* more… How do you mean?' Simi asked, confused.

'I mean, Jem thinks being with someone takes something from her, like she's only strong alone. We have to find someone that makes her go weak at the knees but in a good way,' said Meagan.

'Yes!' yelped Simi. 'Someone so great she'll fall over herself to be with him.'

'Totes. That's what this is all about. I guarantee it,' Meagan said. 'Come, Simderella. Let's make a list. What does Jemima really, *truly* need?'

CHAPTER 23

Simi

Simi looked up as the door at the end of the familiar, white corridor swished open. She was back at Antonia De Silva's office a week after her previous audition. For some inexplicable reason, she had been invited in for something called a 'chemistry read'. From what she could gather, this casting was to see if she had an on-screen rapport with the leading lady herself, Cameron Christiansen. Simi dry-gulped as an actor she vaguely knew tiptoed over to the signing-in sheet and scribbled her name. She gave her a polite smile then returned to her script. Antonia's office was much quieter today. Before, there'd been at least eight actors lined up in the corridor. Today there were just two and somehow, Simi was one of them.

'Have you ever done a chemistry read?' she whispered to the other actress.

'A few,' she replied.

'How are they?'

'Largely terrifying,' the actress said with a sweet laugh. 'Just do your best and don't think about the fact you're auditioning with Cameron Christiansen and this might change your life.'

Simi gawped at her until she realised – she was joking.

'Don't worry. You've proved you can act or you wouldn't be here. You can't get this wrong.'

Simi nodded, not reassured at all. No matter how hard she tried, things rarely went her way. Usually she only found out she hadn't got the job when she stumbled across the show on TV. And who did she most often see staring back at her from the screen – Sandra Scott. She was everywhere, doing everything from selling toilet roll to delivering bad news in the latest hospital drama. Simi didn't wish Sandra less success, she just wanted a little for herself. And where *was* 'Sandy'? she wondered. Normally, by now she'd have breezed in, shattering all hope. Was it possible for once, she hadn't made the cut and Antonia was in a race against time to fill the role? If that was the case, Simi was more than happy to be the rank outsider stealing a last minute win. She had to focus though. With or without Sandra in the race, this could easily be snatched from her by any one of the great actresses being seen for this role. Simi scrolled through the notes Meagan had emailed her, perplexed. She had only ever had two agents in her career, one of whom had spent most of their relationship trying to enrol her in a colon cleanser pyramid scheme. But though she'd had little experience of what agents did, she was sure burying her under a pile of acting notes, wasn't part of the deal. Every audition Meagan sent her on was the same. The annoying part was, Simi knew Meagan didn't do this with her comedians. She wasn't telling them how to deliver their jokes so why was she telling Simi how to act? She reread Meagan's notes still unconvinced. Meagan, who only ever skim-read scripts had advised her to play Dorothea as angry – because it would be funny. However to Simi, Dorothea seemed happy about her situation evidenced by the line, 'Being in my lady's favour has advanced me beyond my station. I could not have hoped for more!' Why would someone say that in anger? Was she being sarcastic? Simi speculated. Possibly but there was literally nothing in the script to suggest that. Dare she ignore Meagan's advice and follow her own instincts just this once? The very thought gave her the jitters. Moments before the biggest audition of her life was not the time to go rogue.

Inside the audition room, Antonia lowered her glasses as Simi looked at her expectantly, pleased with her performance. She'd made 'angry' work and given *almost* everything, leaving just a little in reserve in case Antonia wanted more. Antonia cleared her throat as the echoes from Simi's angry shouting bounced around the room.

'That was very – interesting,' she said.

Simi smiled hoping 'interesting' was casting-speak for, *you got the job, kid!*

Cameron, who had been lying on a tattered chaise longue opposite Simi stood up and slinked, feline-like, over to the window. She pushed it open and with the ease of a cat, slipped out onto the fire escape and lit a cigarette as long and thin as her limbs.

Simi, who had been trying not to stare at Cameron, now stole a glance. She was stunning. She looked tall in her perfume adverts but in real life she had to be over six feet tall. She had cocoa skin, platinum blond hair, limbs like scaffolding and yet the poise of a dancer.

Antonia cleared her throat again.

'We certainly hadn't thought of Dorothea as being quite so... enraged,' she said.

'Well I was thinking, perhaps she's a communist who doesn't want to buy into this bourgeoisie lifestyle,' Simi offered, her conviction withering at the sight of Antonia's pained expression.

'Communist. I see,' Antonia said.

Simi searched Gabe's face for some clue as to how she was doing. Gabe stared back, gave her an almost imperceptible neck-pop then started tinkering with the camera.

'I mean, she doesn't have to be. I could try it another way,' said Simi, backtracking.

Antonia glanced over at Cameron who was halfway through her extra-slim cigarette. Simi's eyes darted between them as though some sort of telepathic communication was taking place. Cameron raised an eyebrow and closed the window, turning her back on the room.

'Please,' said Simi not noticing that her hands were clasped together in prayer.

Antonia gave an unreadable smile. 'Alright,' she said, then nodded to Gabe. 'Strawberry filter please.'

Simi exhaled with relief. And strawberry filter? Perhaps they were sending her tape to the producers and wanted it to look as good as possible. Come on, Simi, she chanted in her head. Make that strawberry filter count. This time she would discover the character for herself, in the moment. Gabe nodded with a grin and began adjusting the camera settings.

'Will Cameron be coming back in?' Simi asked looking over to the window.

'No, darling, I'll read with you this time. When you're ready,' said Antonia.

Simi looked out at Cameron. How were they going to discover if they had chemistry if she was ten feet away on a rickety old fire escape? Maybe Cameron was checking *how far* their chemistry could stretch. Simi nodded assuredly before reordering her script pages and beginning again. A moment later, Gabe was clacking the viewfinder closed and opening the door for Simi.

'Right… I… you don't need to see anything else?' she stuttered.

'No, that was great,' said Antonia.

Simi gave one last confused look at Cameron who was elegantly staring into nothing, probably having intelligent acting thoughts.

'Thanks again, Simi,' said Antonia and before Simi had finished wittering her twenty-five goodbyes, Gabe had closed the door in her face.

Simi walked down the corridor, stunned. She'd been bustled out of the room so fast, her feet had barely touched the polished wooden floor. Well at least her last attempt had been better and hopefully, Cameron had a sense of how far Simi could project her chemistry.

'Really interesting interpretation. So brave,' said the other actress, though her eyes seemed to be saying something very different, like, WTF was that. Simi felt her mouth go dry and left.

Once outside, she tucked herself into a café's back doorway, letting out a pained, *arrrrghhh! Brave? Brave??* Brave was what actors said to their friends after seeing them do a terrible performance. Either that, or *great energy*.

167

'*Frrrriiiiiiiiiiiiiiggg!*' Simi hissed.

Why had she listened to Meagan?? *Angry* had been the most ridiculous suggestion she could have gone with. She'd have been better off playing it like a clown again or a psychopath. In fact, psychopath was probably what her performance looked like and why Cameron had escaped onto the balcony. And even though she'd managed to get a do-over, it was obviously too little, way too late. Oh, God, Simi whimpered as she crouched down into a ball. This whole thing was a disaster. Simi hadn't wanted to audition in the first place and when she had she'd ruined it by listening to Meagan's terrible advice. Why didn't she trust herself and, worse, why didn't Meagan trust her – about anything? Whatever she thought, people overrode or just dismissed it. The only important choice Oscar had let her make was which joint Christmas card to send! No one trusted her choices. Simi gasped as a realisation struck her. That's exactly what the dating game was! She had basically given the girls power-of-attorney over her. She was telling them she didn't trust herself and that they were better placed to choose a date for her than she was. What had Meagan once said? *People treat you how you let them.* Meagan had talked at length about boundaries but it hadn't occurred to Simi that one of those boundaries might have to be between her and her girlfriends. Her stomach lurched at the notion. They were her backstops, her confidantes, her wingwomen. But even so, that didn't mean they got to decide everything for her. She needed to start deciding for herself. Even if she got it wrong, she had to try. Tonight, when they meet up for another round of the game, Simi would bow out. She had to make some changes and perhaps this was the place to start. She stood up, confidently striding to the end of the block. As she reached the corner, she spied Sandra Scott trotting up the street towards Antonia De Silva's office and darted back into the doorway.

'Sandra-Flipping-Scott,' she seethed, punctuating each word with a pathetic, flailing punch.

As she flung her arms about, a flurry of white flakes floated down in front of her. Snow? she thought, reaching out to let a flake settle in her hand. But instead of melting it disintegrated into a grey smudge. Simi looked skyward and saw where it had come from. Above her was Cameron, cigarette in hand, staring down between the metal stairs of the fire escape. Without a flicker of expression, she opened the window and slid back inside Antonia's office. Simi listened as the old wooden window grazed shut.

'Frig,' she grizzled as she stomped off to the tube and the receptionist job she would probably have for the rest of her life.

CHAPTER 24

Jemima

Jemima looked up from her laptop. Though the Nostromo buzz had melded into a hypnotic hubbub, the *pshhhp* of the opening door grabbed her attention every time. Her phone pinged. She looked at the message.

Let me know when ur back. Could go for lunch? Mx

Bugger off, Miles, she grumbled, flipping her phone over.

Still feeling singed from her recent blunder with Chance, a man-blaze on two fronts was more than she could handle. It had been nearly a week since they'd taken that walk around the park. Since then she'd been in Nostromo practically every day but hadn't seen him once. She shame-shuddered as she remembered the look on his face when she'd assumed he wanted a date and *then* rejected him. That wasn't just throwing the baby out with the bath water. That was throwing out the bath.

All she wanted, in a very low key, no drama way, was to put things right but how could she if he'd disappeared. She could pop up to his practice but that felt like massive overkill.

So here she had sat, all week, partly working, mainly waiting. *Pshhhp.* Jemima glanced at the door as a woman with a shopping trolley nudged it open. Typical. Now she *wanted* to see him, he was nowhere in sight. She just wanted to chat with him, absorb his energy, enjoy watching his face crack into a smile. She wanted to discuss her book with someone who got it and, yes, maybe she could do all that over dinner! Jemima gasped at what felt like such a huge, massive, confession – *wanting* to have dinner – with a man. Yes, she was ready to have Chance as a friend and perhaps even a confidante. Anxiety over her secret – those borrowed stories – was building by the day. She needed to talk to someone, even if it was just to quieten the guilty clamour inside her brain. She didn't often talk about her writing with Meagan and Simi. After reading her first novel, Meagan's note had been, *too much insurance stuff.* But as this novel now had so much of them in it, even if she'd wanted to – she couldn't talk to them. The book was littered with stories from Meagan and Simi's love lives and titbits of their personalities and Jemima *still* hadn't asked their permission. Why couldn't she just blurt it out? She grimaced, knowing exactly why… because she was terrified they'd say no. And then what? Heading to LA, leaving everything and everyone behind might become her only and best option. No, she was in so deep; the only way out was through. She *had* to speak to them. The deadline was just two weeks away. Her one saving grace was that she hadn't used *all* the girls' stories, drawing the line at Simi's college exploits. Even though it would have worked brilliantly, it was a step too far. It was possible Meagan and Simi would appreciate that discretion at least. As she considered this, the door *pshhhped* opened. Jemima instantly recognised his curly brown hair and dipped down behind her laptop screen. The first time he saw her, she had to be engrossed in some moment of literary genius, not a melancholic daydreaming. She eavesdropped as he paid for his coffee and wrapped up his friendly banter with Rania. He wasn't in scrubs today she noticed, but a casual shirt and jeans. Jemima decided her apology would be concise yet earnest then she would make a swift exit. She would leave talk of dinner to another day. As he approached, Jemima raised her hand to wave him over. At that precise moment, a woman behind her yelled, 'Chance!'

Jemima froze, a deer in the headlights of a fast-moving awkward situation.

'Hey!' Chance smiled and headed towards the voice.

Jemima's mind raced. Was Chance on some romantic rendez-vous? That's why he'd been weird when she'd assumed he wanted a date. He was already seeing someone! Jemima glanced his way once more. He still hadn't noticed her. A swift and unnoticed getaway was still possible. She would apologise another time. She snapped her laptop closed and went to get up.

'Jemima!'

She froze again.

'Hey you!' she simpered.

'Over here, Chance!'

The voice behind Jemima sounded female, young and very Australian.

Great. Jemima was now stuck in the middle of a date sand-wich.

'How's it going?' Chance said pointing at her laptop, darting a look towards the voice.

'Oh, you know,' Jemima quivered.

'This is a nice spot to write, eh?' he said.

'Yeah, can get a bit noisy,' said Jemima throwing a discreet but shady eye behind her, just managing to catch a glimpse of Chance's date.

Jemima noted her long red hair, not ginger but dyed red, like a stop sign. She was younger than Chance, perhaps mid-twenties. Her eyeliner looked like she'd put it on three days ago and her hand-painted Doc Martens were almost completely covered by her frayed flares. Jemima smiled politely in her direction. The woman tutted and went back to her tea.

'Yeah. I go to our… that park when I want a bit of quiet,' he said.

'Yeah… ' said Jemima as the two of them smiled clumsily.

'So, despite me almost scuppering your writing with demonically bad book readings, has Beverly found love?' Chance asked.

'Sort of.' Jemima shrugged, wanting to say more but knowing now was not the time.

Chance nodded.

'So… I'm having drinks at my practice next Thursday. Kind of a fundraiser thing. Swing by if you're free,' he said.

'Well, if I'm not busy. You know, writing and everything,' said Jemima shuffling on the spot.

'Sure… Course. Oh, listen, about the other day. The whole date thing. We cool?' he laughed with a silly grimace.

Jemima tilted her head. What was with the face? Was it *such* a strange proposition to date her?

'Totally cool. I mean, *as if* we'd date,' Jemima said as she slipped her laptop into its case. 'I mean, *riiight?* And anyway… '

Jemima threw a look back at Chance's companion. He followed her gaze.

'No, I meant—' said Chance but Jemima already had her coat on.

'You're already... whatever and I mean, as if we'd have been a match. *Pttth*,' she scoffed.

'Right... As if... Well, I'd better get on... ' he said, thumbing in the direction of the crimson-haired foghorn.

'Yeah, me too,' said Jemima before bundling towards the door in the hope it led straight to the gangplank of an LA-bound flight.

Outside, her cheeks felt scorched. Well, that was another name to add to the growing list of reasons to relocate to California. She quickly turned towards home but as she passed Nostromo's window she couldn't resist taking one last peek. She watched Chance's date embrace him. They held each other for a long time, her head buried in his neck. Eventually they sat. His date grabbed his hand, yanking it towards her, staring into his eyes. Though Jemima couldn't see Chance's face she imagined him mirroring her intensity. Good for them, she exhaled. She pulled out her phone and stared at her last text.

Let me know when ur back. Could go for lunch? Mx

Though she wasn't ready to sit face to face with Miles and chat over bruschetta as though nothing had happened, there was no point pretending he was an unknown caller either. Well done, Miles, she murmured as she opened up her contacts list and typed in, *M.i.l.e.s. C.o.n.r.o.y.* As always, he'd managed to wiggle his way in, like a splinter under the skin. Yes, he was a jerk but there was something reassuring about the familiarity. Jemima's fingers tapped the SAVE button. She put the phone back in her pocket and took one final look at Chance before marching home. Not bothered, not bothered, not bothered at all, she declared.

CHAPTER 25

Meagan

Meagan cupped her hand around her phone, making sure Glenn the contractor, was out of earshot. He'd already been privy to far too many of her private calls.

'Todd, I've got this refurb on lockdown. Back off,' Meagan hissed into her phone.

This whole keeping-Todd-at-arm's-length thing was proving harder than she thought.

'I don't get you. Who couldn't use a spare pair of hands?'

'The only thing I want your hands to do isn't allowed because… say it with me, Todd,' Meagan toned like a kindergarten teacher.

'Because you're playing this silly dating game. Fine but don't come running to me when you need someone to paint into the top corners of the room,' he scoffed.

'Have you heard of ladders? Bye, Todd,' said Meagan hanging up.

Meagan kissed her teeth long and hard. She had this sorted and if she did need assistance, of all the people she was going to draft in, her fuck buddy was the last of them. She glowered at the open doorway of her office as Glenn whistled tunelessly in the other room. She'd selected her door three weeks ago yet was still staring at the insufferable drape Glenn had hung in its place. Where was her door, why did everything take so long and *what* was Glenn whistling?

'Glenn,' she growled, unable to take the noise any longer.

The trill warbling stopped and Glenn poked his head into the room.

'Don't you normally head off around now?' Meagan enquired.

'My pilates class isn't for another hour so I thought I'd redo the gloss work.'

His head vanished and the whistling started again, louder than before.

Meagan gritted her teeth as she conceded, Glenn's extended tenure might be slightly her fault. It hadn't dawned on her that scheduling the flooring people on the same day as the gloss work was a page one, schoolgirl error. Glenn's *oh deary, deary, me-ing* had felt like nails on a chalkboard. So she'd made a mistake. That didn't mean she needed a knight in shining armour. She was her own cavalry and always had been. The sooner people got that, the easier life would be for everyone. Sure, it would have been nice to see Todd, mainly because she missed the sex but the refurb first aid, the flowers, the chocolates and heart emojis, she did not need or want. What happened to the cursory 'hi' followed by a frantic quickie? One time they'd got down to it so fast it was only afterwards she realised she still had her handbag on her shoulder. That's what she missed. As Glenn's whistling scored into her soul, Meagan decided it was time to call it a night. Her manicure was scheduled for six thirty and that was the only painting she was interested in. And after, she would meet the girls and play another round of their daft dating game. She shut down her computer and headed out.

Simi had chosen tonight's location and Meagan had known it was going to be something bizarre. She looked over at the other two who were still lacing up their boots.

'Isn't ice skating more of a coupley thing?' she asked.

Simi shrugged as she tightened her scarf around her neck.

'What's up, Simi, you getting cold feet?' Jemima laughed, nudging her.

'Blimey, were you someone's granddad in a former life?' said Meagan rolling her eyes. 'What's the matter, Simster? Me and Jem are gonna find you another quality fella.'

'Yeah… ' said Simi looking towards the rink.

Jemima scanned the crowd. 'Looks like we might reel in a catch here.'

Meagan tried not to laugh as she watched Jemima do a seated shimmy to the loud dance music spilling from the rink outside. It usually took so much alcohol to get Jemima dancing it wasn't cost effective. Simi continued to tie her laces, barely having spoken since they'd arrived.

'Come on, Sim. Spit it out,' Meagan said, folding her arms.

Simi looked back out at the rink. 'I don't want to play the game anymore.'

Thank God! thought Meagan who was becoming convinced the gains were not worth the pains for any of them. She threw a 'finally' roll of her eyes to Jemima who would probably be even more delighted about this than she was. The whole experience seemed to be causing her actual physical pain.

'Well, if you're sure!' said Meagan as she clomped towards the rink. 'They're serving free glühwein. Let's get a glass or ten before they run out!'

'Wait a minute. It's only been a couple of weeks,' said Jemima wobbling to her feet.

'What?' snapped Meagan.

Even if Jemima was opening up to meeting someone, no way was this her preferred method.

'Thing is, I only broke up with Oscar two weeks ago,' reasoned Simi, 'and plus, if I'm going to meet someone I should speak to him myself – start believing in my choices.'

'And who told you to do that?' asked Meagan.

Simi opened and closed her mouth. 'I… just… me.'

Meagan's eyes narrowed. This had Oprah written all over it. Listening to your inner she-wolf and thinking for yourself was fine for everyone else but when Simi did it, it always led to trouble. And guess who had to come to the rescue: Meagan.

'I trust your decisions! I'd never have met these guys without you,' Jemima implored.

'But you hated Lance,' said Simi.

'But I loved what I learned.'

'Really?' said Simi.

'Definitely. They say the thinking that got you into a problem can't get you out of it so that's why I need you guys. New thinking. Your thinking. You and Meag,' said Jemima, taking Simi's hand.

'But, I – don't we need to trust our instincts, make our own choices?'

'No, Sim, we need each other,' Jemima said shuffling closer to her. 'Have you noticed how a three-legged stool never wobbles?'

'I suppose.' Simi nodded. 'Yeah… I'd never thought of that.'

'Well, just like that, we need each other for this to work,' said Jemima.

'You're *sooo* right. We are a massive stool!' said Simi.

'Well, I wouldn't put it quite like that… but yeah!' Jemima said putting her arms around Simi.

Meagan looked on as they hugged. In all the years she'd known her, Jemima had never gushed over relationships not even when she'd been in one. She wanted to play the game yet talking about her love life made her snappy and weird. Something didn't add up.

'Let's just give it one more go,' Jemima said clasping Simi's hand, 'and if you really don't want to carry on, we'll call it a day.'

Simi wavered.

'Come on, Sim. You set tonight up. Now we're here, we might as well go for it!' said Jemima.

'Okay, one more go!' Simi said. 'Come on, Meag.'

'Great!' said Jemima slapping her thighs and standing.

Simi stood too and Meagan watched them clomp towards the rink.

Great, Meagan huffed.

Out on the ice, Jemima and Simi tentatively slid forward. It was just after nine and the rink was buzzing. Strips of lights pulsed to dance music blaring from speakers. Around the periphery, groups of friends whizzed by, their skating confidence lubricated by the free glühwein. Ahead of her Meagan watched as Simi and Jemima, hand in hand, slowly teetered along. As they rocked back and forth, clamping hold of each other to keep their balance, she softened. Like she always said, yes they were idiots, but they were her idiots. She glided in behind them.

'If you hold on to each other, you'll take each other down if you fall,' she said.

'That's the point!' shrieked Simi as she stumbled, instinctively reaching for Meagan and Jemima.

'Simi!' howled Jemima as all three of them collapsed to the floor in a giggling heap.

'I'm sorry!' Simi said as she battled to stand while cackling with laughter.

Meagan clambered to her feet and manoeuvred herself in front of them. She jammed her skate against Simi's, gripping her arms as she tried to yank her back to standing.

'Need a hand?'

Meagan turned to see the out-stretched hand of a tall, black and deliciously handsome man.

'We're good,' she said before turning back to Simi and heaving her to her feet.

'Meagan,' mouthed Simi, 'he's gorgeous!'

'Shhh!' said Meagan before looking back at the man, 'Unless you've got a winch, we're fine.'

'No worries,' he said, smiling.

He hesitated for a moment then glided off to re-join his friends.

'He was *hot!*' Simi grinned.

'Whatever,' Meagan said as she surreptitiously scanned the crowd for him.

He *was* hot. If she had a type, he would be it. Tall obviously. A narrow face with neat stubble. Designer clothes. Tick, tick,

tick. His flaw, however, was that he probably wanted to be another knight in shining armour and that was a hard no.

'You two looked good together,' said Jemima as she gripped the side of the rink.

'He looks like drama,' said Meagan before skating away.

'Everyone's drama. We just have to decide who's worth it,' Simi said tottering behind Meagan before easing into a wobbly glide.

The girls skated for a while with Meagan leading the way and after a few circuits they started to gain their confidence.

'Meagan, can we talk about my audition…' Simi began.

'Yeah, man,' said Meagan. 'My notes must have worked coz you're still in the running.'

'I… I am?' Simi stammered.

'Yaaass, queen. You're welcome,' Meagan said, enjoying the moment.

Despite script reading being a massive ball-ache, Meagan had managed to skim-read the *Clash of the Crown* episode Simi had auditioned for. From the get-go she could see it was missing laughs. Even intense dramas need comic relief. Lucky Meagan had steered Simi towards injecting some much-needed comedy. If she got it right, not only would Simi be a shoe-in for the role but the producers would probably realise their mistake and write in more gags.

'Come on, guys,' said Jemima. 'We've only got thirty minutes before the next session starts. These dates aren't going to arrange themselves!'

Meagan eyed Jemima. Something was *definitely* odd.

'She really is into this,' Simi said gleefully.

'Yeah…' said Meagan as she watched Jemima scope the rink for Simi's potential date.

'So,' said Simi quietly, 'you know what you have to do when you look for Jem, right?'

'What?' said Meagan, still watching Jemima.

'Meag! We talked about this. Our list. Smart, funny, good looking, loves books, makes puns, generous, kind, keeps his feet on the ground and most importantly... '

'Makes Jemima want to do the same. Yeah, yeah I know. And after we'll turn water into wine and feed the five thousand,' said Meagan.

'It's not that hard. And what's the point of all this if we don't find people that make our lives better, add value? She just needs someone with roots who'll make her want to stay put. Got it?' said Simi.

'Yeah, yeah. Got it. I've got to find Jemima a funny tree,' said Meagan.

CHAPTER 26

Jemima

Jemima leaned back on the rink barrier to take a breather. After two embarrassing wipeouts and just as she was about to give up, she had finally found Mo, Simi's next date. She watched Simi wave coquettishly across the rink at him. Jemima was pleased and from the way Simi was slathering in his direction, she was too.

'You seriously don't know who he is?!' Simi whispered so loudly she may as well have put it on a sandwich board.

Jemima shrugged. She was so bad at celeb spotting she'd once spent a whole tube ride talking to an ex-*Blue Peter* presenter thinking they'd gone to school together.

'He's just landed the lead in the new Black Panthers comedy, *Blacklash*. It's gonna be huge. I can't believe you didn't recognise him!' said Simi.

Jemima took another glance at Mo. Nope – she had no clue who he was.

'Mmmm. Six foot two inches of mixed-race gorgeousness,' Meagan said, sneaking a peek. 'I can't believe I'm gonna say this, but next time, *Jemini*, I want you to find my date!'

Jemima laughed. Maybe she was starting to get the hang of this.

The girls looked on as Mo bantered with his friends, his bluey-white teeth giving him that dazzling smile you only ever saw in Hollywood… and Essex.

'*Ohmygod, ohmygod, ohmygod,* this is AMAZING. He's exactly what we talked about. He's in the biz. He's successful and he is hot as a mother monster!' trilled Simi.

'You bagged a good 'un, Jem,' Meagan said winking at her.

'And I'm gonna get you someone even better, Meag,' said Simi leaning against the side scrutinising every skater that whizzed past.

'Well, go on then,' said Jemima tapping her watch. 'They're not going to come to you.'

'Oh… yes… they… are… HEY!' Simi yelled at a passing skater.

As she hollered, the helpful stranger from earlier skidded to a halt and Simi zigzagged over.

'Well played, Simster. Well played,' said Meagan with a conceding nod.

Jemima watched as Simi, after a brief chat with her target, beckoned Meagan over. Why was Meagan so drawn to tall men? Even when she was in heels they towered over her like the Shard. As Jemima pondered, a very excited Simi and less enthused Meagan made their way back over.

'He's a nerd,' Meagan said.

'He owns a tech company and his name's AJ,' enthused Simi.

'He hasn't even got a full name and he's barely six foot,' griped Meagan.

'And you're five four – in your heels,' said Simi.

'Plus he doesn't drink. Where's he gonna take me, a library?'

'Well I think you're going to have a lovely time,' said Jemima poking Meagan.

'With my teetotal midget. I'll give it an hour,' she said.

As the girls continued to rib Meagan, the ice rink speakers crackled to life.

'*Skaters — You have ten more minutes. I repeat, ten more minutes to GET YOUR SKATE ON!*' And with that the music ramped up several decibels.

'I'll get the job done in eight.' Meagan grinned as she skated off at speed.

'I'm gonna go for a victory lap,' said Simi, attempting a twirl. 'You'll be okay?'

'I'll be right here, waiting for Meag to drag over my prey,' smirked Jemima.

Simi gave her a stern look.

'Sorry, my prize, my prince even!'

Satisfied, Simi wobbled off to re-join the stream of skaters.

As Jemima leaned against the sidings she felt her phone vibrate. She pulled it from her pocket and peered at her screen. It was an email from her LA pal, Rebecca. The title read: **House Swap. Interested???** Jemima's pulse quickened as she clicked open the message and read. Rebecca was relocating to London and, as the title suggested, was looking for a house swap. Jemima swiped through the attached photos. She was almost breathless at the images of Rebecca's apartment which looked just as beautiful and bright as she remembered.

'Watcha doin'?' said Simi, clattering against the siding.

'That was a fast lap,' Jemima stuttered, quickly pocketing her phone. 'It was just an email – from my friend Rebecca. It's nothing.'

'Rebecca's the one with the weird lisp?' Simi asked.

'It's just a normal lisp,' said Jemima.

'You stayed with her in LA, right?'

'Yeah. She's been offered a twelve-month contract at their London offices and she's thinking through her options,' Jemima said, her words fading to nothing.

Now was not the time to discuss this. She had enough self-made dramas to handle.

'If she comes to London, I hope she knows, you're ours,' Simi giggled, clutching Jemima.

'One hundred per cent,' she said before changing tack. 'So, tell me more about Mo.'

'Now, are we all happy with our dates? Jem, what do you think of yours?' Simi asked.

'Tim? Yeah, he's nice,' said Jemima.

'You are welcome,' said Meagan with a flourish.

'And don't you think he's a good fit, you know; sweet *like you*, funny *like you* and *grounded*,' Simi enthused.

'I'm not sure I got all that from one conversation but he's definitely nice,' said Jemima as they skated back to the hut.

Simi's face fell and Jemima felt bad. But what could she do? For her, this wasn't about falling in love. This was about a much bigger picture.

'I bet Jem's only dating these poor fellas to get ideas for her book. She probably gets home afterwards and taps away at her little laptop,' Meagan laughed, miming a silly impersonation of Jemima.

'Don't be mean,' said Simi.

Jemima's face drained of blood. She stopped dead in her tracks thinking, for one horrific moment, she had been found out.

'Jem's not *that* shady. She knows I'm joking,' said Meagan as she stepped into the warmth of the hut.

'Course,' said Jemima, forcing out a laugh.

Despite the Baltic temperature, Jemima was sweating. Hanging back, she quickly pulled out her phone, going straight to Rebecca's email. She needed to prepare her exit strategy and this might be the first part of it.

I am soooo interested! Jemima tapped into her phone. She hit SEND and followed Meagan and Simi inside.

CHAPTER 27

Simi

Simi opened one eye and then the other. The bedroom was dark but in the hallway she could see the flickering glow of a TV screen. So, this was Mo's pad. She looked around the bedroom which was enormous, and, aside from some minimalist furniture, empty. Luxurious, long curtains hung against sliding doors that opened out onto a balcony. At the start of the evening, she never dreamt she'd end up in the bed of a famous actor, yet here she was. The night had started with early drinks and dinner at Nobu which Mo had paid for and Simi still felt guilty about. She wished she were more like Meagan who considered such chivalry reparations for the gender pay gap. Then later, outside the restaurant, when he'd put an arm around her and pulled her to him, Simi had actually swooned. But then she'd had a choice.

'Want to come to an exhibition I'm opening next week or… you could come back to mine?' Mo had whispered so close to her ear it felt as though he'd planted the words inside her head.

And now, here she was, in his super-king-sized bed. She looked over at his side which was empty. Perhaps he was fixing them a drink… while watching TV. Simi wondered if Meagan was having similar issues on her teetotal date with AJ. All Simi wanted was for Mo to come back to bed so they could get on with falling head-over-heels in love. While she awaited his return, she star-fished under the duvet, the brush of the silk sheets making her squeal. She looked around the room again, her eyes now adjusted. Where was all his stuff?? They'd basically had sex in an IKEA showroom. Simi spotted her crumpled dress against the cream carpet and her bra, which had somehow hooked itself onto the door handle. She sighed. If Mo wasn't going to come to the mountain, perhaps she would have to get dressed and take the mountain to him. Unsure she wanted to be the mountain in that analogy, she kicked her feet around under the duvet trying to loop a toe through her knickers. Above Simi's head she saw the time, projected from a digital alarm clock on Mo's night stand. 11.05 p.m. They'd only had sex an hour ago and she'd already been abandoned. Maybe it wasn't time to move mountains. Maybe it was time to leave – once she'd found her knickers. Simi clambered out of bed and unhooked her bra from the door handle. Any romance she'd experienced at the start of the date had been shot to smithereens, and really, she only had herself to blame. She'd been so excited about her date with Mo, checking her phone on the hour every hour waiting for his text arranging their meet-up. Her dress was fresh from the dry cleaners that morning and she'd washed and twisted her hair two days earlier so it would be at its most afro plumpness. And for what?

She peeped down the hall where she could now see the television in his living room. As the first-person view of a machine gun bounced around the bottom of the screen, she heard gunfire and a drill sergeant's pained yelp. Simi's jaw slackened. Was he playing a computer game? She leaned back onto the cold, bedroom wall. After kissing the frog in search of her prince, so often she ended up back at his lily pad. She did it because intimacy was supposed to be the start of something yet, once again, for the guy, it was just the happy ending. Was Mo the same? Was *this* what Meagan's whole boundaries speech had been about? And now Simi had surrendered something precious in the hope he valued it as highly. But he hadn't. He was playing shoot-em-ups next door while she manned a search-and-rescue for her underwear.

'What would Meagan do?' she whispered, pacing.

Quickly, Simi grabbed her phone from the bedside table and fired off a text.

I've lost my knickers! Help!

Why was this so much easier for Meagan? When she slept with a guy it made him want her more – like poor Todd. But when she did it, they disappeared off to shoot alien insurgents. Simi tossed her phone aside and crouched down to look under Mo's bed, staring at a jumble of shoe boxes. She pushed a couple aside noticing a price tag. $400.

'For a pair of shoes?!' she inhaled.

She flipped a lid and inspected the contents. Inside were a box-fresh, unworn, new pair of trainers. Unable to resist, she opened one more box. Once again, there nestled among crisp, tissue paper like a couple of sleeping babies was another pristine pair of white trainers.

'A thousand dollars!'

Just one of these shoes was worth more than her first car.

She pushed the box aside and opened another. Yet more unsullied, white trainers. Simi thought of what she would do with that much disposable income – therapy for sure and maybe a fasting retreat where you had coffee enemas and sifted through your poo for old chewing gum.

'Simi.'

She froze, around her now several opened shoe boxes and no legitimate explanation in sight.

'Hi… ' she spluttered.

'Looking for something?'

Self-respect was her first thought.

'Trouble?' she said with a half laugh.

Mo looked at her, confused.

'As in Elvis,' she said, trailing away. 'I was looking for my, you know.'

Mo sat down on the floor next to her resting his arm on her knee. He laughed and despite her abject embarrassment, eventually she laughed too.

'Have you looked under the duvet?'

'Yes… I… '

Mo pulled up the end of the duvet sweeping his arm from side to side. Just then his eyes widened and a terrified expression crossed his face.

'They've got me!'

His head plunged under the bedding as he fought to free himself from the terror-knickers.

'Very funny,' Simi said, slapping his thigh.

At last his thrashing subsided and he pulled out her under-wear, ceremoniously handing them to her. She slapped him again before slipping them on and reaching for her crumpled dress.

'You going?' said Mo, disappointment in his voice.

'Well, I thought you were busy.'

Mo pushed himself up off the floor and went to one of his fitted wardrobes. He pulled out a T-shirt and tracksuit bottoms similar to the ones he had on and put them on the bed.

'Chill for a bit,' he said before heading back to the living room.

After a moment, Simi heard him fire up the game again.

'*This is Collateral Mayhem. Over-eighteens only…*'

Simi slipped on the T-shirt and jogging bottoms and looked down at her shapeless form. In the figure-hugging body-con dress he'd slipped her out of she'd looked hot. Now she looked as though she were heading to the prison gym.

'Come, Simi, I've got another controller,' he called.

'Coming!' she said as though even wild horses couldn't hold her back.

She padded through to the living room feeling the lush, deep carpet under her feet. Perhaps this wasn't a total wipeout. Mo wasn't indifferent. He just wanted to share his passion – for gaming. If she could learn to ride a bike with Oscar, shooting insurgents would be easy. And weren't sharing your interests one of the building blocks of a relationship? Meagan and her boundaries were all well and good but if she'd followed that advice would she be here with Mo playing Collateral Mayhem? Sometimes, love wasn't all hearts and flowers. Sometimes it was covering someone with a suppressive fire while they reloaded. Perhaps, Simi daydreamed, once the dating game was over, something real might be possible with Mo.

'Grab that grenade!' he instructed.

'Love to!' She beamed as her gaming character discharged its weapon aimlessly into the sky.

CHAPTER 28

Meagan

Meagan laughed, bemused that she hadn't checked her phone for three whole hours. She scooped up her arbitrarily selected 'lucky' bowling ball and rammed her fingers into the holes. Here was another first. She was bowling. She held the ball in both hands before swinging her arm back so far, she was barely facing her lane.

'Woah, woah, woah!' said AJ lowering her arm. 'Not such a high swing.'

Somehow, bowling had passed Meagan by. As a teen, her and her friends had spent most of their time trying to pass for 21 and get into nightclubs. And though Meagan was terrible at it, chucking something heavy, it turned out, was very much up her street. AJ gently manoeuvred Meagan into position, pulling her hand back for balance. She nestled into his body.

'Now what?' she said.

'Allow yourself a little half-swing forward, pull back and then release.'

Meagan bit her lip in concentration as she swung her hand with full force. Her arm soared over her head and the bowling ball sailed off her fingers. She yelped as it crashed onto their table behind them sending fries and soda everywhere. She and AJ froze, everyone's eyes on them.

'We're alright,' he said with a placating hand as Meagan stared at the chunk that had been knocked out of the flimsy, Formica table.

'Ooops,' she laughed, flinching at the damage.

A couple of staff members scurried over to survey the wreckage and issue the kind of frail reprimand only teenage part-timers can. After they'd wiped what remained of the table and cleaned the food up from the floor they scuttled back to the reception desk. Meagan clamped her hand over her mouth and dived into their booth, AJ nestling in beside her.

'Do you know what the problem is?' she said hoisting up her foot. 'It's these minging shoes. If I was in my heels, I'd be killing it right now.'

'You'd be killing something,' said AJ.

Meagan dug her elbow into his ribs. He nudged her back and she looked at him, surprised. She'd never had a date like this, like she was with a mate.

'I'm gonna get my shoes. You'll see,' she said sliding out of their booth and heading to the reception desk.

She dumped her bowling shoes on the counter, the shoe-stench radiating from the shelves almost flooring her. She'd rather be a blind knife thrower's assistant than deal with other people's footwear. The team member handed over her suede boots and she stroked them like a beloved pet newly released from quarantine. The Universe's natural order restored, she trotted back to AJ.

Meagan flopped into the booth and thrusted up her feet. 'Prepare to meet thy doom.'

'With those?' AJ said, pointing at her boots.

Meagan elbowed him again and before he could jab her back, she put up a defensive block and stuffed some fries in his mouth. Their eyes locked and she smiled. Much to her surprise, this night had been pretty decent and a total contrast to her evening with Bruno. How had they got so familiar in just a few hours? She'd had no booze, she'd eaten on a date, something she never did and she'd removed her heels *in public*. Was it too early to call the Guinness Book of Records?

'Want to try again?' said AJ pulling her up by her hand.

'You bet your arse I do.'

AJ rolled Meagan's 'lucky' ball aside handing her a smaller, lighter one. She wanted to cut him some side eye but he was probably right. She stepped up to the line, staring down her lane. AJ tucked himself beside her and Meagan began to wonder if she might like this guy. He had a very grabbable butt, that was for sure, and sexy eyes that were also nice, like he'd care if you orgasmed first. Deals had been broken over less. But then, she scoffed at her silliness, almost forgetting her plan. No one was going to distract her from that. Meagan felt AJ's hand rest on her side as he pointed to where her ball needed to land. He was closer than he needed to be. She inhaled. If smells were edible his cologne was fine dining. But it didn't matter how lovely he smelt or how good he looked. This wasn't the plan.

'Are you okay, Meagan?'

'Hmmm, yeah. So, what am I doing?' she said trying not to inhale anymore AJ.

'Bend the knees, breathe, swing, release and remember... '

His warm breath brushed across her face.

'Don't kill anyone.'

Ignoring his deliciousness, Meagan let the ball swing in her hand before releasing it. It thumped onto the lane, then veered in the direction of the gutter. AJ winced as it rumbled towards certain death but then miraculously bananaed away from the edge.

'You've put some spin on it,' AJ gawped as the ball rolled on, now almost centred.

Meagan held her breath as the ball careered into the middle pins sending them flying, knocking all ten down. The pin-setter cleared the deck and their scoreboard broke into a celebratory cacophony. *STRIKE!*

AJ pumped his fist then hoisted Meagan into the air.

'You did it! And no one's dead!'

'I told you, it's the heels!' she laughed.

As she let him spin her around and her laughter ebbed away, she felt vulnerable. It wasn't horrible but it certainly wasn't comfortable. AJ placed her back on terra firma and she looked up at him, his face catching the light in just the way Todd's did. She put a hand on his cheek, pulling him to her and they kissed.

AJ and Meagan sat in their booth watching the staff close the place down. They all looked like students who'd taken this job to get through uni but forgotten to go to uni.

'Can I call you?' AJ asked taking up Meagan's hand.

Her heart thumped in her chest. The hand that AJ was holding usually held her phone and she hadn't looked at it for *five* hours. She pulled it from the side pocket of her bag, horrified at the stack of notifications. Meagan switched to autopilot working through the backlog. Her solicitor, some clients, Antonia De Silva, Todd, Glenn and a weird text from Simi about underwear.

'Fuck it,' she said.

This was what happened when you allowed others to distract you.

As she typed with one hand, she pushed the other into the sleeve of her jacket, chasing it around her seat. AJ reached over and helped her into it as she continued to tap away at her phone, barely noticing. She switched typing hand as he fed her hand into the other sleeve, the only sound the ticky-tak of her texting and the staff vacuuming in the background.

Can we talk.

A text from Todd. More distractions. Unless it read, 'I'm hard. Get over here' it was pointless.

I'm on a date.

She pinged back at him.

That should put the kibosh on his love lunacy. To put a final nail in the coffin Meagan grabbed AJ and took a selfie. Ideally, she would have preferred him not to look like a Pitbull licking a stinging nettle but the photo would still do the trick. Todd needed to know she only wanted one thing from him, good old fashioned, ancient Roman screwing. Nothing more. Nothing less. The photo swooshed off and she got up to leave.

'So that's it?' said AJ.

'Sorry, babe, I've gotta help my friend find her knickers,' Meagan said before heading for the exit, emailing and texting as she went.

CHAPTER 29

Jemima

'Jeeeeeehm, it's *Eeeeeeeeve*,' said Eve.

Jemima listened to the rumble of Eve's exhaled vape mist down the phone and braced herself. Yesterday she'd sent over a draft and since then her phone's every ping, pop and whoosh had given her palpitations. After filth fest, Jemima needed this draft to win so big it obliterated that fateful mistake from Eve's memory. If Hudson Hicks jettisoned her due to her penchant for writing pornography it would not be good. If she got a reputation for being 'trouble', even the Ordnance Survey people wouldn't want her. This call was make-or-break. Jemima just wished she wasn't standing outside Highbury and Islington tube station to take it. The station staff were trained for emergencies but an author's dreams being crushed was probably outside their remit.

'So… ' said Eve, 'have only had a skimeroo but – love, love, *loooove* where this draft is going.'

'Oh my god, that's great,' said Jemima as relief flooded her.

'Yaaaaaah. It's *reeeaaally* good. It's pacy, sexy and Beverly is quite funny now,' said Eve.

Jemima knew why. The part of Beverly that could magic up sarcastic clapbacks was pure Meagan.

'That is great news,' said Jemima, flushed at the thought of the finish line edging closer.

Completing was starting to feel doable. All she needed were a few more nuggets to round out Beverly's backstory and the rest could come from previous drafts. She silently punched the air.

'One thing though,' said Eve, 'I do feel like Beverly needs one last juicy, dark secret.'

'How do you mean?' asked Jemima as the finish line drew away from her.

'Well, I love the traits you've given her. It's *reeeaaahlly* well done coz it's in keeping with the *faaaahst* two books but now I feel like we need to know *why* she's like this. Where did it all begin? You know what it's like. Once you break open a draft it begs more questions! I'm sure you'll figure it out. Anyhoo, gotta fly. Great *waaahhhk!*'

Eve hung up leaving Jemima stunned. Every time she eked nearer to the end, it seemed like another mile was added to the race. *A juicy, dark secret – like what?*

'Jemima?'

She turned.

'Tim. Hi, sorry, miles away,' she said pocketing her phone.

'No worries,' he said leaning forward to kiss her on the cheek. Jemima tried not to stiffen but couldn't help herself.

'So, what's the plan? Skydiving? Wing walking? A balloon ride?' she rattled.

Tim's face fell, 'Oh. It's a school night, I thought… pizza?'

'I'm joking.' Jemima smiled.

'Phew.' Tim sighed, relieved, 'I figured it's first date. Pizza's safe, isn't it? Unless you're gluten and lactose intolerant – and vegan. Are you vegan?'

'I'm actually a fruitarian,' Jemima said. 'We only eat what falls from the tree.'

She looked on as Tim's mind scrambled before a grin spread across his face.

'You're joking. Excellent,' he said as they both laughed.

'I love pizza,' Jemima said. 'Let's go.'

And with that, they headed off.

Pizza was a great choice, thought Jemima, as she walked alongside him. In the time it took to scoff one down, she would glean whatever might be useful for the book then head home.

'Here we are – the best pizza in North London,' said Tim.

Jemima took in the unassuming little pizzeria. Inside, the place was empty aside from the stripy-shirted staff prepping ingredients. After placing their order, Jemima and Tim planted themselves at a corner counter. Jemima edged her stool closer to Tim. They were only half an hour into the date but she could already see he was a much better fit than cynical Lance from last week. There was an openness to Tim that Jemima rather liked.

'You've a lovely smile,' he said tearing himself a slice of pizza.

Jemima looked away coyly instead surveying the quiet pizza parlour.

From the flickering fluorescent lights to the plastic tables and hand-scrawled menu boards, nothing about Nove di Nico said, 'amazing pizza' but she had to concede, it was yummy.

'What I don't get is, if this place is so good why is it so quiet?' she said navigating a slice towards her mouth.

He smiled. 'It's early. You'll see.'

Jemima nodded with pretend scepticism. On the wooden pizza paddle between them, there was only one slice left and she really, really wanted it. In reality, she could have demolished another whole pizza, they were so good.

'Want that last piece?' Jemima and Tim said in unison before laughing again.

'Jinx,' said Jemima.

'Jinx, my claim,' Tim shot back.

'Jinx no return!'

'What's that?!' chuckled Tim.

'The secret ammo anyone who went to an East London girls' school has in their back pocket for an unexpected game of Jinx,' said Jemima as she took a pizza cutter from the utensils container on their table.

'Fair enough,' laughed Tim as Jemima cut the last slice in half.

She pushed a half-slice across the paddle towards him.

'I think he does it as a conversation starter,' he said, 'cutting it into nine and not sixes or eights.'

'Ah, Nico's *nines*. Cute,' said Jemima as she bit into her piece.

Though earlier, she'd decided the end of the meal would be her signal to make a quick exit, actually she was enjoying Tim's company more as the evening progressed. She had discovered he was a keen chess player and manager of a bread factory, something more interesting than she'd anticipated. And what with the walk to the pizza place, ordering their food and chatting about everything from bread to books, they'd been together for nearly two hours. Jemima had shared the ups and downs of the literary world whilst Tim had explained the ins and outs of producing the nation's favourite staple. Jemima had been fascinated.

'So you make the *same* loaf and at one store they'll sell it as a premium product while another will sell it in their budget range?' Jemima asked.

'Loads of manufacturers do it. Baked beans, cornflakes, sugar. It's called private labelling. If you like you can come and see behind the wizard's curtain sometime,' Tim said wiping his hands and pushing away their empty pizza paddle.

Jemima squirmed. It was a nice offer but that meant meeting again, and meeting again sounded very much like a second date. Being on *this* date was already a landmark.

'You know, the last factory I worked at burned down,' said Tim breaking the silence.

'Really?' said Jemima, grateful he'd chosen to breeze over her lack of a response.

'Yeah. The stock was toast.'

'Oh my god, how long have you been waiting to say that?' Jemima groaned.

'Since the ice rink!' Tim winked.

'That was three days ago!'

'Don't I know it,' said Tim as he placed his hand on Jemima's.

She stared at it. The warmth was nice but alien. Perhaps she'd let it rest there for a minute before sliding her hand away, she calculated as her anxiety ascended.

'What are you thinking about Jemima Abeson?' Tim murmured.

Jemima could almost feel the blood coursing through her veins. Was holding hands first date behaviour? Pizza and a chat was fine. This was not. Just then he leaned over to kiss her. Jemima yanked her head back.

'What are you doing?!'

Tim blinked in shock. 'I thought… '

'What?' Jemima said tugging her hand away.

'I'm sorry,' Tim back-pedalled as Jemima stood. 'I thought – Look, I live around the corner. Why don't we have a coffee and just chat?'

Jemima's cheeks grew hot. 'Thanks but I have to go. Early start.'

She grabbed her bag and headed for the door, Tim darting between the tables behind her.

Outside in the street, Tim manoeuvred in front of Jemima. 'Are you okay?'

'I'm sorry. It's not you,' Jemima said, grimacing at her clichéd excuses.

She wished she could have given him more but even she wasn't sure what was happening.

'I know *that*,' said Tim. 'I thought we were having a nice night. What's going on?'

Jemima tightened, her breath hard and heavy.

'It's too much. I'm sorry,' she said, sensing the tingle of tears.

Tim rubbed his forehead. 'The kiss?'

'No, everything. It wasn't supposed to be like this,' Jemima blurted.

'What was it supposed to be like?'

'I don't know. I'm not here to… date,' Jemima gabbled.

'You're not on this date, *to date*?' Tim said, shaking his head in confusion.

'You don't understand. It's for my book… '

Tim took a step back from Jemima, hurt etched across his face.

'You mean this is *research*?' he asked.

Jemima looked down at the pavement where a light dusting of winter snow had settled.

'Oh wow, okay,' Tim laughed bitterly. 'Right well, nice to meet you – I think.'

He paced off in the opposite direction leaving Jemima standing in the cool, green glow of Nove di Nico's florescent lights.

As her breathing gradually slowed she felt a flush of embarrassment. She had essentially told him he was an *experiment* – just as Lance had said to her on their date. And why, when she had genuinely enjoyed his company? If it hadn't been for that kiss, everything would have been fine. But something about it had made her feel… weak, like she was collapsing from the inside, her strength draining away in that single moment of contact. Getting out was the only thing she could think to do. It was always the only thing she could think to do. But it wasn't just the feelings of weakness that troubled Jemima. Another feeling had surfaced too. Was it *pleasure*? she wondered, half laughing, half crying. What a cruel joke life was, that with pleasure could come such pain. Yes there was one truth that kiss had unearthed. She *did* want more – yet the impulse to run was still so strong. In her mind, there were so many reasons why she was single, why disappearing was necessary, why she needed to keep her life so very small but ultimately did it come down to one thing: fear? Is that why giving Beverly a love life was so terrifying, because Jemima was scared for herself?

'Wow,' she murmured.

Not only was she getting in her own way, she'd been an obstacle to Beverly too.

She propped up her collar and turned in the direction of home. She had to walk, be on the move, do something to clear her mind. Five minutes from home Jemima rounded the corner, her head turned down, staring at footprints on the snow-covered streets. As she passed the familiar cobbled pavement opposite Nostromo, she willed herself not to look over because if she did, she would then look up. But try as she might, as always, her gaze was drawn to Chance's practice where the lights were still on. Inside she could make out the shadow of a lone figure. It was the night of his fundraiser. She'd told herself she couldn't go because of her date but the truth was, once again, she'd been gripped by her own fear. Was that going to be the story of her life? Before she could answer she felt her feet move and soon she had crossed the street. Her hand wavered over his intercom buzzer before pushing it.

'Hello?' came Chance's crackly voice through the speaker.

'It's me. Jemima.'

'Hey! Come on up!'

He buzzed the door open and she went inside.

Jemima ascended the stairs, noting how quiet it was – no other voices. She pushed open the reception door into his practice. Chance had already shut off some of the lights ready to lock up and was collecting plastic cups and paper plates of canapes. His practice was not what she expected. She assumed it would be clinical and blokey but instead was neat, uncluttered, warm and inviting.

'Hi. Sorry I'm late, I—' said Jemima.

'Don't be daft. I'm glad you made it at all.'

'About five hours after everyone else,' said Jemima. 'Let me at least make a donation.'

She pulled her purse out but Chance put a hand on hers, stopping her.

'It's fine.' He smiled, his hand lingering a moment.

Once again, Jemima was taken by his eyes. Even in this dim light they seemed to glow. Finally, Chance moved his hand.

'Take a load off,' he said, dusting off a couple of chairs and pulling them together.

'Cheers and I'll definitely donate… next time.'

'Yeah. Next time. Let me get your coat,' Chance said helping her out of her mac.

Jemima swayed as she picked up his soft, earthy scent.

'Care for a plastic beaker of wine?' he said holding up a screw-top bottle.

She grinned. 'Thought you'd never ask.'

Jemima re-crossed her feet which were propped up on a chair in front of her. Chance had slipped his shoes off too and put his feet next to hers. Every now and then, their toes would touch sending a bolt of electricity through Jemima. How was it the briefest of contact could do that? she wondered as she watched him read from her phone, occasionally uttering a quiet, 'hmm, mmm.'

She took a sip of wine dying to know what he was thinking but scared of what he might say.

'You don't have to read the whole thing,' she said.

'Nearly done… ' murmured Chance, his eyes wide as he read.

Jemima now regretted letting him see her book. Though it was only a couple of chapters it felt as though he were performing open heart surgery on her.

'Wow,' he said finally handing Jemima's phone back.

As their fingers touched, *crackle*, another shot of electricity. Jemima shifted in her seat as thoughts of kissing him surfaced in her mind. She shook her head, burying them.

'So… ' she said steering her meandering mind back.

Chance was the first civilian to read any of her new draft and she so wanted his seal of approval. He was her canary down the mine shaft but she couldn't tell if he'd been poisoned by noxious gas or would live to read another day.

'It's, I mean… I effing love it, pardon my Greek but wow,' said Chance, reaching over and patting Jemima's ankles, resting his hand there.

'Really?'

'Yeah. I mean firstly, Beverly is – sexy.' He laughed, his cheeks flushing.

Jemima exhaled quietly as he squirmed.

'It's like old school Beverly from book one and then some. You've added this awesome layer to her. How did you do it?' Chance asked.

Jemima hesitated.

'I *borrowed* the stories – from my friends' lives. The friends-with-benefits thing, that's Meagan and the absent father moment, that's Simi,' Jemima said, surprised at the relief of saying it out loud.

'And the sass, that's pure Meagan,' she continued, 'and so is the fixation with a life plan. There's more of that in the next chapter but you get the idea.'

'And they're good with this?' Chance said in wonder.

'How do you mean?' Jemima asked, her breathy excitement fading at the question.

Chance looked away thoughtfully.

'What? What is it?' Jemima said sitting up.

'I dunno. Just seems a bit… harsh. I mean, the bit where you say she's *using* the, you know, fuck buddy, doesn't seem like you. And won't your mate be pissed when she reads it?' he said sitting back.

Jemima's lips tightened. 'If you knew Meagan, you'd know she's not much of a reader. And anyway, it's a character. I'm saying it about Beverly, not her. Meagan'll understand that.'

Jemima felt a pain in her hand as her nails dug in hard. Even she knew, just because Meagan hadn't picked up a book since the *Yellow Pages* went online, this wasn't really a defence.

'So you haven't asked her?' Chance said.

Jemima stared back at him, not in the mood for twenty questions. It was time to leave.

'I am going to tell them. It just hasn't come up,' she said, rising to her feet.

'Look, I know it's Cheeseville but honesty's the best policy, then everyone knows where they stand, but what do I know. Look at me telling you how to do your job,' Chance laughed awkwardly jumping up and pushing the chairs back to their place against the wall.

'I think I know my friends a little better than you,' said Jemima tugging her coat from its hook.

Chance looked at Jemima, her words seeming to broadside him.

'You're right. It's none of my business,' he said opening the door with one hand, rubbing his temple with the other.

'Listen, Meagan said the dating drama from our game would be good for my book,' said Jemima, her throat tightening.

'Her dating drama – or yours?'

'Her drama *is* my drama,' Jemima said, irritation growing.

He was right. This was none of his business. When the time came, Jemima would tell Meagan and Simi and they would understand.

'It's your call,' said Chance holding the door open wider.

Jemima's lips went taut. 'That's right. It is.'

The moment the words left her mouth she regretted them.

Chance pushed his hands into his pocket.

'Cool. Well, thanks for stopping by,' he said, primed to close the door as soon as he could.

'Right, bye then,' said Jemima as she made her way down the stairs.

'Yep, bye,' said Chance, his hard, clipped words dropping like pebbles as the door closed.

Jemima turned. Through the frosted glass she could see Chance running his hands through his hair. *He* was frustrated? What about her, having some smarty pants half-doctor critiquing her book? He gets a couple of mentions in his brother's autobiography and thinks he's A.A. Gill. Jemima clumped down the stairs. Everything felt heavy; her limbs, her head, the air. She stepped out into the street now aware of the incessant ringing of her phone. She yanked it from her pocket and peered at the screen. With no fight left, she answered.

'Hi Miles,' she said as she walked off towards her flat.

CHAPTER 30

Meagan

Meagan stepped back to survey her half-painted office wall. DIY wasn't her ideal way of spending a Friday afternoon but at least since she'd turned it into a painting party, it felt less like accepting help and more like just a messy get-together. And now she'd accepted six hands were better than two, the overhaul was finally close to completion and she was here for that. After many raised voices with Glenn, the door was hung, the fittings would be installed on Monday and once the paint work was finished she could bring in her new furniture. Soon things would start to feel normal. The office would be done along with the dating game and, fingers crossed, Todd's temporary madness. Meagan poured two whiskies, handing one to Jemima and passing Simi a can of pre-mixed gin and tonic.

'Thanks,' said Simi tugging at the ring pull. 'Do you guys realise, we've only got a week left of the game?'

'*Have we?*' said Meagan with blistering sarcasm.

'Come on, Meag. It's been good. I've learned loads and we've dated some really interesting men,' said Simi.

Meagan scoffed. Bruno, her snuffling suitor had been many things but interesting was not one of them.

'Thing is, now that we're coming to the end I think we need to up the stakes,' said Simi sipping her gin and tonic. 'The guys have been nice but this game is about new possibilities.'

'Good point. Maybe we should give it another week or two,' said Jemima, pushing and pulling her roller across the wall.

Meagan wiped her hands on a cloth and tossed it aside. She didn't need new possibilities. It was these two dolts that were all over the place. From across the office, Simi gave her most persuasive doe eyes and Meagan begrudgingly caved.

'Okay, Sim-Simma,' she sighed. 'What did you have in mind?'

'Really?! Right,' Simi said gesticulating with her paint-stirring chopstick. 'We've all *talked* about what the others need but I think it's time we *felt* it. Some real, from-the-soul truths.'

'I don't get it,' said Jemima.

'We did it in an acting class once. Meag, sit,' said Simi planting herself on the floor, cross-legged and beckoning Meagan to join her.

'Why am I going first?' Meagan squawked.

'Just because. Now sit down and close your eyes,' commanded Simi taking Meagan's hands in hers.

Meagan reluctantly sat, closing her eyes. In front of her, she could hear Simi take several deep breaths before letting out a low moan. Great, thought Meagan. Instead of finishing her office, she was now in some bizarre love séance.

'What are you doing?' whispered Jemima.

'I'm communing with her aura,' said Simi as she splayed her hands and began to rock.

'FYI, when you commune with mine, it might go to voice-mail. Just leave a message,' Jemima said.

Meagan smirked.

'Shush!' said Simi, rolling and rocking even more, her ban-shee moans making Meagan giddy.

Simi's voice seemed to be swirling around her, coming from all directions. Suddenly, Meagan felt Simi's movements stop.

'Well?' Meagan said opening her eyes.

Simi starred back, her face expressionless.

'You need a strong heart,' she said.

'Exactly. Don't want him conking out halfway through bumping uglies,' Meagan snorted going to stand.

'No, Meag,' said Simi pulling her back, 'You know what I mean, like a strong box, that can hold you.'

'Like a safe… ' ventured Jemima.

'Sounds like a prison,' Meagan said, this time making a con-certed effort to loosen herself from Simi's grasp.

She wobbled to her feet, steadying herself on her filing cabinet. Whatever Simi had done had made her feel – odd. And what was all this talk of hearts and safes. She already had safety – her plan. That's how she was taking ownership of her life so no one could let her down again. And no matter what the other two thought, the plan wasn't a response to Parker. It was about life, the world, how things were for a woman and what they had to do to protect themselves especially when you came from nothing. Meagan would never forget being placed on free lunches at school, wearing second-hand clothes and never being able to afford what her friends could. Far from being a burden, however, it was all fuel to her flame to ensure she was – and always would be – self-sufficient. All at once, Meagan became aware of the hush in the room.

Simi turned to Jemima. 'From now on, when we look for Meagan, that's what we have to find – a strong heart. Now, Meag, you do the same for Jemima.'

Meagan exhaled. 'With all that wailing and rocking? No way, Sim. Not today.'

Simi pushed Meagan down until she was sitting on the floor again and cautiously Jemima sat opposite her looking as though she were about to have an anaesthetic-free tooth extraction.

'Take Jemima's hands,' said Simi, sounding like a birthing coach.

'Simi, is there any sense in which this might be overkill?' said Meagan as she unceremoniously grabbed hold of Jemima.

'No.'

Meagan closed her eyes and huffed, taking a deep breath. Instantly her mind flooded with images of trees, acres and acres of them in a forest. She sprung her eyes open.

'Don't tell me,' said Jemima, her eyes still squeezed closed. 'I need a millionaire with his own publishing company.'

'Shush,' instructed Simi. 'Meagan, what did you see?'

'I don't think I'm doing it right,' said Meagan, uncertain. 'All I saw was a bunch of trees.'

Simi nodded sagely, 'That's what you said at the skating rink.'

'Yeah but I was joking.'

'What's going on?' Jemima asked, opening her eyes.

Meagan shook her head. The images in her mind had been so vivid, so clear. Just trees, rooted, still, strong in all weathers, immovable. Jemima looked at her.

'I dunno. Perhaps you need to meet someone from Forest Gate,' Meagan said, quickly standing.

Having someone, even one of her besties, seemingly able to peer into her soul or being able to peer into theirs had unnerved Meagan.

'More booze?' she said hoisting up the whisky bottle.

'It's Jemima's turn to do me,' said Simi as she positioned herself back on the floor.

'What exactly am I doing though?' Jemima asked as she took Simi's hands.

'Just ask the question and listen for the answer,' said Simi as she closed her eyes.

Meagan topped up her glass as Jemima took a deep breath and closed her eyes too.

'Four hundred years ago they'd have called this witchcraft and burned us at the stake,' Meagan scoffed uneasily.

Jemima's face creased in uncertainty. She opened her eyes and pulled her hands away.

'What is it?' Simi asked.

'All I kept getting was – a break,' said Jemima.

'You mean like a chance or opportunity?' said Simi. 'Do you want to take another look?'

'I probably wasn't doing it right,' said Jemima, hopping to her feet and stretching her legs.

'Do you think it meant a break from my old patterns? I'm confused,' said Simi.

'Look, I just did what you told me,' said Jemima, flustered.

Meagan had had enough. Everything was starting to feel way too serious.

'Come on, man. This is meant to be a painting *party* not Mad Nanny McFanny's Witchcraft Coven. If I'm gonna drag Simster here on her day off, we should enjoy it,' said Meagan raising her glass. 'And, Jem, aren't you glad of an afternoon away from the book?'

At Meagan's words, the pressure seemed to ease out of the room.

'To be honest, I'm so close to finishing, it's almost become fun again. The time flies by,' said Jemima.

'It's true,' Simi piped up. 'Sometimes I don't see her for hours. She's in her room just writing and writing and writing like she's plotting. Won't even let me read anything.'

'It's not… ready.'

Meagan watched as Jemima seemed to momentarily disappear inside herself. She knew writing could be pressured but her publishers really were making Jemima work for her money.

'Let's take a breather,' said Meagan wandering over to her window and looking down on the alley below.

Meagan loved her window and particularly her view of this quiet Soho alleyway where, after dark, people got up to all kinds of things their parents wouldn't approve of. Jemima leaned on a patch of unpainted wall next to Meagan, as Simi perched on the windowsill beside her.

'So, how *is* the book going?' Simi asked as they all watched the toing and froing below.

'Beverly's backstory is coming along,' said Jemima after some thought.

'Excellent,' said Simi.

One day, thought Meagan, she would definitely finish one of Jemima's books – but there was just *soooo* much insurance stuff and, furthermore, reading anything longer than a cocktail menu made her brain ache.

'Good for you, mate,' Meagan said.

'Actually, I have to say thanks to you guys,' Jemima continued. 'You've inspired my writing.'

'Wow,' said Simi, beaming.

'How so?' Meagan asked.

'I mean, you gave me ideas about who Beverly is… ' said Jemima.

'Well as long as you don't do a Troy on us,' said Meagan nudging her.

'Course,' said Jemima, draining her drink and going back to her painting.

'Jem's not like that,' said Simi as she trotted back to her roller tray.

Meagan bristled at the thought of Troy, remembering the time she'd been stupid enough to open up about her dad's bankruptcy, about the day the bailiffs had taken their things, moving through the house like locusts. She'd quipped that the only thing she'd been bothered about was her Xbox but they'd taken it anyway. And after sharing all that privately, Troy had stolen it, neatly weaving it into a new routine she performed the following evening. An Anderson Shelter couldn't protect Troy from Meagan's wrath when she had found out.

'But you know, sometimes you absorb information,' mumbled Jemima almost to herself.

'It's okay,' said Meagan, 'we'll just kill you and you can explain afterwards.'

'That's not funny!' said Simi, waving her roller at Meagan.

'Oh relax, Sim. I'm not gonna kill anyone – just horribly maim them.' Meagan winked.

Simi frowned at her, rubbing her rose quartz in Meagan's direction. Before she could respond, her mobile rang. Meagan pulled it from her overalls trying not to get paint fingerprints on it. She looked at the screen and withered. It was Todd. Again. She pocketed the phone, letting the call go through to voicemail but just as she picked up her brush, it started ringing again.

'Allow it, Todd!' she cursed.

This had to stop. What was wrong with him? No level of hotness could excuse this behaviour.

'Something happened?' Jemima asked.

'Yeah, I've got myself a stalker,' said Meagan.

Simi looked away and carried on painting. 'Maybe he just really likes you,' she offered.

And that was lovely, thought Meagan, but too much. What weirdo would call after receiving a photo of her out with another guy?

'It's getting on my wick,' she said dragging her brush back and forth over the wall.

'It's been four years. No wonder he's got attached,' said Jemima.

'Why? I haven't.'

'You and Todd have lasted longer than any of my relationships,' said Simi.

Meagan let her brush drop down, 'There is no "me and Todd". There's just me and then this whole other weirdo that won't quit.'

'Wouldn't it be funny if you ended up together, you know, like married,' said Simi.

Typical, Meagan simmered. In Simi's mind, life was all church bells and bouquets.

'Todd is NOT marriage material. He's not even boyfriend material. If there weren't laws about street sex, I wouldn't have even set foot in his flat. I'd be doing yoga poses with him in that alley,' said Meagan pointing out of the window.

'Downward dogging?' said Jemima.

Simi spluttered her drink as they all broke into laughter. Thank God, thought Meagan. This day had become way too fraught. It felt good to finally have something to laugh about. As a second wave of giggling struck, Meagan's office phone rang. Her laughter abruptly subsided. Todd was pushing his luck. She swiped the cordless phone out of its cradle.

'Listen, I don't care what you can do with your tongue, I want you to – Antonia. Hi!'

Meagan pushed the receiver into her chest and facepalmed before composing herself.

'Sorry, Antonia, no I said, *tongs* not tongue. I just sacked my hairdresser and he's taken it badly. Anyway, what can I do for you?'

Meagan listened, occasionally nodding as Jemima and Simi watched on.

'Okay, got it… I see. Right. Thanks,' she said before hanging up.

She turned to Simi, her face sombre.

'Are you doing that thing where you pretend it's bad news – but it's not,' Simi asked.

'I'm sorry, angel. They went another way,' said Meagan. 'They're idiots, obviously.'

'Obviously,' Jemima added rubbing Simi's back.

Simi nodded and returned to her wall, paint dripping down her arm from her roller.

'I don't understand,' said Meagan pacing, the dead receiver still in her hand. 'You played it exactly how I told you?'

'Yup,' said Simi still staring at the wall. 'They even put on a special filter. A blueberry or... gooseberry... '

Meagan stopped pacing, 'You mean a *strawberry* filter?'

'That's it.'

Meagan's head dropped. That was not good at all.

'What's a strawberry filter?' asked Jemima.

'It means,' said Meagan, 'they weren't recording. It's an old trick they use for street interviews. If someone's being weird, the director will ask the cameraman for a strawberry filter.'

'As in, *don't record them*?' asked Jemima.

Meagan nodded. 'What did you do, Sim?'

The room went quiet.

'I did what you told me to and that's why they thought I was bonkers! The second time round, Cameron didn't even want to read with me... in a chemistry read! Your notes were way off,' Simi blurted.

'Excuse me?' said Meagan.

'They're always off. The only reason I do them is because you took me on when no one else would and I'm grateful for that, but what's the point if it's making things worse? And now I'm stuck, like, if I don't do what you say, I'll get in trouble even if what you say is completely wrong,' said Simi quivering.

Meagan took a long breath. It would be unfair to unleash on Simi who was clearly high on paint fumes and not in her right mind. Simi looked at the floor.

'I mean, you could just do your own thing, Simi. It is your audition,' said Jemima.

Meagan threw a silencing glare across the room and Jemima went back to her painting.

'I want your input, Meag, I really do but just... read the scripts

– properly. Not everything is about comedy,' said Simi playing with the handle of her roller. 'Sometimes I wonder if your notes might be why I'm not getting anywhere.'

Meagan felt her lips tighten across her teeth.

'You know what kills me about actors. Nothing is *ever* good enough. And when everything is *juuust* right you don't want to audition because life's not quite working out. Well, boo hoo! That's how the world is, Simi. Shitty things happen but we crack on. I work eighteen hours a day, six days a week and all I hear is whining. Not *thanks Meagan, great job, Meagan*. I tell you what, comedians aren't perfect but they're a damn sight more grateful!'

Jemima upped the intensity of her painting.

'So, instead of telling me my notes lost you the job, how about a modicum of gratitude, a smidge, a drop, a wee dram!'

Simi blinked in shock before stepping out of her overalls, grabbing her rucksack and leaving. Jemima looked over at Meagan before putting down her roller and going after Simi.

'Oi!' Meagan hollered. 'You haven't finished your wall!'

CHAPTER 31

Simi

Simi glanced around Nostromo at all the creative types beavering away in various corners of the café. She could see why Jemima loved working here. It certainly made Simi feel better and anything that helped put Meagan's painting party behind her was more than welcome. Coffee orders placed, they took a seat by the window and waited for their drinks.

'I got it first thing,' said Simi, showing Jemima a text.

'"Sorry about Friday. Good luck at the audition. At least SS isn't in the running,"' read Jemima. 'Well, she apologised. That's a big step for Meagan.'

Jemima handed the phone back. Simi reread the message unconvinced and frankly, still smarting from Meagan's harsh words.

'If she's sorry, why did I get such a dressing down? She knows I'm grateful,' moaned Simi.

'Do you tell her?'

Simi's brow furrowed. She had assumed her appreciation was obvious but evidently not.

'Might be worth letting her know. Looking after actors isn't really her thing. She's doing her best,' said Jemima.

Simi's heart sank. It was true. Meagan was doing her a huge favour and in return, all she did was criticise her.

'So, who's SS? Is it this Sandra Scott woman?' Jemima asked.

Simi's mood darkened as she remembered that once again, Sandra 'bloody perfect' Scott with her flawless everything, had swooped in, nabbing the role of Dorothea.

'I'd do better in a flying competition with Superman than auditioning against her,' grumbled Simi.

Why did Sandra even go up for roles like Dorothea, Simi stewed. For her they were chicken feed but for Simi, they were a chance to take her career to another level or any level for that matter.

'Remember what Luke from our comedy class said. What's meant for you won't go by you. Plus, Antonia can't think you're all bad. She's invited you to audition for another role,' said Jemima.

'I guess,' Simi said, searching Jemima's face for reassurance.

'Hey, Jem, your coffees are ready!' called Azi.

'Come on, chin up.' Jemima smiled as they collected their drinks.

With their to-go cups in hand, the girls headed out. Simi kissed Jemima goodbye and watched her head back to her flat, probably to continue cooking up her secret literary masterpiece. Aside from when they were playing their dating game, it felt as though Simi saw Jemima less and less. Even though they were living under the same roof, she missed her and hated the sight of Jemima's almost-permanently closed bedroom door. Simi hoped she hadn't outstayed her welcome. Jemima had been so kind, letting her stay. The thought she was desperate to claw back some personal space made Simi shudder.

Well, whatever was going on, Simi prayed it was a lone cloud casting a brief shadow which would soon pass. Maybe once the book was delivered, they could hang out like they used to and this would all be forgotten. In the meantime, she had to focus on today's task – her audition with Antonia. She marched off towards the tube, determined and ready.

In less than an hour, Simi was sitting in Antonia De Silva's corridor of doom, staring up at the new *Clash of the Crown* poster mounted on the wall. She was back on the dreaded casting carousel but at least some things were different. Yes, there was the usual row of actors muttering lines and that one girl who always struck up distractingly loud conversation. All that was the same but what was different was that Sandra Flipping Fabulous wasn't in the running. It still stung that she'd got the Dorothea role but at least that gave everyone a fighting chance for the role of 'Cake', the part Simi was auditioning for that morning. Simi looked at her script page again. She loved creating characters – even though she'd only done it professionally a handful of times. Usually it was with dialogue like, 'You're fifteen centimetres dilated,' or 'Could you describe the person who assaulted you?' But with this one page of dialogue in her hand, she really wasn't sure what to do. And worse, the character Cake only uttered one word… cake. What was she supposed to do with that? At a loss, Simi opened Meagan's email and scrolled down. Just as she suspected, there they were. After the time, date and details for the audition – Meagan's notes.

Even after everything that had gone down on Friday, Meagan had still sent her 'thoughts'. Simi read and reread them, now steeped in uncertainty. No, Simi thought. This was why no one trusted her. She didn't trust herself, always defaulting to other people's opinions. She wasn't going to do Meagan's notes, she was going to figure this out by herself. She gasped, thrilled at her tiny act of rebellion. Simi looked up and down the corridor again. Either side of her, the other actors seemed to have made clear character choices, several arriving pretty much in costume. Simi looked down at her own clothes, jeans and a chunky knit sweater. What if the problem wasn't her interpretation? What if the problem was – her? Maybe, success would come if she were like someone more successful… like Sandra. If Antonia and so many other casting directors loved Sandra, that could be the path to a sure-fire win. She glanced down at her one page of dialogue wondering how Sandra would handle Cake, a simple girl who worked in the kitchens and loved… cake. Sandra would probably stride in with a big luxurious swish of her hair. Simi patted her afro which was far from swishable. She would need to try something else. She didn't have time to buy donuts but maybe she could slather on some quintessential Sandra Scott charm, a suitable sickly-sweet substitute for donuts if ever there was one. She would give toothy smiles and nauseating bonhomie to everyone in a fifty-yard radius. Why hadn't she thought of all this before? She would ignore Meagan's idea that Cake was a mole from a neighbouring kingdom *pretending* to be a simpleton. It *wasn't* funny and it didn't even make sense. Instead, Simi would just be *Sandra*, she decided, as the casting-room door opened and Gabe peered out.

'Tolu?' he said and an actress at the other end of the line followed him in.

'Good luck!' Simi beamed with an enthusiastic thumbs-up.

Tolu gave her a perplexed look before closing the door behind herself.

How *Sandra* was that? Simi smirked.

According to the signing-in sheet, Simi was next. She instinctively looked to her phone for Meagan's usual good-luck message but there was nothing. Simi really hoped their rift would soon pass because she was starting to miss Meagan too. What with one thing or another, things were getting out of kilter between all three of them and Simi didn't like it one bit. To take her mind of her friendship woes, she practised flashing a Sandra Scott grin. As she hit full-beam, Antonia's office door opened. Tolu came trotting out, thanking them profusely. Simi watched her pace down the corridor.

'All the best!' Simi whispered, waving crossed fingers at her.

Tolu sneered at Simi before disappearing through the double doors.

'Simi Oladipo,' an expressionless Gabe called as he poked his gaunt face into the corridor.

Go, go Sandra Mark II, Simi intoned as she swished her imaginary weave and sauntered into the casting room.

'So,' said Antonia clapping her hands on her thighs. 'Bit of a weird one, this.'

'I love weird!' Simi simpered as Antonia's smile hardened.

Wasn't she loving this second coming of Sandra? Not a problem, Simi decided, ramping things up by randomly throwing her head back and laughing at nothing.

'Are you okay, Simi?' Antonia asked.

Simi stopped laughing.

'Must be a sugar rush from the donut I had. I'll bring you some next time!' Simi cawed.

Antonia cleared her throat. 'Actually, I'm trying to get my cholesterol down. So, as I was saying, this role is a bit of a weird one. Obviously, she doesn't say much so I thought we'd improvise.'

Gabe glared at Simi who had broken out into a cold sweat. Every actor had a fib on their CV like ballet or long-swording and Simi's was improvisation. She couldn't improvise her way out of a supermarket car park.

'Great,' she lied, stealing a glance at Gabe who had a tiny smirk on his skinny face.

Simi was certain he knew. Gabe dragged the camera tripod back to give Simi more playing space – or room to hang herself. It was time to drop the Sandra imitation, Simi realised. Playing a role to get a role was not going to help. She could do this. Besides, how wrong could it go if all she had to say was 'Cake!'

'Don't look so worried. You don't just have to say "Cake". Let it go wherever it wants,' said Antonia as she limbered up with some gentle neck rolls.

Was this an improv session or a kick-boxing fight, Simi panicked. Whichever, she was going to get battered.

'Okay, imagine you're in the kitchen probably baking a cake,' said Antonia chortling at her joke.

Simi tried to smile back but it manifested as a wide sneer due to her mounting terror. This is ridiculous, she thought. This character is in one scene and says literally the same word over and over again. Why were they improvising?

'Ready?' said Antonia rolling up her sleeves.

'Cake!' said Simi before crumpling in embarrassment. 'I mean, cool!'

Simi braced herself. *Yes and*, is what they taught you in drama school, Simi remembered, quivering on the spot. Gabe started the camera rolling, the smirk spreading across his face like a contagion.

'What were you doing in her ladyship's latrine, Cake?' said Antonia regarding her with suspicion.

Simi's face contorted as the machinery in her brain shut down. Antonia may as well have been speaking Portuguese backwards.

'Cake,' Simi said eventually.

'I said, what were you doing in there, Cake? You're supposed to be making our lady's pudding.'

Simi could almost hear her brain call the emergency engineer only to be told they wouldn't arrive until Tuesday due to the bank holiday.

'Cake!'

'Okay, pause a second,' Antonia said to Gabe. 'So remember, you don't have to just say, "Cake".'

Gabe, who could barely contain his arch grin, hit record again.

'And *action!*'

'What are you doing in her ladyship's—'

'I'M A SPY!'

Simi dragged her swivel chair towards her desk, the insistent ringing phone a welcome distraction from thoughts of her Cake audition that morning. It had replayed in her head on a cringe-creating loop for the past hour.

'Good afternoon. Ahuja, Cohen and Cooper Surveyors, how may I direct your call?'

Simi punched numbers into her switchboard. She replaced her handset and went back to staring out of the window. Some actors called jobs like this survival jobs but for Simi, it was a lifeline, especially after *that* audition. Furthermore, she liked working at ACC. She had lovely bosses, they were generous with bonuses and the office was close to the shops. And this was all good because, given how her audition had gone, she would most likely be working here for the rest of her life. It wasn't so bad. In a decade or ten, she might get promoted to junior assistant office manager and earn enough to buy a boxy studio flat in zone sixty.

She thought back to a few hours earlier. After the 'spy' interlude, luckily she'd calmed down enough to offer up a passable improvisation. Then again anything was reasonable after trying to turn the character into a medieval, cake-loving 007. As Simi had backed out of the room with *thank-yous* that were really apologies, one thing had become abundantly clear; she didn't have what it took. Acting was too tough. She'd been to every type of class, pretending to be a giraffe, a man, a house mat and a baby, all in search of her inner self. She'd shelled out for accent classes, elocution lessons and Alexander Technique training, which just seemed to make her cry. And to cover all this, she'd borrowed hundreds, possibly thousands of pounds from Jemima. She had hoped one day to land a job with a big, fat cheque to pay it back. But there'd been no cheque. Just rejection heaped on rejection. And finally when she'd got into the room for a huge show, she'd blown it. Big style. So yes, this reception desk was as good a place to be, given acting wasn't where she was going to end up. As self-pity threatened to consume her, the main front door opened and Simi pulled herself up into a vaguely professional posture, pasting on her amiable receptionist smile.

'Good afternoon. How may I help?' she said as a young man approached her desk.

'Simi?' he said.

'Yes… ' she replied sitting even more upright.

'Todd,' Todd said resting a hand on his chest.

Simi gawped at his tailored navy suit, fitted shirt, strong hands, and chiselled features.

'What are you doing here?' she said suddenly tensing.

As lenient as her bosses were, one thing they never allowed were personal visitors. She looked down the corridor towards the partners' offices.

'And how did you find me?' she whispered, panicking about getting caught while simultaneously drinking in Todd's handsomeness.

Meagan had painted him as this hairy, human bindweed, slowly wrapping itself around her but the guy in front of Simi was like a luscious ivy, luxurious and strong.

'Meagan mentioned you. Said you worked at a surveyor's in the area and I… '

God, even his voice was like a sunset stroll in a glade, Simi fawned.

Down the corridor she heard Paul, the senior partner, locking up his office. Immediately, Simi snapped herself out of her Todd love-in. Once Paul had said his goodnights and grabbed his pre-commute cup of water he would pass through reception and he absolutely could not see Todd.

'Thing is, I'm not supposed—' Simi murmured.

'It's Meagan,' Todd interrupted. 'Well really, it's me. I think I might have to let her go but I can't shake the feeling she wants more but won't let herself. How do I convince her without becoming some kind of stalker?'

'That doesn't make you a stalker… does it?' Simi asked.

'Well, if they're not reciprocating… '

'Reciprocation is open to interpretation… ' Simi argued distracted by the glug, glug, glug of the water cooler at the end of the corridor.

Todd shrugged. 'All I know is, I've tried everything, including pretty much whatever she wants to do in the bedroom and had things done to me that—'

'Yeah, okay,' Simi said raising a hand.

Some things were best left between a girl and her fuck buddy.

'Four years we've been doing this and we had a good thing but lately, she's been acting weird. Ghosting me one minute. Texting me pictures of her on a date the next.'

'Okay. Idea!' blustered Simi as she heard Paul heading towards reception. 'Why don't we talk about it – over a drink, perhaps after *six*?'

'I mean, we make each other laugh, we have fun, the sex is… mind blowing.'

'And I bet that's not all that gets blown,' Simi blathered as Paul's footsteps advanced.

'I just miss my mate,' Todd said propping himself on Simi's glass-topped reception desk, 'and I know she misses me too, otherwise why the texts? What do you think she wants deep down? Is it to feel wanted, needed, safe? I can give her all that.'

Wait, safe? thought Simi. Isn't that what had come up at the painting party? She knew it. Todd *was* what Meagan needed!

'She doesn't know what she wants. You need to catch her unawares. Surprise her,' she gabbled.

As Todd was about to reply, Simi's boss rounded the corner.

'Look, *I've told you*, we have a franking machine!' Simi yapped in Todd's confused face.

Paul hovered for a second. He looked Todd up and down as though trying to sniff out any personal connection. Finally satisfied he nodded a good night to Simi and headed for the exit. Simi listened as the heavy door clicked shut then collapsed onto her desk.

'You okay?' asked Todd.

'Fine thanks,' she wheezed. 'Just resting my face.'

CHAPTER 32

Jemima

Jemima slipped the to-go cup from her morning coffee run with Simi into the recycling. In her heart, she had hoped Chance might have materialised at Nostromo but perhaps it was best he hadn't. What with the book and the game, life already felt like a tangled web without him and Simi crossing paths. And LA was yet another thread in Jemima's ball of confusion. She'd been playing email ping pong with Rebecca for several days, teasing herself with the prospect of a clean break. Though she hadn't made her final decision, it was feeling more and more real. The knots of Jemima's confused life were becoming tighter. The one good thing was, if LA was her only escape from the mess she'd created, it meant her conversations with Miles couldn't make things any worse.

By finally taking his call, her longing for a connection with *someone* had opened a door and Miles had amiably strolled right through. The first time they spoke, Jemima had let him carry the conversation, absolving herself of responsibility. She listened, remembering how much she liked his voice with its rogue northern vowels that occasionally pushed through his London accent. She shivered at what Meagan would say if she knew. Simi wouldn't be too chuffed either, which is probably why Jemima had retreated to her room, under the guise of work, to speak to him. However, now four days and several conversations later she was not only responsible but culpable even. She scrolled though her recent calls and dialled his number. This was new. She was calling *him*. 'Hey you,' she said.

Definitely culpable. Definitely wrong.

'Hey, gorgeous. How's tricks? So, I was passing Nostromo. Don't worry, I didn't go in,' he said, reassuring her. 'How long have they had those airplane seats?'

'A year? I like them – a lot,' Jemima replied.

'They look fun I suppose but you could get a whole table in that space. More cashola,' said Miles.

Jemima's ears pricked up as she heard Simi's key in the front door.

'Hiya, Jem!' Simi called from the hallway.

She was back from work. Was it that late already? Jemima looked at her closed bedroom door praying Simi wouldn't come in. 'Hey, Sim.'

'Fancy a glass of vino?'

Jemima hesitated. 'Maybe later.'

'Simi's living with you? Blimey, I thought she was all over the place when *we* were together,' said Miles.

Jemima glared at the phone willing herself to hang up. That's what she should do. Tell him, 'Good luck with everything,' which was British for *I have no intention of seeing how your life turns out*, and ending the call but she didn't.

'It's just temporary,' said Jemima.

'Sure, we'll see in a year's time. Anyway, I'm glad you called.

I wanted to ask, have you, perchance, got a plus one for Hudson Hicks's spring party?'

Jemima sank into her pillows with a hollow laugh. Miles was always hustling for something and this time it was to get his hands on *the* hot ticket in town. Though they were a relatively boutique publisher, one thing Hudson's did well was throw a party. Authors, agents, publicists and marketing people all wanted to be on the guest list and Miles was no exception.

'I always take the girls, Miles. To be honest, I'm surprised Eve even invited me this year,' Jemima murmured.

'Ah yes, I heard all about your saucy draft,' Miles laughed.

'What? How?' Jemima panicked, almost dropping the phone.

'Darling, you know what the lit biz is like. Everyone knows someone who knows someone who likes to chatter,' said Miles.

'Shaheena,' said Jemima through clenched teeth.

'Sounds like you rocked Eve's world though. If thrillers don't work out, you'll have an illustrious career in erotica,' Miles chortled.

'It was a political gesture,' said Jemima correcting him.

She held the phone away from her ear as his tinny laughter seeped through the speaker.

'You and your politics, sweetness,' said Miles. 'There's always something.'

Jemima's grip tightened around her phone. At least she had a stand point. She'd met 5-year-olds more politically engaged than Miles. The only parties he ever supported were the ones serving canapés.

'Shaheena shouldn't have told you about that,' said Jemima trying to rein in her annoyance.

'Shaheena couldn't keep a secret if it was by court order. Don't worry. Mum's the word. But I have to say, Jem-Jem, how come you weren't this naughty when we were together?'

Jemima looked at her open window wanting to hurl her phone through it. She wanted to tell him to piss right off using a maps app to get there but still she didn't. He was as annoying as junk flyers but as much as he got under her skin, he also made her feel… alive – another paradox that drove Jemima insane. Yes, he made her feel alive yet when they broke up two years earlier, something inside her had died. That night would always be fresh in her memory. She and Miles had been at the premiere of a film he had tenuous links with having sold the book rights to the production company. Halfway through the movie Jemima had felt a god-awful pain in her abdomen. When the pain became unbearable, she'd set social niceties aside and excuse-me'd her way out of the auditorium. Fifteen minutes later a flustered Miles arrived in the foyer trying to coax Jemima back inside.

The next thing she remembered was coming to inside an ambulance.

'Miles?' she'd asked the paramedic, a short, round Asian woman.

'About two miles. There was a bit of traffic because of that premiere,' she said.

Jemima's eyes darted around the ambulance.

'No, I mean my boyfriend, Miles. Where is he?'

'Oh he said he'd meet you at the hospital. Didn't realise he was your fella,' said the paramedic as she strapped a blood pressure band around Jemima's arm.

Jemima's eyes began to burn and before she could stop them, tears flowed. Lying on the thin ambulance mattress, her body was weak as though its vitality had leeched away. The love she'd had for Miles that held her up day to day was gone. And as the crack in her heart opened, she sobbed for all the time she'd given Miles, for the hope she'd had that he was, underneath it all, a decent guy. She sobbed for letting in someone so unworthy. She sobbed for the one who'd been too scared to love, who'd waited and waited, never opening up, who finally had, then made the choices that led her here, lying alone in an ambulance. She sobbed for the woman that had trusted Miles to love her. She sobbed because though whatever ailed her would heal, her shattered heart was something no surgeon could fix.

'Jem?' Miles said.

Jemima looked at her phone. She was back in her bedroom. 'Hmmm?'

'You were a million miles away. I said, what did Eve say about this filth draft?'

Jemima listened to the sound of her own breathing. She did feel alive but it was the alive you experienced standing on a dangerous precipice. Was Miles her certain death? Surely the constant threat of a fatal fall was no way to live? She deserved better but where was that better going to come from? Hopeless cynic Lance and his Christmas cracker jokes? Tim who probably thought she was a crackpot? Or Chance who was so, so far out of reach?

'Jem-Jem. You okay? Tap once for yes, twice for no,' Miles chuckled.

'I'm fine. It's fine. Eve appreciated the draft as a political manifesto so—' said Jemima bringing herself back into the room again.

'And then gave you a month to get her a proper draft or they'll drop you,' said Miles laughing.

Fucking Shaheena, Jemima seethed. She was unbelievable. What *else* had she told him?

Suddenly, Jemima's face went cold. What if Shaheena had told him about using the girls' stories? Jemima slapped her forehead as she recalled a recent conversation when, like an unadulterated imbecile, she told Shaheena how she'd finally managed to execute Eve's notes.

'What else did Shaheena tell you?' Jemima asked.

'Not much. Just that your deadline is a week away,' said Miles.

Jemima sighed with relief. Perhaps, for once Shaheena had exhibited a modicum of discretion.

'And that you nicked stories from Meagan and Simi's lives.' Jemina deflated like a three-day-old balloon. Great.

'Fear not, Jem-Jem. Your secret's safe with me and at least you found a solution. Ten out of ten for innovation.'

'Yeah and it'll only cost me two best friends,' she said cradling her head in her hand.

'They'll get over it. The main thing is Eve is happy, yes?'

'Almost. Now I've created this complicated past, she wants one final, dark secret to tie it together.'

'No sweat. One of those girls is bound to have something depraved lurking in their pasts.'

Jemima grimaced at his judgement but then wavered as once again, Simi's stalker story barged its way to the forefront of her mind. It was ideal and would give Eve exactly what she wanted. It was dark, had edge and motivated so much of Beverly's new backstory but it was also a step too far.

'That sounds fantastic!' Miles whispered in awe before Jemima had even finished explaining.

She began to feel woozy. He was right. It was fantastic in an awful but perfect way. But if she went for it, she would be done. Yes, the book would be finished but so would her friendships.

'They will hate me for this. Chance, a friend of mine, said it's too harsh.'

'Blimey, you showed an unfinished manuscript to someone? They must be special. What have you done with the real Jemima Abeson?' snorted Miles. 'My dear, if you've written Beverly as an interfering know-it-all or hopeless love puppy who dates duds and the girls recognise themselves in that, that's a good thing. Sometimes honesty is necessary.'

Jemima repositioned herself on her bed, drinking in Miles's words. That was what Chance had said but coming from Miles, the words felt less like sage advice and more like scheming justifications.

'Even if that were true, who am I to put their past in print?'

'Jem-Jem, what kind of friend would Simi be if she *didn't* donate that story to you? Think about how you've supported *her* career over the years. The money, the time learning lines. For Christ's sake, you've given her a place to live, rent-free… She owes you.'

Jemima rubbed her temples. Miles truly was a master of spin.

'I've got to go,' said Jemima, hanging up before Miles could respond.

She fired up her laptop and began typing, her breath heavy as words poured onto the page.

CHAPTER 33

Meagan

Meagan took a bracing gulp of her afternoon coffee and looked around her freshly painted but still unfurnished office. If it weren't for the girls she wouldn't have got this far and so for that, she was thankful. However, for the ongoing headache Simi was giving her, she was not. She checked her emails then texts. Not a dicky bird from Simi since her Cake audition that morning. That's gratitude for you, Meagan sighed. She perched herself on the filing cabinet she'd borrowed from the PR company up the hall, her coffee mug precariously balanced on a pile of actors' headshots. Every week forty more arrived in the post from thespian hopefuls. They weren't to know Meagan already had her dream team, twenty-three comics – and one actress, their headshots mounted on her new headshot wall. Her eyes drifted to Simi's photo, a black-and-white portrait that was damn near faultless, even if Meagan did say so herself. She'd directed the photo shoot and yes, her first impulse had been to do what she does with her comedians and have Simi mug for the camera in a charming, post-watershed, yet approachable way. However, in the end, Simi had educated her on what was actually required of an actor's headshot and the end results were stunning. They captured Simi's kindness and vulnerability but also her underlying tenacity. Meagan studied the photo as a realisation dawned. If Simi hadn't intervened, this image of her would never have existed. Casting directors would never have seen her true essence and that would have been because of Meagan. She suddenly felt a heaviness. Did she really know what she was doing when it came to managing Simi? Acting was a whole new ball game and one she was in danger of messing up with all her interfering. She paused mid-sip of her coffee as a sobering thought coalesced. Was the reason she didn't need to intervene with her comedians because they were doing well or were they doing well *because* she wasn't interfering? The very notion made her nauseous.

Meagan studied Simi's photo. The girl looking back at her rarely stood her ground but the Simi from the other day had. All at once, Meagan could see what a fighter Simi truly was – the epitome of the old saying, fall down seven times, get up eight. Meagan blew a kiss at the photo imagining Simi pretending to clutch it to her heart as she always did. But if Simi was so strong, why *did* Meagan interfere? Rather than helping her friend's career take off, she was keeping her grounded. And by default, weren't Simi's career failings stopping Meagan's own life moving on? Her plan criteria had always been clear, *all* her clients needed to be working before she could move onto the next stage, a relationship. As Meagan rubbed her sweating palms together, she couldn't help wonder, were Simi's apparent failings getting in the way of her plan or was she using her plan to get in the way of Simi? Her mind swirled at the very thought. Now that the next phase of her plan was possible, in fact, according to her schedule, imminent, Meagan realised – she was terrified. The elevator at the end of the corridor shushed open, yanking Meagan from her ruminations. She shook the thoughts away and went back to clearing floor space for her new furniture.

'Knock, knock,' said a voice.

Meagan almost choked at the sight of Todd standing in her doorway.

'Todd? What. The. Actual. Fuck?' she growled.

'Slow your roll. I've got you a surprise,' said Todd, holding up his hands in placating defence.

'And I've got a surprise for you,' Meagan murmured as her hand balled into a fist.

'Just hear me out,' he said as he took a silver envelope from inside his suit jacket.

Meagan's eyes narrowed, 'And that is?'

'Glad you asked,' said Todd, a smile breaking. 'So I thought, you've been working hard. How's about a spa day at the Worthington followed by a gourmet dinner *aaaaand* a night in one of their luxury suites… '

Trying to ignore his newly grown-out hair which made him even more handsome, Meagan looked at him in utter bewilderment. Despite sending him a photo of her on a date then ignoring his calls, here he was. This had to stop.

'Take a seat, Todd,' she snarled.

He looked around the empty room before sitting on the corner of the filing cabinet.

'You look nice. Have you changed your hair?' he asked.

Meagan kissed her teeth. 'We need to talk.'

'You've put some tracks in or added some highlights?'

'Todd!' she barked.

'Okay, alright. I just wanted to surprise you. I thought go big or go home but it backfired royally… ' Todd said as he ventured towards Meagan.

She held up a hand stopping him.

'Yes, mate. Royally. If you had a kingdom it would be called Fuck-up-shire.'

Todd laughed.

'It's not funny.'

'Sorry,' he said, trying not to grin, edging towards her. 'Look, someone put a stupid idea in my head and it tanked. Point is, we've been at this for four years but we're still in the same place.'

Meagan lodged her hands on her hips. 'Did I say we were going anywhere though?'

'No, but you didn't say we weren't,' said Todd taking Meagan's hand in his.

Her temples began to throb. Why didn't he understand, regardless of how phase three of her plan was looming, he wasn't going to muscle his way in with his soft hands and gorgeous face. Todd lightly pulled Meagan towards him, his eyes locked onto hers.

Meagan pulsated, as she peered back at him, the fight in her faltering. She loved looking up at tall men, craning to kiss them, leaning on them – but now was not the time for craning, leaning or kissing. She tried to pull away. He needed a nice girl to settle down with. Someone like Simi. Perhaps Meagan would re-gift him, solving all their problems. Granted he was a bit too young for Simi and she was a bit too actory for him but other than that they were a great fit. Why hadn't she thought of it before?

'Meag, I know you think it's just physical…' said Todd sliding his other hand around her waist.

As Meagan leaned back into his grasp she felt her lust shift up a gear. With her free hand she hitched up her mini skirt and entwined a leg around his calf.

'No, Meag,' he said easing her leg back down. 'I want more than just that.'

Meagan stared at him, stupefied. This was the longest they'd talked without winding up in bed, on a sofa, her desk, his desk or his kitchen worktop and this is what he had to say?

'You think sex with me is a *just*?' she said pulling away. 'Fam, you're getting the best of me.'

'Why don't we find out? It's your birthday next week. I'm going to take you on a date. Something simple like bowling?'

Meagan threw her head back with a sour laugh. 'Bowling? Birthdays, *dates*. My friend, if you *reeeaally* knew me, you'd know Meagan don't do birthdays – and *bowling*?'

'Whatever, Meag. Let's just see. If you hate it, if we both hate it, I'll walk away. End of. I'm serious. Don't throw out something you know we both want.'

Meagan stepped back. She looked into his brown eyes, noticing laughter lines she'd never seen before, a small spot of vitiligo under his chin and an old scar on his neck that told its own story. She sighed, gently kissing him on the cheek.

Meagan pulled the duvet up to her waist as the warm wave of her third orgasm washed over her. She had learned early on how to wring the maximum gratification from her sexual encounters.

And while Jemima loved watching old French cinema and Simi loved to cook, Meagan's hobby was teaching lovers to bring her pleasure. Training session over, she relaxed into the soft pillows and smiled to herself, the hint of that delicious cologne brushing past her nose. This was the perfect full stop to her exchange with Todd that afternoon, she concluded as a hairless arm flopped onto her hips. She looked down at it, momentarily surprised by its unfamiliarity.

'*Hmmf,*' sniffed Bruno. 'I didn't expect to hear from you, naughty Meagan but I'm glad I did.'

Meagan tensed at the sound of Bruno's snort. Now that Todd was officially catching feelings with his talk of birthday dates and bowling, it was time to get herself a new trainee lover. For a first attempt, Bruno had done well though Meagan had been taken aback by how, at the point of orgasm he'd strained, 'Thank *youuuu.*' Also, if she were honest, Bruno wasn't as gentle as Todd who was much more patient. Her pleasure *was* his pleasure – a rarity, Meagan had to concede, and one she would miss. She also wasn't a fan of Bruno nodding off immediately after thanking her. Oh well, he would learn eventually she reassured herself. And at least she wouldn't have to listen to him wittering on like Todd always did, asking her a million questions about herself.

Bruno stirred, flopping his head towards Meagan.

'So, listen, sweet lady,' he said, eyes still closed. 'I must put you out. I have a 5.30 a.m. flight.'

Meagan's eyes widened. Put me out? *Put me out..?* she gawped. Like a cat… ? Like Dino at the end of *The Flintstones*? No one had ever 'put Meagan out' in her life. If anything, she was the one who did the putting out. Was something being lost in translation? she fumed, glaring at his dozing face. Well, maybe, I'll put you out, make you orgasm so hard your eyes will be on stalks. Sniff *that*, blondie. She began massaging his smooth chest. Where was all this man's hair? she puzzled as her hand banked southwards. He stopped her, gently but firmly putting her hand back on her own tummy.

'*Hmmf*. I only cum one time each night. I'm conserving my chi, you know,' he said as he set the alarm on his phone.

Meagan watched, baffled and infuriated. She threw back the duvet and paced the room gathering up her clothes, almost stumbling as she slipped on her skirt. This was not okay, she seethed hopping towards the door trying to slide on her stiletto at the same time.

'Right. Well, bye,' she said lingering.

'Sure, Hmmf. The white button in the hall – this is the door release,' said Bruno as he turned out his bedside lamp. 'Call me, sweet Meagan. We do this again.'

Meagan stood in the dark, stunned. Finally, she turned to leave, thumping into the bedroom door.

'*Fuuuuuck*,' she hissed.

In the corridor, she drilled at the elevator button as it made its laborious ascent to the penthouse. Tap, tap, tap, tap, tap, tap, tap, tap. TAP, TAP, TAP, TAP!

Eventually the doors opened and she stepped inside. Only once out in the street did she exhale, letting out a bitter laugh. Tears welled as she bent double trying to catch her breath. Between the laughter, the anger and the crying, she wanted to scream in Bruno's face, how *dare* you? Do you know how much other men want this? Do you know how much *Todd* wants this? But she couldn't say any of that because he had put her out – like the bins. She wiped her eyes with the cuff of her coat. It was his loss and tomorrow on his 5.30 flight to Düsseldorf, he would realise that.

Meagan exhaled again, her breath a white column against the black sky.

'FUCKING MEN!' she screeched before pounding off down the street.

CHAPTER 34

Simi

'This is nice,' said Simi blowing her freshly painted nails. 'Been ages since we've chilled.'

'Hmm, mmm.' Jemima nodded as she tapped out a text message trying not to smudge her manicure.

'And what with my audition this week and you with the book, the dating game… and all your phone calls, it'll be great to let our hair down at the Hudson Hicks party tomorrow,' Simi continued as Jemima chuckled at an incoming message.

'Totally,' said Jemima, finally turning her attention to Simi. 'I know I haven't been around much.'

'That's okay. You're busy. It's just lovely to have my advice guru back coz I need to talk to you about something,' said Simi cautiously.

'Funny. There's something I need to ask you too,' said Jemima but before she could say more her vibrating phone cut into the moment like a hot knife through butter.

'Sorry, Sim, I've gotta take this,' Jemima said, scooping up her phone and padding through to her bedroom, laughing with whoever was on the other end.

Simi strained to listen. If she didn't know better, she would swear Jemima was flirting. But with who? Simi blew on her nails again. Jemima wasn't the devious type but things were definitely different of late. Maybe it was just the book though that didn't explain the mysterious phone calls. Twice, Jemima had seen her phone ring and closed her bedroom door to take the call. Was Jemima dating one of the men from the game? Simi glared at her closed bedroom door just as Jemima traipsed back into the living room, plopping herself onto the sofa.

'Fancy a movie?' Jemima said clicking on the TV.

'Mmm,' said Simi, noticing a tiny smile on Jemima's face. 'Who was that?'

'Publicist. Boring strategy stuff for the book launch,' said Jemima, scrolling through her Webflix account.

'Working on a Saturday – dedicated,' Simi probed.

'Well, you know – Ooooh, *Fatal Attraction*. I haven't seen that in ages.'

Simi looked at Jemima who was giving nothing away. Perhaps that was because there was nothing to give away. Maybe Jemima *had* just spoken with her publicist and, knowing how boring Simi found all that stuff, was simply sparing her the dull details.

'Obsession is so interesting, don't you think?' said Jemima, eyes still on the screen. 'I mean… Meagan told me about Terry, at college… '

For the first time since she'd sat back down, Jemima looked at Simi. 'Did you know that what you were doing was… '

Simi watched Jemima hesitate, searching for the least hurtful word.

'Weird?' offered Simi.

'That's not what I meant.'

Simi sighed. Her pursuit of Terry had been a low point and, with the benefit of nearly two decades of hindsight, pretty bloody humiliating.

'I wasn't weird. I was desperate. Jem, I know this dating thing just looks like fun but in these few weeks I've discovered a lot – deep things, like stuff about my dad. When he left, it triggered something. I've spent my whole life searching for his love. Thing is, I've been looking in completely the wrong places, ready to fall at any opportunity. That's desperation.'

Simi was almost giddy from saying what she'd felt so deeply but had never before articulated.

'After I slept with Mo, I finally got what Meagan has been talking about – the boundaries, how people treat you, men, the hunt – all of it,' Simi said.

'Did Mo say something?'

'Kind of. Early on, he said he loved dating and it's only just clicked. I thought that meant he would love to date me, so I slept with him but he literally meant he loves going on dates – with different people.'

'Then he's a scallywag, Sim. That's not your fault,' interjected Jemima.

'Yes, it is. He told the truth it's just I wanted him to want me so badly, I didn't listen, not properly. Just like with Terry and then Oscar, I heard and saw what I wanted. You see, desperate,' said Simi.

The women looked at each other. This was huge for Simi.

'Jem,' she said at last.

'Yeah,' said Jemima, leaning forward, concerned.

'I think we need to open this now.'

Simi grabbed an unopened bottle of red from the coffee table.

Jemima laughed, holding up two empty glasses. 'You read my mind.'

Simi popped the cork and poured the wine while Jemima shook popcorn into a bowl.

'My dad left when I was 7. I'm 35. So, when you ask, did I know if my behaviour with Terry was strange, no, I didn't. I was just looking in the wrong place for what I'd lost a long time ago,' said Simi taking a big sip of wine.

Finally, she could see that her entire relationship profile, her outlook on love, her longing for a man had all been shaped by the absence of just one.

'Babe,' said Jemima kissing Simi on the cheek, 'you're amazing and I bet you'll find someone great who deserves you.'

'I wish for it every day,' said Simi.

'Then it will happen,' said Jemima offering up her glass. 'And it'll happen because you're ready – not because you think you need it.'

'Cheers,' said Simi tapping her glass against Jemima's, 'but maybe I should have a time-out from boys? Remember what came up when we read each other's auras. You said it yourself – a break.'

'I suppose,' said Jemima. 'Look, darling, whatever you need, I'm on board.'

'Thanks, lovely,' Simi said, resting her head on Jemima's shoulder. 'What's your wish?'

Right away, Simi could feel Jemima squirm.

'I…'

'You know I mean about love, right?' said Simi, playful but firm.

She wasn't going to allow Jemima to side-step the question as she normally did.

'I know.' Jemima nodded.

Simi searched her face for a clue. Clearly she was wrestling with something. 'Just say it. I promise, I won't tell.'

Jemima caught Simi's gaze and straight away, Simi felt the weight of Jemima's sadness.

'I want someone who makes me want to keep my feet on the ground,' Jemima said.

'I knew it!' Simi whispered. 'You will meet that person. I promise you.'

The girls hugged, Simi aware of just how tightly Jemima was holding her. She kissed her forehead, willing that special someone to find Jemima and bring her back down to earth.

'You're an amazing friend, Simi,' said Jemima, 'and you're an amazing person.'

'Oh, Jem, you are too.'

'I don't know about that,' murmured Jemima loosening her hold.

'Are you mad? There is literally not a bad bone in your body. I can't even imagine you doing something horrid and even if you did, I'd forgive you for *anything*.' Simi beamed.

Jemima nibbled on a piece of popcorn. 'Bless you.'

'So, while we're having a Saturday confessional, what did you need to ask me?' said Simi.

'It was nothing,' Jemima said shaking popcorn crumbs from her lap. 'But what can I do for *you*, Ms Oladipo?'

Simi's smile waned as she searched for where to begin.

'Okay, here's the thing… I'm thinking of getting a new agent,' she blurted as though a hasty delivery would deaden the impact.

'What?' exclaimed Jemima.

'Shhhhh. I'm just thinking about it. I haven't done anything.'

But Simi knew that wasn't true. Just that morning, with the trepidation of a teenager looking for porn on their parent's computer, Simi had googled, *London acting agents*. She needed someone who was used to the plodding and rather traditional reality of managing actors. Meagan was all about the fast-moving world of comedy and it just wasn't working. This temporary favour was becoming a long-term headache for both of them.

'What do you think?' Simi asked, desperate as always for higher wisdom.

Jemima blew out her cheeks. 'Sim, this is a big deal. Can you talk to her?'

'*Hello?* Did you see what happened at her painting party?' Simi replied spreading her hands in frustration.

'Fair play.'

'I drafted an introduction letter. Would you take a look?' Simi said handing her hefty old laptop to Jemima.

'You said you hadn't done anything!'

'It's just a letter,' said Simi, avoiding Jemima's gaze.

She reached for a notepad, poised to jot down any and all pearls of wisdom imparted.

'I didn't know whether to make it corporate and serious, you know, talk about growth quarter on quarter? Or funny. I was going to put confetti in the envelope so that when they opened it—' said Simi.

'Picture Meagan getting an introduction letter with confetti inside.'

Simi nodded, crossing confetti off her shopping list as the reality of what she was doing struck her. How would she explain to Meagan she no longer wanted to be her client? And what would happen to their friendship? Would they even have one after that bombshell?

'The letter's fine but the real question is, are you ready for what may come if you send it out. Agents talk and Meagan may find out before you're ready to tell her.'

Simi stared at her letter.

'You never know, she might be happy about it,' Simi said, reaching. 'We've talked about keeping work and friendship separate for ages so in a way I'm helping. Plus, it would mean she could move on with her life plan.'

'If that's what she really wants.' Jemima tutted, tapping at the TV remote.

'How do you mean?'

'It just seems an unfair pressure on you that you have to be working before *she* can move on. She made up the rules for this plan. She could break them,' said Jemima as she scrolled through the TV menu.

'But, Jem, if you keep changing the rules that's not a plan. That's just – life!'

'Well, life always gives helpful nudges. Maybe you should move on so there's nothing standing in the way for either of you,' said Jemima at last selecting *Scandal* on the Webflix menu.

'I suppose… ' said Simi, clouded in even more uncertainty.

Was it possible Meagan was using Simi to scupper her own life plans or was it the other way around? Out of her own deep insecurities, was Simi sticking with Meagan to hold herself back? Was Meagan *her* crutch?

CHAPTER 35

Jemima

All day, Jemima had had a growing sense of doom. That afternoon, with one click, she'd sent the finished draft of *Beverly Blake Discoveries* to Eve. Yes, she'd put an end to the saga she'd been living in for months but in doing so, had put something much bigger in motion. In the end, she'd used more stories than she had intended. By including the stalking details, she'd needed to balance things out so had borrowed even more from Meagan. In the days before sending the draft, she'd felt like she was going crazy. One minute she'd be certain her actions were terminal and only fixable with a one way ticket to LA. The next, she'd laugh at the fuss she was making, reassuring herself the girls would be fine. But whatever the outcome, one thing was true. The deed was done and Jemima felt no jubilation – just dread.

Right now, copy-editors were notating, marketing people were brainstorming cover designs and Jemima was sitting on a ticking timebomb she had failed to stop countless times. Now she had no choice. She *had* to tell the girls. Obviously not tonight though as they were heading to the Hudson Hicks party. Somehow, Jemima had to slap a smile on and get through it. She exhaled wishing she could uninvite Simi and Meagan – just this once. But that wasn't possible. They'd been her guests every year since she'd signed with Hudson Hicks. It wasn't just a highlight in her calendar anymore. Simi picked her outfit three months in advance.

Jemima eyed herself in the mirror as she slipped on her cream blazer. From the living room she could hear Simi getting ready. She popped in an earring. Tonight was the first time Simi and Meagan had seen each other since their fallout and that was another reason why it was not the night to drop more manure over everything. After the painting party, Meagan had disappeared into a spiral of work, the game had fallen away into the background and it felt like their lives were moving onto diverging paths. Jemima hoped Simi and Meagan would put their issues behind them but with Simi now seeking a new agent, how long would that last even if they did?

Jemima put in her other earring and as she looked at her reflection, she became aware of how tense her body was. Her shoulders were rigid and her jaw tight. She shook a little, trying to loosen up but an unease remained in her stomach. That afternoon, she'd frantically briefed Shaheena to keep quiet about the book or better yet, avoid the girls altogether at the party, but a free bar and loose lips were a terrible combination. There was nothing Jemima could do but hope. She stared at her closed door realising she was stalling. In here she was safe but out there was her proverbial dead body by the fire escape – there was Simi and Meagan, Miles, the dating game, Hudson Hicks, her book, everything. She sighed gloomily knowing that, with one email to Rebecca saying 'yes' it could all go away and yet she still hadn't been able to do it and there were only two reasons why – Simi and Meagan. Life without them didn't feel like any kind of life at all. Jemima took a moment then finally went through to the lounge. There, Simi was made-up, dressed-up and ready to go. She looked stunning, regal almost.

'Ready?' Simi beamed.

'Ready.' Jemima nodded taking another breath to still the turmoil within.

Jemima walked down the long, pink, corrugated tunnel into the venue, eyeing her surroundings.

'The decor is always so brilliant,' yelped Simi as they followed the other guests inside.

'Drink, madam?' said a waiter, thrusting Bloody Marys in their hands and ushering them towards the main room.

Simi gawped at the elaborate design. 'This must have cost a fortune!'

Jemima nodded as she peered around her. She'd been to this venue before, a Grade II listed music hall. But tonight, its shabby Aldgate chic and peeling walls were hidden behind sheer pink drapes in all directions. Jemima noted the elongated cerise and red lilies between each drape and the tiny cherubs peeping through. Every year, the party was themed as a cryptic homage to one of their authors but Jemima was at a loss as to who this one could be.

'Please tell me you're this year's author?' Simi asked, taking another drink from a passing tray.

'It's definitely not me,' Jemima scoffed, doubting she'd ever be that in favour with Hudson Hicks.

'Next year, *one hundred per cent*,' said Simi inspecting a tray of canapes. 'Yikes. Mini fish and chips!'

Jemima studied the drapes and flowers again. Now she was curious. What was the theme? After a moment, she scanned the room. Meagan had said she was coming straight from work but Jemima still hadn't spotted her.

'Have you spoken to Meagan?' she asked Simi.

Simi shook her head, her mood clouding.

'Are you going to?'

Simi shrugged.

'Simi? She'll be here any minute and I have to go and press the flesh,' Jemima said.

'Fine. I'll speak to her – for you,' conceded Simi.

'No, Simi. Speak to her for you. Look, Meagan elbows, knees and barges her way in to every situation regardless of whether she's needed or not but she's not doing it to hurt anyone. It's how she shows her love.'

'But it's ruining my life!' wailed Simi.

'Says the woman who's about to fire her.'

'Oh, yeah.'

'If you want that to go well, make nice now. Find her. Say sorry,' said Jemima shoving Simi off. 'I have to mingle.'

Simi plonked her glass down.

'Fine – Oh mini pizzas. Cute!' she said as she moved off into the crowd.

Jemima watched her leave. Simi and Meagan had fallen out before but always made it back. She just hoped Meagan could make room for this new Simi who spoke up for herself. While Simi circled with her olive branch, Jemima steeled herself for the task ahead. She hated the grubby business of networking but Shaheena had insisted. She swiped a glass of prosecco from a drinks waiter and began her tour of duty.

An hour later and Jemima was networked-out having spoken with everyone Shaheena had instructed her to. However, now that business was over, she wanted to find Simi and Meagan who had hopefully buried the hatchet. And more importantly, she wanted to spend time together as a trio. They hadn't done that in over a week. She wanted to enjoy this time, a time when they didn't know about the book, where it was just them being mates, how things used to be.

'Watch out, hot coffee,' said a voice behind her.

Jemima froze. She knew it was Chance.

'Hey!' He beamed giving her a hug.

Tensing, she hugged him back.

'What are you doing here?' she said, anxiety radiating from her like solar flares.

This was more worlds colliding than she could handle.

'I'm with Pete,' said Chance. 'Wait, are Hudson Hicks your publishers?'

Jemima gave serious thought to lying.

'Yes.' She confessed.

'Wow. How come you never said?'

'Well, you know, Pete's all the way over there in autobiographies and I'm here in female-led insurance-based thrillers for the 25 to 45-year-old demographic – different worlds,' Jemima gabbled with a nervous chuckle.

Chance grinned.

'You're hilarious. Wait 'til I tell Pete. He'll be stoked,' he said pointing over to a pink Black Jack table in the corner.

Jemima spotted Lula first, then Pete's walking stick, and then Pete. Even from across the room she could see the family resemblance. Though Pete was stockier than Chance, he had the same Mediterranean complexion and of course that same killer smile. Just then Pete threw his arms up in celebration, folding them around Lula. He'd clearly won at the table and even though they were only playing for tokens, from his smile you would have thought he'd won the lottery. Even unadulterated delight ran in their family.

Chance turned back to Jemima.

So, listen I feel like I'm always apologising but I am genuinely sorry about the other night. I spoke out of turn,' he said.

'It's fine. Really.'

'It's not. Who am I to tell you about your friends or your book? Am I forgiven?' Chance said placing his hand on his heart with a boyish grin.

Jemima leaned in. 'It's finished.'

An enormous smile spread across his face. Jemima thought she'd seen it at full beam before, but this was dazzling.

'That's fantastic!' he said taking her by her shoulders.

He kissed her on the cheek and she blushed.

'Anyway,' she flustered, 'I'm sure I'll get a tonne of notes.'

'But you've done what ninety-nine point nine nine per cent of people can't. You finished.'

Jemima felt herself blush again. It was true. Finishing the book had taken its toll but the one thing she could say for sure was that it existed. She'd done it. She placed her hand on his arm. As they talked, she let it slip down until eventually she could feel the warmth of his hand near hers. Their eyes met and Jemima became breathless. How was it that just the gentlest of touches, the briefest of looks could make her feel like this? Pleasure and pain once again. Did Chance feel the same, weak yet strong, excited and scared? But then she remembered the red-haired woman. The flushed feeling subsided and she put her hand back by her side.

'Jemima? You okay?' said Chance.

'No – no, no, no, no,' she hissed as she glared over his shoulder to an ice sculpture luge at the back of the hall. There, a reunited Simi and Meagan were slamming vodka shots – with Shaheena.

Jemima's heart pounded. Chance evaporated from her thoughts as she watched them like an unexploded firework. Just then Shaheena and Meagan gasped, pointing over at Jemima. Her knees buckled.

'Anyway, Chance, lovely to see you,' she prattled as Meagan advanced.

Jemima scurried over to meet her in the middle of the room.

'Everything okay?' Jemima asked, voice quivering.

'Who was that?' said Meagan.

'Who?' said Jemima doing a terrible job of pretending.

'The hottie you were just chatting with,' said Meagan turning Jemima's face towards Chance.

Jemima shook her head free. 'He's the, a… he's the medic. In case of emergencies. Soooo, what have you and Shaheena been talking about?' Jemima asked feigning ease.

'Jeeez,' said Meagan rolling her eyes, 'she was carping on about your writing process. No offence. I'll eat the sausage but don't show me how it's made, d'ya get me?'

Jemima's shoulders dropped two inches.

'You look stressed as fuck, mate. Your agent's gone. Come get a shot from that sculpture thing. And quick before Simi drinks straight from it and gets her lips stuck to the ice,' said Meagan dragging Jemima back to the luge.

Once there, Jemima thrust a glass under the sculpture and the bartender threw a shot of vodka down its icy shoot. She closed her eyes as the liquid burned coldly in her throat.

'Better?' said Meagan.

Jemima popped her eyes open. The girls were staring at her.

'Yeah,' she said, remembering to smile. 'More importantly, how are you two? Everything cool?'

'Cool and the gang, baby,' Meagan said linking arms with Simi.

'Sim?' asked Jemima.

'Brill!' Simi said grinning hard.

Jemima scrutinised her face. Something was off. Though they'd got their friendship back on track, it was evident Simi was still going ahead with Operation: New Agent and Meagan didn't know. Jemima tensed. That had a blast radius she would stay well clear of.

'I was thinking,' said Simi surveying the party guests, 'there are loads of quality guys. Like-minded, successful and hopefully single. We haven't played the game for ages. Let's do it here!'

Jemima's breath caught. 'But you said you wanted to take a break from guys,' she stammered.

'I can't keep up with you, Sim.' Meagan laughed.

'After tonight, Jem, definitely,' said Simi, her attention on the men in the room.

'But it's a works do,' Jemima pleaded.

Just then, the music ramped up several decibels, the lights

dipped and a huge neon sign saying 'DISCO', began to flash above a black-and-white dance floor.

'Not anymore it's not,' said Meagan as she teased Jemima with a *Saturday Night Fever* pose.

'Come on!' said Simi tottering off in search of prey, with Meagan trailing behind.

Jemima's feet felt nailed to the floor. Now the book was finished the pressing matter for her was not the game but confessing her actions.

'Come on, Jeminator. If there's one place we'll find someone who matches you, it's in a hall chocker with book dorks,' prodded Meagan.

'Yeah, plus we've got new intel now about what we *feel* you need,' said Simi.

Jemima still couldn't move.

'I can sense it, Jem,' Simi whispered. 'The one that will make you stand still, is here.'

Simi grinned before shimmying towards the dance floor.

'Chill, Jem. It's a party!' Meagan winked as she followed Simi, grabbing Jemima to complete their train.

Perhaps this was penance for all she'd done, Jemima sighed as she trailed behind them, a down payment on their forgiveness.

'I know exactly who I want you to pick for me,' said Simi swivelling playfully towards the girls.

Jemima tracked Simi's gaze through the crowd and came to a grinding halt. She was looking directly at Chance.

'You're not allowed to choose your own date,' Jemima flustered.

'Maybe we should start trusting Simi to know her own mind. That's what I just agreed, right, Sims?' said Meagan flopping her arm around Simi.

'Well it's a work-in-progress but yeah. I've got a feeling about him and I need a good man to practise my boundaries with.'

'You can't,' Jemima said stepping in front of Simi and blocking her view. 'He's married.'

'How do you know?' Simi asked looking past Jemima.

'Because I… read his book,' Jemima lied. 'Hey, guess what they've got in the other room? Rocking horses!'

Simi skirted around Jemima to take a better look at Chance.

'You said he was a medic,' Meagan interjected.

Jemima opened and closed her mouth.

'I know your game,' Meagan said pointing an accusatory finger.

The back of Jemima's neck went cold. How did Meagan know what she had only recently acknowledged for herself, that she had feelings for Chance?

'You don't want us showing you up in front of your fancy literary chums but look around you. You're the most uptight person here,' said Meagan waving in the general direction of the party goers. 'Don't worry, Sim. I'll talk to him before this one comes up with another excuse.'

And with that, Meagan tipsily trotted over to Chance.

'Yipppeee!' said Simi applauding.

Jemima, a helpless bystander, witnessed the scene unfold like a car skidding across black ice. Meagan approached Chance effortlessly striking up a conversation. Jemima cringed as he looked over, his eyes piercing her, his expression dejected. Finally, after an epoch, Chance's gaze shifted to Simi. He waved politely to her but the moment his eye caught Jemima, his smile collapsed. Jemima's heart plummeted – this was unbearable.

'I think he has a girlfriend,' Jemima said, turning to Simi.

'Married, single. Which is it, Jem? You must be thinking of someone else. Besides, he doesn't look the cheating type,' Simi said.

'And you can tell?' Jemima hissed in quiet desperation.

Simi glared at Jemima who recoiled. That was an awful thing to say and she knew it.

'What I meant was… was… ' she stammered.

Simi straightened her dress, hiding her hurt.

'If he had a special someone, don't you think she'd be here?' said Simi.

Jemima went to speak but the words got trapped in her throat as Meagan brought Chance over for an introduction.

'There was a woman. Red hair. Angry looking. They kissed!' Jemima gabbled but it didn't matter.

Simi wasn't listening. Her eyes were on Chance and as he approached, she let out a tiny squeal. Jemima had no choice. She had to disappear. She raced to concoct an excuse. Meagan and Chance were feet away but she was still tethered down.

'Jeeeeeeeeeeeeehmmmm!'

Jemima span on her heels as Eve advanced, open armed, a tall champagne flute in one hand and vape pen in the other.

'Daaaaaahling!' said Eve as she air-kissed Jemima four times.

Jemima had never been so relieved and delighted to see Eve in her life.

'Sorry. Gotta go,' Jemima said to Simi as she peeled away, thanking the universe for its impeccable timing.

'My dear girl, I cannot tell you how happy the team are with your *final* draft,' said Eve raising her champagne glass to Jemima.

Jemima beamed. These were words she never thought she'd hear but had longed to for months. She wanted to cry.

'Well? Don't leave me hanging,' laughed Eve.

'Sorry!' Jemima effused, clinking glasses.

'Beverly has some guffaw-out-loud lines and that whole stalker backstory, *maaaaaster*stroke,' said Eve puffing out a cloud of strawberry-scented mist.

Jemima's eyes darted over to Meagan and Simi who were still within hearing distance. She had yet to formulate a plan for her confession but the girls overhearing like this was not an option.

'And that whole married-man history and *the life plan*,' said Eve. 'She's such a loon but *I loooove* Beverly. Genius, Jem. Genius.'

'Wow, thanks Eve,' said Jemima, trying to walk her away from the others.

This was high praise, but also high risk, discussing the book with Simi and Meagan so close by.

'This decor, huh? It's *amazing*,' Jemima said, changing the subject.

'You likey?' said Eve proudly.

'I love it. The flowers and cherubs. Very… Grecian,' said Jemima as she peered over at Simi and Chance who were deep in conversation.

How was any of this happening? Was this night punishment for the wicked deed she'd done?

'Grecian? Ha! You silly sausage,' shrieked Eve. 'They're not lilies, they're labia! The cherubs are babies being born. You're in *The Cave*.'

Jemima's eyes darted back and forth. The pink tones everywhere were not subtle and delicate as she'd first thought but cervical.

'This room is the interior of a womb,' said Eve sweeping her arms in all directions, 'and the corrugated tunnel at the entrance is—'

Jemima gulped. 'A vagina?'

'That's right!' said Eve pleased with herself. 'Guess what the ice sculpture is?'

Jemima looked over at where her and the girls had been drinking shots from moments before and laughed drily. 'It's a clitoris.'

'Yes! It's a ginormous, icy clit!' laughed Eve.

Jemima forced a grin. Thank God she hadn't drunk the Bloody Mary earlier.

'We wanted it to be low key. Nothing offensive. Never know, next year, it could be you! BTW, have you seen the ball pits? They're in the shape of ovaries and the balls are eggs! It's so much fun!' Eve said as she grabbed Jemima, dragging her towards an adjacent hall.

Jemima slowed, glancing back at Chance as Simi spoke animatedly to him.

'Come on!' said Eve tugging at Jemima's jacket sleeve.

Jemima turned away, allowing Eve to lead her.

Eve wove through the hallway crowd greeting various guests with air-kisses and promises of lunch.

'Oh, I haven't seen that rascal for ages. You must meet him,' said Eve, waggling a finger at a man across from them. 'He sells screen rights and could help get a TV deal for Beverly. I'll bring him over!'

Jemima looked, faltering for a moment.

'Come here, you!' Eve called across the hallway. 'Milesy, there's someone I want you to meet.'

CHAPTER 36

Meagan

Meagan glared at Jemima and Miles from the doorway. Half an hour earlier, she'd stepped off the dance floor for a pee break and on her way she'd caught a glimpse of them chatting together in a bar across the hallway. Since then, she hadn't been able to peel her eyes off them. As far as she knew Jemima and Miles hadn't seen or spoken to each other since their break-up yet here they were gassing like old friends. Was this just a chance encounter? With all Miles's industry connections, crossing paths at some point was bound to happen. However, what Meagan could not and would not stand for was him socialising with Jemima as though nothing had happened. And why, Meagan thought, was Jemima giving this waste of skin the time of day? Weeks before she was cowering under a table at the mere mention of his name. Meagan's anger began to simmer, *why do people never learn?* Simi's life was like the scratched record of a terrible heartbreak song and here was Jemima, drinking and laughing with the man who had driven rough shod over her heart then reversed back for good measure. Meagan was not having it. If she had to, she would go over and separate them. So what if it annoyed

Jemima? That's what tough love looked like. One of them had to have their wits about them and as usual, it was Meagan. Just then she felt a body nestle up beside her.

'Whatcha doin'?' said Simi with a broad smile.

Meagan turned to see Simi who looked like the cat that hadn't just got the cream but bought the dairy. She rolled her eyes. Love fools, every one of them.

'I'm waiting,' she said taking her attention back to Jemima and Miles.

Simi started dancing on the spot, 'Aren't you going to ask me about him?'

'Who?'

'Chance.' Simi grinned.

'What chance?'

'Silly,' said Simi nudging her, 'you just hooked me up with him. And may I say, brava.'

'His name is *Chance*?'

'Short for Chancellor,' said Simi excitedly, 'and I think it's a sign. Remember when Jemima said the word *break* came up when she communed with my aura. I thought it meant a break from guys but a break is also an opportunity or a chhhh… '

Simi's words withered as she followed Meagan's gaze across the bar.

'Oh.'

'Yeah – oh,' said Meagan. 'He's got exactly three minutes to walk away or I'm going in.'

Without looking she clicked her fingers and a waiter scuttled over to replace her empty glass.

'It looks like she's having a nice time,' offered Simi.

Meagan tutted. Cocktails had clouded Simi's memory. She'd

clearly forgotten Jemima's post-Miles devastation, one that dwarfed even Simi's recent pain.

'This bloke is shit on shit's shoes. If shit were wearing shoes, Miles would be the crap shit stepped in and said, "oh no, I've stepped in shit". That's how shit he is.'

'That's a little strong.'

Vesuvian rumblings brewed inside Meagan. Simi was about to get covered in lava and only had herself to blame.

'Have you forgotten what she was like when they split up?' said Meagan.

'I… I have not,' said Simi.

'And the things she wanted to do to herself?'

'But Meag—'

'And how, for three weeks, we couldn't leave her alone?'

'Of course, I remember! But maybe she wants this… I think they've been talking – on the phone.'

Simi's words lingered like a bad fart.

'What?' Meagan seethed, volcanic tremors rising.

'I mean, I think so. I'm not sure. It could have been British Gas. Her boiler's been on the blink and the water sometimes runs cold when I'm in the shower. Actually, maybe she's got the kitchen tap on. You can never be sure, can you? Plus—'

'She's been talking to him?'

'Well anyway, let's find *you* a date!' said Simi shifting to return to the other hall.

Meagan yanked Simi back.

'I *knew* she was up to something. Since when?' said Meagan ignoring Simi's pained grimace.

'Just leave it,' snapped Simi pulling her arm back. 'She's a grown woman making her own decisions.'

Meagan steadied herself. Simi normally crumbled under interrogation.

'We both are,' said Simi appearing to amass confidence, 'and it's not your place to interfere. Earlier you said you were going to butt out. So please, do as you promised because I don't know about Jem but I've had enough!'

'Really?' said Meagan preparing to bury Simi so deep that in years to come, archaeologists would add her petrified body to the People of Pompeii exhibition.

Meagan had bitten her tongue too many times and frankly, she'd had enough of *that*.

'You need me, Simi. You couldn't decide your way out of a one way street. You use tarot cards to choose your breakfast!'

'I trust the cards more than I trust you,' Simi spat back.

'Is it?' said Meagan popping her neck. 'If it weren't for me, do you realise how many *more* failed relationships you would have, how many fewer acting jobs you would have landed? You can't even take a decent headshot without someone holding your hand.'

'Acting jobs? You and your insane notes have lost me at least the last two I've gone for.'

Meagan could take just about anything but criticising her efforts was the rawest betrayal of all. Yes, being an acting agent was harder than she'd anticipated but she'd given Simi a lifeline when no one else would. To have that flung in her face wounded bitterly.

'Well maybe you should find yourself another agent who knows what to do with your "talents"!' said Meagan viciously waving air quotes at Simi.

'Maybe I will,' Simi said, flouncing off towards the cloakroom.

Meagan watched as Simi shook on her coat and stomped down the vaginal tunnel and out into the street. The space where she had been quickly filled with party goers who zipped to and fro laughing and chatting together. Meagan went to move but was unsure where to go. In the side bar, Jemima and Miles were still engrossed in conversation, oblivious to her presence. Shaheena was enjoying a school-disco style snog behind the cloakroom and Simi was, by now, probably writing wedding vows for her marriage to Risk or Gamble or whatever that guy's name was. All at once, Meagan felt so alone.

CHAPTER 37

Simi

'Jem,' Simi called down the hall.

There was no reply. Jemima was out and the flat was empty. Simi puffed her cheeks, relieved. She had barely seen Jemima since the party three nights ago but given all that had happened, maybe it was best. Her date with Chance had finally arrived and she just wanted to focus on that. Her tummy fluttered at the thought of him. He was her best date of the game so far. And to think, if she'd taken that break from men, she'd have missed out on this kind, almost-doctor with the gorgeous smile who was *fit* as.

He was so wonderful Simi decided she was *not* even going to sleep with him. She wasn't going to do what she had done with Mo because this was not a sprint. Besides, someone as lovely as Chance would not be in a rush. He was a good person. Simi could tell from little things like how lovely he had been to her friends, well, Meagan. Jemina had run away before they'd been introduced which was kind of rude – and strange. At the weekend, Jemima had toasted to Simi finding the man of her dreams yet the second someone materialised, Jemima hadn't wanted to know. Was she only happy when all three of them were as terminally single as her? Perhaps that's why she'd told Simi to take a break! And why she'd turned to Miles. It was out of a fear she'd be the last to meet someone. That could also explain the strange stuff she'd said about Chance having a girlfriend or a wife. Sabotage! Maybe Meagan was right all along about Jemima being up to something.

Maybe Meagan was right about a lot of things. Simi crumpled at the mean words she'd said to her at the party. As liberating as it had been to get it off her chest, it had also been unfair – especially when Simi had questioned Meagan's abilities as an agent. Meagan had twenty-three successful careers under her belt. Simi didn't even have one. She suddenly felt painfully foolish. Meagan was successful. It was Simi that was failing and trying to blame everyone but herself for it. She didn't have a clue what she needed. Furthermore, standing her ground only made things worse. Involving other people in her choices was a good thing. Besides, Meagan only did what she did out of love, but instead of gratitude Simi had thrown it all in her face. She planted her head in her hands. It was time to just do as she was told and accept other people's wisdom. Throughout her life not doing that had messed up one thing after another and it had to stop. It had messed up everything with Meagan and derailed her relationship with Oscar. If she had let him take the lead and not expected so much from him, he wouldn't have fallen into the arms of another. And in the deep recesses of her soul she couldn't help feel that if she'd been a good girl and done as she was told, her father would not have left either. She was seven when it had happened but all her life the thought that it was her fault had gnawed at her. If she'd been a quieter, less flamboyant, more obedient little girl, perhaps he'd have stuck around. From now on, she concluded, she would toe the line and just do as she was told. Sometimes other people just knew best.

As her new reality sunk in, her phone pinged. Meagan's name glared at her from the bright screen. It was their first communication since the party and could have been anything from a warning saying she'd taken out a contract on her to an invoice for services rendered. Simi reached for her phone, wondering if she should read the text *after* her date. If Meagan had put out a hit on her, it would put a real downer on the evening. She paused then swiped open the message.

'Oh,' she said as she read it.

you got the job.

A broad grin spread across her face.

'Do as you're told? Screw that!' Simi laughed, as she flung on her jacket and strode out of the flat to meet Chance.

Simi peeked from behind her hand as the London Eye capsule continued its ascent. She gripped the railing and took a long inhalation.

'I am so sorry, Simi. I should have asked,' said Chance.

'No, no, no,' she said, trying to control her trembling. 'You weren't to know I'm scared of heights and anyway, we'll be on our way down soon, won't we?'

As the city lights twinkled in the distance the irony was not lost on Simi. Having vowed not to get horizontal with Chance, she was now battling to stay vertical – and conscious.

'I think I need to sit down.' She quivered as the zenith loomed above them.

'Course,' said Chance, scrambling to her assistance.

Simi closed her eyes as he led her to the middle of the capsule where she lowered herself onto the bench. Once her breathing had returned to normal, she opened her eyes.

'So, should I cancel our dinner reservation at the top of the Shard?' Chance smiled, kneeling in front of her.

Simi felt the blood drain from her cheeks.

'I'm joking. Sorry,' he said as he rubbed her arm.

Her face broke into a smile and they laughed at the ridiculousness of it all. As the capsule finally approached ground level, Chance helped Simi stand. Despite her wooziness, his touch felt good. No, better than good. It felt amazing.

CHAPTER 38

Jemima

The girls were at their usual brunch spot, Des Oeufs! a bustling Upper Street café where the staff knew them well. They were in their usual booth having their usual order but today everything felt different. Where once the atmosphere was light, now it was thick like tar; dark and unforgiving. Meagan's refurb update had been monosyllabic. Congratulating Simi on her new job had been heartfelt but perfunctory as was the praise for Jemima completing her book. So much for a nice birthday brunch for Meagan, Jemima thought as she swirled her mimosa. Things were beyond tense and she had no idea how to untangle this ungodly mess. There were so many things she wanted to ask, like what had happened on Simi's date with Chance two days ago? Normally, information poured from Simi like a waterfall but today there was nothing. Then again, Jemima hadn't exactly been forthcoming about the secrets she held. All at once, her shoulders became heavy with her unsaid burdens – stolen stories, her feelings for Chance and conversations with Miles. And piled on top of all that, Rebecca had been in touch – again. She'd received an offer on her apartment but was giving Jemima first refusal. She had three days to decide. Though everything that made Jemima want to stay was crumbling, she still couldn't pull the trigger. The centre of her world was sitting right in front of her and whatever rocky terrain she encountered, all roads still led to these two women. How could she give them up?

Simi pushed her plate aside and cleared her throat.

'Sorry to bring this up now but I'm stopping the game. Definitely this time,' she said at Jemima.

'Good,' Meagan said, draining her mimosa.

'What? You can't. Why?' said Jemima.

The game couldn't end like this. Simi finding Chance was like watching the ball on a roulette wheel bounce into the one gulley you absolutely did not want it to. Black. Thirty-five. The game couldn't end on Simi with Chance. It just couldn't.

'But we didn't all get dates last time. Let's give it one more week?' said Jemima in desperation.

'Come off it, Jem. We've had enough. You should be pleased,' snipped Meagan.

Jemima recoiled. There was nothing she could say that wouldn't also reveal her heart.

'No, Jem. Me and Chance have our second date tonight. I think it's serious,' Simi said.

Jemima jolted as Simi's words hit her. A *second* date? And what did she mean by *serious*? Had Chance said this or had Simi misread the signals again? Jemima's lips moved but nothing came out, Simi's cold and unrevealing expression stopping her. Well, if Chance did want Simi, Jemima would just have to pack away her passions and accept he was lost. Under the table she dug her nails into her hand, wanting to run. Finally, Simi peeled her gaze away and Jemima was able to breathe.

'Plus, with me going away on this *Clash of the Crown* job and you moving to LA we'd have to stop anyway,' Simi said.

Meagan turned sharply to Jemima. 'What?'

Jemima looked to Simi. 'What do you mean?'

'I needed to print a script so I took some paper from your recycling tray. There was an email from Rebecca. Pictures of her flat and stuff.' Simi shrugged.

'Secrets and lies,' said Meagan, eyes locked on Jemima.

'She was just offering it. I'm not doing anything about it,' Jemima flapped.

'Really? "*I am sooooo interested*",' Simi quoted. 'You got that email at the ice rink. You said it was nothing.'

'Told you she was up to something,' murmured Meagan.

Jemima crumbled, trapped. 'Listen, we've all got side-tracked. Let's restart the game—'

'Stop telling me what to do,' Simi spat, 'and Meagan, I think you're right.'

Meagan's eyebrows arched practically to her hairline.

'We should separate work from friendship. I'm getting a new agent. Thanks for that advice, Jem.'

Meagan threw a piercing glare across the table, deep hurt pulsing across her face. She slid out of their booth and before Simi had even finished her sentence, two bank notes fluttered to the table.

'Meagan, wait—' Jemima pleaded but Meagan was already halfway to the door.

She stared into the space where Meagan had been. Where once there were three, now there were barely two. Simi gave a nod to their waiter for the bill.

'You know, Jem,' Simi said slipping her jacket on and taking out her purse, 'it's almost like you don't want me to be happy, I mean really happy.'

Jemima tried to answer. Simi's pain was the last thing she wanted and the very suggestion left her reeling.

'It's like I'm this joke to you. *Simi, the love klutz, Simi the broke actress, Simi the unfixable problem*, and just when I meet someone I like you do everything to put me off, ruin it.'

'I was protecting you. You don't know him,' Jemima implored.

'Do you?' said, Simi, a frost in her words. 'Do you like him?'

All at once, Jemima was on a shore, a tsunami accelerating towards her. Waves of emotion crashed, battering her. She so wanted to deny, to reassure her friend but nothing came. And with her silence, she had made everything worse.

'Thought so,' said Simi as she placed a couple of notes on top of Meagan's and left.

'Simi,' Jemima said but she was gone.

Jemima was numb and aware of only two things – the futile desire to run and the beating of her devastated heart. Was it shame she felt, hurt, guilt or an astringent cocktail of all three? She shook as she picked up her phone and dialled.

'It's me,' she said, cupping her hand around the microphone, as much to block out the café noise as to conceal this dreadful deed.

'Jem-Jem,' said Miles.

She knew he was toxic but as with so many noxious substances, a little poison often brought pleasure. This would be the first and last time, a final fling before disappearing to Los Angeles. And before she departed, she would confess all to the girls then be out of their lives forever.

CHAPTER 39

Meagan

Meagan pulled her hair into a bun. After that chronic brunch with the girls earlier, she was glad to be on her own. She looked around Bar Dodgem before scribbling down her song choice.

'I won't need the words,' she said, handing in her slip of paper.

Had Meagan known it was karaoke night, she would have gone elsewhere but now she was here, she was well up for belting out something vengeful. From the flyers scattered around, she quickly discovered that Bar Dodgem's annual karaoke event was their one concession to cheesy naffness. As a result, the bar was actually busier than usual. It was filled with its usual hipster-types in 'casual' outfits that in fact were more curated than an exhibition at the Tate Modern. The rocking horses had been moved to the outer edges. The brightly coloured equine spectators now watched disinterestedly from the shadows over the main area which had become a mosh-pit-cum-dance floor. On stage, there were no crumby speakers, wobbly lyrics screens and cruise ship crooner comperes. This was karaoke, Bar Dodgem-style. There was a band and they were tight and well rehearsed. This was not their first rodeo. They'd already belted out several subverted covers. Rap tracks transformed into Eighties pop, reimagined as rock anthems. Meagan rubbed her hands together. This was how to celebrate her birthday, unencumbered and free. She would drink, sing and forget. Forget herself, Todd, Miles, Simi and Jemima. She would forget everything except one thing – relationships meant giving away a piece of your heart and it was never, ever worth it. Even if they didn't mean to, people always trampled and destroyed your love. Jemima and Simi were just as bad as Parker, two more people who could not be trusted with her emotions. She'd always suspected life was easier as a solo pilot and these last few weeks had proved it.

'Fuck 'em!' she bellowed just as the band rounded out the final bars of the last song.

The crowd whooped as a bandanaed woman who'd sung the hell out of an Amy Winehouse track tiptoed off stage.

'Next up, Meagan! Where are you, Meagan?' said the keyboard player.

'Here!' she yelled draining her beer.

She nudged her way through, still getting used to the soft, flat padding of her new trainers. Only at the age of thirty was she discovering that flat shoes were actually comfortable. Out of sight of everyone she knew, she'd decided to wear them as an experiment and they were *brilliant*. What a trap she had created for herself, the designer cage of a sassy, hard-arse business woman. It was understandable though. Coming from nothing, the look meant everything, be it her postcode or the shoes on her feet. Well if it was a cage of her own making, tonight she would bust out of jail. As she bounced onto the stage, she looked down at her T-shirt, loose and creased and her ripped skinny jeans. These clothes were *soooo* comfy! Microphone in hand she saluted the audience, playing up to the applause and wolf whistles.

'Right, Meagan is gonna sing 'You Need Me, I Don't Need You'!' boomed the keyboard player.

'Yeah!' screeched Meagan as the speakers whistled discordant feedback.

The keyboard player went back behind her electric piano and gave a nod to the band. 'Okay! One, two. One, two, three, four!'

Luckily for tone-deaf Meagan the half-rapped track was in her range but even if it weren't, she didn't care. All she wanted to do was dance herself free. She wanted to feel happy, alone and alive – to throw off her pain like a sportswoman running off an injury. She twisted, bopped, leapt and turned, taken by the music. She didn't need the words. The sentiment was etched into her heart from the life she'd already lived. From leaning on a man who would never give her what she wanted, from watching girlfriends rely on unreliable guys, from the painful betrayal of Simi and Jemima, from realising even her parents couldn't support her. She punched the air and jumped up onto a speaker. This was what life was about – rocking and rolling on her own terms, she affirmed as she launched into a flying kick across the stage. The crowd roared in appreciation as she landed. She was crushing this performance.

It was the pain she was aware of first. A cold, shooting bolt from her ankle. She crumpled to the floor in what felt like slow motion, the crowd still revelling in her daredevil manoeuvres. Meagan was sure – something was broken. A leg, an ankle, her pride? But whatever had happened, she was going to finish this song. She had to, she grimaced, pushing through the final bars on her back. The band crescendoed to a close as the crowd roared.

Meagan waved from the floor, high-fiving any hand within reach.

'Thank you. Cheers, guys,' she boomed into the mic before beckoning the keyboard player over. She grabbed her charity-pin laden lapel, and pulled her close. 'Babe, call an ambulance and call my… friend, the one who texted me last. Tell them to meet me at the hospital.'

Unable to bear the pain any longer, she flopped back onto the stage – defeated.

Meagan stared up at the standard-issue ceiling tiles. She hadn't been in a hospital since Jemima's appendectomy after Mile's premiere. How did hospital staff do it? The uniform and smell were enough to put Meagan off let alone the hours and pay. Just then, the curtain swooshed back and Meagan's exhausted junior doctor popped her head in.

'How are we doing?' said Dr Blandy as she flicked her floppy purple fringe aside.

'Just give me the bad news,' said Meagan.

'Really it's just news, isn't it? It's how you feel that makes it good or bad… '

'Just spit it out.'

'You're pregnant. Yay,' said Dr Blandy going in for a flaccid fist bump.

'What?' gawped Meagan propping herself up on her elbows.

'What?' said Todd.

Meagan almost jumped out of her skin. What the *hell* was he doing here?? But then she remembered. Numb with pain and beer – she had told the keyboard player to contact the last person who'd texted. She'd thought it was Jemima but it had actually been Todd. This was beyond a disaster.

'Wait, this is bed nine?' said Dr Blandy consulting her notes. 'Damn. I've done it again. I am *sooooo* sorry. I'm like, super tired. You're the ankle – so, not broken. Yay. We'll get you bandaged up, give you some anti-inflammatories then you're good to go.'

While Meagan sat in shock, Dr Blandy made her getaway, briefly popping her head back through the curtain.

'*Aaaand* if you could keep that little snafu to yourself that'd be aces. I'm sort of, completely on a final warning. Cheers,' she said before disappearing again.

Meagan puffed her cheeks, too stunned to be angry.

'The fuck was that?' she said falling back onto the bed.

Well, at least her ankle wasn't broken. There was too much going on for her body to fail her now.

'Wow. Can you imagine us having—' Todd began.

'Don't. Listen, thanks for coming but I can handle it from here.'

'How are you going to get home?' he asked.

'I was thinking of trying out this new thing called a cab,' said Meagan, nixing any and all attempts to be her knight in shining armour.

'You need help—'

'Seriously, mate.' Meagan grimaced. 'Look, sorry if I've been a bit of a—'

'Bitch,' Todd said. 'It's okay.'

Meagan lay still. What was with everyone backchatting her? As she studied his face, formulating her acerbic response she noted that something was different. There was a grit to him that hadn't been there before or maybe she hadn't noticed.

'I just wanted to make sure you got home okay. That was all,' he said standing.

'Wait, where are you going?' she said, reaching out.

'Back to my date… '

Meagan's face froze. *A date*? Lying on her hospital bed, that same loneliness she'd felt at the Hudson Hicks party began to close in on her. She turned away unable to watch him leave. Out of the corner of her eye, she noticed him sit back in the visitors' chair as tears splashed onto her pillow. Todd pushed a crumpled tissue into her hand.

'Dodgem dust,' she sniffled, wiping her eyes.

Meagan manoeuvred herself to face Todd again.

'Thank you,' she said, the strange sensation of vulnerability almost overwhelming.

'No problem,' he replied taking her hand. 'Anytime, Meagan. You know that… Anything for you, even this book thing.'

'What book?' said Meagan dabbing the last of her tears as the curtain swooshed open again.

'Hiya. I'm Camilla. Going to pop this bandage on,' she chimed.

'Whatever,' Meagan said turning back to Todd. 'What book?'

Todd shifted in his chair as Camilla pottered, neatly laying out her bandage and Tubigrip.

'I was going to talk to you about it at the Hudson Hicks do but I thought I'd be the last person you'd want to see… '

'Todd, seriously. What the *fuck* are you talking about?' said Meagan wanting to shake the information out of him.

'Look, I know how you girls sometimes overshare after a couple of glasses of wine. I get it.'

If Todd didn't get to the point soon, he was going to get something, Meagan quietly growled.

'Okay, so, crime fiction isn't my area but I was curious. I knew Jemima was your buddy and I heard about her run-in with Eve so I thought I'd read it,' Todd said.

Meagan gestured for him to continue.

'Anyway, as I was reading I spotted this... phrase you used to use to describe my... ' He looked at Camilla whose entire focus was on securing Meagan's bandage.

'Your *what*?' said Meagan.

'You know,' said Todd glancing at his groin.

Camilla's eyes crept over and then back to her bandaging.

'Cams. Give us a minute,' said Meagan as politely as she could, given she might kill someone.

Camilla went to speak but then received a full wattage Meagan glare and left, swishing the curtain behind her.

'Can you explain, using the smallest words you know, what the hell you are talking about?' said Meagan in a menacing whisper.

'"Package like a clenched fist... like going ten rounds with Anthony Joshua..."' he said shifting in his seat. 'There were some other things – about you that sounded familiar too but, like I said, I don't mind. It's not every day your old fella gets immortalised in print.'

Meagan threw her legs off the bed and pushed herself into a sitting position.

'What are you doing? You need your anti-inflammatories.' Todd panicked.

Meagan leaned forward and grabbed Todd by his jumper.

'Fuck anti-inflammatories. Get me a copy of that book… *NOW*.'

CHAPTER 40

Simi

Simi revelled in her deep, deep attraction to Chance. She gazed across the kitchen counter at him wondering what she might say were he to propose there and then. Yes, it was only their second date but the signs were *so good*. He'd already shown how in tune they were with his choice of date – a Mexican cooking class. Clearly, he'd intuited her love of world food. It was sweet too that he'd wanted to make up for his faux pas with the London Eye. Despite taking twenty minutes to recover after, Simi was pleased that had happened. It had brought them closer *and* scored her a second date – which was shaping up very nicely. The only thing she was slightly nervous about was the tequila tasting later. She just hoped, as with wine tasting, you got to spit it out – but by the way everyone was going on about it, she suspected not.

'Okay, guys, after you've put your filling on the tortilla, roll it up like a big J. You know?' their cooking teacher, Carmen, chuckled as she paced between the counters.

The class laughed along as she mimed smoking a joint, giving one woman a playful nudge.

'I mean it's not my thing but *el campo fértil no descansado, tórnase estéril.*' She winked at Simi with a playful flourish.

'Right. *Cinco!*' Simi beamed before turning to Chance, nonplussed, 'What did she say?'

'Basically, *All work and no play,*' Chance whispered.

'Ohhh!' Simi whispered back, 'And what did I say?'

'Five,' Chance said.

'Right.' Simi grimaced, focusing on her tortilla as her cheeks burned with embarrassment.

'*Muy bien.* Now put your lovely enchiladas in the pan! This is fantastic munchies food,' said Carmen, with a clap of her hands.

As Simi positioned their rolled-up tortillas, she glimpsed at Chance imagining what her married name signature would look like – amazing, obviously – just like their wedding, their kids and their chocolate Labs. Everything with Chance would be amazing.

'So, how did you and Jemima meet?' Chance asked as he poured sauce into their pan.

Jemima – again, Simi frowned. This was the third time she'd come up in conversation and they hadn't even got their food in the oven. They were supposed to be falling in love not picking over the potted history of Simi and Jemima's frazzled friendship. Simi decided to smile through it. She'd answer his question then steer them back to more important matters such as how many children they were going to have.

'Stand-up comedy class. She's not really a performer though, obviously,' said Simi, her tummy knotting at her meanness.

'Maybe, but she is funny,' said Chance.

'You got that from seeing her for two minutes the other night?' Simi asked.

'No, we've met before.'

Simi's expression fell.

'I mean, I've seen her around. We go to the same coffee shop and, well, she seemed… funny.'

'Yes, she's funny,' Simi replied.

If he was starstruck, she wished he'd just ask her to get Jemima's autograph so they could get on with setting each other's worlds on fire.

'We don't need to talk about her,' said Chance whisking their pan into the oven.

'No,' said Simi as he returned to their counter.

However, Jemima was now in the conversation and Simi couldn't help recall what she'd said about Chance at the party.

'She did say something interesting though,' Simi said.

Chance's smile flickered.

'She mentioned a woman with red hair… '

'How did she know about… ? Ah, the coffee shop we go to, I mean, our Nostromo. What I'm saying is… the woman's name is Joy,' he blustered.

Simi slapped on an amiable smile. It was as though Chance and Jemima had this whole history she knew nothing about. He knew how funny she was and where she bought her coffee. Jemima knew about this red-headed woman and maybe more. Simi indicated for him to continue in the vain hope he'd tell her, *Don't worry about Joy. She can be a flower girl at our wedding* but his expression seemed to indicate otherwise. Simi tensed, mad at Jemima who, even in her absence, was ruining this evening.

'So, who is Joy?' she finally asked.

Chance tensed. 'She's my brother Pete's ex. When they broke

up and he went to Mexico she latched onto me. When her visa ran out I thought she'd go back to Oz but well, now she thinks we're an item,' Chance said, embarrassed.

'Are you?' Simi asked, baffled by his explanation.

'No but it's weird. I was in Oz when her and Pete broke up. I comforted her while I was there. Seemed the right thing to do. Anyway, I head home to London and next thing I know, she's flying out to the UK too. Like I say, it's weird,' he said shaking his head. 'She's got boundary issues. She gets attached to someone without knowing how they feel. That's why Pete broke up with her. It's like, she just decides, it's you and that's it. You don't get a say.'

Simi felt herself buckle, mystified. Carmen tapped a spatula, quietening the lively room.

'*Bueno*! Guys, I'm going to teach you to make the best, I'm not joking, *the* best guacamole. Honestly, it's an aphrodisiac. Know what my magic ingredient is?' She grinned bumping the man beside her with her hip.

'Wanna put money on it being marijuana?' Chance murmured trying to lighten the mood.

'Mmm,' said Simi distracted. 'You should say something to Joy, shouldn't you?'

'How? I don't want to hurt her.'

Simi spooned avocado into her bowl. So, Chance *was* single it's just that this red-haired loon hadn't got the memo. 'But you're not… '

'No,' he said.

Simi pounded the avocado mush. 'Have you kissed?' she asked after a while.

Reluctantly, Chance nodded, throwing coriander into their

292

dish. 'That's how it started. It was just this one time. Straight away I knew it was wrong. Now, I just meet her for a coffee or a beer from time to time. That's it,' he said looking into Simi's eyes.

She could see he was telling the truth. There was an honesty about him but there was something else too or something missing. Though he was convincing it didn't feel like it was her he was trying to convince. But if not her, then who?

Simi looked up at him. 'Let's change the subject.'

'Fine by me,' he agreed.

'You know what is my special ingredient? *Amoooorrr*,' said Carmen. '*Love*. What you think I was gonna say? Come on. Keep chopping!'

Simi glimpsed over at Chance who dutifully began dicing tomatoes.

'And you know what would go so well with this one?' asked Carmen.

'Tequila!' everyone shouted.

Thoughts of red-haired temptresses were set aside as Simi threw an anxious glance around the room. Everyone, including Chance, seemed thrilled about washing all this down with tequila, all fifty-seven varieties on the menu if they could. Simi wanted to join in but the last time she drunk neat tequila she'd woken up on the Eurostar. She would politely decline. There had to be another way to show Chance what a great match they were.

From across the counter, Chance handed Simi a brimming shot glass. 'I'm so glad you're up for this. I love a girl who appreciates a quality spirit.'

'That's me!' she said, sweat beading on her forehead. 'Down the bottom! I mean up the hatch!'

'I think I'm allergic to tequila,' Simi slurred as spittle bubbled in the corner of her mouth.

'Maybe,' said Chance as he readjusted his grip of her.

Simi's head flopped forward onto his shoulder as he ascended the hallway stairs to Jemima's flat. Thank God he was strong enough to give her a piggyback. In these shoes and this state, she wouldn't have made it to the station let alone back here.

'You're amazing,' she hiccuped into his ear.

'Thanks. Is this the one?' he whispered, stopping outside Jemima's door.

Simi peeled her head off his shoulder.

'Yep!' she said before thumping it back down.

'Keys?'

'Yesssss! Keys, keys, keys. Shhhhhhh!' Simi said shushing herself.

She rummaged in her bag. Finally she found them and jabbed in the general direction of the lock.

'I'll do it,' said Chance, taking them from her.

'Chance, I think you should do it,' Simi said as she slid down his back onto the floor.

Chance pushed the door open and hoisted Simi up as best he could. He tucked an arm around her waist and led her through to the living room where she flopped onto the sofa. After removing her coat and shoes, Chance dragged the duvet over her.

'Okay, mate,' he said. 'I'm gonna shoot.'

'Can you get me some water *pleeeease*?'

Chance took a deep breath and smiled before going through to the kitchen, quickly returning with a glass. Simi tried to drink but nausea threatened like the growl of an approaching train.

'You okay?' said Chance feeling her brow. 'You're hot.'

'Thanks, babes, so are you.' She winked, stroking his face.

'No, I mean, you're sweltering. In fact, this flat is like an oven. I'll turn the heating down or you'll get dehydrated and make your hangover even worse.'

'Thanks, Doc. It's by the door,' said Simi gulping down another nauseous ebb.

Chance went over, keeping half an eye on her as he adjusted the thermostat.

'Would you stay, just until I'm asleep?' Simi whimpered.

Chance lingered, throwing a furtive look down the hall then back at Simi.

'Pleeeeease?'

'Sure.' He nodded, shaking off his jacket.

Simi listened as the boiler grumbled to stillness and Chance wedged himself on the edge of the sofa on top of the duvet. As she nestled into the crook of his arm, she quickly drifted to sleep.

Simi opened her eyes. Outside it was light but still early. Chance had fallen asleep, arm still around her. He really was lovely. She could see why Jemima liked him. In the cold light of day she could deny that no longer. Equally, only a dunce could fail to see, he liked Jemima too – a lot. As always, however, Simi had fought for a different truth that gave her what *she* wanted. She gulped as she remembered what Chance had said about Joy, *she just decides, it's you and that's it*. Wasn't that what she did? In every relationship she ignored the signs – the real signs, because it wasn't what she wanted. She'd come a long way since cowering in Oscar's basement yet that deep desperation not to be alone still haunted her. Just days before, she'd been talking about abstaining from men but just like that, she was planning an imaginary wedding. She thought of her cosmic ordering book and the many married name signatures she'd scrawled in it and then crossed out. That was not normal. She thought of the pets and the parties and photos she'd pinned to her vision-board before she'd even had a first date. She was trying to quench a thirst that could never be satisfied. Would she ever find a relationship that would leave her feeling complete?

But then Simi's mouth slackened as it dawned on her – perhaps that fundamental question was the root of the problem. Since her father's absence, she'd been searching for someone to fill the gaping hole he left. However, in the hazy morning light, she finally saw that this space didn't need to be filled. It needed to be healed. Rather than searching for a replacement, she needed to let her father go. She needed to forgive herself, reminding herself daily if she had to, that what happened was not her fault. That's where her sense of completion lay. She had done nothing wrong and no relationship, no person could make her whole. That sense of completion could only come from within.

Simi blinked away tears and smiled. How had it taken 35 years to realise she *could* stand up for herself, make her own choices *and* she didn't *need* a man. She was complete as she was. She looked over at her boxes, bags and suitcases in Jemima's living room. It was time for change. Firstly, she would step aside and let Jemima and Chance figure out whatever was going on between them. She would make peace with Meagan and get her career on track. But this time, instead of waiting for an agent to fix her problems, she would take control. It had been ten years since their stand-up course. It was time to be brave and give it a try. A lot of her favourite actresses came from a comedy background. There was every chance it might open doors for Simi too.

And lastly, it was time to find a place of her own. She had to start navigating the world without depending on others. It would be hard but that was what it meant to be a grown-up, not a girl desperately seeking her daddy's love. Even if she failed, it was time to try. As the sun peeked between the curtains, Simi could feel her new dawn rising, a second chance at a different way of living. She was going to embrace it with both hands. Happy tears trickled down her face.

CHAPTER 41

Jemima

Jemima prised her eyes open and looked over at Miles. He was sitting up in bed reading *The Observer* on his iPad, looking content, as though their two years apart had never happened.

'Morning, sleepy head,' he said, eyes still on his article.

Oh god, thought Jemima, murmuring a generic reply. She scanned the room like a scene-of-crime officer. Clothes strewn across the floor. Empty wine glasses. Tissue flowers on the bedside table. Nether regions that felt like a pounded chicken escalope. Yep. Sex had taken place. And though she would testify otherwise, the fact was, she had instigated it. She had made the phone call after that hellish brunch and like Bruce Wayne responding to the Bat-Signal, Miles had been over like a shot – that evening.

Jemima also couldn't deny, however, that it had been what she needed, something familiar, distracting, disposable. But now, she wanted him to leave. Their night together was the coda to a series of awful decisions which needed to end with him dressed and out the door. Things were awkward enough without Simi bumping into him going for her morning pee. Jemima glowered as he took a leisurely sip of his coffee. Perhaps, she calculated, if she surfaced it would encourage him to do the same. She tried propping herself up but that made her head pound like the bass bin at a warehouse rave.

'You really put it away last night,' chuckled Miles.

Jemima felt a swell of nausea but this time it wasn't because of the three bottles of wine they'd sunk. It was him. She flung back the duvet and lurched to the window, scrambling to open it. Thunder rumbled in the distance but the cold, brutal breeze felt good.

'Says it's gonna rain most of today. Course, that needn't bother us when we're in LA, eh?' said Miles as he swiped through the rest of the newspaper.

Jemima froze. '*We*'? As the first splatters of rain fell, her addled brain began to piece together fragments of their drunken conversation from the night before. She'd confessed her LA ambitions to Miles and he'd carped on about how he'd love to move there too. *Oh god,* Jemima murmured. She'd said moving would be great for his career and that he would love it there but he'd taken it to mean they should love it there *together*! This was madness. Jemima hadn't even confirmed she was going! She clasped her hand over her mouth. It was LA that had initiated the sex. Miles had said how the dry LA heat made him horny and in her drunken haze Jemima had cranked up the heating to full blast. Next thing, they were entangled under her sheets while Miles negotiated the terms of his expatriation. Jemima deflated into a ball. LA was about getting away from everything she'd screwed up not taking it with her. If Miles was going to hijack her great escape, she might as well charter a plane and take Simi, Meagan, Chance, Shaheena, Eve and the staff of Hudson Hicks with her too.

'Think of it, Jem-Jem,' said Miles sliding in behind her at the window. 'In a few months we could be doing this looking out at the Pacific Ocean.'

'Mmmm, It's still just an idea really. I haven't actually confirmed anything,' she said.

'Well you need to. Rebecca's offer won't be on the table forever. Isn't it great that with our jobs we can work anywhere?' he laughed. 'This could be amazing for me. I mean for us.'

'Mmmmm.'

'And I don't want to jump the gun but with your dual citizenship, my green card should be a doddle,' he said.

He put his arms around her, his grip feeling like a boa constricting its prey. Jemima shivered.

'I'm so glad you called, Jem-Jem. To be honest, I thought you just wanted to shag. Which is fine. Girl power and all that but, well, inviting me to LA, it's amazing. And look, I know I screwed up before but I promise – this is going to be different.'

'Mmmmm!' Jemima cringed.

But she hadn't invited him! He'd invited himself and now she was trapped in his tightening grasp, desperate for an exit strategy.

Jemima jumped at the sound of a loud clackety *thump! thump! thump!* at her front door.

'Blimey, the God Squad are getting aggressive,' Miles joked as he nuzzled her neck. 'Who could that be? It's eight o'clock on a Sunday morning.'

'Whoever it is, they're probably not going away,' Jemima said freeing herself from Miles and throwing on some clothes.

The thumping grew louder and more urgent. Jemima put a hand on the bedroom door knob but as she went to turn it, she heard Simi's muffled voice in the corridor. Jemima pressed her ear to the cool wood and listened.

'*Where is she?*'

It was Meagan. What was she doing here at what was technically still Saturday night in her world?

'What's going on?' said Miles.

Jemima span round, all at once surrounded.

'I know you're in there!' Meagan hollered.

Jemima listened at the door again. It sounded like Meagan was pacing but every step was accompanied by a loud *thunk*. Did she have a baseball bat?

Jemima gulped. Meagan knew.

'Stay here,' she hissed at Miles, 'and whatever you hear, do *not* come out.'

'You better get out here or I'm gonna kick that door in with my one good foot!' Meagan screeched.

Jemima braced herself and opened the door, swiftly closing it behind her.

'Oh, here's Sleeping Beauty,' Meagan cawed.

'What's going on? What happened?' said Jemima pointing at Meagan's trussed-up ankle.

Meagan leaned on her crutch, her normally flawless hair wet from the rain, her face as thunderous as the impending storm.

'Never mind that. How's about you tell us about your little book?'

Simi looked to Jemima. 'What's going on?'

'Would you like to explain?' said Meagan, one hand on her hip.

Jemima's breath quickened. How had she found out? Against all odds Shaheena had kept her mouth shut at the party. In fact, everyone who knew Jemima's dirty secret had been there that night and none had said a word. So how the hell did Meagan know?

'Why don't we go into the living room,' said Jemima hopelessly attempting to deescalate.

'Let's talk here!' Simi piped throwing a concerned glance towards the closed living-room door.

'Fine by me. Let's talk about how Agatha Christie here has been stealing stories for her book!'

'You mean plagiarising?' asked Simi.

Jemima could barely bring herself to look at Simi. Her innocence and confusion was crushing.

'Come on, let's have a cuppa,' Jemima pleaded.

'Urm, there's something *I* should explain,' said Simi as the living-room door opened.

All three girls turned to see… Chance.

'I should probably—' he said shuffling towards the door. 'Hey, Meagan. Jemima.'

Jemima watched Chance edge between the three of them. The front door clicked shut behind him and her heart fell through the floor. This was awfulness squared. Her knees weak, she turned to Meagan and Simi.

'Can we please just talk?' She quivered, heading to the living room, praying they'd follow.

After an eon, Simi then Meagan clacked in behind her.

'Jem, what's going on?' Simi asked. 'What's Meag talking about?'

Jemima steeled herself. There was still a slender chance they would understand.

'Sit down and I'll tell you everything… ' she said. 'Tea?'

'Fuck tea, Jemima. Fuck sitting down. Fuck listening to you try and wheedle out of this,' blasted Meagan. 'So here's what's up, Sim. Your girl Jemima has been using stories from *our lives* to finish her book. That's why she wanted to play the stupid dating game. She didn't want to meet anyone and she wasn't bothered about *you* meeting anyone either. She just wanted intel.'

Simi searched Jemima's face, her eyes clouded in bewilderment. Jemima tried to hold her gaze hoping somehow Simi would see the good in her as she always did and not the betrayal.

'No, Meag. This must be a mistake. Jem?' Simi whimpered. 'Or a coincidence? Writers absorb stuff all the time, don't they? That's what Shaheena said at the party. I mean, how do you know for sure, Meag?'

Sweet Simi, thought Jemima. She so wanted it to be 'them against the world', when the truth was, the enemy had been among them all along. Jemima's head bowed in shame as Meagan clacked towards her.

'How do I know?' said Meagan, hovering, '"*Package like a clenched fist*."'

Jemima's stomach lurched. *Todd*. How could she have overlooked the fact that Todd worked in marketing and might read the book – *and* recognise that description. She felt herself go light-headed. She'd been so preoccupied with not letting it slip to Meagan and Simi, she'd forgotten to keep her book out of Todd's hands, too.

'I don't understand,' said Simi, her voice shaking.

Meagan lowered herself into a seat and placed her crutch across her lap.

'Sit, Simi. It's my turn to tell a story. Remember when Jemima was whining about how her editor wanted her to sort out Beverly, her frigid flop? Well, she did it by using us, our experiences, our lives, to give her a backstory,' said Meagan jabbing her fingers into her own chest.

Jemima stared at the floor as Simi listened, horrified.

'Ever wonder why Jemima always asked questions about our love lives but brushed us off when we asked about hers? I *told* you she was up to something,' Meagan said, spitting the words out.

'How did you find out?' Simi asked.

'Ah, ha,' said Meagan waving a triumphant finger like a TV detective revealing the killer's fateful error. 'Jemima did a good job of getting everyone to keep schtum but she forgot one person: Todd. He doesn't normally read all the new novels but this time he did. So he's reading away and he says, there's this character called Rodd who had a—'

'Package like a clenched fist,' finished Simi.

Jemima's entire body collapsed as she realised how foolish she'd been to think that keeping Shaheena quiet and the girls away from Eve was all it would take to stop them finding out.

'By the way, sweetheart that he is, Todd said he's okay to be in your book,' said Meagan smiling archly. 'I, however, am gonna sue you inside out. You're gonna be like a chew toy in a dog shelter when I've finished with you.'

Meagan eased herself off the sofa and went to stand.

'Hold on, Meagan. Shouldn't we let Jemima explain? If she's only put in details about Todd and he's fine, that's okay, isn't it?' said Simi.

Jemima stared into the middle distance as Meagan laughed.

'Darling, Todd isn't the half of it. She makes Troy look like the archangel Gabriel. She put in stuff about my mum and dad, about Parker, you and Oscar, oh and a lovely little backstory about that time Beverly stalked a guy in college. She didn't even change his damn name!'

'J… Jemima?' Simi spluttered.

'You've got to understand, I was *inspired* by your stories but… the deeper I got the harder it became to speak to you about it. Instead I just hoped you'd forgive me. I mean that's what best friends do, right… forgive each other's missteps,' Jemima said as she noticed Meagan's grip on her crutch tighten.

She braced herself, ready to duck.

'Misstep?!' You used our lives to turn Beverly into an obsessive, home-wrecking freak,' bellowed Meagan.

Jemima watched as rain streaked down the living-room window, wishing somewhere in those rivulets she could find the right thing to say. She looked back at Meagan who was close to tears, her face burning red. Meagan's vulnerability was almost more terrifying than her fury.

'I was desperate and because you said the dating game would help with my book, I thought that meant it would be okay,' said Jemima.

'I meant *your* experiences. Not mine!'

'I tried to use my stories. I did but – it was too painful,' Jemima whimpered.

'So, what? You decided using our stories wouldn't hurt *us*? We've all been through shit, Jem. You're not the only one who's had their heart broken, lost something they wanted. I wanted Parker but he didn't want me. Simi wanted a family but Oscar didn't. We got over it. You're the only person I know who thinks their only option is freeze or flight. You're not a fucking deer. You're a 42-year-old woman yet you still run away like a 5-year-old,' said Meagan slamming her fist on her lap.

'It's because of my mother,' Jemima began, her voice barely a whisper.

'I swear down, if I hear that dead-body-in-the-street story one more time! It's because of you! The reason you couldn't do what you needed with your book isn't because of your mum. It's because you were too afraid to take on your own life, own what you've been through and make it count for something. You had everything you needed in your own history but you were too shit scared to use it! The only reason your precious Beverly had a stick up her arse in the first place is because you do. She can't love because you won't,' bawled Meagan.

Rage brewed inside Jemima. Meagan knew nothing and was more of a love cripple than she was.

'What about you with Todd?' sneered Jemima before she could stop herself. 'You've got a man who loves you yet you use this ludicrous plan to avoid commitment. Truth is, *you're* scared. You're too scared to lean on anyone that's for sure. No one's allowed to do anything for you yet you think you know best for everyone else, well you don't!'

'Jemima, that's not cool,' said Simi holding her hands up.

'She's been hiding behind this Parker-didn't-want-me-thing for years! It's a set-up. She picked a married man, so she would always have a get-out and you've been using the plan as an excuse ever since! You think I've got a stick up my arse? You're a bloody shish kebab!'

'Jemima, stop!' implored Simi.

'No, Simi. This whole, *if I can get this last client over the line then my life can start*, it's bullshit. That's why she sabotages you, so you don't succeed and she has an excuse to never start living!'

yelled Jemima. 'And you let her because you're too scared to be responsible for your life.'

Simi wobbled, the force of Jemima's accusation knocking her onto the ropes.

'Meagan was helping me and at least she didn't try and sabotage my love life,' said Simi glaring at Jemima. 'I know why you told me lies about Chance. Because you're in love with him.'

Meagan drummed her nails along the metal frame of her crutch. 'Wow, you are hashtag squad goals. Stealing our men, stealing our stories. You want to steal my crutch coz you clearly can't stand on your own two feet.'

Silence descended as the girls fumed in their own corner of the ring.

'I just don't know how you could do it, especially after Troy,' Meagan continued. 'I knew something fishy was going on but I thought you were going to church or something.'

'I was desperate,' whispered Jemima.

'Yeah, well, you'll be hearing from my lawyer first thing. After I've finished, you won't be able to get a job writing product descriptions on the Tesco website.'

'Oh, give it a rest, Meagan.'

Everyone looked over.

Jemima's face drained as she saw Miles standing in the doorway, arms crossed with a towel around his waist. Meagan turned back to Jemima.

'Yep, desperate,' she said pushing herself up.

She clacked towards the door, barging Miles out of her way.

'At least when we move to LA we won't have to put up with any more of your shit,' Miles sneered at Meagan before winking at Jemima.

'You're going with *him*?' said Simi.

Jemima folded back into her seat and closed her eyes as the horror washed over her. Waking up next to Miles had been as bad a start to the day as she could imagine but clearly the Universe had seen that as a challenge. She exhaled hard suddenly aware of the tense quiet. She opened her eyes. Miles had gone, by the sounds of things, to the bathroom. Meagan had left, leaving the front door wide open in her wake and Simi was stuffing clothes into her black holdall.

'Simi,' said Jemima approaching her.

She continued packing, ignoring Jemima, who tried to put a hand on her shoulder. Simi brushed it off.

'You and Miles – in LA?' Simi snorted.

'I'm not going to LA with him. I promise you.'

'And the stories. How could you?' said Simi as she collected up her toiletries.

'I'm an idiot,' said Jemima, her heart heaving.

Simi stopped.

'You could have asked. It might not have been okay but you should have tried,' said Simi, her eyes glistening with tears.

Jemima stood back helplessly as Simi packed. This was unbearable. Simi's pain felt like emotional craters that plummeted down into the core of her soul.

'Alice's flatmate is on a theatre tour so I'll stay there,' said Simi sucking in her emotions.

'Please, you don't have to—' Jemima said grabbing her arm.

Simi yanked herself away.

'Yes, Jem. I do. I can't bring Chance here now, can I? You'll probably steal him too.'

Jemima's stomach churned at Simi's words. So, she and

Chance *were* serious? She tried to catch Simi's eye, searching for confirmation but Simi avoided her gaze, instead looping her bag strap over her head.

'I'll be back for the rest of my things,' said Simi before taking one last look around and leaving.

Jemima stood, rooted to the spot. She couldn't cry, she couldn't shout, she couldn't even be angry. Her pathetic desperation had ruined the one great thing in her life. Jemima fell to the floor as guttural sobs rocked her body. It was the end. As she throbbed with sadness, she felt a hand on her back. Miles scooped her up and pulled her to him, the warmth of his breath, soothing. He stroked her hair as her sobs ebbed and she slowly calmed.

'It's okay, Jem-Jem. Meagan won't sue. She loves you. She's just angry, as per,' said Miles.

He rocked Jemima, and at last the sorrow which had enveloped her subsided.

'You know what would make you feel better? Breakfast,' he said brushing hair from her face.

Yes, that was exactly what Jemima needed. She was emotionally as well as physically hungover and a great, big, greasy fry-up would most certainly ease the pain.

'That would be amazing,' she said smiling up at Miles.

'Good girl. Grab yourself some eggs and bacon. I've got a brunch thing to go to but, when I get back we can research my green card application. Best to start now because—'

'You're going out?' Jemima said pulling away.

'It's just a thing,' he said trying to haul her back into their hug. Jemima broke free from his grasp.

'Get out, Miles. Now,' she said.

'What?'

'Get out and don't come back. Don't call me. Don't text. Don't even think of me. Unfriend me on Facebook. Get out. We're done.'

Miles hesitated, 'Come on, sweetness.'

Jemima's eyes narrowed as she spotted a vase Shaheena had given her as a moving-in present. She picked it up, tossing it from hand to hand.

'Jem-Jem, you're upset,' said Miles.

'Too right I am. Now get out!' she said, pulling the vase back ready to launch it at his head.

Miles raised his hands and took a step forward. The vase whistled past him, shattering on the living-room wall. He turned to look at the fragments on the floor.

'JEM-JEM!'

'GET OUT!!' she screamed as her gaze jerked around the room in search of more missiles.

She hurled a dirty plate. It span through the air like a flying saucer piloted by a drunk alien. Alarm pulsated across Miles's face as he skidded into the hallway, one hand holding his towel the other slamming against the wall for balance.

'Have you lost your—!'

The plate smashed against the wall inches from his head.

'That's it, Jemima. You've lost me forever too!' he said as he ducked a metal tealight holder, which thudded into the wall sending plaster dust into the air.

'GOOD!' Jemima yelled as Miles bustled out of the front door.

She watched him spill down the stairs and out into the street, darting around, unsure where to go or what to do.

'You'll always be alone, Jem-Jem! You'll always be running away. Go to LA. No one cares!' he hollered from the street.

Jemima marched through to the bedroom, gathered up Miles's clothes and stomped back to the living room. She yanked the window open and threw everything out, enjoying the sight of his underwear fluttering to the ground.

'You're a lonely, pathetic lunatic. Always have been. Always will be!' Miles wailed.

'Here, catch,' Jemima said as she balled up his designer jeans and threw them out too.

She pushed down the window blocking out the sound of Miles's banshee-like cries and exhaled. Running her fingers through her hair, Jemima looked at the shards of glass and ceramics scattered everywhere. How had she made such a god-awful mess?

CHAPTER 42

Meagan

Meagan loitered in the corridor outside her office, watching the lift. It was less than twenty-four hours after the showdown at Jemima's and she had already set the legal wheels in motion. The only missing piece of her puzzle was Todd. She glanced at her watch. He was three minutes late. If they were going to stop Jemima's pile-of-crap novel going to press, they had to act fast.

Jemima had messed with the wrong people and it didn't matter how far she ran, Santa Monica, Saint Lucia or the Sea of Tranquillity, Meagan was coming for her. With every recognisable trait, conversation or story Meagan read, her fury had grown. She was not just angry at Jemima's full-blown betrayal. She was furious at herself for ignoring her instincts, which she'd done for weeks. Now, it was all so embarrassingly obvious. Why would a chronic singleton suddenly want to start dating? Well, it was over now. At the end of the corridor, the lift doors opened and Todd paced towards her, his face fixed. Good, she thought. He means business just as much as she does.

'What's going on?' he fumed.

'Don't worry, I've got it all worked out,' she said, hobbling behind him into her furniture-less office. 'We can get her on defamation of character, invasion of privacy and unreasonable publicity. That's just for starters. There might be something we can do around libel too.'

'Meagan, *we* can't do anything because you're not supposed to have read the book,' said Todd.

'Then why did you let me see it?'

'Look,' said Todd standing even taller than normal. 'I get that you want to have it out with your mate but this cannot happen.'

Meagan pounded her fist on a print-out of Jemima's manuscript which still sat on top of her filing cabinet. 'I'm going to do more than have it out with her. I'm going to bury this.'

Todd pressed his fingers into his temples, angering Meagan even more. He was behaving as though *she* was the one missing the point. His question shouldn't be why was Meagan suing but why wasn't he? If anything, he should be leading the charge.

'Meag, I've breached company confidentiality sending you that draft. I could lose my job,' said Todd.

'You'll lose a lot more if you don't get on board, mate,' Meagan hissed.

'Meagan?'

'*We* are going to make this book toast,' she said jabbing a finger into his firm chest.

'Meagan,' he said moving her hand.

She pushed him aside and began a maniacal circuit of her empty office.

'Once Hudson Hicks hear about this, they'll drop her like a rubber brick in a swimming pool,' she cackled.

Todd stepped in front of her. 'Meagan, stop.'

'What?' she said looking up at him. 'Look, this has "settle out of court" written all over it.'

Todd stepped aside, pushing his hands deep into his pockets.

'Don't worry. Hudson Hicks won't fire you. They'll thank you for saving them the embarrassment,' Meagan scoffed, hobble-pacing even more manically.

'Think about what you're saying.'

Against her will, Meagan's hand began to contract into a fist.

'What do you want me to think about? The betrayal or the theft or both?'

'How about me? My job,' said Todd.

Meagan felt that same burning sensation in her eyes she had that night outside Bruno's and at Jemima's yesterday morning. Despite her best attempts to quell them, tears came. But she knew better than to give in to them. They were just a bodily function like coughing or having a wee. As the hardness in Todd's expression fell away, her upset was replaced by anger.

'Don't you dare pity me. My eyes are crying but I'm not!' she said as a huge sob burst from her without permission.

Todd took a step towards her but she put her arm out, locking it at the elbow. He wasn't using this as a way in.

'Meagan,' he said, moving her hand from his chest.

'No,' she sobbed, squeezing her eyes as though trying to wring the tears from her body.

'My God, do you have to do *everything* yourself? You won't even let someone comfort you,' said Todd. 'Right, I need to go. I've got my Monday team meeting – if I've still got a job that is.'

'*What do you want?*' Meagan wanted to yell. Whatever it was, she couldn't give it to him.

Todd buttoned up his jacket and looked towards the door.

'Have a nice life with your new girlfriend!' Meagan scoffed as another sob burst from her.

'It was a date, Meagan. It was just a date,' he said reaching out to comfort her.

'Well, good riddance anyway.'

Todd pulled back.

'Wow. Okay, you know what, good luck,' he said before heading to the lift.

Meagan hobbled after him, scrabbling for something to say. Before she could think of anything, the elevator doors closed behind him and the noise of computers and conversation from the other offices seeped into her awareness. Once again, Meagan was on her own. She limped back into her office and leaned against the wall sliding down until she was seated on the floor. Feeling the coarse carpet tiles under her hand, she slipped further until she was lying in the foetal position and she wept. Meagan wept like she had never wept in her life. She wept for herself, for the loss of her friends, her heart, for the betrayal, the deep betrayal, and out of sheer fatigue.

She was exhausted.

Meagan had worked since the age of 16 and never leaning on anyone had left her without the energy to even stand. She looked around her empty office, desperately wishing it were filled with nice things. Nice things took the pain away but in this room there was nothing, just her immense misery. She hated nothing. Nothing was the space left behind when debt collectors took the family TV. Nothing was what was in her mum's purse when she wanted a new top or to go out with friends. Nothing was the contents of the fridge when she got home from school not just once but many times. 'Nothing' had made a 16-year-old

Meagan decide not only would she always have 'something' but she would most certainly amount to something too. Life had let her know, it was all down to her. But after fourteen years of grafting, on her empty office floor, what did she have to show for it? Even if she owned all the possessions money could buy, unshared things meant – nothing. Tears welled from the pit of her tired, broken heart, a heart that had never trusted the world, and instead coped by controlling *everything*, even who she loved. Was that why she was alone, why that arm's length she kept between her and everyone else suddenly felt like a chasm?

She laughed wearily at her oh-so-clever plan, a worthless fantasy as unreachable as any of Simi's cosmic wishes. Her plan wasn't a strategy. It was a futile attempt to strangle the spontaneity and glorious messiness out of life. Jemima was spot on. Even with Simi's acting Meagan had wrung out all natural impulses by trying to control it. Furthermore, it hadn't been to help Simi but to protect herself. She'd created that absurd, arbitrary rule so she didn't have to move on with her life plan because now the next step was upon her, she was terrified. From here on in, every phase involved leaning on someone, trusting them with no guarantees. They involved being vulnerable, which, like eating sushi and riding a bike, Meagan did not do. She curled herself into a tight ball on the floor. She didn't have a life plan. She had a cryogenic chamber. In work Meagan was fearless, but in life taking care of someone else's heart and letting them care for hers was the most terrifying prospect of all. More sobs poured from her, but this time it was a release, one that had been a long time coming. She sobbed as she realised all she had lost by controlling *everything* – Simi and Todd, a bigger life that didn't gravitate solely around work. In fact, if she weren't such a control freak, she might actually have a desk and chair to cry on but she'd controlled that out of existence too.

Just as her misery threatened to consume her, the landline phone rang. She groaned into the floor and snivelled her way across the carpet to hit the speaker button.

'Yes?' she blubbed.

'It's Denise on reception. Your lawyer's here. Are you—?'

'Send her up,' Meagan whimpered.

She ended the call and rolled onto her back.

CHAPTER 43

Simi

Simi piled up the remainder of her belongings in Jemima's hallway and she stared wistfully at her tiny tower of things. Had it really been seven weeks since she'd moved out of Oscar's place? And now she was moving again. This time it was into Alice's Norwood flat on the dreaded south side of the river. Just days ago, the thought of living so far from the girls had been unthinkable. Now, it didn't matter. Simi checked her watch. Her cab was due at quarter past giving her ten long minutes to decide what kind of farewell Jemima deserved. When she'd been packing earlier, she'd felt so incensed, an apartment-shuddering door slam was all she could have managed. Now her departure loomed, however, a curt 'bye' from the other side of Jemima's closed bedroom door, seemed only fair.

Simi looked around the living room, her home for almost two months. Without her clutter, it was decidedly neater. Simi felt pangs of guilt at Jemima's generous hospitality. She owed her a thank-you for that, at the very minimum. Unless, thought Simi, as a creeping suspicion gathered momentum, Jemima let her stay so she could harvest intel? Two months' rent was a small price to pay for such priceless data. Simi stomped towards Jemima's bedroom door, thumping hard. She listened to her move across the room. When the door finally opened, Simi stopped. Jemima's eyes were puffy and drained, her body slumped. Simi wanted to hug her and tell her everything was going to be alright. She wanted to stroke her ashen face and reassure her that before she knew it they'd be sipping cocktails at Ripley's like none of this had happened. She wanted to say all that. But she couldn't. She was still so, so hurt.

'Did you want me to stay here so you could get more stories?'

'Of course not,' said Jemima visibly crumbling.

'Hmm.' Simi nodded, studying Jemima's earnest expression. What she had done was unspeakable but even Simi knew she wasn't *that* underhand.

'Can I help you with your things?' said Jemima.

'I can manage,' Simi said, more brusque than she'd intended.

As tough as it was seeing Jemima unravelling, Simi still couldn't access the warmth and love she'd always had for her. Was it gone forever? She didn't know. Forgiveness was certainly a long way off. They'd bickered in the past, even fallen out for a few days but nothing like this had ever happened and the sense of loss was numbing. Good girlfriends were so hard to find, friends with whom you could be totally you, who would love you no matter how ridiculous the things you did, said, loved or wanted. Why had Jemima done this to them all?

'I know what it is. You think I'm a wally, a soft touch. That's why you thought it would be okay.'

'I don't,' Jemima pleaded.

'It's like you preferred me unemployed, single and with my

life in a mess. But now I've landed a job, got a place to live and finally found a good man, you don't like that.'

Remorse flickered through Simi as the lie tumbled from her. The truth was, she knew Chance's true feelings for Jemima. That didn't stop her wanting to push the dagger in just a little, make Jemima hurt as she was. The reality was Simi hadn't seen or spoken to Chance since he'd left on Sunday morning. She also suspected the only reason he'd arranged that second date was as an apology for the London Eye incident. He really was a good man. If only Jemima could bring herself to let him in. Simi shifted her gaze. If she was going, she had to do it now. As much as she couldn't inflict any more pain, neither was she ready to give Jemima the absolution she desperately wanted.

'Please, Sim. Tell me how to put this right,' Jemima begged, holding out her hand.

Simi wished she had the answer but her mind and her spirit were blank. With nothing more to say she turned away from Jemima's outstretched hand, scooping up her bags. She yanked open the door and began hauling everything downstairs as a heart that had previously beaten as one was unnaturally torn in three.

CHAPTER 44

Jemima

Jemima's phone blared for attention and she knew its klaxon ringtone meant one thing. It was Shaheena. She scrambled around in the folds of her bedding to silence her phone – again. It rang through to voicemail and she collapsed back into her pillows. She had been in bed for three days getting up only to say goodbye to Simi, pee and eat what she could scavenge from her bare cupboards. Last night she'd eaten baked beans from the tin and, if she didn't get her act together, today it would be sauerkraut for breakfast again. Make that lunch, she sighed. It was already 2.15 p.m.

Jemima forced herself out of bed. She padded to the window to pull the curtains open and grimaced. It was a bright, crisp day but all she wanted was to block out the sun and extinguish its joyful rays. She wanted to pretend the world wasn't happening, like somehow, existence itself was some huge, clerical error. Defeated, she slipped back under her duvet. She felt exhausted, as much by the daylight as her futile attempts to put right the waking nightmare she'd created. Her reconciliatory overtures to Meagan had been met with a nuisance-caller-whistle blown down the phone at her. She'd tried calling Simi but every time it had just rung and rung. She had even called Todd but as she'd listened to the ringing tone, she'd realised she hadn't a clue what to say – *sorry for outing your southpaw penis?* In the end she'd hung up, eaten a mouthful of sauerkraut and gone to bed. Once more her phone klaxoned. Again, she let it ring through to voicemail purgatory. Straight away, a text message whooshed in.

We need to talk lawyers. URGENT

Jemima buried her face in the pillow. So, Meagan's lawsuit was happening and once she'd finished with Jemima, not even deep-sea rescue divers would be able to find the wreckage. Jemima felt like Atlas but instead of bearing the weight of the world on her shoulders, she was carrying a steaming pile of shit. Filth fest, a juvenile political statement, had been a colossal waste of time and upset the one person who'd given her a chance. She'd abused her friends' trust, using them and because of paralysis in her own love life, she had all but killed Beverly's. To win, Jemima had lost – massively.

She laughed sadly, realising how closely Beverly's romantic journey mirrored her own. In her first book, which Jemima had written when she and Miles were still together, Beverly had been in love, entangled with her boss, Kane. That minor storyline had been sensual, dangerous. However, by the time Jemima started writing *Beverly Blake Mysteries* she and Miles were no more. She killed Kane with a heart attack, leaving him to die in an abandoned lock-up. He was slain in the same way a part of her had died, abandoned and with an unfixable heart. That's when Beverly had become a single-minded workaholic with no room for anything but the job. Jemima's push-back at Eve's notes had been totally disproportionate but only now could she see why. Jemima had always thought she was defending a principle but really she was protecting herself from delving into waters she felt too weak to swim in. There were so many ways she could have handled Eve's note, a deep dive into her own romantic past was just one solution. Damn it, there were probably YouTube videos on how to write romance but she had done nothing. Instead, she convinced herself that because of the deadline she had no other options. But this didn't come down to time. It was about Jemima's unshakable fear that love, true love, breaks you and that hadn't even started with Miles. That had come from losing her dad. Jemima pulled herself up in her bed as the fragments of her life's puzzle began to order themselves in her mind. After losing the love of her life, her father, Jemima had constantly settled when it came to relationships. In Miles she'd fallen in love with a compromise because the fear of finding and falling for a great man scared her so much. It scared her because if you loved, you lost – and that pain was unbearable. And this fear had bled into her writing. She had made Beverly so cold and closed off that readers never truly knew her heart. Jemima gasped as the penny dropped so loudly it practically clanged inside her head. Eve wasn't asking for her to make Beverly need a man. She was asking for her to *want* one. It wasn't even about a man. It was about passion, feeling and being fully alive. That's why the backstory detail had worked so well, because readers could finally connect with Beverly through what she had once desired. Jemima wanted to laugh – a pain-filled, ironic, Alanis Morrissette guffaw.

She looked at Shaheena's text again. If this was the end of

Beverly, Jemima wanted to enjoy one last moment with her. She would call Shaheena later but while the executioner's keys still jangled in the distance, she would head to Nostromo. Azi and Rania would say kind words and make her a nice, milky latte with a piece of cake she hadn't asked for but would gratefully receive. Yes, Nostromo was ideal. It was where Beverly had come in to being and therefore the right place to hold her wake.

Jemima pushed open the café door. The blissful relief of being somewhere warm and welcoming, was instant.

'Am I pleased to see you! My usual please, Azi,' said Jemima as she went to sit in the airplane seats.

'I've a good mind not to serve you,' Azi stropped.

Jemima blinked at her, bewildered.

'Is this… Are you joking?' she spluttered, looking to Rania for clarity.

Rania shrugged and busied herself taking cups out of the dishwasher.

'You threw away your chance, you silly girl,' Azi fumed.

Jemima shuddered. She knew Azi had a temper but never imagined she'd be on the receiving end of it.

Rania rested a hand on her wife's arm. 'Az, you said you would leave it.'

'Yes, well, I say a lot,' Azi said wriggling from Rania.

'He chose Simi. I didn't do anything,' said Jemima.

'No, you didn't. This is my point. Eight pounds,' said Azi holding out her hand while pointedly turning away.

Shaking, Jemima rummaged in her pockets for change. 'Have you put your prices up?'

'Chance tax,' said Azi as she cluttered about, preparing Jemima's drink, 'because he probably won't show his face in here anymore in case he bumps into *you*.'

'Well, that's not exactly right. He said he was getting ready for a training thing... ' said Rania as Azi shot her a glare.

'A training thing he's doing to avoid bumping into Jemima!' she snapped and with an indignant swish, she disappeared into the back room.

Rania gave Jemima an apologetic shrug. She picked up the metal jug Azi had abandoned and continued steaming the milk.

A second later Azi stuck her head back around the doorway, 'And she's having that to go.'

'Yes, my love.' Rania smiled forlornly at Jemima as she replaced the mug with a take-away cup.

Jemima backed away from the counter, shaking. She pulled out her phone going straight to Rebecca's last message. Her hand waivered before typing, I'm in. This wasn't running away. It was pragmatism. Why stick around if you're not wanted – anywhere.

'Here,' said Rania, putting Jemima's coffee on the counter before beckoning her close. 'I saw him heading to the park for a break.'

Jemima looked up at her as she gripped the cardboard holder. Rania was sweet but it was too late.

'Cheers,' she said as she added two more names to her list of people to escape.

'Don't forget, Jem, the park,' said Rania.

Jemima shrugged and left.

Out on the pavement she took a sip of her coffee, its sweet, milky warmth taking the edge off her sorrow. She looked at Chance's practice, her eyes drawn, as always, up. Could either of them tolerate a goodbye? Of all the people entangled in this mess, he was the only one not angry with her – she hoped. With America now a certainty, a final farewell to Chance could be the best full stop to this sorry car crash she could expect. Just then the 11a bus rumbled past her. She knew its route well. After the post office it took a right and went straight past the park – their park. She hesitated for a moment, then made a dash for the bus stop.

Jemima held the railings, her breath shallow. As she scanned the children's playground and ornamental garden, she spotted Chance. He was sitting by the pond, pulling apart a sandwich and throwing scraps to a hungry congregation of pigeons. She walked around to a side gate and approached him.

'Made some new friends,' she said nodding towards the pigeons.

He looked up and a smile broke which he quickly buried.

'Hey,' he said going back to ripping up his sandwich.

'I, umm, I just wanted to say sorry you got caught up in the thing on Sunday,' she said, hovering awkwardly by his side.

An apology was a safe place to start given she owed one to pretty much everybody. Chance shrugged, tossing the remainder of his lunch aside. One by one, the pigeons waddled towards it. Jemima wished her life were that simple, just carb-loading and trying not to step in your own shit.

'From the little I heard, it sounded like a nightmare,' he said, dusting crumbs off his hands.

'A nightmare would have been preferable. You can wake up from those,' said Jemima as she tore at the rim of her coffee cup. 'Someone with less scruples than you suggested I did it.'

'Miles?' Chance asked.

Jemima looked away. Discussing Miles was like discussing the *Titanic* with passengers on the *QEII*. No one would feel better after that.

'Simi mentioned him the other night. Said he was your big love and that you were back together.'

An uncomfortable silence descended as Jemima foundered.

'So is it true? Are you back together?'

'We're not but... ' she begun then stopped.

It wasn't that simple. Now she was committed to a new choice, to standing still – in LA. She had given Rebecca her word; a promise had been made. Soon deposits would be sent and flights booked. And after that, there would be no more running away. No reneging. She would put down roots and finally stand still, out of everyone's way.

'Well so you know, nothing happened with Simi. She got a bit tipsy so I carried her home and nodded off on the couch,' said Chance.

'What you two do is none of my business,' Jemima said, regret quickly following as Chance recoiled.

'Well, aren't I the dumb arse,' he said, standing.

'The thing is, Chance. I'm going to America, a house swap,' said Jemima standing too.

'You don't have to explain to me,' he said turning for the exit.

'I know,' said Jemima, gently pulling him back. 'I want to. All my life I've been running away. It's time to put down roots.'

'In LA?'

'Yes.'

'What about your roots here, your family, your friends?' he asked.

'You saw how royally I've screwed that up. I need a fresh start,' said Jemima.

'Well, I hope Beverly makes it,' Chance said, his tone softening. 'I liked her.'

A despondent smile briefly crossed his face then he turned to leave. The moment he was out of sight, Jemima's knees buckled and she slumped back onto the park bench, too in despair to even cry. LA could not come soon enough. Now she was almost at rock bottom it was time to call Shaheena. Delaying the descent any longer was more agonising than simply thudding to the floor. She dialled, awaiting the inevitable.

'Bloody hell, Jemima, where the hell have you been? I've been calling you for three days!' barked Shaheena. 'Anyway, more importantly, guess who got caught in the gender-neutral toilets at the Hudson Hicks party getting a blowie off of—'

'Aren't agents supposed to be discreet?' Jemima interjected.

Shaheena gasped. 'When have I *ever* been indiscreet?'

Jemima bristled, 'You told Miles about filth fest.'

Shaheena went quiet.

'He tricked me! Said he was interested in selling the TV rights for you!'

'Shaheena, just tell me what Meagan's lawyer said.' Jemima no longer possessed the energy to even reprimand her.

'*Meagan's* lawyer? *Whatchu talkin' 'bout, Willis?*'

'You sent a text about lawyers,' said Jemima losing the will to live.

'Yes, I blinkin' did. Okay, are you sitting down?'

'Yes,' said Jemima bending forward to give the executioner a clear view of her neck.

'Right. First of all, Hudson Hicks want you to come in and discuss ideas for more Beverly books. If you have any stories up your sleeve, I would pull them out *tout de suite* because my waters tell me there could be a two, possibly three book deal in the offing,' Shaheena giggled.

Jemima blinked, trying to take in her words. A moment ago, her entire career was heading for the bottom of the ocean but somehow it had been thrown a lifeline.

'Shaheena, that's amazing. I—'

'That's not even the best part. You know IPC who do all those book adaptations? They're doing *Clash of the Crown* next and rumour has it, *The Cave* as a limited series. Well, they're interested in buying the rights to the Beverly Blake franchise,' she squealed.

Jemima sat up. 'What do you mean?'

'They want to turn Beverly Blake into a series. We need a contracts lawyer coz this is *money moves*, girlfriend!'

Shaheena whooped down the phone but before Jemima could join in the celebrations, reality sunk in. If the girls were going to veto the book, a TV adaptation would be out of the question.

'That's great news, Shaheena, but it's not going to work,' said Jemima.

'What? You no likey money?' said Shaheena. 'Jem, this is it. You've made it. There's nothing standing in our way.'

'Yeah,' said Jemima, 'about that.'

CHAPTER 45

Meagan

Meagan watched her printer slowly spew out each page of Simi's *Clash of the Crown* contract. All the while, behind her she could hear Simi fidgeting.

'Still no furniture?' Simi said into the void.

'Oh my God, I've been robbed,' Meagan gasped sarcastically before snatching Simi's contract from the printer.

Though she wished she could verbally eviscerate her, Meagan had to keep Simi onside. After Todd declared himself out of the lawsuit earlier in the week, she was her last ally.

Meagan pasted on a rigid smile and handed the contract over. 'You set for filming on Saturday?'

'They're flying me to Dublin tomorrow afternoon,' Simi said looking around for a flat surface, eventually smoothing out the paperwork on the nearest wall.

Meagan watched Simi jiggle her pen to draw down the ink, embarrassed. She didn't even have a horizontal surface for clients to sign a few crumby papers on. This is what her life now amounted to – a shitty, deskless vacuum.

'Just sign pages three, eight and ten. I can fill out the rest,' said Meagan suddenly wanting Simi to leave.

'I'll fill it out. You don't know my new address,' Simi said, shuffling through the contract.

Meagan frowned. Who was this efficient, business-like Simi and what had she done with her bubbly, fun friend?

'So, are you excited?' Meagan asked.

'No notes, okay?' said Simi eyes still on her paperwork.

Meagan swayed, momentarily speechless.

'I... I... ' she stammered. 'All I was going to say was, having *Crown* on your CV will impress your new reps.'

Had this been any other client, Meagan would have left a size-four footprint on their arse as she booted them out of her office.

'I don't have a new agent,' Simi confessed, handing back the signed papers.

Meagan's tummy fluttered.

'I see,' she said searching for what to say.

'Well, I better get going. Got to pack,' said Simi slipping her handbag into the crook of her arm.

Meagan shifted her weight. Part of her wanted to tell Simi good riddance. She wanted to point and laugh from the bleachers as Simi tried to make it with no agent, but even Meagan knew that was coming from her hurt.

'If you don't have a new agent... I can still, you know,' Meagan hazarded.

'Meagan... '

'No more notes. Promise. My only job will be making sure the world knows how brilliant you are and once they meet Cake, they will,' said Meagan.

Standing in the middle of her bare office, she had never been surer of anything. She loved the woman standing in front of her and would do whatever it took to keep her in her life. She wasn't going to let ten years of friendship slip away just like that.

'And we'll keep business and friendship separate. It got messy but we can clean that up. I want you as my client and I need you as my friend. You're the best, you frigging idiot,' said Meagan as tears flowed.

She searched Simi's face for a sign, but this time, her expression was unreadable.

'What do you want from me, Sim?' said Meagan throwing up her arms in frustration.

'I don't know!' Simi said. 'Just, stop. Stop... pretending to know everything and how to do everything... Stop acting like you don't need anyone, that you can do it all yourself. Everyone needs someone. You are a beautiful, capable, intelligent, generous black woman but no one said you have to do it all alone. Everyone around you wants to support you but you never let us in. Not me, Jem, Todd, anyone! If you don't need us, why do you even have us in your life!'

'It's not that simple. I've been on my own since I was 16. I relied on someone once and they let me down. Never again,' Meagan said, her body tightening as memories crowded her.

'Meagan,' said Simi, a firmness in her voice, 'Parker was a married man. You were too young to understand but he wasn't yours to rely on. You must see that.'

Meagan trembled at the mention of his name. But as much as she wanted to scream, Simi's words were true. Parker was never hers and she'd got burned not because of what he had done but because of what she'd expected. And after, she'd re-orientated her whole life because of that.

'I don't know how to do it any other way,' said Meagan, 'I don't know how to let people in.'

'There is no *how*. You just allow the people waiting to be there for you, to be there for you,' Simi said reaching out to Meagan.

As Simi's words sunk in, Meagan's noble island, which she'd dwelled on for so long, began to feel like a lone mass drifting out to sea. Unable to sustain her remoteness anymore, Meagan collapsed into Simi's arms, each clinging to the other for dear life.

'I'm scared, Sim,' sobbed Meagan.

Simi enveloped her arms around her. 'That's why I'm here.'

And with that, Meagan let go fully, falling into Simi's kind embrace.

An hour into her newfound vulnerability, Meagan was still finding her feet. One thing she was sure of, to make this journey she needed Simi by her side. And as she looked around her sparse office, she realised, friendship was the only thing she had ever needed. But now she and Simi had begun to get themselves onto an even keel, it was time to get down to business.

'So my legal team will be getting in touch with Jemima tomorrow,' she began, reaching for the paperwork her solicitor had left with her.

'You and Todd are really going to sue her?'

Meagan laughed drily. Was there any other option? The punishment had to fit the crime.

'Well, Todd bailed but two plaintiffs are still enough,' Meagan continued.

Simi looked at her confused. 'Two?'

'Yeah. Me and you.'

'But—'

Annoyance brew within. Did Meagan once again have to explain why this was not just necessary but justice.

'Simi, you are about to do the biggest show of your career. Even for the small roles, hack journos will sniff around for gossip like a mutt up a poodle's arse. As your agent and *your friend*, I'm telling you, we have to shut this down,' she ordered, laying on her best Meagan glare.

Simi cleared her throat but said nothing and Meagan seethed. As usual, she would have to take this on by herself – the story of her life. Why did she think today would be different? she bridled as her thoughts spilled into a resentful eddy. But then, she stopped herself, dumbfounded. Her loner mindset was so ingrained she was almost powerless in its face. She reeled at how quickly the anger had surged as though it had a life of its own, possessing its own spiteful intent.

'Sorry, Simi. Old habits.' Meagan shuddered.

'It's hard, Meag, I know,' said Simi laying a reassuring hand on her.

Meagan smiled. 'Look, I can't force you to join this lawsuit. It's your call.'

Simi puckered her lips side to side, weighing her decision as Meagan waited, her breath bated.

'Jemima was out of line,' Simi began.

'Exactly.'

'But it's a big step. Plus, it's expensive and she is… sorry, *was* our best friend,' Simi continued.

'I'll take care of the money and if we win, which we will,

she'll have to pay our expenses anyway,' said Meagan trying to rein in her frustration.

'Not that it's about the money,' Simi pondered.

Meagan balled her toes inside her shoe, wanting to scream in Simi's face but she held it in. That was old Meagan. New, sensitive Meagan would give Simi all the time she needed – whilst biting her new, sensitive tongue.

At last, Simi slapped her hands on her thighs. 'I'm in. I think. Yes, I am. Let's shut it down.'

'Yes, mate!' yelped Meagan, high-fiving Simi.

Strong-arming people had always been Meagan's go-to tactic. She was stunned to find there were actually other ways to get what you wanted. She would have to try this *patience* malarkey again sometime.

'This is the right thing, Simster,' she said, clocking Simi's downturned demeanour. 'It'll be fine.'

Meagan leaned in for a fist bump.

'Cool. I think. Yes, cool,' Simi said, tapping her fist against Meagan's.

CHAPTER 46

Simi

Simi waited until she was alone before letting out a giddy squeal. After weeks of bizarre auditions, notes, waiting and uncertainty, she was finally on location. She laughed as she twirled around her huge trailer, arms outstretched, her fingertips not touching a single wall. After a few bounces on her sofa, she inspected her kitchen including a fully stocked fridge, and her bathroom, complete with power shower. This trailer was nicer than her first flat and all this for someone doing just one day of filming. As she soaked up her surroundings, there was a knock at the door. It was Kelly, the production runner.

'Ready for some breakfast?'

'Sure. Where do I go?' Simi asked.

'No, I bring it to you, unless you're not hungry,' said Kelly about to move on.

'No, no. I am. Umm, I'll just have fruit and porridge… with some seeds. Aaaaand,' said Simi pretending to ponder, 'a bacon and egg sandwich with ketchup.'

'Cool,' said Kelly scribbling shorthand on her pad. 'Also

make-up are ready for you so if we could get you in your costume that'd be great.'

'Copy that,' said Simi with an unnecessary salute.

Kelly smiled before disappearing off to the next trailer.

'Make-up are ready for me,' Simi mimicked as another delighted squeal burst from her. Quickly gathering herself, she pulled her freshly pressed medieval tunic from its hanger. 'Okay, one cake, coming up.'

Simi ogled the huge spread of salads and food warmers brimming with all kinds of deliciousness. She'd been waiting in her trailer fully made up and in costume for so long it was lunch time. With a full plate, Simi stepped onto the dining truck and looked around for her fellow kitchen wenches who she'd met in make-up that morning. Joining a new set was always daunting so having a mini-tribe made the day just a little easier. Having spotted them she headed over but as she was almost upon them, she noticed a familiar face towards the back of the truck. Without her usual nails, lashes and weave, she looked different but there was no mistaking, it was Sandra Scott. Sitting alone, picking at her food, she was far from the ray of sunshine that burst into audition rooms dazzling everyone. Today Sandra looked more like the shadow than the sun. Simi took a deep breath and shuffled between the tables towards her. She passed a huddle of electricians complaining about overtime, the director chewing his camerawoman's ear off about their next shot and the make-up team laughing naughtily at an in-joke. Finally she reached Sandra.

'Hey,' said Simi.

Sandra looked up. 'Simi?' she said, trying to raise a smile. 'You're on this too? That's fantastic.'

'Yeah. Well, I was just coming over to say hi,' Simi said turning to join her kitchen posse.

'Fair enough,' said Sandra, her voice weak. 'Cameron said I was to sit by myself anyway.'

Simi paused. 'Why?'

This was meant to be a dream gig not a bullet to dodge. She was intrigued.

'Because she's decided my character is a loner,' Sandra said jabbing at a tomato while discreetly wiping away tears.

Simi set down her tray opposite Sandra, no longer intrigued but concerned. 'She shouldn't be making choices for your character. That's not fair.'

Sandra rested her head in her hand. 'She never *stops*. That's why we're overrunning. The director tells me one thing then she says another. It's like I'm a puppet, *The Sooty and Sweep Show* but instead of Matthew Corbett with his hand up my arse, it's bloody Cameron Christiansen.'

Simi offered Sandra her napkin to wipe her eyes, knowing all too well what it was like being bombarded with unsolicited advice.

'I wish I was one of the kitchen girls. You all seem to be having so much fun,' Sandra said.

Simi blinked at her, stunned. After years of envying Sandra, now Simi had something *she* wanted? Life – it made no sense. Sandra Scott was the walking, talking epitome of an unobtainable perfection. Everyone from classmates to family, the media and more had drummed into Simi that fair skin, straight hair, long nails, good eyelashes, thin waists, long calves, hairless arms, thin ankles, small ears and a million other traits, were

338

good and what Simi had wasn't. Perhaps it would help Sandra to know just how revered she is, thought Simi.

Sandra stopped nudging her food around and seemed to deflate. 'The funny thing is, Simi, I was always jealous of you.'

Simi stared back at Sandra, dumbfounded. Of *what?* she puzzled.

'You're naturally gorgeous. You've got this beautiful, thick hair, lovely, clear skin, You never have to bother with false anything. I was always intimidated by that. At auditions, I feel like I have to compensate,' said Sandra.

Life from Sandra's side of the table didn't look anything like Simi had imagined. Sandra wasn't like Meagan, using her beauty embellishments to reveal herself. She used them to hide. Simi listened, agog as Sandra explained that she kept her lank hair under a weave because it was getting greyer by the day. Her nails were brittle so she covered them with gels and though it did her dry skin no good she always wore make-up – even in the gym. And all of that was shrouded behind a big, confident smile. Simi squeezed Sandra's hand.

'You are beautiful and a brilliant actor. Speak to the director because what Cameron's doing is bullying and no one should have to put up with that.'

They sat, holding hands in a bonded stillness.

'Call me Morenike. That's my real name,' Sandra whispered with a vulnerable smile.

Simi blinked. 'You're Nigerian?'

Sandra nodded conspiratorially and Simi squeezed Morenike's hand even more.

'We have *so much* to talk about. We should totally hang out,' she said, excitedly.

'I would *love* that,' Morenike replied.

As the two of them sat grinning together, the dining truck wobbled and Kelly stepped on. 'Okay guys, that's lunch. Sorry for the delay but, Simi, girls, we'll be coming to the kitchen scene next.'

'Right,' replied Simi.

She got up and squished round to Morenike's side of the table to give her a hug. 'It'll be alright,' she whispered.

Quickly, Simi shovelled down a mouthful of food and stuffed a bread roll in her apron. A moment later, zigzagging between the cluster of Winnebagos, she wondered how she had got Sandra so wrong. Far from being this impeccable, impenetrable automaton, Morenike was just as vulnerable as she, if not more. Simi was looking forward to getting to know her new friend, Morenike.

She stepped onto her trailer and immediately was struck by a beautiful aroma, the glorious scent of two enormous bouquets on her coffee table. She dashed over, plucking a card from the first bunch.

You've got this, with love, your agent,
your friend, your Meagan xx

Simi kissed the card and slipped it back into its envelope.

Her hand hovered over the second card nestled between an array of beautiful lilies and long-stemmed roses.

Eternally sorry. When or if you
forgive me, I will be waiting. Jem x

Simi ran her fingers along the card, feeling the love infused in each word. She clutched it to her chest, rereading it, her heart filling up. Yes, Jemima had messed up but she'd apologised a million times in as many ways as she could. Even though Simi was yet to respond, Jemima had not stopped calling, texting and emailing since their fateful fallout a week ago. More importantly, she showed no sign of letting up any time soon and Simi didn't want her to. The pain of what Jemima had done was huge but the pain of losing her was far greater. If she and Meagan could make peace after their bust-up, there had to be a way back for Jemima and suing her was not going to help that in any way.

Kelly knocked on Simi's trailer door. 'Ready for you, Simi,' she called.

'Got it,' said Simi as she hastily dialled Meagan.

'What is it? Is Cameron being a dick? Do you want me to come and——?'

'Meag. I haven't got long. I needed to tell you on the phone. I can't do the lawsuit. I'm sorry.'

Kelly knocked again, rattling the frosted glass on Simi's door.

'I'll talk to you later,' Simi said hanging up.

Jemima was by no means forgiven, but Simi was not going to punish her further either. She had suffered enough.

Outside her door, she could hear Kelly radioing ahead, telling the onset team she was on her way. She positioned herself in front of her full-length mirror and struck a Wonder Woman pose. Alice had sworn this was good for confidence.

'Cake!' she barked.

She was ready.

CHAPTER 47

Jemima

Since her call with Shaheena the previous afternoon, Jemima had played out every scenario and they all led to the same dead end. If she didn't take the deal, that was the end of the road with Hudson Hicks. If she did, her friendship with the girls would be irreparable. And the reality was, even in LA, there was no escaping whatever vulture lawyer Meagan sent circling. The worst part was, she still hadn't heard from them and the wait was becoming more excruciating by the day. Jemima's head span at the possible outcomes. Was there a chance Hudson Hicks would back her? Or would they join the litigation congo line and sue her too? At the very least they'd want their advance back and that was long gone.

Jemima took an out-of-date pack of coffee grounds from her cupboard and heaped a couple of tablespoons into her old cafetière. This was her new rock bottom, not even being able to go to Nostromo for her morning pick-me-up for fear of being torched by Azi's wrath. As she poured the water, she realised, she had control over nothing. The horse hadn't just bolted, it was darting around the field, taking a massive dump over everything. Prior to sending that final draft to Eve, she could have stopped this. Now, she couldn't even go to her favourite coffee shop. She pushed down the plunger and the coffee swirled through its wiry mesh. Jemima paused. Whether Meagan sued or Hudson Hicks dropped her was out of her hands but there was one thing she still had power over. She searched the recent calls on her phone and dialled.

'Shaheena, it's me.'

'Have I got some juicy goss—'

'I'm not taking the deal or the adaptation. I'm not taking any of it,' Jemima said interrupting her.

The other end of the phone fell silent.

'Shaheena?' Jemima said.

'Shush. I'm thinking.'

Jemima waited, quietly surprised that contemplation was something Shaheena even did. Maybe she was weighing up whether to sue her as well.

'This is about Meagan and Simi finding out they're in the book?' Shaheena asked.

'Yes,' Jemima said, as her misery surfaced all over again.

'Have you actually heard from Meagan's lawyer?' Shaheena pressed.

'No, but… '

'No buts. She hasn't got grounds, Jem,' Shaheena interjected.

'But… '

'Do you name her?'

'No.'

'Does Beverly look like her?'

'Well, no but—'

'Ah, ah. No buts. So, the similarities are, what?' Shaheena asked, almost triumphant.

'Well, they both had a friend with benefits,' explained Jemima.

'Who *hasn't* got a friend with benefits, or should have one, no names mentioned, *Jemima Abeson*?'

'But… '

'Jem, it's *coincidental*. We don't include that page one disclaimer for our health. It's precisely to stop morons like Meagan doing this kind of thing,' Shaheena said.

'There's a hell of a lot of coincidences,' said Jemima, not daring to dream Shaheena might be right.

Certainly, in terms of characteristics, Beverly was now a fusion of all three of them with the fastidious, clinical aspects of Jemima, the forthrightness of Meagan and Simi's vulnerability. No one person, not even Jemima could claim the character was solely based on them. Even Beverly's romantic paralysis belonged to all three of them.

'You're a creative. You take inspiration from everywhere. I bet I'm in there somewhere!' said Shaheena.

How ironic Shaheena wanted to be in the book while everyone else wanted out.

'Yeah,' Jemima lied.

'I knew it, you little tinker,' Shaheena giggled. 'Look, Meagan's got nothing, okay. So, no more talk of turning down book deals.'

Jemima leaned against her kitchen counter. Even if Meagan didn't have a case, which would give her a professional reprieve, personally she was still in the doghouse, cowering in the canine cathedral and that was a much, much bigger deal.

'Maybe,' said Jemima taking a considered gulp of her coffee, 'but I'm still going to LA.'

'Man alive, Jemima. Why?' Shaheena wailed.

Jemima massaged her neck, feeling drained. Suddenly she realised, for LA to truly be a new beginning, a chance to leave everything behind, that everything had to include Beverly. Taking her to LA would just be an agonising reminder of all Jemima had lost. A sorrowful gloom descended. She and Beverly had been on a journey that had started nearly fifteen years ago in Jemima's imagination. She was as much a part of her world as any living, breathing human and now, just as Beverly was finding her stride, she was about to become another casualty of Jemima's own selfish stupidity. She held the phone from her face as tears of bereavement fell.

'You've lost your bloody marbles, darling,' said Shaheena elbowing into Jemima's pity party. 'You can't leave those girls. Not Beverly, Meagan or Simi. Meagan is clearly a workaholic lunatic. Without you, she'll have no one. She'll just work herself to exhaustion and that Simi *definitely* needs you.'

'They don't. More accurately, they don't want me. I can't even get Simi to take my calls,' said Jemima with a morbid finality.

'Jemmy, don't do something you'll regret. Nothing is broken forever. Besides, what about me? I need you.'

Jemima fell silent. This was the sweetest thing Shaheena had ever said to her but it was too late. She had to do this.

'Hey, did I tell you about the waiter I snogged at the party?' said Shaheena.

Jemima groaned to herself. Only Shaheena could one-eighty like that on a heart-to-heart.

'Shaheena, I have to go,' said Jemima.

'He's into all that Tao stuff and he told me a story about this girl who tried to run away from her shadow. You heard it?'

345

'No,' said Jemima, rolling her eyes.

'So this woman wants to escape her own footsteps and her shadow,' began Shaheena.

'Why?' Jemima asked like a cranky teen.

'I don't know. That's just what happens in fables. Anyway, she wanted to escape her footsteps and her shadow so she decided to run but every time she put her foot down, there they were, her footsteps and her shadow, so she ran faster and faster until she dropped dead.'

'Well, you know I love a happy ending,' Jemima grizzled.

'The point is, Jem. She didn't realise, if she'd just stepped into the shade, the footsteps and the shadow would have disappeared. She just needed to find herself a big old tree and stay still.'

Jemima sighed. 'Listen, Shaheena. I really have to—'

'Look, usually I hate fables. I'm like, no one sleeps for a hundred years, stop demonising old women and under normal circumstances, the hare would have won! But I heard this one and straight away, thought of you. Just chew on it, okay? Laters,' said Shaheena, and she hung up.

Jemima set down her cup, massaging her brow. Maybe Shaheena had a point and this was fixable. Maybe too, this wasn't the time for running away but to take on her life, walk past that body and look. As she contemplated this, her phone pinged with a text message from her local taxi firm.

Your airport pick-up is outside. You have five minutes of free waiting.

Well, she couldn't think about that now. Life would just have to take its course. Only time would tell if she was making the right choice, she thought as she headed for the door.

346

CHAPTER 48

Simi

Simi watched the carousel trundle past, battling the urge to clamber on and get carried around the baggage reclaim hall.

'Don't you just want to sit on that thing?' said Morenike as she waited for her bag next to Simi.

'I was just thinking that!' Simi chuckled.

How things had changed since the catering truck, she thought. After filming their scene, which Simi was relieved had gone well, all the kitchen girls and Morenike had gone out together. Had they not had such an early flight, Simi was sure they'd have stayed up all night. After raiding their minibars they'd retreated to her room where they'd shared acting horror stories. Simi had had them howling at her impression of Gabe. They'd discussed creepy directors, lovely producers and everything in between until they'd noticed the sun creeping up and reluctantly called it a night. On the plane, Simi and Morenike had sat together and hardly stopped talking and laughing the whole flight home.

'Oh, there's mine,' said Morenike.

She hoisted a Louis Vuitton case off the conveyor belt then turned to give Simi a hug.

'Okay, lovely, thanks so much – for everything.'

'Thank *you* and don't be a stranger, Morenike!' Simi said with a playful wag of her finger.

'It's Sandra though,' said Sandra, plastering on her professional smile. 'What goes on in Dublin stays in Dublin.'

Simi felt time stop. 'Oh… right.'

And with that, Sandra about-faced towards the exit and was gone.

Simi stood by the carousel in a stupor watching bag after bag drift past her until, finally, the conveyor belt regurgitated her holdall. She yanked it off the carousel. What had just happened? Did Sandra consider her heritage a dirty secret not for public consumption? Simi remembered a girl at school who had done everything to hide her African heritage, even pretending she was from French Guyana not Ghana. And in her teens, Simi had been teased for everything from the tight kinks in her hair to her shapely behind and defined muscles. No one told her those strong Nigerian features were beautiful. She'd had to discover that for herself and was still learning. After so long undoing those negative messages, how could she befriend someone who wanted to bury that ancestry?

'Bye, Sandy,' Simi said under her breath as she too headed for the exit.

As usual, the arrivals hall was a criss-crossing confusion of bewildered travellers. Simi braced herself for the trek across town to South London. By the barriers were rows of private hire drivers. She examined their nameboards, teasing herself that someday one might be waiting for her. As she did, her attention was caught by a board behind all the drivers. Clearly written in black ink on a wipe-clean slate was her name. Her face creased. Was it possible another Simi Oladipo was travelling at this exact same time, to this exact same airport, on the exact same day? But then she looked up at who was holding the board. Shock turned to surprise which became a smile then a grin that gave way to tears as she hastened through the crowd towards Jemima.

'What are you doing here?' Simi gasped.

'Trying to make your dream come true,' said Jemima, uncertainty in her eyes.

Simi bit her lip, hoping somehow to contain her sobs but she couldn't.

The girls held each other as though holding on for their own survival, as though the harder they held on, the more love they could squeeze from each other.

'I am *so* sorry,' said Jemima wiping tears from Simi's face.

'I'm sorry too,' said Simi. 'I want you to use those stories. You've given me so much and I know Beverley means the world to you. It's the least I can do. They're yours and I won't take no for an answer.'

Simi held Jemima again. Ultimately, she could see, no one would ever know the source of these stories and they were great stories. They would simply become part of the Beverly Blake canon. But this wasn't only for Jemima. Just as Meagan had said, this was a chance for everything Simi had been through to count for something, help others to grow, do things differently. After all, why learn from just your own mistakes when you can learn from someone else's too. Simi pulled away from Jemima for a moment, sensing that the news hadn't landed as she'd imagined.

'That's so kind of you, Simi, but the book is dead. I've decided to withdraw it and go to LA. No Miles, just me. I'll be packed and ready to go in a fortnight.'

'No, Jem, you can't!'

'I can and I am,' said Jemima, 'Now, let me take that bag for you, madam.'

'Wait,' said Simi taking her holdall back. 'What about Chance?'

Jemima stopped. Simi knew, the truth was long overdue.

'There's nothing going on with me and him. On that date, he talked about you *all* night. He's in love with you and, unless I'm going mad, you're in love with him too, right?'

Jemima went to speak but nothing came out.

'Right?' said Simi.

'It doesn't matter. Even if, and it's a big *if*, there were something between us, Meagan hates me and that's more important than falling in love with some guy,' said Jemima heading towards the car park.

Simi's mind whirred. So, it wasn't Chance, as she'd previously thought, who could persuade Jemima to stay. It was Meagan. Without the love of her best friend, Jemima was convinced there was nothing to stay for.

'Wait. Let's talk to Meagan. I mean, *reeeeally* talk and if she still wants to shut the book down and can't see a way back, then you can go to LA with my blessing – as long as there's a couch for me when I visit.'

Jemima looked around the airport as though she might sprint off there and then. Simi edged towards her. 'Stop running, Jem. Face this.'

After a long silence, Jemima sighed. 'Fine but if she murders me, I'm going to kill you.'

'Yes!' said Simi, punching the air. 'Not the killing me bit but yay to everything else.'

Jemima hunched her shoulders, adjusting her grip on Simi's bag. 'Come on. The taxi's waiting.'

'Home, James!' Simi trilled following her.

As they walked, she heard someone clear their throat, loud and close behind them.

'Oh, hello… *Brutus*,' came the voice, stopping them both in their tracks.

CHAPTER 49

Meagan

Meagan stood glaring as anger coursed through her veins. Even her idea of meeting Simi at the airport had been stolen by Jemima. The woman was shameless. Clearly she'd realised, of the two of them, Simi was the soft touch and had started working her to save her libellous blood-money book. Well, she would not be such a pushover, Meagan sneered, as Simi and Jemima span around in shock.

'Meagan!' Simi exclaimed. 'What are you—'

'I came to welcome my favourite kitchen maid home. Didn't realise she'd become a turncoat,' Meagan snarled shoving her name board in her bag.

Simi looked her up and down.

'Wait. Why are you so small?' she said as her eyes fell to Meagan's feet. 'You're in flats! And a T-shirt!'

'A lot's changed, bitches,' she retorted. 'So, Jem, trying to save your little book?'

Not that she had to ask. It was obvious. Why else would she haul her ass to Gatwick on a Sunday morning? Well she was too late. All Meagan had to do was hit the kill switch and her lawyers would incinerate her. She laughed to herself at how, just that morning, she'd questioned if legal action was a step too far. However, seeing Jemima pull this weaselly manoeuvre made Meagan even more determined to bury her.

'So what have you got to say for yourself, *Jem-Jem*?' Meagan sneered.

'Hudson Hicks offered me a two-book deal.'

'You never said that,' gasped Simi.

'Big whoop. Once they find out about my case they'll withdraw quicker than a catholic lad having a fumble with his girlfriend in the back of his parents' car,' shot Meagan, enjoying that zinger.

'I'm turning it down and *I'm* withdrawing the book,' said Jemima with a calmness that irritated Meagan.

'So there's no need for court and lawyers and stuff,' said Simi.

Meagan shrugged. Though this was an unexpected plot twist Jemima was not off the hook.

'What about your advance?' she rallied.

'I'm taking a loan to pay it back.'

Meagan floundered. That would be a millstone around Jemima's neck for years and with no book to generate an income, would leave her struggling.

'What about Hudson Hicks's expenses, Shaheena's commission?' Meagan said, flailing inside.

She had been sure this book was the most important thing to Jemima given what she'd sacrifice to finish it. How could she now forsake it? This had to be a bluff.

'Shaheena keeps her commission. I'll return the advance and pay Hudson Hicks's expenses as soon as I can,' Jemima said.

'It's true,' Simi chimed.

Meagan looked at Jemima as her uncertainty built. Jemima always talked about how much she enjoyed being a writer, how much she loved Beverly. Could she really throw all that away?

'What will you do?' asked Meagan, now on shifting sands.

'Go to LA. Start again.'

'No!' said Simi. 'You said you'd try!'

'And I did, darling, but this isn't working,' Jemima said going to leave.

Meagan shoved her hands in her pockets. She wanted to turn away too. She wanted to not care and for this image of Jemima to be her last, but...

'What will you do in LA? You only know Rebecca,' Meagan blurted.

Damn. Why couldn't she just let her go? She was angry, so very angry but there was something else too. Was it love? God, she *hated* giving a shit about people!

'Get a part-time job. I'll still write, maybe try my hand at comedy,' Jemima said.

'You could write about this,' Meagan snipped.

'Meag.' said Simi.

'You're right. No one would believe it anyway.'

Jemima faced Meagan, the two of them standing like monuments as the world zipped and raced around them. Meagan wanted to forgive but the hurt was profound.

'Can I ask you something?' she said. 'And be honest. Why didn't you ask?'

Jemima stared at the floor. 'I tried so many times but, Meagan, you are a bloody scary woman.'

Meagan glanced over at Simi who was nodding in sombre

agreement. *Fuck*. Meagan knew she was formidable at work but how was it her two best friends were scared of her as well. Instantly, Meagan recalled the conversation they'd all had in the rocking horse bar when she'd torn into Jemima for questioning her high standards. At the time Meagan had felt under attack but Jemima hadn't been critiquing her. In her own fearful and peculiar way, she was asking for forgiveness. Had Meagan become that much of a tyrant that she was practically unapproachable?

'Jem,' said Simi into the silence, 'I need to ask something too. Why didn't you use your stories?'

Jemima began to shake. 'I tried but where I'd shut down a chance of… something… you two hadn't. Simi, those butterflies you get when you like someone feel like dread to me. That smile a stranger gives you, terrifies me. Whatever you'd been through you could still let a man in – even a little. Beverly was dying with me but with you guys, she could breathe again. And I want to breathe again too, stop running and just… stay still.'

All three of them fell silent as the airport crowd navigated around them sensing this was something delicate, not to be disturbed.

'I read the book again,' said Meagan. 'I was making notes for the case. It's… it's really good.'

'You think so?' Jemima said, a smile breaking through her sorrow.

Meagan smiled back. Just like bowling, reading was never going to be her thing but Jemima had written a real page turner. Even in the world of comedy, Meagan saw on a daily basis how narratives were still so male-dominated. But in Beverly Blake, here was a strong, female lead that was smart and now sweet, funny and sexy. There was no way she was going to stand in the way of that.

'You should publish it,' said Meagan.

Simi gasped.

'What do you think, Sim?' said Meagan.

'Like, totally. Completely and utterly!' Simi chimed.

Jemima clasped her forehead, her eyes searching Meagan's.

'Are you serious?'

'Yes!' clapped Simi.

'Absolutely. But on one condition,' said Meagan.

Simi stopped mid-clap.

'Name it,' Jemima said, seeming about to hyperventilate.

'Don't go to America,' said Meagan.

There was no way she was going to let Jemima go. Simi needed her, she needed her, and she knew Jemima needed them too. Good girlfriends were a rare and precious thing and in their womanhood they had a matchless kinship. After ten years they were so entangled it was impossible to tell where their love for each other began and ended. They'd seen each other at their lowest ebb and highest highs. They'd celebrated together, commiserated together, briefly lived together, fought, wrestled and primal screamed together. From the stream of disparate souls that moved like bouncing atoms through each other's lives, these girls had, like atomic fusion, clung to each other to create a greater whole. Jemima and Simi made Meagan a better, happier, wiser and now, hopefully kinder, person. No, she would not allow Jemima to disappear from her life. She couldn't. She *was* her life.

'Deal and thank you,' Jemima said choking down her emotions.

'Thank *you*,' said Meagan hugging her.

'Ohmygod, ohmygod. Yay!' Simi yelped as she threw her arms around them in sheer joy.

CHAPTER 50

Jemima

Jemima took in deep life-affirming breaths, still reeling. In twenty-four hours she'd gone from having nothing to feeling like the world was at her feet and she had everything – almost. She'd been lurking around the corner from Nostromo for an hour. Every now and then she'd edge closer only to scuttle back to her hiding place the moment the door opened. She had called Chance's practice but it had gone to his answer machine every time. He wasn't at the park which left Nostromo as her only other option but that meant seeing Azi. As the sun peeped from behind the clouds, Jemima watched curiously as her shadow crept across the pavement. No more running, she reminded herself. No more running. She threw back her shoulders and strode towards the front door.

'Jem!' Rania whispered, scurrying over. 'How you doing?'

'Good, I think. Is Azi about?' Jemima whispered back.

'She's at the cash and carry.'

'Then why are we whispering?'

'Good point,' Rania chuckled. 'A latte to go?'

'No. To have in, please. I'm going to wait,' Jemima said pointing to the airplane seats which had just become available.

Rania gave Jemima a knowing nod and busied herself at her coffee machine. As Jemima watched her, she mulled over the mess she had made and how lucky she was to be surrounded by such amazing and, frankly, forgiving women. She had taken them for granted but never again, she affirmed as she took her coffee to the airplane seats. Around her, in the café, friends chatted, yummy mummies and daddies wrangled their children and the usual collection of lone creatives beavered away at their laptops. The one person Jemima wanted to see, however, was nowhere in sight. And even if he were here, she had no idea if he still felt the same way about her after her awful behaviour. All she could do was be still, be here, experiencing the most agonising wait of her life. As Jemima pulled off a chunk of her cinnamon swirl, the door swished open and she practically snapped her neck turning. She looked on as Rania had a brief exchange with someone asking for directions. After, the door closed behind them and Jemima sank back into her seat. Was she too late? From the moment they'd met she'd known he was special but had wasted so much energy pushing him away. Who could blame him for finally writing her off. Jemima glanced over at Rania who gave a consoling smile, then went back to her cleaning. This was going to be a very, very, long wait. As Jemima settled into her seat she heard Azi bustle in through the back door.

'Oh my god, Ran, the lines at that bloody cash and carry. I thought I was queueing for a Beatles reunion not coffee grounds!'

Jemima sank down further, praying she would somehow go unnoticed but the moment Azi came through, she spotted her and stopped. Jemima gave her a feeble wave. Azi ignored her, instead entering into an animated exchange with Rania. Every now and then, one of them would point in Jemima's direction before diving back into their agitated back and forth. Jemima tensed as her flight instincts went in to overdrive. As she considered knocking over her cup to create a distraction so she could flee, Azi and Rania headed over.

Jemima stiffened but before she could even stand, they were upon her.

'Azi, lovely surprise. Can't stay, I was just leaving,' yakked Jemima, pushing herself out of her seat.

'It's okay, Jem. Azi has something to say, don't you, darling?' said Rania.

Azi glared at her feet as Jemima wondered what the hell was going on.

'Sorry,' said Azi still burning a hole in the ground with her gaze.

'Go on,' said Rania.

Jemima blinked in bewilderment, her eyes jolting between them.

'I'm sorry I shouted at you. I just care for Chance,' said Azi looking up at Jemima.

'We both do,' said Rania putting an arm around her wife. 'We just want him to be happy.'

'So do I,' said Jemima, still clinging to the hope she might add to his happiness not take from it.

'Do you?' Azi prodded.

Rania muttered something to Azi in Arabic and she softened. Rani was like the Azi-Whisperer, able to calm even her most skittish outbursts.

'The thing is, Jem, in our country, it's not easy to just love who you love,' Azi said as she wrapped an arm around Rania, resting her head on her shoulder.

Jemima looked on feeling like spare change. It had never occurred to her what these women had given up to be together.

'How often do you find someone who fits you so well? I just got frustrated because it seemed like you were throwing that away,' said Azi reaching out and taking Jemima's hand.

At her touch, almost by osmosis, Jemima could sense what Azi and Rania had experienced by simply loving each other – the obstacles, the judgements, the fear. Jemima knew only fragments of their story but enough to realise, if people around the world were suffering as they had, only a fool would turn away from love when their path was clear.

'Do you know where he is?' Jemima asked, her intent rekindling.

Azi shook her head. 'He's gone, darling. Took a flight to Mexico to be with his brother.'

'Azi… ' said Rania before being nudged silent.

Jemima's legs gave way beneath her and she fell back into her chair. He hadn't even said goodbye. She buried her head in her hands as the load of another self-created disaster bore down on her. For the first time, she had allowed herself to care for this good, patient, kind and funny man who celebrated her, lifted her up rather than projecting his own insecurities onto her, loved passionately, was unafraid of his emotions and Jemima had blown it.

'Azi?' said Rania, now a scolding tone in her voice.

'Well at least we know how she feels about him!' Azi said planting herself next to Jemima, brimming with excitement.

'He hasn't gone to Mexico. He's on a training course in

Welwyn Garden City and he'll be back this afternoon. We've got a package for him. He'll be coming in to collect it. Wait for him, angel. Don't go anywhere.'

Jemima looked from Azi to Rania not knowing what to believe.

'Are you serious?' she said.

'I am, darling. I'm sorry. You know I've got a horrible sense of humour,' said Azi.

Rania nodded, her face testament to the many pranks and wind-ups she'd endured over the years.

'I'm sorry I was cross with you. We love you, Jem. We want you to be happy too,' said Azi as she threw her arms around her.

Jemima hugged her back as Rania patted the two of them.

'Okay, I need a coffee! You want a basbousa, Jem. On the house,' Rania said as she headed back to the counter.

'Yes, please!' Jemima nodded.

This drama had sent her blood sugars through the floor. Azi stood and kissed Jemima's forehead. 'Remember, this is Chance not Miles. Chance – good. Miles – plonker. Got it?' said Azi.

Jemima nodded. Satisfied, Azi headed through to the back room.

Jemima leaned back into the soft leather cushions. Even Azi could see she had projected Miles's failings onto Chance. Her history was stuck to her like glue, casting a shadow ahead of her, wherever she went. In some ways, it reminded her of her downstairs neighbour's toddler, Nia, who'd fallen in love with a local black and white cat. Nia's mum had named the moggy Sylvester, but unable to pronounce that, Nia always called him Cester. One day, a ginger tom came around and Nia had called out, 'Cester!' It wasn't that Nia had mistaken this cat for her old pal, it was just, to her all cats were Cester. Jemima exhaled. That was what she did with men. Every guy she encountered was Miles, no matter his shape or form, no matter how good a person he was. Could she break out of this self-made trap? Could she disappear that shadow in the cooling shade of a life that included her amazing girlfriends, the career she'd always wanted and maybe, just maybe…

'Is this seat taken?'

She turned to see Chance. His hair was tussled and that same kind smile was spread across his face just as it had been the day they'd first met. She rose from her seat.

'Hi.'

'Hey,' he said, taking her hand. 'You looked like you were miles away.'

'I was but I'm back.' She smiled, daring to take his hand in hers too.

Wordlessly, he moved closer while she stayed still. The background murmur faded as they looked into each other's eyes and an electricity crackled around them.

'So, I'm not sure of the etiquette here but I really want to kiss you. That cool?' said Chance.

Finally, Jemima moved towards him resting her hand on his face. His stubble was soft, his skin warm. Chance pressed his cheek into her palm and closed his eyes as Jemima leaned in and let her lips meet his. His kiss was like the cool shade she'd been seeking for a long, long time.

★

A few days later, Jemima watched the sky for ominous clouds, but there were none, just the red and golden shimmers of a beautiful spring sunset. Since the café, she hadn't been able to stop thinking about her kiss with Chance. Were kisses meant to be *that* good? Well, she would soon find out. She smiled, as she arrived nervously at his place for their first official date.

'Okay, don't be weirded out, but shut your eyes – and no peeping,' said Chance, as he opened the door taking her hand in his.

Jemima paused before screwing her eyes shut.

'Don't let me fall,' she replied, flailing her free arm as she took one tentative step at a time.

She realised she wasn't just physically searching for a foothold, but emotionally too. It felt as if she was standing on the precipice of a whole new world.

'I've got you,' said Chance as he coaxed her forward through his flat.

Jemima allowed herself to plant her feet with more certainty.

'Okay,' he said, still holding her hand, 'now a small step down, and we'll be in the garden. Then you can open your eyes.'

She gently placed each foot on the lower level, then slowly blinked her eyes open. Above, the sun had all but set leaving just a few rust-coloured clouds, and in front lay a blanket laid out with a full picnic.

'I'm making you a Greek feast. Kebabs, tabbouleh, dolmadakia, hummus – I made that myself but, full disclosure, I bought the pitta,' he said leading Jemima towards the blanket.

From the small grill he'd assembled, embers glowing within, to the champagne chilling on ice, it was perfect. And the flickering candles made Chance's tiny back yard seem almost dream-like, a timeless sanctum into which they could both dissolve. Jemima's hand went to her chest almost as though she were trying to slow her heart.

'Just a minute,' said Chance as he pressed play on his phone and cello music drifted from a wireless speaker.

'Is that—?' said Jemima straining to listen.

'Your favourite, right?'

Jemima had never fantasised about romance but if she had, it would have looked like this.

'You like it?'

'I love it,' she said.

'Great, now, there's one last thing,' he whispered, drawing her close. 'I think you are magnificent. You're beautiful inside and out and I want you to know, I've got your back, okay?'

Jemima began to panic. Was he about to tell her he loved her or something else equally mad? Her palms went damp despite the nip in the air. Chance took Jemima by the hand and she tensed.

'It's okay,' he said, standing in front of her. 'You know I love—'

'Wait—' she said pulling back, casing her escape routes.

'Jemima. Chill,' he said.

She let his gaze bring her back down to earth and eventually her shoulders dropped. Unlearning those fear-filled impulses was going to be a long journey.

'Sorry,' she said, laughing at herself.

He smiled, unfazed by the minor squall that had passed through.

'As I was saying. You know I love Beverly but I admire you so much for letting her go even though you don't have to. So, to mark that, I thought we could have a ceremony,' he said revealing a sky lantern he'd hidden away earlier.

On one of its papery sides Jemima could see the face of a woman she instantly recognised.

'I hope this is how you imagined Beverly.'

'You drew that?' she said, blinking at the face staring back at her.

Chance nodded.

'She's… amazing,' said Jemima soaking in Chance's imagining of her leading lady.

This was the first time she had ever seen Beverly's face. Her book covers had always been abstract images probably created by some marketing algorithm but looking at this drawing was like looking into a mirror – but one that reflected the past. Chance placed a box of matches in her hand as Jemima stroked Beverly's face, feeling a rush of deep love and loss all at once. Maybe this was premature. There might be one last book she could squeeze out of Beverly. Eve for one, would be thrilled. But as Jemima looked at the face on the lantern, she knew this was the end of her journey with Beverly, not the beginning. It was time for a new adventure.

Jemima struck a match, its flame sending dancing shadows across the garden. She hovered it on the lantern's wick. Within seconds Beverly had floated out of Chance's hands and up into the night sky.

'Bye,' Jemima said as she watched her drift higher and higher.

She turned to Chance, snuggling close.

'Did you make a wish?' he asked, kissing her forehead.

As the lantern disappeared across London, she looked up at him and smiled. 'I don't need to.'

The girls

Jemima surveyed the beer garden, eyeing up the table of guys ahead of them.

'What about the one in the navy top with the cute dreads?' Jemima said turning to Simi.

'There's already a special new someone in my life… Ellen,' said Simi sipping her prosecco.

'Finally, you're sampling some lady lurve,' said Meagan raising her glass.

Jemima tutted. 'It's her therapist, you wally.'

'You don't know what you're missing.' Meagan shrugged with a grin.

As the sun set on the warm May day, the girls sat, side by side on their wooden bench observing the early evening drinkers. Simi slipped her arm through Meagan's and reached for Jemima's hand as they shared a knowing smile.

Meagan snuggled close, leaning on Simi, 'What about the tall one in the paisley shirt?'

Simi giggled. 'Honestly. I'm looking forward to being on my own.'

'Good. That was a test,' Meagan laughed. 'Every now and then I like to see.'

'Well it's been two months since the game and I haven't cracked yet. Anyway, you shouldn't be worrying about me. We should be talking about your date – with one Todd Paxton,' Simi said as she and Jemima fluttered imaginary fans like Elizabethan courtiers.

'Last name terms at last. Must be serious,' Jemima simpered.

'Well, now my office is finished, I needed a new challenge,' Meagan winked.

The girls laughed knowing that she and Todd would be a challenge – for each other. At least now Meagan had abandoned her 'plan', her love life was an open road rather than electrified rails that could not be deviated from.

'And how are things with Chancellor?' said Meagan making a meal of saying his full name.

Jemima's cheeks flushed at the mention of him. From their first date until now, it had been – amazing. It wasn't easy but Jemima had pushed through old habits and in doing so, allowed something new to emerge, for one, the feeling of being on the same team.

'It's… great.' She grinned.

'Oh, Jem, I'm so happy for you and I've been thinking, I want you to have this,' Simi said.

She reached into her bag and pressed something cool and smooth into Jemima's hand.

'This will make what you have last and last.'

Jemima looked down to see Simi's beautiful rose quartz crystal glint back at her.

'But, Simi, you've had this for years,' she whispered.

'And now it's yours. He adores you. I want you to go for it,' said Simi hugging her.

'You sweet, sweet girl. Thank you,' said Jemima as she felt Simi's blessing in her embrace.

'Look at you two,' Meagan cooed as she patted them both.

As they eventually untangled themselves, Jemima snuck a peek at them all, contented and peaceful, oblivious to the hubbub around them. She hated the thought of disturbing this moment but there was one final piece of business she could no longer put off. She pulled two hardback copies of her book from her bag, and placed them on the table. Eve had kindly rush-printed them but now the books were in front of her, Jemima's anxiety had returned with a vengeance. While Simi and Meagan had agreed in principle to the publication, she had no idea how they'd react finally seeing it in print. Simi picked up one of the books and flicked through its crisp, white pages.

'So many words,' she said in quiet awe.

Meagan stared at her copy, drumming her fingers on its thick cover.

After an age she winked at Jemima. 'Congrats, babes. I will read your books from now on.'

Jemima laughed out of sheer relief. This was everything she'd wanted but daren't hope for – no resentment just pure love which she felt in overwhelming abundance. Her throat constricted as she searched for what she had to say next, words that could ruin all this.

'I need to tell you something,' she said. 'Well, a couple of things actually. This is definitely the last Beverly Blake book.'

'What? No!' gasped Simi.

'Why?' Meagan asked running her hand over the cover. 'She means everything to you.'

'She does but it's time to let her go and I couldn't ask for a better sendoff than this,' Jemima said. 'But would you guys check the first page?'

'Go on, Sim. I haven't got my reading glasses,' said Meagan.

'You don't wear glasses!' said Jemima.

'Oh, Jem. I'm not a reader. If you don't know that by now, we ain't gonna make it,' Meagan squawked.

'I'll read it! Just be quiet!' insisted Simi.

Simi carefully pressed her book open. She scanned the title, usual copyright information and page one details no one ever reads. 'Wait, I'm not spell-checking, am I?'

Jemima pointed to the acknowledgements. 'Here.'

Simi read the brief paragraph then gasped as tears welled.

'What is it?' said Meagan. 'Read it out loud!'

Simi wiped away her tears, clearing her throat. '"*And lastly, I dedicate this novel to my dear, darling companions, Simi and Meagan, without whom this book would not be and neither would I. You are my sheroes, my muses, my heart and I love you.*"'

Jemima watched Simi and Meagan stare at their dedication. She had named them and as heartfelt as it was, this yanked them out of anonymity.

'Is this okay?' Jemima said flushed with doubt. 'I can get your names removed. It's not too late.'

'I can't believe it,' murmured Meagan looking at Simi.

'Me neither,' Simi replied unable to peel her eyes from the page. They both turned to Jemima and screamed, 'We love it!'

'We're in a published book! We're in a published book!' Simi sang as she danced around their table, clinging to Meagan.

'Come through, Jem-J!' cackled Meagan, yanking Jemima out of her seat to dance alongside them.

Jemima exhaled, the release immense. It was okay. It was all okay.

'Honestly, that was not necessary but thank you,' said Meagan as she smothered Jemima with kisses. 'You really are a gem – Ha! Look at me, making one of your puns!'

'I'm so flipping happy!' Simi said as she jiggled and gyrated around.

It didn't matter that people were staring. It didn't matter that they were the noisiest group. All that mattered was they were together and would be for a long, long, *long* time to come.

The Dating Game – The Rules

1. You never ask someone out for yourself.
2. No fibbing or exaggerating about the person you're finding a date for.
3. No falling in love (good luck with that).
4. No vetoing a date someone has got for you.
5. No one gets left behind – so no dates on the night of The Game.
6. No breaking the law!
7. No side pieces.

If you and your fellow wingwomen go out and play The Dating Game, be bold, be careful, be lucky – hit me up on Instagram (@theandioshow) and let me know how it goes!

ACKNOWLEDGEMENTS

Firstly thank you, my glorious readers for taking time out of lifing to read my debut novel. It means the world to me. I never got to do a stand-up DVD (ha, DVDs, remember them?!) so I'm thrilled to have created this little piece of me for you.

And trust me, this book has a ton of me in it. I won't spoil your fun guessing which bits but there are a lot. However, even though there's a lot of me in this book, it wouldn't have been possible without my incredible team so let me take a moment to thank each and every one of them.

Thank you, Charlotte, my amazing editor who encouraged, advised and supported this newbie through the twists and turns of creating my debut novel. To Lisa, Katie and the HQ and Harper Collins team, thanks for everything including taking a punt on me. You changed my life. I'm a bloody author now. I mean, what?!

Anja, thank you for helping me make sense of this jumble of words and for your patient encouragement. You made a seemingly impossible task, possible. And, thanks for being a gorgeous mate too!

A huge thank-you to Richard Scrivener, my literary agent who put this whole thing in motion. Richard, you're more than an agent, you've been a friend and ally through this whole thing. Thank you too to my glorious talent manager, Victoria. Guuuuurl, you rock. What a journey we've had. Here's to ten more years! And Robbie and Tim at Beaumont PR, thanks for helping the world hear about my three favourite girls, Jemima, Simi and Meagan.

Yo, Tedd. *Muchas Gracias* for the Spanish translation.

And lastly some personal thank-yous. My friends on FB and IRL who have been there for me, read my book updates, sent prayers, good wishes, and congrats as I've progressed along this journey, you're the best. I couldn't have done this without you. And p.s. the 'book questions' comments threads gave me jokes. If you know, you know.

And to my gorgeous family, you're unbending love and support got me to the finish line and beyond. Mum, Zeke, Phil, Sarah, Charly, Emi, Xander, Julia, Harrison, Bisi, Funso and Demi – you give me life! Love you all.

ONE PLACE. MANY STORIES

Bold, innovative and
empowering publishing.

FOLLOW US ON:

@HQStories